MORE BY THE AUTHOR

THE RAVEN'S JOURNEY

Book 1: See Me
Book 2: See Me Revealed
Book 3: See Me Go
Book 4: See Me Believe
Book 5: See Me Overcome
Book 6: Hawk
Book 7: Ronan
Book 8: Stolas

LOOKING THROUGH THE SHADOWS

The Underbelly
After the Wreckage
We Always Fight

I S.P.I.

I S.P.I. Mischievous Magic (Volume 1)
I S.P.I. Spicy Sorcery (Volume 2)

SHORT STORIES & MORE

Where Realms Collide
Unnerving Descent
Unnerving Eclipse
Unnerving Wicked
Super: Unexpected Heroes Arise
Rise Reflection
Rise Resurrection
Rise Revolution
Rise Recreation
The Space Between Us
The Pulse (The Haunting of Orchard House)

Michelle Lee on the Web

Michelle on Facebook at
tiny.cc/MichelleLeeWrites

or write to
MichelleLeeWrites@gmail.com

THE RAVEN'S JOURNEY
BOOK FOUR

SEE ME BELIEVE

Michelle Lee

BLUE FORGE PRESS
Port Orchard, Washington

See Me Believe
Copyright 2020, 2022
by Michelle Lee

First eBook Edition August 2020
First Print Edition August 2020
Second eBook Edition May 2022
Second Print Edition May 2022

Cover photograph by Michelle Lee
Cover design by Brianne DiMarco
Interior design by Brianne DiMarco

ISBN 978-1-59092-888-2

For information about film, reprint or other subsidiary rights, contact: blueforgegroup@gmail.com

This is a work of fiction. Names, characters, locations, and all other story elements are the product of the authors' imaginations and are used fictitiously. Any resemblance to actual persons, living or dead, or other elements in real life, is purely coincidental.

Blue Forge Press is the print division of the volunteer-run, federal 501(c)3 nonprofit company, Blue Forge Group, founded in 1989 and dedicated to bringing light to the shadows and voice to the silence. We strive to empower storytellers across all walks of life with our four divisions: Blue Forge Press, Blue Forge Films, Blue Forge Gaming, and Blue Forge Records. Find out more at www.BlueForgeGroup.org

Blue Forge Press
7419 Ebbert Drive Southeast
Port Orchard, Washington 98367
blueforgepress@gmail.com
360-550-2071 ph.txt

For my Grandpa Jack,
who made the beach
the best place on earth.
I know I can always
find you there.

For my Grandpa Mike,
who has always been
a living legend to me
and my whole family.

And for my both of my grandmas.
The lessons, memories, support,
and love are invaluable.

See Me Believe

Michelle Lee

Chapter One

Jax wasn't sure what to think. "She let me go," he said to Ronnie.

Ronnie's head snapped around to look at him. "What are you talking about?"

"Back there in the gym, you know, when we couldn't move. I heard Airiella in my head. She was talking to me, telling me that she trusted me to fight for myself, and she let me go," Jax looked down her. "She didn't kill the guy she was fighting either."

"Is that why you said love wins?" Ronnie gave him a dubious look.

"Yeah. I wanted to say something to Airiella to let her know I was okay and to remind her not to do something she would end up hating herself for," Jax reached out to stroke her arm. "She wanted to kill him."

Jax could tell that rattled Ronnie. "How do you know that?"

"She told me. If that thing couldn't get to me, it was going for you, and you were too close. She was reading its intentions," Jax's hand shook, and he pulled it back. "I thought I was going crazy for a second there, that the darkness was just fucking with me. It was Airiella, though, talking to me."

"Can you still talk to her?" Ronnie looked down at her. She looked like she was sleeping peacefully.

"No, I've been trying." Jax wanted to know if she really was asleep or if she had somehow been hurt by what happened.

"There was a point back there where she scared me. I thought she was going to strike the guy dead, and that isn't her at all," Ronnie admitted somewhat cautiously.

"You told me she willingly dies for me, what makes you think she wouldn't sacrifice what she is for you?" Jax asked his tone borderline anger.

"I don't know. I didn't know I was in danger, honestly."

"Pretty sure that was demon possession," Jax said bluntly. "We were all in danger."

They pulled up to the house, and Jax helped Ronnie get out, following as he took Airiella upstairs to her room. They all gathered and sat around her. "Touch her skin," Mags told them as she grabbed one of Airiella's hands.

Jax felt a pull on his energy as soon as everyone was touching her. Then he felt it change from a draw on them to flowing throughout all of them. "This is insane." He felt what each person brought to the table in the stream of energy running through them in a loop.

Her eyes flew open, "Jax!" she called out frantically.

Startled, he moved, letting go of her. "I'm here."

"You fought it!" she cried. "Where's Ronnie?"

"I'm right here, Angel, I'm okay," he sounded confused. "Can't you see me?"

"I can't see anything," fear crept into her voice.

Jax reached out and touched her again. "You're blind?" he guessed that answered his question on if that had hurt her or not.

He saw her eyes focus. "Wait. Jax, move your hand."

He took it back off her. "What's going on?" he asked, bewildered.

"Touch me again," she said. Her eyes were looking

at Jax but not seeing him. He put his hand back on her, and they focused. "I can only see when you all are touching me."

"Batteries," Smitty said suddenly and removed his hand. "You can't see us now, right?"

"No, it's a little scary," her voice sounded small to Jax.

Smitty moved his hand back, and Jax could see his mind was racing. "You used all your energy doing that back there, didn't you?"

"Maybe? I don't know. I didn't even really know what I was doing," she said sheepishly.

Smitty looked at Jax, "You felt it when we were all touching her, right? The pull of energy?" Jax nodded. "We are recharging her."

"I'm draining you?" Airiella tried to pull away.

"No, I don't feel drained. I feel a flow of energy circulating through all of us," Jax tried to explain calmly to ease her worry.

"Honey, stop worrying about us," Mags put in.

"Baby girl, we are fine," Smitty reassured her, stroking her leg.

"What aren't you telling me?" she glared at Smitty, then Jax.

"I think that was a demon possession," Jax answered quietly. He watched as Ronnie picked her up again and moved to sit on the bed with her leaning against him. Jax was relieved to see her relax more.

"Rest, angel. Taklishim is on his way. That means if you rest now, you'll have enough energy to talk to him when he gets here," Ronnie tried to reason.

Jax removed his hand from her and signaled Aedan and Mags to go ahead and leave. Smitty was giving him a look that said not even to try to get him to leave. "Scoot over, Ronnie," Jax told him.

"What are you guys doing?" she asked.

"We are going to lay here and rest with you," Jax said firmly, not giving her a choice.

"That's right, we've got you, baby girl," Smitty's tone was gentler than Jax's.

She turned around in Ronnie's arms and rested her head against his torso as he scooched down to get more comfortable. She put a hand out to Jax and Smitty on either side and was out cold in a matter of seconds.

"She's stronger now," Jax whispered, running his fingers over her knuckles. "Fierce too."

"What did she do with the demon?" Smitty asked, his tone unreadable.

"I think she pulled it out of Matt," Ronnie replied. "Remember when the room went black? I think that was the demon without a host. Remember the one investigation we had where a demon was present and left its host? It went dark in the room like that."

"Jax, did she kill it?" Smitty leaned up on an elbow to look at him.

"I don't think so. I'm not sure," Jax admitted. "I was still trying to fight to keep the darkness down." He paused to kiss her hand. "She's a living weapon, though, not a disaster."

"I don't give a fuck what that piece of shit called her. The bottom line is, she's ours, and they aren't getting their hands on her," Ronnie whispered roughly.

"Agreed," Jax and Smitty answered firmly at the same time.

"Now, we learn to fight demons," Jax added.

Aedan tugged Mags to be on top of him more as they lay in their bed. He was trying to come to grips with everything that happened. He needed to get over his fear of Mags having been there. His brain flooded with panic again at the thought of something happening to her.

"Aedan, relax a little, please." She rubbed circles on his stomach. "There is no way she would have let anything happen to any of us."

"She was protecting Jax," Aedan argued. "You could have caught blowback, or something else."

"She was protecting all of us, not just Jax. Not only that, but she was also fully in control of the situation."

"If that were the case, she wouldn't have gotten hit the way she did," Aedan refused to budge.

"Why are you acting so stubborn? We saw the same thing. She reacted to Jax's flare up at the same time the guy hit her. Shit, Aedan, she put her damn arm back in the socket, she froze all of us, even the other people in the gym. Somehow, she wiped their memory of the whole damn thing, *and* she took out whatever the hell that was, with no one getting hurt. I think Smitty was right. It just drained her energy."

"You still could have been hurt," Aedan repeated for the hundredth time. His argument was a lot weaker now, and he knew it.

"I'm safer around Airy than anywhere else. I fully believe that," Mags said stubbornly.

"She turned into lightning," Aedan whispered.

"Pretty fucking amazing, if you ask me," Mags told him.

"She didn't scare you?" Aedan was shocked.

"Not at all. I have complete faith in her, and I knew she would never let anything happen to us. She sent a clear message to whatever that was, if it was a demon like Jax thinks, then it's understood she's a force," Mags said proudly.

"All I could think about was you and the babies," he trembled. "I couldn't even move to stand in front of you."

"Faith isn't that tricky, Aedan. You either believe, or you don't. If she froze us, that means she didn't want us to move for a reason. I fully believe that. Everything I've ever heard from you guys all points to her doing exactly what is right for others, never herself. Why is that so hard for you to believe after all you've seen from her?"

"I don't know," he admitted truthfully. "It's just not the way the world works."

"You still believe she's from this world?" Mags pushed.

"Well, I don't believe in aliens," he fired back at her.

"She's not an alien. She's a divine being," Mags kept pushing.

"She's not a god. She's human." Aedan was getting frustrated.

"Her body may be human, but her soul is something else entirely. Life is rooted in science; you need to believe it also has roots in faith. Imagine what would have happened if she hadn't been there. What if one of you guys got attacked while out looking for someone that could pull off the test? What would the outcome have been?"

"I don't know, Mags!" Aedan pushed her off him gently and stood up to pace.

"One of you would have gotten seriously hurt, that's what would have happened!" Mags kept pushing him, her frustration easy enough for Aedan to see. "Yes, I understand that this stuff happens around her or Jax, but it's also the safest place you could be. She will always put herself between you guys and danger. She has every single time! Do you need to watch the YouTube videos again of her running into that house? She got you out before anything happened to you."

He sunk on to the bed, despair rolling in waves off him. "I'm just so damn scared, Mags."

"I think that's a natural reaction to have. You don't seem to believe Airy has your back."

"That's not it. I know Airiella has our backs. She's proven that time and time again. I just don't understand any of it. I know I work investigating the paranormal, it's different to live it, though. I'm constantly afraid I'm going to lose Jax. Now I'm afraid for Airiella, on top of mounting fear for you and the babies. It's like everywhere I turn there is something else to scare the hell out of me with things I have no concept of how to process. Smitty and Ronnie both have changed. Jax has changed. Hell, even we've changed since she's been in our lives." Aedan threw his hands up in the air.

"It's the change that's scaring you the most, isn't it?" Mags tugged him until he lay down next to her.

"Probably. I can't predict what's going to happen. If there is something I can do to control it or steer it away from danger. Airiella talks about freezing and not being able to respond, and that's what it feels like I am doing. Ronnie ran into a burning house. I stood there and watched." Aedan held his hands over his face. "Jax almost died, and I did nothing. She *did* die, and I did nothing."

"Believe, Aedan. Believe in her." Mags rubbed his arm.

"What if she doesn't come back? I don't want to watch her go through what Smitty and Ronnie did. I can't watch her die." Aedan started shaking again.

"Oh honey, I wouldn't want to see that either. If Airy needed me there, though, I would do it in a heartbeat. It would suck, no doubt about that. But I wouldn't let it hold me back."

"If I even let myself wonder how I would feel if that were you, blind panic takes over. I have no idea how Ronnie did that. I can see how he feels about her, Smitty too. You saw Ronnie after. Hollowed out, destroyed looking." Aedan couldn't let it go.

"I think you might be looking at it wrong. Yes, Ronnie looked bad, but I also felt the strength of his love for her, and that brought him through it. Look how close they were before, and look how much closer they are now. He fully believes in her, trusts her, and stands by her no matter how he feels about it."

"Today," his voice broke, "was my fault. I put Airiella in that situation. I put Ronnie and Jax in that situation. You and Smitty too. If I hadn't pushed them, none of us would have been in danger. Because of me, our babies were in the presence of a demon."

"Every day that you all are here, our babies are in the presence of an angel. Did you ever think of it that way?" Mags said gently. "You had no way of knowing that something would possess that guy. You can't shoulder the blame for things like that. She doesn't blame you. I don't think any of them do."

"I hate the what-ifs. I hate that I feel this scared all the time. Logically speaking, none of anything that happens has made sense. Emotionally, it's me that's the disaster, not Airiella." Aedan was crumbling, and he knew it.

SEE ME BELIEVE

"Trust her, Aedan," Mags prodded him.

"I do trust her. I'm just a captive to this fear right now," Aedan muttered.

"Then believe in her as the rest of us do."

"I'm trying, Mags. I am." She snuggled up to him, and he let her warmth soak into him. He needed to figure out how to believe as they did. He couldn't live like this.

Chapter Two

ow many normal women wake up with a bed full of sexy men? I thought to myself as my brain came out of its fog. I guessed if I was going to be fair, I couldn't accurately count myself as normal. I cracked open my other eye and latched on to the deep gaze of Jax.

I spoke in his mind, I remembered. A bevy of new things happened today. Oh boy, and they were all there to see it. They also all saw Jax fight for control and win. A massive success in my book. I smiled at that, at him.

Ronnie's hands were under my arms and over my back. I didn't know if he was asleep or not, and if he was, I didn't want to wake him by moving. Being suddenly dragged up the rest of the length of his body answered the question if he was asleep or not.

"None of us are asleep, siren," Jax said as if he read my mind.

"How long was I out?" I was almost afraid to ask.

"A couple of hours," Smitty patted me on the ass.

"Today was interesting, angel of mine," Ronnie kissed me slowly. My libido woke up faster than my brain did.

"Share, you Neanderthal," Smitty griped. He pulled the top half of me off Ronnie and gave me a kiss of his own.

I swore, if Jax kissed me next, it was going to be all over. There would be an orgy right here on my bed whether Jax was ready or not. I heard him laugh as I tried to get my body under control.

"I think if your walls are down, I'll be able to hear you after today," Jax answered my unasked question. "Don't know for sure, but your thoughts are definitely interesting."

I groaned in response. "This is not a good thing."

I sat up so Ronnie could get more comfortable, and I could see all of them at once. I immediately noticed the bloody knuckles on Ronnie's hand and grabbed it. "It's fine, angel. I only broke his nose."

"After you delivered the most vicious kick to the balls I've ever seen," Smitty added with pride.

"I was ridiculously was proud of that one," Ronnie grinned. "Now, let's talk about this freezing us in place thing."

I held up my hand. "Sorry. I did that to keep you out of danger. If you had gotten closer, that guy would have come after you."

"I could have easily taken him," Ronnie growled.

"The Matt guy, yes. Whatever was in him is a different story. If that ball kick didn't stop him, I didn't want to take the chance," I argued. "I know you don't like it, but a lot happened at once. I was able to read his intent, and you were closer than Jax was, and once he saw Jax was in control, his focus changed to you." I wasn't going to cave on this, no matter how much Ronnie hated it.

"You let Jax go, first," Ronnie said as a statement, not an accusation.

"He needed to believe he could do it. It was a strategic move on my part. I knew he had it," I defended myself.

"That was a big leap of faith, siren," Jax answered quietly.

"I wouldn't have done it if I didn't believe in you,

Jax. If I'm still breathing, there is no way I would let something happen to any of you."

Smitty cleared his throat. "The, um, the voice thing, speaking of siren," Smitty looked flustered. "What was that?"

Ronnie leaned forward and took my hand. "Yeah. I truly felt fear then. Like an all-encompassing fear."

I thought about how to word it since I wasn't entirely sure what happened or how I did any of it. "I asked the raven for guidance. The voice thing felt like I was relaying a message. You were scared of me?" Ronnie's admission kind of shocked me.

"Not really of you, of the contrasting emotions coming from your voice. It was sweet and musical almost, but the intent I felt was cold and deadly." He looked uncomfortable, saying that.

"It felt pretty deadly when I said it," I agreed, and he relaxed. "Don't be afraid to be honest with me."

"Okay, so you felt like you were relaying a message then. What about the lightning thing?" Smitty went down his mental list of questions he had for me.

"After the fire in that house, that one seemed almost instinctual to me. I knew lightning hit outside, and I remember thinking I need the lightning in my skin. Then it happened precisely when I needed it to," I also remember how weird it felt to contain that much energy.

"It, uh, well, it almost felt painful through the connection," Ronnie stuttered.

"It felt that way to me, too. It almost felt like when I was releasing the energy I took from Jax," I shivered a little remembering the feel of trying to contain it all. "Kind of like it was too much for my skin, and it wanted to peel, but didn't."

"It scared the shit out of me. It was the first thing I thought of when I saw that glow come over you," Ronnie said, squeezing my hand.

"That was all you then, not the raven?" Smitty might as well be taking notes.

"Almost certain. The ground moving was the raven

showing me what to do to the energy. The air thing just happened. Maybe it's a byproduct of everything else I was doing at the same time; I'm not sure. Or maybe it was just that I was almost out of control." I had as many questions as Smitty did.

"That is not a thought I want to entertain after seeing what you can do today," Ronnie was quick to say. "Don't lose control."

"What about people not remembering anything?" Smitty went on.

"The raven. She told me that they shouldn't remember this, that if they did, I wouldn't be safe. She showed me a little trick with the flow of energy in the room. It hadn't felt right to me to play with their minds like that, yet at the same time, I understood why she thought it needed to happen."

"And the black cloud that swallowed everything?" Smitty stared at me.

"That was the thing I pulled from the Matt guy. Jax thinks it was a demon, right?" Jax nodded. "Whatever shape it normally takes, it couldn't. I damaged it, but the raven told me it wasn't dead. She told me how to pull it without harming Matt. It wasn't easy, and it made me so dizzy."

"Well, you dropped after that. So I think that my guess earlier was right. All that stuff totally drained you of energy," Smitty said smugly.

"It wanted you dead," Jax added. "When I was watching you spar, the darkness in me kept filling my head with dark thoughts. It told me he was going to hurt you, and that thought took over me so fast I didn't even have any warning. I need better control. If you hadn't felt that surge in me, your focus wouldn't have shifted."

"Jax," I held up my hand to stop him. "Don't even continue that thought. None of this was your fault, nor was it Aedan's, as I somehow know he is blaming himself right now, too. This situation was the work of whatever demon or spirit that was. You did fantastic today at fighting that, plus, you telling me that love wins, it gave me an extra boost of strength. This thing had already set its plans in place and would have used any of you to carry them out. Ronnie was his target when he saw that the darkness in you wasn't in control. Do not try to carry guilt for this."

"Your shoulder dislocated," Jax pointed out, his tone even, his emotions ratting him out.

"It was a sparring match. I was bound to take a hit that would knock me on my ass," I let the sarcasm fly.

I felt Ronnie and Smitty tense up at that. "You need to let me take a look at that shoulder, angel."

"Oh, for fuck's sake," I pulled my shirt off, doing my best not to wince at the overhead motion I used. Damn. I refused to look at it.

Smitty paled and was off the bed and out of the room in a flash. Ronnie kept his face neutral, but his jaw ticked. Jax just crossed his arms and gave me a look. Smitty came back in with an ice pack and towel and held it on my shoulder.

I could be just as stubborn as them. I refused to flinch, but my traitorous eyes watered, though. Damn these shoulders. "Look, my shoulders are already bad. It's a weak spot, and that was a lucky hit. I've felt worse."

"Do you actually think that helps your case?" Jax glared.

"Just fix me some of the magic juice Taklishim left me. Or Degataga, whoever. Just mix that up, I'll be fine. There's a bottle of anti-inflammatories in my purse, get that please." Now that I was physically relaxed, the pain was setting in.

"Angel," Ronnie leveled a look at me that was firm. "There might be a tear in there from that. You'll need to get it looked at, and with that, tell me how you knew to put it back in place like that."

"Don't ask questions you don't want to know the answers to," I said quietly. "Besides, it's already torn. It can't get worse than it is."

A strange look drifted across Jax's face, and a warning bell went off when he stood. "Do. Not. Discuss. Her. Past."

Ronnie and Smitty went rigid. I gave them both a look. "You need to trust him that he can fight this." I stood and crossed to Jax. "Look at me," I demanded him.

He locked eyes with mine. "It's too close to the surface right now. I can't hear or talk about that shit you went through."

"That's fine. I understand that. Just fight it down. Fight for you," I reminded Jax.

He took my chin gently in his hand and turned my head to look at my shoulder. "That isn't helping."

Ronnie was at my side, pulling my shirt back down over my head. "Sorry, man, I wasn't thinking."

"Please go sit back down and ice it," Jax pleaded with me as he dug through my purse, looking for the bottle of pills. He shook a few out and brought them to me as Smitty held the ice to my shoulder.

They were overbearing, but they meant well, I reminded myself. "Aedan!" I shouted as loud as possible, making them all jump. "Oops, sorry." I wasn't sorry. Not even a little bit. I was feeling a tad ornery.

I heard the pounding of his feet. "Is everything okay?" he sounded panicked.

"Yep. I just wanted to tell you to stop being an asshole and blaming yourself for things that are outside of your control. Everyone here needs to keep hearing that. I am not fragile. I will protect you all, doubly for unborn babies. Those things, demons, spirits, whatever, they can't beat me when it's someone I love on the line. Got it?" I felt kind of badass throwing orders around.

He opened his mouth, looking like he was going to argue when Ronnie interrupted. "Dude. Don't argue. You saw her pissed off earlier, did you learn nothing?"

Smitty's laughter broke the tension. I grinned. Aedan just nodded and shuffled off out of the room, looking like a scorned child. "Well played, Ronnie."

"One question, siren," Jax's voice was quiet. I braced myself for the utterly disarming way he cut through my layers straight to my heart. "Who protects you?"

There it was. Cut right open. I didn't have an

answer ready, and my traitorous eyes pooled with tears. God, I loved this man. A strangled moan escaped his lips, and he crossed the room to stand in front of me.

"I can see your thoughts, siren." He tucked a strand of wild hair behind my ear. "Let me try, please," was his hoarse whisper. All I could do was nod.

Chapter Three

Smitty was ready. He had his laptop, a paper notebook he had been using to take notes as they came to him, pens, and his phone. They decided to meet in the dining room as it had the table with the most workspace. Except, the three council members bypassed everything and went straight upstairs to Airiella's room.

Smitty paused to check his connection with Airiella to make sure she was okay and didn't feel anything alarming, then followed them. Had he missed something? Onida passed Airiella's room and went to Jax's, where she was doing something in the doorway.

Tama and Taklishim went into Airiella's. Tama wandered the room while Taklishim motioned her to take her shirt off. She didn't even argue, though she struggled a bit, and Smitty crossed to help her. The bruise was hideous.

"How'd you get her to do this without arguing with you?" Smitty asked Taklishim, who just laughed at her scowl.

"I promised magic juice," Taklishim gave a small smile.

"Shit, you are going to need to teach me that recipe

if it gets compliance," Smitty muttered.

"I don't always argue. Just when you guys are acting overbearing," she grumbled.

"I'm assuming that's all the time, Raven," Taklishim said with a bigger smile. "Relax, I need no resistance in the arm to check. You'll feel a weird heat, so I've been told, when I'm using my ability. Stay relaxed."

Smitty watched in fascination as Taklishim's eyes went out of focus, and he moved Airiella's shoulder around. Her face was a clever mask of nothingness as she tried to hide the pain from Taklishim, though Smitty felt it. He was sure Taklishim felt it, too.

Tama was now mixing up some herbs to make what Smitty assumed was what Airiella called the magic juice. She handed it to Airiella and told her to drink it all. She downed the brown water fast, wincing at the taste.

"Tama, this will take two of us," Taklishim said quietly. "Raven, this is going to hurt. I'm sorry about that."

She gritted her teeth, "I'm used to it. Just do it."

"Whoa. Wait," Smitty interrupted. "What are you doing?"

"I need to separate the joint to pull the pinched tendon out that got caught when she popped the joint back in place. There's quite a lot of damage in there. However, this is the only one I can assist with right now. She is correct in saying she's used to it, from what I can see." His words came too easy for Smitty's taste.

A wave of empathy washed over him, "Baby girl," Smitty said, moving to stand behind her, "I've got you."

She nodded. "Just do it."

Tama stood perpendicular to Airiella and braced her collarbone, holding her in a grip while Taklishim pushed against the shoulder and was doing something Smitty couldn't see. He could feel the intense pain that she fought against, and Smitty ground his teeth together.

It didn't take him long, and he released her gently and backed her up to the edge of the bed. "I'm going to put this rub on it; it won't do much against that kind of pain. Hopefully it will take the edge off. It will help with the inflammation, though."

She was pale and had broken out in a cold sweat, her uninjured arm trembling slightly. Smitty held her hand, "Tell me what you need."

"I'm okay," she assured him, though the voice was weak.

"I can feel that's not true," he said into her ear, her hair tickling his nose.

"It's just pain. Trust me. I'm used to it."

"Can you engage your shoulder, Raven?" Taklishim's eyes were sympathetic.

"Be more specific. I can force any movement you need me to. If you are asking if it hurts, then yes."

"No, I need to see the movement while it's engaged instead of passive," Taklishim explained.

Smitty held her other hand as she forced a movement that he knew without feeling it through the connection, set her teeth on edge. She swung her arm overhead like she was swimming, but only rotated it once, squeezing his hand painfully hard as she moved.

"That's enough. It's no longer pinched, though that bone is tearing the cuff even more. I spotted several tears, only one new. You should consider the surgery," Taklishim explained gently.

"It didn't fix the other one," she argued.

"No, it didn't fix it. But it did slow down the damage and cleaned it up a little." Taklishim patted her hand.

Smitty saw by the shutdown expression on her face that she wasn't going to consider it, at least not yet. He wisely kept his mouth closed and watched as Taklishim spread some sort of gelled substance over her shoulder; it had a slight mint smell to it.

Smitty helped Airiella get the shirt back on and led them downstairs to the dining room. He brought up his list on the computer of questions and waited for the others to get settled.

"Okay, I've compiled a list of information together, along with questions about what's going on. That way, we can try and get a better understanding of what we need to do. Do you mind if I just list out the questions?" Smitty started.

They all agreed. "What are we facing other than Jax's darkness? Why can Jax hear Airiella in his head? Will every new ability she gains drain her like it did this last time? How much more will she gain, and will we know in advance? How do we fight it? Is there a solution to help Jax get rid of this energy without Airiella pulling it and killing them both? What was that thing she faced today? Will she be able to sense them as she can with Jax's thing, so we don't get blindsided by a psycho wanting to kill her?"

Taklishim had a good poker face, Smitty decided. All he got in response was an eyebrow raised. "Is that all?"

"I'm sure I'll have more depending on your answers. I'm putting together a list of what we know that I reference to try and piece things together. I'll give you that first. We know Airiella's abilities have grown, though we don't know the extent of it until faced with sudden life-threatening situations. Through her efforts, Jax is more himself than ever before, and he has started to be able to fight back against it for control over himself. Airiella has made significant progress in healing, which leads me to believe that is why she can do more now, and she has wings that make appearances at odd times. She communicates with the raven, and after this last little go-round, Jax can hear her thoughts."

"Can you explain in better detail what happened today?" Tama asked.

Airiella leaned forward, and Smitty noticed her keeping the injured arm close to her body and using it very little. "I can. We were at a gym to test me on fighting reflexes against someone that isn't known to me to see if I froze and was able to predict movements. It felt off to me before it even started, though it wasn't something I could pinpoint. During the match, I felt Jax's energy flare up fast, and my focus shifted, resulting in the shoulder injury. Everything happened super fast after that. It lasted probably not even five minutes though it felt like hours. The guy's name was, well is, Matt. His voice changed, and it wasn't him speaking through it. Matt had become something else. He threatened Jax, which set my bat-shit crazy temper off, which is never a good thing. Then threatened me, which I didn't care about, but then I was able to read his intent. I had frozen the group to keep them from moving closer to me, which was the danger zone. I also needed Jax to trust himself to fight it, so I released him. When this thing inside Matt saw Jax was in control, it shifted its focus to Ronnie. Temper once again flared hot. I asked the raven for guidance. Forgive me if I'm out of sequence with a few of these things, it happened fast. It called me a disaster and a beast and wants to destroy me and was going to use whatever means it could to do that. Jax and Ronnie being the first two targets. That wasn't going to happen if I could help it. Lightning struck outside, and I remember thinking that I needed to have the lightning in me, and it happened. I somehow also made the ground shake, and wind appear inside the building. I knocked all the bystanders in the gym out, threatened the thing inside Matt and managed to pull it out of him, and somehow was able to manipulate the energy of the room to wipe the memories of those I knocked out. I know I didn't kill whatever it was. Then we both dropped. Did I miss anything?"

"Well, somewhere in there, I started hearing your thoughts. From my end, it happened after I was in control of myself," Jax added. "Not only that, but I could also feel the energy flows she was using and how they changed directions."

"Yeah, I felt that, too," Ronnie said. "I could feel when she pulled and when she pushed and kind of where it was heading or drawing from the source. Also, the temperature in the room became ice cold. And at one point, so did Jax's skin. She also started to glow as soon as he threatened Jax, and right before she moved towards him, that glow turned blue."

"Bright electric blue," Mags added to that.

"Smitty also thinks that she passed out because all that drained her energy. And when we touched her after getting back here, that we were recharging her," Aedan put in sounding skeptical. "The other thing was if one of us took our hands off her, she couldn't see."

"Wow, I sound like a circus act," Airiella's voice became subdued. Smitty stretched his legs out under the table and sandwiched her ankles between his. He saw Jax and Ronnie both put arms behind her. "One-woman freak show, right here folks. Step up and get your tickets."

"Knock it off. You aren't a freak show, angel," Ronnie glared at her.

Tama pulled the framed picture from inside her sweater that she must have taken from Airiella's nightstand. The one Jax had taken on the beach. "Tell me, hon, did this picture have something to do with any healing inside that happened?"

Airiella nodded. "Jax took that picture. That entire day was a big day of reconciling some of my past. The beach allowed me to release a lot of that stuff I'd held on to. Then, when he gave it to me yesterday, he healed something else. The part of me that avoided mirrors, the way I see myself, and how I thought I looked to others."

"Jax, can you send me a copy of this photo? It's stunning," Tama asked. At Jax's nod, she continued. "That last piece that healed yesterday may have been one of your biggest issues. That also could be why you were able to do so much at once. You believed in yourself."

"Tama is right. I think this is part of what Jax struggles with, and also, I believe Aedan. Belief. Jax, belief in yourself, Aedan, belief in others. There are still fractures within this bonded group though they are becoming smaller each time I see you all together. Airiella, with that new internal strength, the tides in this have easily changed," Taklishim told them.

Onida joined the conversation. "From what I have been able to gather from the other side, what you dealt with was a mid-level demon. They have declared an all-out war against Airiella. The news of her existence spread like wildfire through the veil. They covet her power. If they can't kill her, they want her blood," she looked directly at Smitty.

"Tak had mentioned that before," Smitty said, typing. "Any more info on what her blood can do?"

"They can do rituals to harness her power. While they can't possess her, they can make a trap for her and, through her blood, try to control her movements, her thoughts, like that which resides in Jax, which is why they also want him. The combination of the two of those in the wrong hands is devastating," Onida went on. "They will stop at nothing to get it, and they have minions here watching and reporting."

"Those necklaces won't work against demons," Tama pointed at Smitty's neck. "Those only work against spirits. Airiella, what you did by harnessing that lightning inside you is incredibly powerful and unheard of from what we can tell. It will work to pull the demon from a host, though I am unsure of how to kill a demon. The one you managed was badly hurt, though he still exists. It will also drain you fast, the amount of energy needed to sustain that I can't even imagine."

"Two of the backers of your show are pretty strong talents. I can't divulge their information, but they are the reason this council exists. They have both spoken with me, and the reason they support your show is they want to prove that these things exist and want you to be able to show people they can fight back against it." Taklishim sighed. "While I don't agree with this next part, I was not able to change their minds. They want Raven to do an interview, a radio show that deals with paranormal things. Those videos that got put online have triggered some questions that we, here, don't want to be answered."

"Wouldn't it put her in more danger?" Smitty felt a wild surge of protectiveness pop up.

"Yes. And we also don't want it known what Airiella is. That was the primary reason we headed here anyway when you called. We want to coach you on what to say or how to answer. This other little development solidifies that need," Taklishim growled out.

"You told me she was the most unconventional angel ever," Smitty recalled.

"That she is. She curses like the devil, has the temper of a hurricane, and abilities that far surpass anything we've ever been able to dig up. Her emotional capacity alone is far more than any other empath recorded throughout history. Though, those were Degataga's words, not mine. The unconventional part that is."

Smitty saw Tama reach out and touch Taklishim's arm and shake her head with a gentle nod to Airiella. Smitty looked over at her and saw the expression on her face. Then, that of Jax's next to her. "Do you need a minute, baby girl?"

"Yeah, I need to use the restroom," her voice was wooden. She stood and walked out of the room.

"She's feeling like a freak," Jax whispered harshly. "The more you point out how different she is, the louder her thoughts get about it being impossible for people to love her."

"Tak, her wound may have started to heal with this picture, but it's still quite fresh. You may need to reinforce that these aren't bad things. Gently. I know your intent behind the words; she doesn't. Thank you, Jax, for the insight," Tama responded quietly.

Smitty felt her emotions roll through him. "She's hurting," he looked at Ronnie, who was immediately out the door, followed by Mags.

Taklishim's poker face cracked a little. "I apologize."

Smitty switched subjects while she was out of the room. "You said something about Aedan needing to believe."

"Yes." Taklishim seemed to think about his words before continuing. "He's having a hard time believing what is real, am I right?"

Aedan nodded, shame drifting over his face. "I'm trying."

"You don't need to conform to a religious belief or commit yourself to study ways to change your life to believe in her. You can see the goodness in her, feel the love, and know it is real. These abilities are astounding, even us. No one can fault you that. You do need to trust that she is stronger than these forces that work against her," Onida said bluntly.

"If even *you* don't know what she is capable of, how do you know that?" Aedan challenged.

"I believe," she replied simply.

Smitty felt her before he saw her and knew she had calmed down. He shot a look at Jax, whose face was still hard but softened as soon as she came into sight. She sat back down quietly, and Smitty saw Jax pull an Airiella move, and he put his hand under her shirt against her back. Ronnie gave a small nod at Smitty and settled down next to her as Mags took her seat.

"Raven, I apologize for my words and not realizing how they would fall on you. While you are unconventional, you are nonetheless amazing in every way I have seen. Along with Degataga, the three of us are the most powerful on the council. Maybe in this country even, and we are all in awe of you. It's my selfish abject fascination that has kept me at a distance while I analyze everything, and I've failed to express how impressed I am. You outshine us all, combined," Taklishim let his emotions seep through to his words.

"Would it help if I reigned in my temper and stopped swearing?" she asked, looking down at the table.

"Not even a little. Those are qualities I happen to find oddly endearing. Raven, never change yourself for anyone who thinks you fall short of their expectations. Only allow love to shape you and heal you," Taklishim's voice was soft and gentle now.

Smitty saw the impact of those words land and personally thought they carried more weight than his previous ones. His throat thickened as he watched her push through the doubt that was waging war inside her.

"Thank you for that," she told him softly.

"Never doubt our allegiance, beautiful girl," Tama joined hands with Taklishim. "We don't always see eye to eye with the board or the council. We will deliver the message as promised, but we stand behind *you*, and our goal is to aid you; however, we can. While we may deliver news that none of us like, we will find a way to do as asked without giving away information they truly want. We've gotten good at the smoke and mirrors game where it concerns you."

Smitty cleared his throat again, "So how do we beat demons back?"

"If it's you guys alone, without Airiella, the methods Father Roarke uses can be of assistance. We've made him aware of the need for this knowledge, and he will be in contact. If Airiella is with you, my suggestion is to do exactly what she says and let her handle it. The innate knowledge of how to do this is already in her bones and makes itself known when the time is needed," Onida provided.

"We have to stand by, and do nothing?" Ronnie didn't like that answer and Smitty wondered if he'd push.

"I didn't say that. If Airiella freezes you, as you call it, then it's for a reason, and you need to trust her judgement. If she stands between you and someone else, don't get angry with her. The essence of what she is, has knowledge that none of us know. It's the reason we believe she was created. As you tell us things, we learn. We can record for future generations. We also have to trust that she will believe enough in herself to follow through with the knowledge that comes. Maybe she will ask for help in ways that Father Roarke can teach you. I can't say," Onida firmly stated.

Smitty didn't like standing by any more than Ronnie did. "I guess that means we won't know if she obtains any more abilities until the situation calls for it then."

"It's a guess on my part, but I think that is correct," Taklishim answered.

"I am leaning towards believing that she will be able to sense the intent of one of these beings. Certainly, the stronger it is, the more she will sense it. I can't guarantee it, and it's the feeling I get when I look inside her," Tama answered another of Smitty's questions. "They aren't human, so they don't have human emotions, and though they use a human, their intent will carry an energy that triggers the essence inside her."

"That intent can also trigger the energy inside Jax," Taklishim looked at Jax, and Smitty observed his face, looking for a sign he wasn't in control. "It wants to. The spirit world knows her weaknesses are those she loves. What they don't understand is what they consider a weakness; it is also one of her strengths. You *all* make her stronger. By threatening you, they unleash the power in her that they both fear and covet."

"What about Jax hearing her in his head?" Smitty reviewed his questions.

"I think that has to do with their connection," Tama fidgeted a little. "I don't know a lot about what you all share. For Tak and me, it's more than a connection; it's a mate bond. We can talk to each other through that. For us, we only ever have one mate, when we lose them; it breaks us."

"Jax is her mate?" Ronnie asked. Smitty couldn't read the tone.

"We don't know," Tama answered. "It's one of the many things we are hoping to learn. In previous lives recorded about others like Airiella, there has only ever been a mention of one connection."

Onida leaned forward and rested her elbows on the table. "This is what I hear from the other side. It could be, the reason there are so many of you is that whoever is causing imbalance may be much greater in power than has happened before. It's not something I have been able to confirm." She looked at Ronnie and Jax. "You two have the strongest bonds with her I've ever seen. I don't know what that means, other than she needs you."

Smitty wasn't bothered by that, nor was he jealous. What he shared with Airiella was perfect for him. "Assuming logic, that would also make them the biggest targets?"

"Possibly." Taklishim looked at Mags. "You aren't on the shooting locations with them. I would assume if we can get Father Roarke to bless this house and surrounding land that you and the innocent lives you carry will be safe. I have seen no reason for you to fear for your safety. There is nothing etched in stone. In your case, I would speak to Father Roarke about ways that you can keep yourself protected. Likewise, I will work with Degataga and Kalisha to see if there is anything we can do from our side."

"Thank you," Aedan breathed out, clutching Mags's hand.

Tama placed the picture of Airiella on the table in front of Airiella. "When you feel doubt, look at this. Believe."

Smitty felt the emotions roll through her again like a choppy sea. "Is there anything new on ways to get that shit out of Jax without killing either of them?"

"We haven't figured it out yet." Taklishim looked over at Jax. "Keep working on you, because it helps. You now have rock-solid evidence of that. Did you, by any chance, go in the water while you were at the beach?"

Smitty wasn't sure why that hadn't occurred to him to check. "No, I felt the occasional mist coming off the surf, but I didn't get wet," Jax confirmed.

Taklishim looked at Tama, and Smitty wondered if they were talking to each other. Tama nodded at him, and Taklishim looked back at Jax, "Tama and I believe that if there is no other choice and she has to pull it from you," now he looked over at Smitty, "her blood might be able to save him."

"Tell me you do not mean that I would have to drink from her like I was a vampire," Jax got agitated.

Smitty silenced Jax with a look. "Let them finish."

"No," Tama answered. "I think even a few drops on your tongue from a finger prick might do the trick. I don't know how long it would take for the effect to sink in, so my suggestion is, if at all possible, to have a little blood on him before you pull it, then maybe a little more after."

"Like when you get a paper cut and stick your finger in your mouth," Onida added.

Smitty made a note on his computer. "What about Airiella?"

"We don't know," Taklishim answered glumly.

Smitty didn't have anything else to ask after that, and they wrapped up the conversation as Airiella's phone went off in a medley of text messages and a phone call. He watched her excuse herself as she looked in confusion at her phone as she answered it and walked away.

It was a light bantering conversation now that the heavy stuff hand ended. Smitty was saving his documents and shutting down his computer when a wave of grief and fear slammed into them and staggered them all, and a shattered looking Airiella stepped back in.

Chapter Four

Ronnie was about to lose his mind. The picture painted for his angel was not a pretty one. He also had no idea what that phone call was, but she was not okay. "Angel, what happened?"

"My grandpa," she started, and her face crumpled, "he's dying. A drunk driver just hit my parents, who were on their way to the hospital to see him. My brother said my mom's hurt, but he doesn't know how bad."

"Fuck! I'm so sorry. I'll go with you, we'll get a flight out now," Ronnie told her, starting to steer her upstairs.

"If I may," Onida interrupted. "Airiella, we chartered a plane, and since we are going to the same place, we will take you with." She looked at Ronnie with a pained expression. "I do think you need to stay here and learn as much as you can. If someone goes with her, it's my belief it should be Jax."

Shock tore through the entire group, not just Ronnie. Even Jax was stunned silent. Taklishim butted in, "She's right. Airiella is much better off with Jax with her. Simply because she won't worry about him, and she is uniquely able to help him and keep the danger from him.

Ronnie, physically you are the strongest and best utilized here keeping yourself and this group safe while you learn from Father Roarke."

"Can't they all come with me?" Ronnie's heart broke at her tone.

"We don't have that much room on the plane. The rest could certainly follow behind on a commercial flight," Tama said gently, giving Taklishim and Onida a look. "The two who don't think with their hearts didn't explain their reasoning well. They do have a point about learning as much as possible with things speeding up as they have. The decision is entirely yours on who you bring with you, or if you bring no one. Regardless, we will get you home."

Ronnie hated it. He hated every bit of it. He knew she needed him, that she needed all of them, and it hurt like hell to admit that they were right. "Is Jax really safer with her? Or is that a giant beacon for whatever it is to single them out in a vulnerable situation?"

"He is safer with her," Tama replied, her tone sympathetic. "The demons know her power now and will approach with fear. They'd have to find a willing host near her to get through, and in the limited places she will be, that won't be easy."

Airiella clung to his arm as she shook. "I don't need to pack. I have clothes at home. I just need my purse. Jax go pack a bag," she said, deciding for Ronnie. "Give me a minute with Ronnie, please," her voice cracked.

He let her pull him down the hallway into the office, closing the door behind them. "Angel, do you want me to follow behind?" he held her as she cried silently.

"No, learn how to fuck these things up. I know you and Smitty are the best at this stuff, and both of you together is the best thing for everyone else. I'll keep Jax safe," she choked out.

"Back to his question from earlier, who will keep you safe?" Ronnie's heart clenched painfully at the thought of being so far away from her.

"You will. Jax will. All of you will. Because if shit goes sideways like it always seems to do, you all are there picking me up and dusting me off, putting me back together. I might have to do the ugly stuff, but your job is much harder than mine." She audibly swallowed. "The thought of losing my grandpa hurts so fucking bad."

"Angel, loving you isn't hard. I trust in you completely to make the calls you think are best. I'm gonna be honest; I hate this. I fucking hate the thought of not being there with you," he kissed her tears.

"Me too. It scares me." Airiella pressed her lips over his heart.

"Jax will take care of you," Ronnie hugged her tight.

"I know he will. I'm just going to miss you being this wall behind me that never lets me fall, especially when I know something like this will push me right over."

"If you change your mind, call, and we will all be on the first flight out," he made her promise. "Go get your purse, I'll check on Jax. Call your brother back and tell him you're on your way."

Fuck. Airiella walked away in a defeated posture. He stalked off to find Jax in his room, pacing wildly. "What if I can't be what she needs?" he blasted out as Ronnie walked in.

"Jax, breathe. Did you pack a bag?" Ronnie tried to make his voice calm.

Jax picked it up, "Yes, I'm not clueless."

"She's going to need you in ways that I know scare you, just be there. That's all you have to do." Ronnie encouraged him. "Call if you need us to come. Call me if you freak out. Her family is the only thing as important to her as we are. I know you can feel what she's going through."

"I'm not you, Ronnie," Jax argued.

"No, you aren't. Airiella still needs you, though. She chose you to go with her, Jax. Remember that. She could have ignored any suggestions made; she usually does. You know that. Just be there. I trust you and know that you will take care of her. Trust yourself."

Ronnie hoped and prayed that Jax came through on this. "What if this breaks her?"

"Then you pick up her pieces and keep them safe until she's ready for them," Ronnie answered. "Let's go."

Ronnie walked him downstairs, keeping his hand on Jax's shoulder for support. As soon as he saw Airiella, Jax went and took her hand, holding it. Ronnie let out a sigh of relief as they all hugged her making her promise to call with any news.

Ronnie went last and kissed her softly with a promise sealed in there for her that he would take care of things here. He could do this for her. He could do this for Jax. "Remember how much I love you; carry it with you."

Onida stepped over to him, "While they were checking on Ariella, I performed a shamanic blessing on each of your rooms and the hallways for when you are asleep at night and vulnerable. This house should remain a safe zone once Father Roarke does his thing."

"Thank you for that, Onida," Ronnie said gratefully.

"Please don't fear for her. We will take care of your angel while she is home," Onida touched his hand briefly and walked away with a grace that defied gravity. He stood there and watched them drive away. It felt like a part of himself was being torn in half as the two people that mattered most to him left.

He could do this. He turned to Smitty, "Our angel is expecting us to learn what we need to learn, so let's do this, so she isn't fighting on her own."

Smitty had a determined look on his face, "I've already talked with Father Roarke, and he's going to take a red-eye flight and be here early tomorrow morning."

"Perfect. I'm starting research tonight," Ronnie added.

"Guys, I met her grandpa when we had dinner with her family. We should send flowers or something," Mags fell in step beside them. "He's quite amazing."

"He'd have to be, look at his granddaughter," Ronnie smiled at Mags, throwing his arm over her shoulder. "Do what you think is best on this one, Mags."

"Absolutely. You two do your thing. I'll work on Aedan."

"Don't leave visible bruises," Smitty joked, making Ronnie wince at the memory of Airiella's first relationship. "Sorry, bro. Wasn't thinking."

"It's fine. The first serious relationship Airiella had, that's what the guy did. Hit where the bruises weren't visible."

"Did you find out his name and where we can find him?" Smitty was no longer joking.

"No. I thought about asking. I knew Airiella wouldn't like that, though." Ronnie rolled his shoulders to try and ease the tension that was creeping up. "Should we order a pizza?"

"Already done. Way ahead of you," Smitty clapped him on the back as they settled in the office. "I also texted Aedan to answer the door when it arrived and to serve us."

Ronnie laughed. "Good. Time to become a demonologist."

I hated leaving them. It felt so wrong, and I was scared shitless about being away from Ronnie like this. It wasn't that I didn't trust Jax because I did, and I knew he would do everything he could to keep me from falling apart. I also knew that if I did fall apart, he would take care of me. Ronnie had become exactly what I had told him. That supporting wall that holds the structure up during a hurricane, and I knew this was going to be a giant hurricane.

"I can still hear your thoughts, siren. I know this hard," Jax whispered in my ear. "I do promise to be what you need. Or, rather, I promise to try my best to be what you need."

"I know Jax. I'm sorry." I twined our hands together and sat as close to him as I could without crawling in his lap. He kissed my temple in response. "I need to call my friend to tell her I'll be back and need my room and see if she can pick us up."

"We will see you home, Airiella," Taklishim told me.

"That's the opposite way for you," I told him, my

brow furrowing. I pulled my phone out to call Mel.

"Hey, you," she answered.

"Mel, I'll be home tonight, family emergency," I rushed out, afraid to say the other words that were on the tip of my tongue.

"Your brother was just by to make sure I knew, I'm sorry, hon. There have been a few weird things happening you should know about here. I found the front door unlocked when I came home one day and the screen door to boot. Since I don't go in and out that way, it stood out. I couldn't see that anything was moved, or out of place. Both cats were acting normal too."

"My parents have a key, but they would have told me if they were coming by. My brother doesn't have one. Did you ask any of the neighbors if they saw anything?" A shiver went through me at the possibilities that popped in my head: my ex-husband or his son, Michael, or some random demon-possessed person.

I felt Jax stiffen. "Shit, sorry, Jax," I whispered. "Just that, or anything else, Mel?"

"The gate to the backyard was open a few weeks ago," she added. "I also know that it wasn't me because I don't go out there. I relocked both the bottom and the top locks. I did ask the neighbors if they'd seen anything, and no one had."

"Well, damn. It's a quiet neighborhood. If there'd been a rash of crimes, the neighbors would have known."

"Yeah, I figured. The neighbors are pretty nosy. There were also a couple of nights where the doorbell rang in the middle of the night. My first thought was your ex-husband, or the last one. I don't think Michael has the balls for that, does he?" Mel asked.

"Maybe. I'm inclined to agree with you, but Michael was sneaking in the apartment after I fell asleep to just fuck with my head. Maybe I'll get one of those doorbell cameras when I get back, and we can try to install it." I'd just have to make time. I didn't want to deal with a crazy ex-any of them.

Taklishim was motioning at me, and I raised my

eyebrows in a silent question. "We will take you home. If something is happening there, I want to check it out."

"Mel, I won't need to be picked up, and I won't be alone. You don't have to wait up," I informed her. Knowing things had been happening, I wasn't going to argue with Taklishim.

"You know I will anyway. I want to hug you. I know how close you and your family are," she told me. She was one of the few friends I could count on anymore. "See you soon, hon."

"Is that why your reaction to someone in your hotel room was so extreme?" Jax asked slowly. "Your ex and his head games?"

He could see my thoughts. I couldn't lie. "Yes. If it's him, well any of them, I'll handle it. Don't worry." I put my walls up and sealed them tight, hoping it would help. If it was my ex-husband, that would be easier to handle than Michael. I didn't want to face Michael.

"Do I want to know which one Michael was out of the ones I saw in that dream?" his voice held a dangerous edge. Shit, walls didn't work. "Nope, they didn't work."

"Onida and I have a way of looking in both worlds. That would show us a trace, or an echo of a spirit that was up to something. It will also give us a chance to perform shamanic blessings to keep the space safe. On top of those, I think you should enquire about a priest coming to do the same thing," Taklishim interrupted before I could have the uncomfortable talk I didn't want to have.

"Thank you, that would be appreciated. I don't want to think my friend is unsafe in my home. I still think I will do the doorbell camera thing too." I hated to feel paranoid.

"Wise move, I think," Taklishim smiled at me.

"Before we get to the plane, we never discussed the interview. I'll set it up with Aedan, so you don't have to worry about that part. We think that based on what the videos show, don't go farther in any abilities other than great intuition and the ability to read emotions. Empaths are not unknown, and it isn't a lie. It's also why they hired you." Tama laid out her thoughts. "If they bring up the glow, it was a camera or piece of electronic equipment Jax had with him. It's easy enough to fabricate not knowing what he had in his hand since that isn't your part of the team. Stick with giving away no personal information. They will ask and pry repeatedly. Don't talk about reading energy or any of that, just emotions."

"Easy enough," I said, not enthused about the idea of talking about anything that had to do with me. "It's something that I can't get out of doing?"

"No, they'll push it however they can. If you keep refusing, the backers would probably invite the press to a shoot. At least this way, it's on your terms, not theirs," Onida spoke candidly.

"Airiella," Tama's voice was gentle and kind, "tell me about your grandfather."

Grief washed through me again, and Jax stroked my hand in response. "He's amazing. His parents immigrated here from Italy. He and his brother were the first ones born over here that survived. He's the last of his family that's left, sadly. He's worked at pretty much everything; he has lived through incredible history, and his memory is damn near perfect. My nanie and grandpa are the pillars of my mom's family," I started to choke up.

"I've got you, siren," Jax kissed my temple again.

"We grew up being around them all the time. My brother and I grew up with the old school Italian values that people don't often practice over here. My grandpa was integral in that. The memories of him I have are so precious. I can't even begin to imagine him not being here." Hot tears streamed down my cheeks.

Tama leaned forward to give me a tissue. "Did they say what is wrong?"

"He's old. His heart is failing; his kidneys are failing; you can't treat one without adversely affecting the other. My brother said that he keeps having spells where he can't breathe, like it's asthma, but it's not."

Taklishim started to say something, but both Onida and Tama silenced him. "Has he lived a long life?"

"He's 96, yes he has," I admitted. It didn't make me

feel better to know it wasn't being cut short.

"He won't be gone, beautiful girl. Just his body," Tama told me.

I knew that. Not seeing my grandpa smile or hearing him laugh or tell a story was ripping a hole in me. I buried my face in Jax's shoulder, ashamed at the display of emotion I couldn't contain. I felt someone sit next to me.

"Raven, it's okay to grieve. Losing your grandpa will be a heavy loss for you. I wish that one of us could heal him for you to save you the pain. We can't. This situation is the work of his maker calling him home," Taklishim stroked my hair in a rare display of emotion from him.

"You are a raven, an angel in his faith," Onida spoke. "You will have the ability to speak to him from beyond. You carry messages, and he lives through you. Death will not be the end for such a man. It is only the beginning of a new time."

I openly sobbed. "I'm so sorry, beautiful girl. Death is a journey that marks us all. You wouldn't be who you are without him. Remember that," Tama said gently.

Jax unbuckled my seat belt and pulled me on to his lap, wrapping his arms around me. "I'd take this from you if I could, siren," Jax held tight.

"Sadly, we all unite in pain," Taklishim put his hand on my shin that lay on the seat next to him. "Would you like us to make you sleep, Raven?"

"Would I be able to think?" my voice came out muffled.

"No, Airiella, we can make it so that you don't dream of this. It won't go away when you wake up, but it will give you a few hours of peace," Tama answered.

I nodded gratefully, missing the comfort of my new family. Poor Jax. "Wait until we are on the plane, please," Jax told Tama. "Siren, don't feel sorry for me. I'm right where I'm supposed to be."

I love you, I thought to him, knowing he'd hear me. He kissed my head and held me until we pulled up to the private gate. He got me settled in a seat and held my hand. "Please, knock me out. I don't want to think right now," I pleaded with Tama.

"I understand," she smiled sadly. I felt warm, then nothing.

J ax was thankful for the few hours she'd have of peace. He'd been in no way prepared for the deep well of grief and pain she was experiencing. He nervously ran his hands through his hair and looked at her for the hundredth time in five minutes.

"She's okay, I promise you, Jax," Tama reassured him.

"The depth of her emotions is constantly catching me off guard," he admitted, surprised with himself.

"She has that effect on us, too," Taklishim said wryly.

"Do you mind if I delve into your personal life?" Tama probed.

"I'm shocked you are asking for permission," Jax responded. "You usually just ask anyway, whether I want to share or not."

"True. The reason is for my personal interest, though. I'm curious about what is between you two. I know there is a connection there because I can see it. You haven't made it permanent yet, have you?" Tama pushed him.

He felt a little embarrassed talking about it. "No, not yet. Not in the way of sexual intercourse," he grudgingly admitted.

"Why? The connection looks frayed from what I can see, despite that, it's incredibly strong already." Tama went all out in that one question.

"Why?" Jax scoffed. "You've met me. *I'm* the disaster here, not her. She's already died for me. I've been able to feel her since before I even set eyes on her for the first time. I felt her walk in the room and blew up at her. I'm fucking terrified, that's why."

"I can sense the fear, but I don't understand the fear. What is it that scares you? Being permanently connected to someone?" she pushed harder.

"No. I'm not afraid of commitment. Especially not to her," Jax mumbled. "I'm afraid to believe it's possible for someone like her to love me. I'm afraid I'll hurt her. I'm afraid that the feeling of need I have for her will go away, worse, I'm afraid that the feelings she says she has will go away once I do it."

"Does she know this?" Taklishim asked, joining in to make it even more uncomfortable.

"Yes," Jax sighed. "So does Ronnie. I know it's irrational, and I know none of that is true. I wanted to be better inside before I saddled her with me. I wanted to be more stable for her. A better person than those in her past," Jax just let the honesty flow from his lips.

Tama looked at him thoughtfully. "You speak from love, yet you can't tell her that you love her, can you?"

Jax shook his head. "Are you afraid of those words?" Taklishim pushed as hard as Tama.

"Yes, in a way. The feelings I feel toward her dwarf anything I ever felt for Winnie. There is a part of me feels guilty for that. Another part is scared of that because it's so intense. There are times it rules me. I feel so strongly about her. I want to run far away and not look back, but I can't, because not being near her is physically painful. It makes me feel no better than those in her past that used her, controlled her, tried to possess her. I don't want to do that to her."

"Do you love her?" came the quiet question Jax was terrified to admit. She already knew the answer; she wanted him to say it.

"Fuck. I do. So goddamn much," Jax looked down at her sleeping form.

"The connection will give you peace of mind," Taklishim told him. "It's a feeling of comfort, of constant love that doesn't weaken. It carries you when you think you can't go on because you can still feel her. You feed her soul; she feeds yours. It's a bond that doesn't break, Jax."

"You make it sound so easy," Jax said dryly.

"It is," Tama explained. "You will see. It will also bring you closer to Ronnie through her. Ties that won't break. It will also help to heal a large part of what remains broken in you. Put you closer to where you want to be. You are nothing like those from her past, do not let that stop you."

Jax could only nod. He wanted nothing more than to simply curl up with her right now and make it all go away. In the dimmer lighting of the plane, her skin was a dark tone. It spoke of years in the sun, yet it was a natural color for her. Her hair was dark until a stray ray of the fading sun poked in through the window and made it glow red.

"Jax, that picture you took was pure magic," Tama broke into his thoughts again.

He reached into his bag and pulled out his framed copy and handed it to her. "Take mine. I'll print another."

Taklishim traced a finger over the outline of her wings. "We will do our best for her, Jax. She's not only your world; she's the grace in ours too."

"What do her wings look like?" Tama asked.

"Perfection. Ink black and silky soft. They reflect the light like her eyes do. Makes me think of starlight," Jax closed his eyes and pictured it all.

"They must be beautiful," Tama breathed. "They are huge."

Jax stood suddenly and pulled his shirt off and turned. "This is a drawing I did from memory," he showed his tattoo.

Onida and Tama gasped, even Taklishim widened his eyes. "Jax, this is breathtaking work." Her tone changed. "You claim her then?" he figured she saw the name that was there, hidden in plain sight.

"I do, she's mine," Jax bluntly stated. "She told me that. She also said she was Ronnie's."

"It's you, Jax. Never doubt that." Tama touched his back softly.

"How do you know?" Jax sat back down.

"It's written on her soul," Onida answered for Tama.

"Time for you to start believing," Taklishim added,

staring out the window at something Jax couldn't see.

"Why do you call her siren?" Onida wanted to know.

"Her voice haunts me. Makes my body react, my heartbeat funny. I told her it's like a siren song. I also called her a witch," Jax smiled. "I told her that because at first, I wanted to believe it was some sort of spell she had me under."

Tama only smiled in response to that. Jax picked up Airiella's limp hand and held it for the rest of the flight. He napped here and there, and soon they were landing and rolling down a runway that wasn't at the airport. Jax sent a quick text to Ronnie to let them know they landed in Seattle.

"Arrangements we made," Taklishim explained at Jax's look. "Tama is going to pull her out now. Be prepared; the emotions will come back just as strong."

Jax nodded, holding her hand as she woke with a gasp. "I'm home, aren't I?"

"You will be soon," Jax kissed her forehead. "We just landed."

"It's all so very real now," she whispered sadly.

"Call your brother, baby. Let him know you landed," Jax kept his hand on her at all times.

Chapter Five

Aedan walked into the office to find Smitty and Ronnie hunched over computers and stacks of printed pages between them, with various sections highlighted. They'd been busy. "Any word?"

Ronnie lifted his head, his eyes rimmed in red. "They just landed. I got a text from Jax."

"Did you ask why suddenly her emotions went dark?" Aedan sat in the armchair and kicked his leg over the arm.

"No. Go ahead and text him," Ronnie went back to his screen.

"You aren't curious?" Aedan pushed.

"Of course, I am. If something had been wrong, Jax would have told me," Ronnie snapped.

"Sorry, Ronnie. The drastic separation is hard on all of us," Aedan replied glumly.

"Is it physically hurting you?" Smitty turned then and asked.

"No, it's an ache in my chest, but not painful." Aedan rubbed his chest.

"It's a physical pain for Ronnie," Smitty told him.

"It's more than an ache for me, though not quite as bad as Ronnie's."

"I get it. I get it. Stop pushing. Anyway, Tom just hung up with me, and they pushed our shoot schedule out a week. Taklishim pulled some big strings from his end. They tried to tell Tom to do the shoot without Airiella and Jax, but Tom stood his ground this time. So we have an additional week now on top of the already scheduled time off."

"That gives us more time to learn some stuff at least," Smitty leaned back in his chair, closing his eyes.

"Tom is an avid Airiella fan," Aedan continued. "He flat out refused to shoot an episode without her."

"Smart man," Ronnie commented.

"They also want her to do the radio interview while she is home at one of the Seattle radio stations," Aedan added, hoping they weren't paying attention. He should have known better. Both men turned to look at him.

"So she'd be doing this alone? Without us?" Smitty crossed his arms over his chest.

"Apparently. I doubt Jax would let her go at it alone," Aedan hoped that would ease the rising tension.

"No, he wouldn't. That's beside the point," Ronnie commented. "Does Tak know this?"

"I'm not sure. I sent Taklishim the info. If they just landed, then he's probably driving home right now and can't check." Aedan fidgeted. "I think the interview is a good idea."

"I'm sure you do," Smitty snarled.

"Guys. Stop. We need to work together," Ronnie said, tired.

"We need Aedan to be on board with the rest of us," Smitty argued.

"He's not wrong, Aedan," Ronnie looked at him. A surge of guilt washed through him at the look on Ronnie's face.

"You guys know I love Airiella," he tried to defend himself.

"No one questioned that," Smitty stood and

stretched. "You just seem to be taking a back seat on things, and not putting any effort into helping either her or Jax, figure this shit out."

"The paranormal gig was always Jax's thing, not mine," Aedan stood, feeling like he was on uneven ground. "I believe there are things we can't explain, and my role in this group was always the skeptic. All this that's happened, all this stuff, it's fucking with my head. Making me disbelieve in my thoughts."

"You don't think I went through the same thing?" Smitty asked aggressively.

"I'm sure you did. You've also been present for things that I can't wrap my head around. You both have seen things I haven't, things that seem to have solidified this belief. Before you jump down my throat, I am not saying I want to see her die," Aedan replied hotly.

"Look, chill. Both of you," Ronnie stood straight to his full height, his back rigid. "The last thing we need is to be divided. Today was a scary-ass shitshow, and we need to work together. Evil entities and demons are part of the reason we do this show. It was that way before we met Airiella. Having confirmation of them is great, and yes, terrifying. If we want to help, we need to learn. Aedan, focus on that. Focus on learning what we need to learn to keep ourselves and the ones we love safe."

"Easy enough." Aedan was tense. "Lay off about the rest then, until I can come to terms with it in my way. Mags riding me about it is enough."

"Fine," Smitty spat.

"Seriously, you two. Stop. Aedan, be the skeptic, that's fine. Stop letting it keep you from doing what we need to do the rest of the time. It would also be wise for you not to doubt Airiella in front of Jax or us. If you have questions about what I saw that night when I was with her, then ask. For now, knock this shit off. Smitty, ease up." Ronnie pulled on his hair in frustration.

"Sorry. I'm just tired, and I don't like being away from Airiella," Smitty backed down.

Aedan looked thoughtful, "Is that why we're all so

tense and at each other's throats? Because she's not here?"

"Probably. Which should be further proof for you to believe," Ronnie fired at him.

"Go get some sleep. You guys look exhausted," Aedan stepped away.

Smitty shrugged, clapped Ronnie on the back, and headed out of the room. He stopped in front of Aedan and held out his fist for a fist bump. Aedan let out a little sigh of relief at the gesture, which told him Smitty wasn't acting unreasonably.

Ronnie rolled his shoulders. "I mean it, Aedan. Be ready to learn tomorrow and not take a back seat. We are all needed in this. All of us."

Aedan got the message loud and clear. They weren't going to take excuses from him anymore, nor make excuses for him. "If you call her, tell her Mags, and I are thinking about her."

R onnie sat on his bed, his body hurting in ways it never had before. He felt like he was missing limbs. His heart ached like it had taken a beating. He grabbed his phone and called her.

"Hi, angel," her voice wrapped around him when she answered.

"Heracles, I miss you," she sounded numb.

"Me too, sweetheart. It hurts being away from you," he wanted to cry it hurt so much.

"We are on our way to my house now, all of us. They want to check for signs of spirit energy since weird things have been happening there." He could hear the worry in her voice she was trying to mask.

"Jax doing okay?" he hoped so. He wondered what weird things, but he would ask Jax about it instead, so she didn't get any more overwhelmed than she was.

"Yeah. I think Jax's missing being near you, too. Yep, he just nodded to me."

"You had some intensely emotional moments earlier, and then you went dark. What happened?" Ronnie settled back on the bed, trying to get comfortable.

"Tama asked about my grandpa, and I was talking about him. It just got to be too much, and she asked if I wanted to be asleep, so I didn't think. I took that option," she explained. "How are things there?"

"Tense without you. Smitty and Aedan are bickering like children. We got some good research started, and found a few interesting things we've highlighted to talk to Father Roarke about. He'll be here in the morning," Ronnie filled her in. "Any more news on your family?"

"No. My brother will be over in the morning to check in with me," the sadness he heard earlier was more evident now.

"I love you, angel. Can you feel me the same way I feel you right now?" he got up and went to her room and lay on her bed.

"I can, that's how I know you aren't okay, Heracles."

"I'm on your bed now, that helps. I may wear your clothes just to feel next to you," Ronnie tried a feeble joke.

He could hear the smile in her voice. "Definitely take pictures of that." He heard Jax chuckle in the background.

"I'm going to sleep here tonight if it's okay with you," he told her, his mind soothed by the smell of her here.

"Of course, it's okay." Her voice softened. "It's hurting me too to be away. At least I have Jax. Maybe you should snuggle with Smitty." The laugh he heard from Jax was louder now.

"Would it have been worse if Jax was here and I was there?" Ronnie ignored the Smitty comment, already plotting a picture to take of them cuddled up in her bed to send her to make her smile.

"I think it would be a lot worse for both of us," she admitted quietly.

"I think so too. But I'm not going to go and sleep in Jax's bed. Call me if you need to talk, angel."

"Love you, Heracles."

"I love you too. Stick to Jax like glue, baby." Ronnie

hung up, stripped his clothes off, and slid between the sheets. She needed him to be strong. That's why she kept calling him Heracles, to remind him.

I felt the turbulence rolling through Jax. I knew he heard the thoughts that were in my head, and I also knew he was stuck on the one about being away from Ronnie. "Jax, I don't regret you being here, stop."

Please trust me, I thought to him.

"It's just hard to believe you could love me as much as you love him," Jax whispered in my ear.

I was tired of having the others hear my conversations with Jax and thought that to him, so he understood why I wasn't answering. We were close to my house now, so I directed Taklishim the rest of the way and fought back a wave of emotion as we parked in my driveway.

"There's spirit presence here," Onida remarked as we got out.

"Loving one's," Taklishim clarified. "I suspect a human is doing the things happening here. We'll check inside as well, then bless both inside and out."

I nodded and walked up to the front door as it opened, and Mel threw her arms around me. "You didn't tell me you were bringing Gandalf, two beauty queens and someone so hot they shouldn't exist," Mel exclaimed, her eyes wide.

God, I loved her. "Mel, you are so good for my heart," I laughed softly. "I called him Gandalf too. His name is Taklishim. The other two are Tama and her sister Onida." I introduced the council members.

"She's not kidding, she really did call me Gandalf," Taklishim shook Mel's hand.

"This behind me is Jax," I introduced him.

Mel stared at him over my shoulder. "Are you and him?" she started.

"Yes, we are," Jax interrupted her. "Hi, Mel, nice to meet you," Jax shook her hand.

Stunned at Jax's comment, I became frozen to the spot. "Damn, girl," Mel grinned. "Wait, if you're an ass, you can't come in," she said protectively.

"Mel," I warned, pushing her out of the way. "Guys, come in. Taklishim, you have free rein."

"Free rein to do what?" Mel asked.

"He's going to check out the place, make some suggestions to me on how to protect it better," I skirted around the truth.

I walked to the kitchen and grabbed a bottle of water for Jax, and one for me. "So, when did this little development happen?" Mel gestured between us.

Jax smiled one of those damn smiles of his that undid me. "I knew from the first moment I laid eyes on her, but I denied it. Now, I just can't. She's mine." His hand had never once stopped touching me since we'd left California.

"Wow," Mel shot a look at me that I couldn't decipher. "I thought you were with the other one."

I honestly had no idea if Jax was putting on a show or not. "Not a show, truth," he said into my ear, his tone low for only me to hear. Damn this mind-reading thing.

Tama appeared by my side, "Can I have a moment?"

Jax looked like he was going to argue. "Talk with Mel a minute. I'll be right back."

I followed her back to the front door. "Is everything okay?"

"Yes. I just wanted to tell you that if you want Jax not to hear your thoughts, you have to picture the connection in your mind and close it off, like you do when you put up your walls. Just with the connection instead. You'll be able to feel him still, probably even feel him beat on the wall, so to speak, to let him back in, but your thoughts will be your own."

"Will this start happening with the others?" I asked, curious.

"I'm not sure. It's identical to a mate bond, in our culture. Those of us who shift into our spirit animal, we've only ever had one. It's possible since Ronnie is feeling the pain of not being with you that you might develop that with him, I can't say. Jax did not lie though, he was sincere," Tama said, gently touching my arm.

I studied her face, my mind carefully blank. "Thank you, Tama."

"They're almost finished. Then we will go. Taklishim will be in contact regarding the interview. The latest he heard was that they would do it here at a station in Seattle. If that is the case, either him or I, maybe both, will be there."

"Okay," I seriously didn't want to do the interview. Maybe it wouldn't be that bad if Tama and Taklishim were there. Jax and Mel came around the kitchen and headed towards us, as Onida and Taklishim walked down the stairs.

"Raven, all is okay. I'll check outside, and we'll go. I'll be in contact," Taklishim said carefully.

"Why is Gandalf calling you by your last name?" Mel interrupted.

"It's, uh, it's just what he does," I stammered, as warning bells went off in my head. "Mel, go upstairs and go to bed," I focused on using the tone that got people to listen to me.

She gave me an odd look but went upstairs with the promise of talking to me more tomorrow. "Oh, the cats are probably under my bed if you are looking for them."

"I figured," I stuck my hand out to hold Taklishim in place. "Goodnight, Mel."

"What is it, Raven?" Taklishim was on guard.

"I feel something outside and get the sense that you need to stay right here for a minute," I answered quietly in case Mel was still in earshot.

"Focus it, Raven. Ask what the danger is," Taklishim's skin cooled under my hand.

Jax had his hand on my back, and I turned inward, opening my senses and asking for direction and guidance. "Someone is watching us," my voice came out like it was automated.

"Human or spirit?" Onida asked.

"Human. Specifically, you three. You three are the

targets." That was all I was saw.

"Give it time, Airiella. You'll be able to hone that warning soon," Tama explained. "That is the raven talking to you, passing messages."

We all heard a car start and the sounds of it leaving, then the warning in my head receded. "It's gone now," I released Taklishim. "You don't look bothered by what I said," I stated.

"I suspected that some of the council and board were curious about my involvement with you. When we notified the board that we were bringing you back with us due to a family emergency and that the shooting needed to wait, there was a little pushback. Asher is terrified of you, Dr. Stone, on the other hand, dislikes you intensely. Aminda fears what your presence means, but has not spoken the truth of what you are. Dr. Fields is suspect. She plays a dangerous game of information gathering, and Onida watches her closely," Taklishim explained.

"The warning you gave came with good timing. If whoever that was, had seen us blessing the house, they would have known something more was going on other than the concern for your well-being that we have stated," Tama added to Taklishim's statement.

"The fact that you had a warning at all tells me that the intent was not good," Onida said.

"I can tell you that's true. Those warnings only go off when something is wrong," I confirmed.

"We will separate and bless the house and property fast and be on our way. I don't think they will continue to watch you as their interest is in us, but stay on guard nonetheless," Taklishim placed his hand on my shoulder. "I'll be in touch."

Tama and Onida gave me brief hugs, whispered something in Jax's ears, and they went outside. I locked up behind them and made sure everything else was closed up downstairs. "Grab your bag," I told Jax.

I led him up to my room and closed the door behind us, locking it as well. "This suits you," Jax looked around my room. It was simple, and it was my favorite room in the house. It made me ridiculously happy that he liked it.

"Ok, Zeus. Spill. What was with the whole insinuating we have a relationship? Was it a cover, so she didn't hit on you?" I asked, dropping to my bed. I had missed my bed.

"I didn't lie. You are mine. I want it known. It's not a jealous thing, either, so don't go there. While you rested on the plane, the three that just left had a pretty candid talk with me and forced me to admit my fears. I realized I could admit them because of you. I told Mel the truth. I knew it when I first saw you," Jax stroked his fingers down my cheek.

"You hated me when you first saw me. I felt it," my voice was low, so it didn't carry.

"It wasn't me that hated you, siren. It was that darkness in me. It still hates you, but I don't. I never have. Every emotion you've brought out in me is the strongest I've ever had. Whether it's jealously, desire, anger, excitement, happiness, protectiveness, you name it. They've all been off the charts."

He laid on his side and faced me. "You certainly know how to keep me on uneven ground with you," I smiled to take the sting out of my words.

"Tell me what you didn't want to say to me in front of them," Jax told me.

Damn it. I wasn't going to get out of this. "You seem to be under the impression that the love I feel for Ronnie overshadows how I feel for anyone else, is that fair?"

"Sometimes," he was hesitant to answer.

"Despite me telling you I love you, you still believe that. Even though I've said, the connection I have with you is by far the strongest of all. And now the added fact that you can see my damn thoughts all point to that being true." I kept the frustration out of my tone; it impressed me.

He had a wary look on his face. "I'm not sure where this is going."

"This is something I am only ever going to say to *you* because it undermines my feelings for everyone else, and I never want to do that. The love I feel for you is so much deeper than what I feel for Ronnie. That's why I haven't pushed you, Jax. It scares me after my past relationships. Ronnie is easy; he never lets me fall. I'm constantly off-balance with you. These words you keep saying strip me down to nothing, and as much as I don't want to admit it, you have my heart in your hands. It's yours. *Nothing* with you is easy, and it makes me value it so much more. Ronnie is my comfort food, a safe place, a deep pool of love I could swim in forever. You are the ocean." The effect this man had on me left me shaking. "Do you see the comparison of a pool to the ocean?"

He stood and lifted my legs on to the bed and settled himself on top of me. "Are your senses open?" I nodded. "Feel me," he kissed me, so gently and softly at first, I wanted to weep with the sweetness of his tongue mingling with mine. Then he deepened it, and it turned into that demanding kiss that left me weak and desperate for him.

I felt the love he wouldn't admit pouring from him through every stroke of his tongue that begged me for an answer to a question I didn't know he was asking. I felt the depth of it pulling me in like the ocean comparison, tossing me around on the waves of that love and threatening to drown me if I didn't surrender to it.

He broke off the kiss. "I love you, siren," he said, staring into my eyes. "I love every infuriating thing about you. You are the reason my heart keeps beating."

A hysterical laugh bubbled up. "Okay, fine, I'll be your girlfriend."

"Like you had a choice," he kissed my nose.

"That's why it scared me," I whispered. "I never had a choice with you. I've been falling down a rabbit hole since you tried to start a fight with me in a hotel dining room."

"Tomorrow is going to be hard, you ready?" He rolled off me and laid back on his side, his hand on my face.

"Not even a little. Why does everything always have to happen at once?" I closed my eyes. "One thing at a time would be nice for a change."

"Do you want to shower tonight or in the morning?

I'm assuming your brother will be by early." He stroked my hair. I wonder if he knew how much I liked that. "I know it now," he answered my thought.

Shit. "I'll shower now, so my hair has a chance to dry, at least," I sat up.

"Hey, I like seeing your thoughts. It helps me," Jax held my hand. "When those doubts inside me creep up and start to fight, your thoughts are the beacon of light showing the path through the dark. That's how I get through."

Hello rabbit hole, I'm still here. "Well, let's see how you handle the insanity of my family. Be prepared for my brother not to like you," I stood and went into my closet to grab a nightshirt. "You might decide you don't love me anymore after that."

"I can handle it. Your family won't scare me away," he promised with one of those killer smiles.

Cold shower it is, I decided as I walked into the bathroom to the sound of his quiet laughter. I made it a quick one. Despite all the resting I had been doing, the emotional exhaustion was taking a toll. I needed a recharge before seeing my grandpa and my mom.

I walked back into my bedroom to see Jax sitting on my bed in only boxers. Maybe I needed a colder shower. He smiled and stood, "Not tonight, baby. We both need rest, and with what I want to do to you, I need far more energy than I have." Maybe an extra-long cold shower.

"Your mind is an interesting place," he gave me a quick kiss. "Now, *I* need a cold shower."

"Towels in the closet to your right by the bathtub," I called after him. I plugged my phone in and opened my windows, staring out into the night. I asked the wind to carry a message to my grandpa that I was coming and that I loved him.

I must have stood there for a while because when Jax slid his arms around me, it startled me. I hadn't even heard the shower shut off. "He knows you love him, siren. There's not any way possible that anyone in your life doesn't know how much you love them. It radiates from you."

I leaned back into him. Holy shit. "Um, are you naked?"

"Yeah, is that a problem?" he pulled back a little, and my body followed.

"No. Nope. Except I might not sleep now," my voice took on a husky tone.

He laughed into my ear, "Yes, you will."

I snapped the curtains closed. "Don't want to share that view. Actually, I don't want to look at that view yet."

"Should that hurt my feelings?" he asked with a fake injured tone.

"No. Definitely not. That's the last of my will power holding on there." I kept my back to him and crawled into bed.

"Be naked, please, let's be skin to skin all night. I will behave," he pleaded gently.

"I'm not worried about you. It's me I'm worried about," was my quick answer, but I complied and pulled the shirt off.

"I just want to hold you. I'm feeling a little vulnerable and need to be close. It's the first time I've told someone I love you in twelve years. Aside from family," he added as an afterthought.

"Oh. In case my cousin in there at the hospital tomorrow, be prepared to be fangirled all over," I told him. "Now kiss me goodnight, Zeus."

He did. Damn, that man could kiss. "I love you, Airiella," he pulled me into him.

This rabbit hole had no end. "I love you, Jax."

Chapter Six

Winnie worried about how Airy was famous over here. It wasn't right. Winnie had a good thing going on with Onida and was able to pass along quite a bit of information. That was how she learned of Airy's grandpa and mom. Winnie had freaked out at the news and tried to find some of the good spirits that had connections to find out if he was going to pass or not.

She couldn't find anyone. Demons had been using this space as a gathering spot before crossing, and the good spirits didn't want to be spotted. She didn't blame them. Some of these demons were horrendous. She hid when she felt the darkness creep in too.

She heard Ronnie call her, so she popped over there. "Is Airy okay?"

"She's emotional as hell. I can't sleep. It hurts to be away from her," Ronnie said. That's when Winnie noticed he was in Airiella's room. "Jax went with her so she could keep him safe."

"That was a good call based on the things I'm picking up from over here," Winnie sat next to him. "He's got a huge target painted on him. You do too, though it's not as big.”

“Have you been able to pick up any names? Their names carry power, and we can exorcise them easier with it, I’ve read,” he picked at a thread on the sheets.

“No, they are separating into groups. All I keep hearing is group one or group two. It sounds like they are going to do it in waves to try and weaken Airy and Jax both.”

“She’s not weak. You should have seen her, Winnie. It was terrifying and amazing at the same time. Not to mention she got a few good hits in with boxing as well,” Ronnie smiled wistfully. “Why does this hurt so much?”

“I’m not sure. It has something to do with the connection and the strength of it. Please tell me that you guys are going to try and figure out a way to protect yourselves? It’s scary.” Winnie put her hand on Ronnie’s arm. “As much as I want to hug you, I don’t want you to be here.”

“Something tells me Airiella wouldn’t let that happen,” Ronnie moved his hand to run it along where he could see her arm was. He couldn’t touch her, but she felt the energy of him.

“No, she would die first. I don’t want that to happen either. Onida has some weight over here and has been working fast and furious to get as much information as she can. I think that something will happen soon. That’s what my gut is saying.”

“I don’t want her to die, Winnie. Even if she can come back from it,” Ronnie’s eye filled with tears.

“I don’t either. We both know Airy will do what she can to keep you safe. They *all* know it over here. If she dies and comes back, they know she has to recover, and that is when you all will be at your weakest. They all know this, and it’s awful.” Winnie fretted and stood and paced.

“Father Roarke will be here in the morning. Smitty and I researched a bunch today, and this is his specialized area. I’m choosing to have faith that we can best this. Losing anyone isn’t an option,” Ronnie pounded his fist into the bed furiously.

Winnie understood. She hadn't had any visions; she didn't know any outcomes. All she had was intuition and instinct. "Onida told me that there was human interference as well. A sudden deeper interest in Airiella since that live show became an internet sensation."

"Are we going to lose her, Winnie?" Ronnie looked at her with utter fear in his eyes.

"I don't know. I know that you have some pretty powerful people on your side and enough love to cover the world a couple of times over. She gets stronger by the day. Sadly, she also finds battles that exhaust her every day too. I fully believe she can do this, Ronnie, I just know she needs help." Winnie heard a whisper from the other side.

"That's my goal. Find every way to help that I can help and do it to fight with her, not watch her do it alone. Not to belittle you, Winnie, I've just never known love like this," Ronnie flung himself backward on the bed.

"Seeing you love someone doesn't hurt me, Ronnie. Just the opposite, it makes me unbelievably happy to see it in both you and Jax. Seeing the love you guys have for her is heart-lifting. Likewise, seeing the way she loves you both." Winnie moved back over to Ronnie.

"I just didn't want you to think that what I felt for you wasn't real," he stated.

"I know it was real, don't worry about that. You guys being happy now is what matters to me. The love we had will always be a part of you and always be with me. It doesn't die, Ronnie."

"I do love you, Winnie," his voice was soft.

"I know. I love you, too. I always will. Please try and get some sleep," Winnie ran her hand over his face.

"Watch over our girl while she's home," Ronnie rolled on to his side and buried his face in Airiella's pillow.

"I'll do what I can, I promise." Winnie sat there until he fell asleep and then popped out to find who was whispering and what the message was. She had work to do.

Chapter Seven

Jax woke up with a naked Airiella sprawled out over his chest, her lengthy hair draped over his arm like a silk blanket. It was the happiest he'd been in a long time despite the circumstances that had brought him here.

He took the opportunity to check her shoulder while she was sleeping and couldn't talk back or argue with him that she was okay. It was a nasty bruise that would have even slowed Ronnie down. He believed her when she said she was used to it and based on what Taklishim had said.

He moved her hair out of her face, brushing it to the side and traced the contours of her face. She still had shadows under her eyes, and he knew how exhausted she'd been. He didn't figure with the added family issues that it would get any better, on top of the learning how to fight demons. Oh, and don't forget that ugly darkness in him, and remember to heal your internal wounds while you're at it.

She stirred under his hands, and he tried to tamp down the emotions to keep from waking her up. She was a light sleeper. He understood why after hearing about the ex that had been sneaking in at night while she slept. Nope, shut that down, that thought didn't help quiet his emotions.

She shifted and moved her hands down around his back, hugging him while she slept. There it was, the happy came flooding back into him, making his heart light. He grinned like a fool remembering her rabbit hole comments in her thoughts last night. It was a great description, now that he thought about it.

"Alice in Wonderland was my favorite book as a kid," she said sleepily.

Startled at the words, he looked at her. "What?"

"You were talking about the rabbit hole I was falling in," she murmured.

"No, siren. I wasn't talking. Those were thoughts," Jax said in wonder.

Suddenly she was wide awake, and those angel eyes of hers locked on his. "I heard your thoughts?"

"Apparently," he replied wryly. "Good morning."

"Think something," she demanded quietly.

He thought about how beautiful she was. He thought about the picture she made sitting there on the beach. He thought about their first kiss and about when he realized he was in love with her.

She groaned. "Thinking those thoughts will make me need another cold shower," she put her head back on his chest.

"This could be fun," he chuckled.

"Two-way street Zeus, remember that," she warned. "Or maybe I should just use this tone when I talk to you from now on," she said in that tone of voice that made him hard.

"Witch. That's playing dirty," he pulled her up to kiss her. He slid his hands down over those hips he found so alluring and cupped her ass, pushing her down on him.

"Who's playing dirty?" she gave him a look and was interrupted by her cell phone going off. "Damn it," she swore, looking at it evilly. "My brothers on his way." She stroked him a couple of times. "Might want to make that go down before he gets here," she said sweetly and stood up.

He swore then and vowed revenge knowing she'd

catch the thought. He grabbed a pair of jeans out of his bag and a plain white shirt, pulling them on as she came walking out of the closet dressed similarly, but in a brightly colored shirt.

"Holy hell, Jax. You wear white t-shirts well," she bit her lip and looked at him like she was hungry. "Shit. Now I don't want to take you anywhere because if some random female hits on you, I might have to strike them down with lightning."

"Ditto, siren. You've got enough men already," Jax was having a hard time calming his body down. He grabbed his leather coat from the bottom of the bag and shut her windows.

Her brother knocked on the screen door right as they came down the stairs. Jax ran his hands through his hair nervously. "Stop worrying," she told him.

She opened the door to a scowling man Jax assumed was her brother. He opened the screen door and snatched her up in a hug. "Ells, this shit sucks."

"Any news?" she asked him as he released her. "Jax, this is my brother Nick. Nick, this is Jax."

"Nice to meet you," Jax held out his hand. Nick hesitated a moment then shook it warily.

"You are on the show, right?" Nick asked Jax.

"Yes, along with three others."

"Why are you here?" he scowled at Jax.

"Nick, stop," Airiella pushed him down the hallway. "I'm the older one."

"It's not like you have a history of picking great men, Ells," Nick threw at her.

Jax bristled, wanting to defend her, but she jumped in with both feet. "Don't start. Jax is here because I want him here. Yes, I'm dating him. He's a good man. You can either be nice or get out. Your choice," Airiella put her hands on her hips in defiance.

"Sorry, Ells. I just worry about you. I'll behave." Jax noticed that Nick still ignored him, but he didn't care. She'd just told her brother about them, and Jax felt proud.

"So, news? Mom? Grandpa?" Airiella reminded

him.

"Mom's banged up pretty good. The pickup hit them on her side as it ran a red light. They did surgery last night to put a pin in her leg, and she has some bruised ribs and a concussion. She looks worse than she is because of the bruising. Dad stayed there all night; he hasn't been home yet."

"Is she at least in the same hospital as grandpa?" she asked hopefully.

"No. Mom is at Valley. Grandpa is at Swedish. Dad's banged up too, just bruises and whiplash though. He's moving slow," Nick warned.

"Okay. So we go there, you take dad home and make him eat and shower. He can come back in mom's car. I'll go to the hospital and see if I can get them to transfer her to Swedish so that she can at least see Grandpa in case he does die," Jax heard her voice break at that.

"Grandpa isn't good. I couldn't go in, Ells." Airiella hugged Nick at that, and Jax felt the emotions roll through her.

"I'll go with you," she said quietly.

"Nanie is exhausted. He wakes up and keeps telling her that he's dying and isn't going to make it and he just wants to hear her voice," Nick's voice broke this time, and Jax shifted when he swayed, thinking he was going to fall. "I'm not used to seeing either of them this way. I don't handle this well."

"I know, Nick. I'm here. You take care of dad. Just make him bring the car, so he goes back home. He can't keep staying in the hospital," she told him, grabbing her purse and keys. She opened the pantry and grabbed a couple of granola bars and some waters out of the fridge.

The thoughts were flying through her mind so fast, Jax was having a hard time following. She was assuming the responsibility of a majority of it, and it boggled his mind. She led them out to the garage and sent Nick to his car while she got in what Jax assumed was hers.

She handed him a granola bar and water. "I'll make sure I feed you soon," she promised him.

"Siren, you don't need to add me to that list of people in your head. I can help you, just tell me what you need, baby."

"Just stick close to me. My mom and brother are both bi-polar and can be very high energy or very draining. The lows are super low. My mom takes meds for it, but my brother doesn't. My dad is about as laid back as can be. My nanie is a spitfire and will run roughshod over anyone in her way. She's also protective and will ask you numerous invasive questions. The rest is a typical family. If my grandpa is as bad as my brother implied, that means that everyone will be there driving the hospital staff crazy. Lots of aunts, uncles, and cousins," she gave him a quick rundown.

"That's good info, but it doesn't tell me how to help you," he put his hand on her thigh, giving it a light squeeze.

"Sticking close to me helps. You'll see. Every family has the person who is the strong one that the others all lean on. In this case, it's me. Mostly because of the empath stuff. But also because I typically have my dad's temperament. I'm easy going, usually, until my buttons get pushed repeatedly. Then my mom comes out of my mouth."

"I've seen the pissed off, and it's intimidating. Yet, I don't think easy is how I would describe you," Jax stated. "Fierce, empathetic, loving, strong, sarcastic, brave, kind, but not easy."

They stopped at a light, and she pulled him over and kissed him. "Definitely, stay close."

I should probably warn you now. I hate driving, and if I offend your delicate sensibilities, I apologize. Once we leave Valley and head into Seattle, road rage will take over." I paused. "Hmmm. I wonder if I can fry the idiot drivers with lightning?"

Jax bust out laughing. "Siren, I have no delicate sensibilities. We should probably try not to end up on the news, though. Let's hold off on the lightning for a bit." I loved it when he laughed like that. "Is Ells a family nickname?"

"Huh? Oh. Yes. My friend in Kansas calls me that too. Ells or Ella is what my family calls me. Airiella, if they are not happy with me."

"I gotta say, Ells suits you. I may have to borrow it."

We pulled up to the hospital and parked. "I hope that my brother can get my dad out of here. If I have to use the emotion thing to get my way, I'd rather him not be witness to it."

"You think that they will push back on transferring her?" Jax held my hand as we walked to the entrance.

"Definitely. Some hospitals, like this one, care feels more of a business than it is concern and welfare of the patient. It's a hot button issue I have. I may have to push or pull some emotions out of people until I can get them to see my way. Or use the voice persuasion thing."

Jax wrapped his arm around my shoulder and pulled me into him. "Warn me if you use the voice thing so I can at least try to stand, so it's not as noticeable that I'm hard as a rock."

I giggled. "Noted." I followed my brother until we got to a room, and he hesitated, shifting uncomfortably. "What's wrong?"

"I don't want to go in. Mom's going to be overly emotional, and I'm tired enough not to be able to handle it."

"I'll send Dad out. Just wait here, then," I squeezed Jax's hand tighter when he went to let go. "Stay close, remember?"

"Are you sure you want me going in from the start?" He pulled his hand loose. "I think you should go first and check to see how she is before I go in."

He made sense. I didn't want to go alone, though. *You're my security blanket,* I thought in my head.

I'll be right here with your brother, he thought back to me.

Damn it. Here I thought Smitty was the logical one. Jax coughed behind me to cover his laugh. I opened the door and poked my head in, my dad struggling to get to his feet when he saw it was me.

"Sit down, Dad," I told him softly.

"Ells!" my mom cried.

"Hi Mom," I walked gingerly over to the bed. She looked like a damn mess. I leaned over to kiss her cheek and give her a light hug. "They have you on lots of drugs?" I asked, looking her over.

"Ells," my dad said tiredly. I walked over and hugged him tightly. "I've missed you."

"I missed you guys, too. Dad, go home with Nick. Shower and change. Eat something healthy too. Then come back in mom's car. I'm going to get her transferred to Swedish," I said, guiding him to the door.

"I tried to get them to do that, but they won't." My dad said, frustration lining his face. "She's freaking out about not seeing grandpa."

"I'll handle it. You take care of you for a few hours, then go to Swedish. I'll make sure they transfer her," I told him gently.

"Thanks for coming, Ells," he hugged me again.

I opened the door, and Nick had a strange look on his face. Jax stepped forward and held out his hand to my dad. "Hello sir, I'm Jax. I work on the show with Airiella."

"Nice to meet you, I'm Spencer," my dad gave me a funny look and shook Jax's hand. My brother was pointedly trying not to smile, and I knew something was up.

"I'd also like to ask you for permission to date your daughter. My intentions toward her are serious, and I'd feel honored if you gave me your blessing."

More hysterical laughter bubbled up, and I bit it back. That explained the look on my brother's face. The shithead knew. Jax gave me a guarded look and I tried to silence my thoughts. They were too chaotic.

"Jax, I could give you my blessing all day long, but if she doesn't want to date you, there isn't a thing I could do about it," my dad said with a smile. "For what it's worth, I appreciate the gesture. Don't hurt her."

Now the laughter came. "Oh, jeez. Dad, go with

Nick. Jax, come with me," I blushed, and pushed my dad.

My brother walked over, hugged me and whispered in my ear, "He did the same thing to me. I like him, but I'll deny I ever said that. Takes balls to ask someone you are meeting for the first time for permission to date their daughter."

"Go. Take Dad, and go," I pushed him too. "I'll see you both in a bit."

I couldn't stop blushing. "I can't believe you just did that," I told Jax.

"I meant it. I want your dad to know I am not dating you to pass the time, that it's serious for me," he dropped a kiss on my forehead. "Some values that I have are old fashioned."

"I'll say. My dad's not the one you should be worried about, though," I tugged on his hand. "Let's get this over with."

We walked back into the room, and my mom looked at Jax with glassy eyes. "Who's this, Ells?"

"Mom, this is Jax. He works on the show with me, and he's also my boyfriend. Jax, this is my mom, Mariana," I introduced them.

My mom just stared at him. She was on pain meds, there was no way to predict what would come out of her mouth, and I was a little nervous about that. "He certainly fills out those clothes well." There it was.

I knew it would be something embarrassing. "Mom, stop."

"Well, he does. Are you going to get me out of here?" My mom tried to sit up, and I jumped forward to push her back down. "You look different, Ells."

"I look old and tired, Mom," I said truthfully.

"No, you have more contours. Is that from athletic sex?"

Oh, my God. Jax was having a hard time holding back his laughter, and I heard him say in my head *if only she knew about Ronnie too*. "Mom, I haven't had sex with Jax. I know you're high as a kite right now, but come on."

"Why the hell not?" she shouted. "Look at him!"

I threw my hands in the air and winced at the pain that shot through my shoulder. "Mom, I'm not here to discuss my sex life with you. I'm going to find someone to talk to about getting you transferred. Stop moving around and sit still."

I yanked Jax back out into the hallway. "Oh siren, I like your mom," he laughed.

"That's not how she normally is. My life is a circus. I can't believe any of that just happened." I looked around for a nurse. "Help me find someone to talk to about getting her moved. I'm not even going to ask. I'm going straight for their emotions and just going to make it happen," I started walking down the hallway.

Jax jogged to catch up to me, still laughing. "Baby, slow down. We'll find someone," he wrapped an arm around me and hugged me to him. "Don't be embarrassed. Although I want to know what athletic sex is."

"Please, do not even ask her," I begged him, my words muffled in his chest.

"Find the humor in it, siren. I doubt there will be much later," Jax kissed the top of my head.

We found a nurse, who directed us to another nurse, who sent us to someone else, and finally, forty minutes later, we ended up in front of an administrator. I did exactly what promised Jax I would do. I found a strand of sympathy and fed it until it lit up like a runway. I pitched the sob story and got a transfer underway.

I texted my brother and my dad to let them know that within the hour, the hospital was moving her via ambulance to Swedish. I then asked the administrator to contact someone at Swedish to see if they could get my grandpa, and my mom moved to a room together, so we didn't interrupt two other families with my large one shuttling between two places. It took a bit more convincing to get that done, but he agreed, and soon I had word that my grandpa was transferring to a different room.

If nothing else, it would ease the frustrations of the nursing staff, with my overbearing but well-intentioned family. I was already exhausted, and we hadn't even gotten to Swedish yet. I promised to write glowing letters to the boards of both hospitals, praising their efforts to aid my family in their time of need.

We got back to my mom's room as her pain meds were wearing off, and her mood was drastically different. *Bi-polar*, I reminded Jax through the connection. I got a nurse to come in and give her another dose as the doctor was signing off on the transfer papers.

Her ride showed up, and I promised her I'd be at Swedish waiting for her, and that my dad would be back. She was back in an emotional mess when they loaded her up. Her mood swings battering away at me.

I trudged back to my car and dug around for my iPod. "I need music. Loud music."

Jax tenderly cupped my chin and kissed me sweetly. "You are doing great, love."

Tears pooled. "I'm not looking forward to this."

"I know. Do you want me to drive?" Jax swiped his thumb under my eye to catch the tears that escaped.

"No. I know the way. Driving here is a shit show anyway, and one that's familiar. Thank you, though."

"I'm going to check in with Ronnie. Blast your music, do what you need to do," he kissed me again.

I got us there in record time, veering off the highway when traffic came to a standstill and taking the back roads instead. We parked and headed in. I needed to check with the directory staff to find out where they had moved my grandpa.

I took the stairs instead of the elevator to burn off some of the tension before we got there. "Sorry in advance. I don't know what we are walking into or how to prepare you. Put your walls up; this will be good practice for you. I'll talk to you in my head when I don't want others to hear."

"Why put my walls up?" Jax asked as we reached the final flight of stairs up.

"Because my family is a lot to take in at once. Even more so in an emotional situation. Plus, you are an empath, too. I don't know how many of them are here, and it's easier to handle if you put them up. I'll leave mine down to get a read. Regardless, you'll know what I'm thinking and feeling. With your walls up, it will be easier to keep stuff away from that energy inside you too. Hospitals drive me batty."

"You really think your family is that bad?" we stopped outside the door to the hallway, and I leaned into him.

"Sometimes, they are. My family doesn't mean anything by it, and they do have good intentions most of the time. They can be protective of me, yet at the same time, suck all the energy out of me with their drama shit. I really would have rather you met them in a family dinner situation than one involving death. Life happens though, and I don't always get a choice," I said in a rush.

"I understand." He tipped my chin up, "I love you."

Even now, he still made me gushy when he said it. "Everything okay with Ronnie?"

"Yes. Ronnie also said you were welcome for the athletic sex," Jax gave me one of his melting smiles.

"Of course, he did," I giggled. "I miss him so much. I'd give anything to be laying in a bed between the two of you right now."

"I know. I can't say I regret the alone time with you," Jax held me for a few minutes.

"Me neither. And you do fill out those clothes very well," I added with a small laugh.

I took a deep breath and opened the door, the smells and sounds of the hospital slamming into me. We wound around the hallway, and I slowed as my cousins came into view. *Brace yourself;* I sent through the connection. They hadn't caught sight of me yet, and the nurses checking Jax out hadn't escaped my attention. I wrapped my arm around him, giving out a back off he's mine, vibe.

Gabby turned and saw Jax before she saw me, which wasn't a surprise since everyone was looking at him. I could have been invisible for all I knew. "You aren't invisible, you are all I see," Jax whispered. That rabbit hole

I liked so much even followed me to a hospital.

Gabby noticed me then and broke into a run and slammed into me, the pain in my shoulder from the impact almost taking me to my knees. Jax kept his arm around me for support. "You're here!" she yelled in my ear.

"Yes, Gabby, I'm here, you don't need to yell," I tried to pull away from her. "Let me breathe."

She looked back at Jax. "Why are you here? And why is your arm around her?"

Sorry, I sent it to him through the connection. "He's here for me. His arm is around me because he's my boyfriend. Satisfied?"

"Wait, I thought you were doing the big hot one. Uh, Ronnie," she spouted off.

Jax leaned forward with that heart-stopping smile of his. "Want to know a secret?" he asked her.

"Always," she said eagerly.

"She's dating us all," Jax smirked.

I cringed. I felt it coming. "You slut!" Gabby shouted.

"Gab, inside voice," I tried to shush her.

"Gabby, is it?" Jax's voice had taken on an edge.

Chill, Jax. She didn't mean it as you think, I sent to him.

"Yeah, you're Jax, the jerk," she crossed her arms and glared at him.

"Gabby," I started, but Jax interrupted.

"Airiella is the farthest thing from a slut that you could get. Even if you were joking, that's not cool. I might be a jerk, but I'm *her* jerk, and I love her."

Gabby's mouth gaped open. "You love her?"

"Time and place, Gabby." I pushed her down the hallway.

"You are one lucky bitch, Ells," Gabby smiled. "He's a jerk, but he's a hot jerk."

"Time and place," I reminded her. "How's Grandpa?"

"Not good. Grandpa asked for you, said you told him you were coming. Did you talk to him?"

"No, I haven't talked to him." *I asked the wind to tell him,* I sent to Jax.

That's a neat trick; he sent back. *Is Gabby always like this?*

Sadly, yes, I sent.

Gabby's two brothers stood slumped against the wall in the hallway. "Those are Gabby's brothers," I pointed them out to Jax. "The partially bald one is Justin, the younger one, Aaron."

I pointed past them to my aunt Elena. "That's my aunt Elena, my mom's older sister, the one in the denim jacket. Next to her is the youngest sister, Amy. Across from Amy is my uncle Joe; he lives with my grandparents to help them out and is my mom's younger brother. Next to him is her older brother, Gene. The little firecracker coming out of that room is my nanie, Florence."

"There's a lot of love in this hallway," he spoke quietly.

"They have a lot of love. As I said, their hearts are in the right place; they just don't always handle things in the best way," I clarified. "They all are amazing in their ways, and I couldn't ask for a better family."

"Ella!" my nanie came rushing over. "You made it! Are you okay?" She squished my cheeks between her hands and studied my face.

"Of course, I made it, Nanie. I'm totally fine," I lied, hugging her tiny four-foot, ten-inch frame.

"How's your mom?" she stepped back and looked over Jax in the way only she could, and I snickered knowing the third degree was about to start for him.

"She should be here any minute now. I managed to get her transferred here, and I sweet-talked them into putting her and Grandpa in a room together to minimize disruptions for other patients."

"That was you that got him moved? You are such a good girl. Introduce me to the nice young man here." She looked up at Jax towering over her.

"Nanie, this is Jax. He's my boyfriend, and he is also the creator of the television show where I work. Jax, this is my nanie, Florence, though we just call her Nanie. It means grandma in Italian."

"Boyfriend?" she looked at me carefully. "I didn't think you would ever date again. He's nice-looking. Do you drink Jax?"

Sorry, I thought as loud as I could.

"No ma'am. Not really. A beer every once in a while, but I'm usually too busy."

"Oh, he's polite! I like that, Ella. Do you do drugs?"

"No, ma'am," he smiled.

"Have you ever hit a woman?" she continued.

"Nanie!" I tried to stop her.

Jax lost his smile. "It's okay, siren." He gave me a soft smile. "Never once in my life. That's a behavior I find reprehensible in people," he said sincerely to my nanie.

"Did you just call her siren?" This woman missed nothing. Gabby had inched closer, hoping to see a show.

"I did, it's a nickname I have for her," Jax said carefully while asking me silently if this was dangerous territory.

Only for me, I thought back.

"Why do you call her that?" Nanie asked him.

"Yeah, why?" Gabby added, butting in.

"Because her voice is like a siren song. It mesmerizes me, soothes me, and it's beautiful," he happily explained.

I winced, knowing what was coming. "That's perfect!" Nanie exclaimed, clapping her hands. "She has the sexiest voice I've ever heard."

Gabby rolled her eyes, "Princess Airiella, everyone. The prodigal granddaughter has returned to the fold."

Jax gave Nanie one of those patented smiles of his, and I watched in absolute amazement as she melted for him. "I agree with you wholeheartedly on that."

"Are you financially secure? Will you be able to take care of her?" Nanie finished off her round of questioning, already won over by him.

"Yes, ma'am." I was blushing furiously by now.

"He's a good boy, Ella. Easy on the eyes," Nanie's

seal of approval complete, her focus shifted behind me. "That must be your mom."

"I think I'm in love with her," Jax whispered to me.

I smiled at him. *Good*, I thought, *because, without Nanie's approval, your life would have started to suck pretty badly.*

I saw my favorite cousin coming out of the hospital room and dragged Jax over. "Stephanie!"

"Hey, Ells, I wondered if you'd make it up. I figured Nick called you, so I didn't."

"Jax, this is Stephanie, my youngest cousin. Stephanie, this is Jax. He's the one," I added, so she knew it was serious.

"Well, that's news! Hi Jax. I'll interview you later. I have a little understanding with Ells that her next relationship has to be approved by me since the others were pretty shitty. This little lady here is my daughter Emma."

I snatched the cutest baby in the world from Stephanie's hands and started cooing at her. "She's gotten so big, Steph. Where's Louis? That's her son," I said to Jax. "He's a wild one. Ronnie would love him."

"He's still in there with Bob and my brothers. Bob is my husband," Stephanie explained to Jax. "The one that is wearing overalls is my oldest brother Pete; the younger one is my brother Mike. Bob will be the one with the wild child in his arms. While we have a moment, Jax, how much of Ells's past do you know?"

"Enough to assure you that none of that would ever happen with me," he answered her simply.

"It's true, Steph. I've got a lot to fill you in on." Jax raised an eyebrow at me. I nodded. *Her, I would tell everything to,* I added.

I waited in the hallway while they got my mom settled in the room. When the nurses came out, I poked my head in and saw my cousins still there. I wanted to give them time, so I leaned against the wall and waited, sitting quietly with Stephanie.

When they came out, I stood. "Go, Ells. I'll keep the

others out. He's been waiting for you."

I took a deep breath and felt Jax's hand settle on my lower back. I stepped into the room and saw the drugs had knocked my mom out. I was thankful for that. I looked at my grandpa, and my heart clenched painfully, and I felt Jax falter.

Easy, baby, he sent me.

Grandpa looked terrible. His lined faced was almost skeletal, bruises up, and down his arms from various blood draws. His typically darker-toned olive skin was now paperwhite and thin. He appeared so frail, so unlike his usual solid self.

I bit back a cry and tried to shut down the emotions that I was sure were showing on my face. Grandpa's eyes blinked open. Watery and almost opaque, he focused on me. "Ella, I knew you were coming. I heard you tell me."

I felt Jax misstep and knew he must be picking up on the emotions I couldn't control. "Hi, Grandpa. Kind of an extreme way to get me to come and visit, isn't it?"

His weak laugh warmed my heart. "It worked, didn't it?"

"How are you feeling?" I sat down next to him and held his hand.

"Terrible. I'm on my way out, Ella." His eyes filled, and grief overwhelmed me: his and mine, both.

"You're pretty stubborn, why do you think that?" I forced a smile.

"I can feel it. I was waiting for you. I talked to your other grandpa, he told me about the job you have to do." His breathing grew harsh, and the heart monitor went crazy.

Jax came up behind me and put his hands on my shoulders. "Breathe slow, Grandpa." Fuck, this was killing me.

"Is this him?" my grandpa asked weakly.

"Him, who? Meet Jax; he's my boyfriend. I finally found a good one, Grandpa," my voice cracked.

"He told me about him." He coughed, his throat sounding fluid-filled. "I always knew you were special, my

Ella. He told me to tell you he will come back. Have faith; he'll come back."

I was losing the battle with tears, and I didn't want them to fall where he could see them. I had no idea who he was referencing. "Grandpa, do you know how much I love you?"

"Yes, baby." He coughed again, and his eyes closed.

My breathing got rough, and I forced yoga breaths in and out, stroking his hand softly. Jax kneeled in front of me. "Look at me, siren. You can do this. Go slow."

My grandpa opened his eyes again. "Ella. My beautiful Ella. Have faith, my girl. We will be there. I love you, my Ella. Remember, don't give up on him."

His eyes closed again, and the heart monitor sent alarms blaring. I stood as nurses came in, and his breathing stabilized, my heart tripping madly. I kissed his cheek. "Don't you go yet, Grandpa."

"Soon, Ella," came the raspy whisper.

Nanie came into the room in a flurry and rubbed my arm. "Did he get to talk to you?"

Numb, I nodded. I walked across the room to check on my mom. "Hopefully, she wakes up soon so she can see him," my voice came out hoarse. I faced the window so they couldn't see my tears. Jax came up and slipped his arm across the back of my shoulders and rested his cheek on my head.

"You don't have to be strong all the time," he whispered. "Lean on me. I got you."

Nanie came up on my other side. "He's right, Ella. They all lean on you. It's okay to lean on him. In fact, right now I'm going to lean on both of you." I wrapped my arm around her, and we stared out the window together, our grief heavy in the room.

Once I felt stable enough to walk out of the room, I helped Nanie sit down between my mom and grandpa and headed out, clutching Jax's hand. The hallway was tense, and Gabby was fidgeting nervously.

"Call me tomorrow," Stephanie came up to me. "I'm taking the kids to my mom's house and going to try to get them settled down. Aaron is up to something, be careful."

I hugged her and shot a glance at Aaron, who was in the same place he was before, only now he wasn't meeting anyone's eyes. "Tomorrow then. I'll fill you in on everything."

Stephanie's eyes went completely round. "Ells. Do *not* turn around. I know what Aaron was up to now. He had to have been talking to your ex-husband. He's here. *She's* with him."

Fucking goddamn son of a bitch, I screamed in my head. Jax went rigid beside me. "Please tell me you are mistaken."

"I wish I was. The bitch just spotted you, so did your ex."

"I can't deal with this right now." I felt rage boiling inside me. Jax tightened his hold on me, and I felt the dark shit in him start to stir.

"I'm so sorry, Ells. Want me to punch her?" Stephanie was only half-joking.

"Believe it or not, I've been learning to fight. Ronnie has been teaching me. If anyone is going to punch her, it will be me," I snarled.

At the thought of Ronnie, I wished with all my might that he was with me right now. I heard Jax's phone go off, and heard Jax ask me through the connection why I needed Ronnie.

"Ronnie would keep me from doing what I want to do. You will let me do what I need to do trusting, that I was making the right choice," I answered him out loud.

"I don't think he would stop you in this case, siren," Jax replied.

Stephanie looked slightly confused, but she said, "He's headed this way."

I turned and saw Aaron, Justin, Gabby, Mike, and Pete block the hallway. I scoffed at Aaron's show of protection since I knew he'd been the one to talk to him. I felt my anger echoing in Jax and tried to force my emotions down.

"Ronnie heard you, that's him blowing up my

phone," Jax commented.

"The timing of this shit is ridiculous," I growled. "Steph, go take your kids home."

"Take care of her," Stephanie said to Jax, and with a touch on my hand, she walked away.

I let Chance walk up to me, my cousins keeping Lolli at bay with Gabby doing most of the work. Jax squeezed my hand in support. "Chance, what the fuck are you doing here?" I ground out, barely keeping the anger restrained.

"I came to see Grandpa," he smirked.

"You thought that bringing her here, where she will cause a scene, during an emergency with my family, was a good idea?" I snarled.

"She made me bring her," the smirk was plastered on his face still.

I wanted to punch him. Immediately I got back from Jax, *me too*.

"Chance, it was a choice *you* made. You always use this excuse. I'm sick of the bullshit. You purposely made a choice that will make my family uncomfortable in an awful situation." My whisper was cold and harsh. "While I'm at it, are you up to your usual crazy psychotic shit and stalking me again?"

"What? No!" he looked shocked.

"If I spot her, or your son around my home, I'll file charges. I'm over and done with the games." Chance looked over at Jax. "Yeah, he's here. He's with me. See how big his arms are? I'll gladly set him loose on you, her, or your son."

"I swear to God, Airiella, I haven't been anywhere near your place," he whined. "That's also rich coming from you. You are with a guy that would hurt a woman?"

"I would do anything to keep Airiella safe," Jax said flatly.

"Chance, you've got thirty seconds to get her out of here," I warned him. "She is not welcome near any of my family."

"This isn't over," he laced his voice with a menacing threat.

"Oh, it's over," Jax moved forward, forcing Chance to back up. "You better hope I don't see you again."

"Airiella, whatever it is you think is me; it's not me. He is out of jail, though. I don't know how he would know where to look for you, or if it's even him. I don't even know if it's her or not. It's not me, though. I just wanted to see Grandpa once more. I swear. He means a lot to me too."

"Airiella Raven, if I don't hear from you or Jax, I'm about to get on a plane!" Ronnie's voice yelled in my head, making me wince.

"Jax, can you call Ronnie, please?"

"Jesus, Airiella, how many men do you have?" Chance sneered.

"Do you think that attitude is going to get you past me?" I asked with a sense of calm that I didn't feel. "Why do you always assume that any male name I utter I'm sexually involved with?"

I could smell the alcohol on him. I knew this was why he was acting the way he was. "Isn't that how you operate?"

"You have me confused with you and her," I was so tired of this. "Gabby, can you go ask the nurses to get security up here and get her out?" I looked at Chance, "If you want to see him, you've got five minutes before I send them in after you. My family doesn't need this right now."

Gabby scurried off to the nurse's station, and Chance gave me a last look before he walked into the room. Aaron walked over to me, "Sorry, Airiella. I didn't know he had her with him. He just wanted to see Grandpa."

"I've never pushed you to not stay in contact with him, Aaron. Right now, you need to choose sides. Family, or the drama and shit he brings everywhere with him."

"I'll make sure he leaves," he promised me.

Nick walked around the corner with Samantha and the girls. I let go of Jax's hands and dropped to my knees as Grace ran at me. "Auntie!"

I swung her up in my arms, "Hi, monkey! I missed you so much."

"Who's he?" Grace looked at Jax as Amanda flung

herself at me.

"That's Jax. He's someone very important to me. Jax, this is Grace." I picked up Amanda, "This one here that I call monkey two, is Amanda."

He smiled and held out his hand, "Nice to meet you, young lady."

Nick looked pissed. "What's she doing here?"

"What do you think?" I stopped smiling. "Aaron is supposed to make sure he leaves. Mom is in the room with Grandpa. She was asleep when I left." I nuzzled Amanda.

"Dad's on his way up. Need me to do anything?" Nick glanced between the door and Lolli.

"No."

"Jax, this is my wife Samantha, and my other daughter Amanda," Nick introduced them.

I fell into the familiar pattern of being the wall my family leaned on as the rest came over one at a time to tell me their woes, draw the remaining energy I had and let me take on their grief. The empath in me pulling them to me like a magnet. I was grateful I didn't have to deal with Chance again; Aaron kept his word.

Chapter Eight

onnie was fuming. Jax had finally gotten back to him. His blood was boiling at the news he'd received of Airiella's ex-husband showing up at the hospital. From the tone Jax had taken, he was pissed too. It had been a long day of learning, and with the pain of missing Airiella and the turbulence of her emotions, he felt like he was unraveling.

When he had heard her voice in his head, it was both a welcome relief and a panic that ran through him. She needed him, and he was over a thousand miles away. When they finally stopped for the night, he went and sat outside under the stars.

That's where he was when she called him. Her voice strained and tired. He listened to her day, told her about his. Told her he was sitting outside and imagining her under the same stars he was looking at to make her feel closer.

He smelled her unique scent on the breeze, and his throat tightened up. "Can you feel that Heracles?"

The breeze had wrapped around him, warmer than the night. "What are you doing, angel?"

"Talking to the wind. I asked it to hug you," Airiella's voice was a warmth that filled his heart. "I gotta get going. I haven't fed Jax all day."

"I love you, angel," Ronnie told her.

"I love you too, Heracles."

He hung up and went back up into her room, where he camped out with all his notes and reviewed everything for the fifth time. Strange energy kept flowing through him, making him feel restless.

Smitty had hung up with Jillian and had finished texting Airiella when he heard Ronnie go back into Airiella's room. They'd had a hard day. It had been informative and overwhelming with a little scary as hell thrown in the mix.

He'd been just as pissed as Ronnie when he'd learned about her ex-husband. He hoped Jax had made an impression on him. Bastard. He got up and paced, nervous energy running rampant through him.

He walked out to Airiella's room. "Hey, let's go spar," Smitty leaned against the doorway. "I need to hit something."

"Great idea," Ronnie bounded up. "Should we grab Aedan?"

"Why not? He could use it too." Smitty went and changed clothes and met both downstairs. "Do you guys feel as off as I do?"

Ronnie nodded. Aedan asked, "You don't think that means a demon is around, do you?"

"No," Smitty thought for a minute. "I think we are feeling Airiella. She's on overload."

Jax watched from his seat on the stairs as she sat in the dark on her front porch. Her head hung down low, hands fisted in her hair. He caught the slight tremble of her body as she fought back the tears. He had no idea how to make this easier for her.

He'd seen firsthand what she'd tried to explain to him about her family, how they drained her, taking the comfort they needed from her, giving none back. She gave it freely, and he felt how heavy it was on her. It wasn't only them either. Random patients had come up to her throughout the day. They told her their burdens, as well as strangers visiting their family. Everyone seemed drawn to her.

He stood and went out to sit next to her. "Let's go eat something, siren. Get something in you to bring a little energy back."

"Okay," she gave no argument. She simply stood and went inside to get her keys and came back out.

He took them from her, and he found his way to a diner that was nearby. She ate a little, mostly pushed her food around on her plate. "Do you need to get rid of all that you took from them today?"

"I did, that's what I was doing outside." She shrugged. "It wasn't the best way possible, but I let it go."

When it was clear she wasn't going to eat anymore, he finished her salad, and they left. She snuggled her cats a little, who was happy to see her. Then she silently headed upstairs. Jax made sure everything was locked up and followed, hearing her in the shower already.

She finished up and came out in an oversized shirt, opened her windows and climbed in bed, staring silently outside. Jax showered after her and briefly wondered why he wasn't hearing her thoughts. The shower felt good; he hated the stink of hospitals and how it stuck to everything.

She waited until he slid in next to her, and she rolled over to face him, her eyes showing just how much she was feeling. "Why can't I hear you?" he brushed his lips across hers.

"Tama told me how to keep my thoughts to myself. You don't need all this noise."

"Siren, let me carry this with you. Let *me* decide what I need or don't need."

"I've never really had anyone that helped me before. It's not something I am used to." Her soul shining through her eyes, and her voice uneven, she said, "Jax, make me forget. Make me forget everything. Even if it's only for a little bit." She sat up and pulled her shirt off, ran her hands along his chest.

His body flared to life under her hands. "Are you sure this is what you want to happen?" he hated himself for asking the question. If she said no, his heart would break.

"More than anything," she lay on her side facing him. "All I want to think about is you and how you make me feel."

His heart skipped a beat. He slowly got out of bed and locked the bedroom door and closed the curtains the rest of the way down. "I'm going to show you how much I love you, siren." He slid back in the bed, "I want you to be open to me, though. Give me your thoughts, drop your walls. I want all of you."

She did exactly what he asked, and her thoughts raced through his mind. A wild, chaotic mix of grief, desire, need, love, pain. Her emotions were hitting like a sledgehammer wielded by someone with superhuman strength. Through it all, one thought stuck out.

She wanted to explore him. He tried to hide the shiver that started in his toes and ran up his body and back down. He'd never let anyone take control before. He'd do it for her if that's what she needed. He'd let her go first, do whatever she needed. Even if he came, he had so much need for her, and he knew he'd be hard again before she ever came once.

"Go ahead, Ells. I heard you. My body is yours to explore," he lay back, putting his hands behind his head.

He saw the tears pool in her eyes. "You called me Ells."

"It suits you. If you don't want me to, I won't," Jax pulled her down on him and kissed her gently.

"You can call me that," she whispered into his kiss. "I can really do what I want right now?"

"Yes. I won't stop you, I promise," Jax groaned as she kissed him with pure need. "My turn is next."

Jax felt her energy shift, and the moment she put

her fingers on him, she filled his every sense, his every thought. She was the air in his lungs, the blood in his veins. There was nothing else for him, only her.

She traced the contours of his arms with those fingertips he loved the feel of so much. The soft, feather-light touch gliding over the sensitive parts of his arms like an untamed fire. Over his collarbone and up either side of his neck. Over the stubble she seemed to love to run her hands over.

She scraped her fingernail over his bottom lip, the sensation driving him wild. No wonder no one else let her do this first. His cock was literally bouncing against him with the need to be buried in her. She hummed deep in her throat, the sexy sound unraveling him even more.

"This is the best thing in the world to me right now, Zeus. Being able just to touch you freely," she kissed him, sucking his lip into her mouth and biting it softly, scraping her teeth across it as she pulled back. "I love exploring the textures," she licked his nipple, "the tastes," her breath across it as she spoke, making it pebble up. "The sounds you make when I touch something that makes your body jump," she dragged her nails down his sides softly, making his belly tremble, and him gasp.

Her words with that voice. Her touch that hadn't even come close to his cock yet. He felt like he was going to explode. He forced his hands to stay locked behind his head. Right now was her time, he reminded himself, he could do this. It was what she needed.

She licked down his torso to his belly button, then traced her finger over his abs and kissed the raven tattoo. She scraped her nails over his hip bones, coming close to where he wanted her to touch the most. She pushed him to the edge of sanity, then rolled him over onto his stomach.

"Sexy as fuck," she whispered as she traced the wings tattoo on his back. Nails scraping down his back, over his ass and down his legs. She followed it up with fingertips going back up his legs. She stopped and spread his legs a little and massaged right behind his balls.

He felt his balls tighten, his body overcome with

sensations, then she backed off. A groan tore through him as she gripped his hips and licked his ass, dragging her tongue to where she had just been massaging with her fingers.

She sucked that sensitive spot, and his hips jerked in her hands. He could swear he heard her purr like a kitten. His entire body was taut, and if she kept doing what she was doing, he would come in a matter of seconds. The connection that sizzled between them making every touch more sensitive than he thought possible.

She rolled him back over and started back up the front of his legs this time, alternating between fingernails scraping and fingertips soothing, punctuated every so often with a kiss. Jax's arms were vibrating, his legs trembling, his belly fluttering, breathing heavy and freely doling out the moans that seemed to fuel her more.

No one had ever touched him like this before. It was exquisite torture, and he loved the way she did it. Every contour, every ridge, every muscle, she lavished that touch of hers on, filling him with the essence of her he couldn't ever get enough of. She was learning his body, leaving no spot untouched.

She sucked his balls into her mouth, and he bucked under her as those fingers stroked down his cock in the gentlest of ways. "Oh, fuck, Airiella, baby," Jax gasped out. "Don't stop, love," he cried out.

She hummed her pleasure, his balls feeling the vibrations of that siren voice, that tongue that was shattering his control. She sat up and straddled his legs, then bent over and ran her tongue up his cock and licked all the moisture that had pooled on his head and belly. It was about to be the fastest blow job ever; he was so close to that edge.

"The first of many, Zeus," she answered him out loud. "I love seeing you react like this. Biggest turn on ever." He swore when her lips wrapped around him and knotted his fingers together, so he didn't move his hands.

"Oh God, fuck," he moaned as she swirled her tongue around his head, over that sensitive spot underneath it, and then sank that humming mouth down on him. His back arched off the bed, and ragged cries ripped through his lips as she bobbed up and down on him, fast, then slow, her tongue never missing those spots that pushed him closer and closer.

When she slid her hand down his leg and massaged his balls and rubbed that spot behind them, it was all over. Control snapped, and his balls tightened painfully fast. She hummed her approval and slid her lips down him again as he came in an explosion, shooting hard down her throat as he cried out her name.

She took it all, massaging every bit she could from him as his hips bounced under her face, and he twitched in her mouth as blue light sparked between them, that connection they shared no longer as frayed as it once was. He felt it rooted deep inside him.

She let him slip from her lips, and she crawled back up him, laying on his stomach. "Jax, watching you come was the fucking sexiest thing I've ever seen," she whispered, kissing his chin. She pulled his arms out from behind his head, rubbing life back into the fingers that went numb he'd been fisting his hands so hard.

"No one has let you do that to them?" Jax's voice was hoarse.

"Not the first time, and not like that," she admitted, resting her chin on her hands against his chest. Those angel eyes looking up at him.

"Their loss," he said, roughly hooking his hands under her arms and dragging her up him. He kissed her, tasting himself on her tongue, another first for him. He found it strangely erotic. "I fucking love you, siren."

She wound her arms around his neck, "Thank you for letting me have that time." She gave him a sensual kiss that curled toes and had him digging his fingers into her hips. Hips that he still needed to bite.

"Now it's your turn, baby," he gave her a wicked smile that had her grinning in response.

I didn't have any doubts about Jax's feelings for me before that, and if in some remote spot inside me there were some lingering that I wasn't aware of, the second he told me I could do what I wanted I fully committed to the rabbit hole I always found myself in with him.

I'd gladly stay here, falling forever. Jax had fully surrendered himself to me and hit every single one of the notes I loved. He was magnificent, and he owned my soul. Not even Ronnie had surrendered himself like that to me. Not from the start.

"I don't own you, Ells," Jax pulled me farther up his body and set me upright.

"You do, Jax. I can't explain it, but you do," I leaned forward and kissed him again. "I am yours."

He growled and pulled me up until I straddled his face. "Brace your hands against the wall and don't move them," came the gruff demand from below me. "Fuck, you smell like heaven." I put my hands on the wall, forcing me to lean slightly forward, giving him complete access.

He dragged his tongue from front to back along my slit, a quiet moan escaping me. "You are the perfect drug," he whispered, his breath floating across that swollen bundle of nerves, sending electric tingles through me. "You taste even better than heaven." He did it again, torturing me the same way I tortured him by avoiding what I wanted him to touch the most.

"Believe me, siren, I'll be touching you exactly where you want it," came his sexy taunt. He followed through. He flicked his tongue across the bundle of nerves with a precision that undid me. Had my hands not been braced against the wall, I would have fallen face-first into it.

With unmatched skill, his tongue played a melody against me that had me shaking in seconds. "Jax," my strangled sob came out. His hands held my hips in place while he wrung an intense orgasm out of me in under a minute, I came all over his tongue my whole body a ball of trembling nerves.

"Don't move," he instructed me, then proceeded to lap at me.

One of his hands left my hip, and I felt him drag his finger through my wetness. My thighs were quivering like crazy, and he turned his head and bit at the insides of each leg. "Fucking delicious," I heard him whisper. His other hand joined the first, soaking his finger inside me.

"Stay still, siren," he said again, and I felt one finger slide between my ass cheeks, as he dragged that moisture back there to lubricate it. I knew he could see my thoughts and I fought against them hard. No one had been there since I was raped. "Trust me, love," he begged.

I held completely still while he slid a well-lubricated finger in my ass, my body trying to fight against my need to relax. My breathing was haggard and harsh sounding, and my thoughts were racing. "I love you, Airiella."

He slid a finger inside me, one in each hole now, and curled his finger into that magic spot, and I lost focus. Then his lips sealed around my bud and sucked while he moved both fingers. Slowly the one in my ass slid in and out while the other curled against that spot. The sensation of all of it together as he sucked and flicked at my button was mind shattering.

"Jax!" I called his name as I started to feel another orgasm build. He increased the pressure of his tongue on me and moved his fingers faster, my body bowing into him as the connection we shared sent pure electricity through his tongue. It built quickly, and the orgasm tore through me in waves so intense I had no air in which to scream his name like I tried to.

He rode it out until I was so sensitive that I couldn't take it anymore and bit my lip so hard that I drew blood. He gently slid me back down his body and rolled me to the side, licking the blood off my lip before kissing me. My entire body went limp beneath him.

"Don't move," he repeated and stood up, lighting the candle on the table. "There is nothing in the world more beautiful than you right now," he stared at me. He stepped back to the bed and rolled me to my back, spreading my legs and then settling between them as he lay on top of me.

He kissed me with one of those kisses that demanded a response, and my body obeyed his command. Heat pooling again like I hadn't just had the two most unbelievable orgasms ever. "I love that the only thing on your mind right now is me," he said against my lips.

He started on my body like I had done to his, touching everywhere, kissing and tasting each spot that made my skin jump. Up and down my body he went, changing directions so many times I had no idea what to expect.

He rolled me over, massaging my back as he trailed kisses down it. Over my ass, back to the insides of my thighs before he rolled me back over. He piled the pillows under my head and arranged my hands to be between them. "Keep them there, siren. Eyes on mine, I want to watch you come," his voice throaty and sexy. His eyes shadowed with heat, the candlelight flickering softly behind him.

He pulled my legs over his shoulders, so they rested against his back. Once again I was spread out before him. I kept my eyes on him as he flicked his tongue out, sliding between the already slick lips and narrowing on that rapidly swelling bud. I bit down on my mouth again as blue light flared up at the touch and worked on keeping my eyes open.

I didn't try to stop the moans he elicited from me as he slowly worked me up and down in a slow fashion, the pressure building. I begged him for release with my eyes, my throat too busy with moans and cries of pleasure to form words.

My legs started to tremble again, and I heard him growl, then he went at me fast and furious as a third powerful orgasm swept through me. My eyes locked on his as he lapped it up and slowly lowered my legs to the bed.

His lips were wet with me all over them. He crushed them to mine, forcing me to taste myself on him as he sucked the blood from my mouth again. "I can't get enough of your taste," he said, licking my lips clean.

He sat back on his heels and drew my hips up to his, wrapping my legs behind him. His cock was already leaking as he positioned it just right and slid into me, his breath hissing out between his teeth. "Fuck, baby, so goddamn tight," he groaned as I locked my legs and pulled him in closer.

He filled me perfectly, and I never wanted this to end. I clenched my muscles around him in a pulsing action, and he groaned, his control slipping. "Please, Jax," I begged him.

He put his thumb against my highly sensitive bud and applied pressure as he shifted beneath me. I arched into him, taking him even deeper. "Tell me what you want, siren," his voice deep and gravelly.

"You," I panted, needing him. "Fast and hard."

He circled his thumb over me again, and I felt the pressure building. Then he gripped my hips with bruising force and pulled out to slam back in, a harsh groan spilling out of his lips. The angle of our hips meeting, making him rub that spot inside me with his cock.

He started thrusting hard and fast, and I lost myself to it. To him. The rhythm of our bodies in sync, our moans in harmony as the connection locked in place, pushing us both over the edge in perfect symmetry. The orgasm was so intense it felt like the house shook as we both lit with a blue glow that formed a solid and stable connection between us, an unbreakable bond perfect in every way.

The emotional blowback on us both had him collapsing on me and rolling me over, still inside me as we cried, our tears mingling on his face. He kissed me and licked at my lip again. This connection had unraveled every thread of my being and knitted it back together with his.

"If this is what they were all like, I am surprised that any of them let you out of their sight for even a second," Jax held my gaze as he licked at my lip again.

"Nothing in my life has ever been like that, Jax. *Nothing.*"

Our bodies still locked together, he rolled us on to our sides, holding me as if he were afraid to let me go. "I can't tell you how happy it makes my heart to hear that."

"What do you feel now?" I ran my hand over his back.

"Everything. I feel everything. The universe, the air around us, I can feel everything. Life, death, and all that happens in between," he whispered against my lips, his tongue licking out again. "I can feel the blood in your body as it flows. Your heartbeat echoes in my head."

"My body, my heart, my soul, my everything, it all belongs to you, siren," he continued. "You are a part of me. Made for me. I love you." Everything awful thing I had gone through in my life had brought me to this moment, here, with him. I'd do it all again if I was guaranteed this.

I touched his face, my heart beating with his, "I love you, Jax."

Chapter Nine

Mags was in bed reading over the notes Father Roarke had left when her body started to feel weird. She looked around the room and touched her protection necklace to reassure herself it was on. What the hell was going on?

She swung her legs over the side of the bed and stood as a wave of pure love washed through her, and her body started to glow blue. She broke into a run heading down the stairs in a panic, worried that something terrible happened to Airiella when she saw blue light radiating from the garage where the guys were sparring.

She jogged out to them and stumbled on the wave of desire that slammed into her. Pure lust tore through her like a hot molten fire in her veins. She staggered inside the garage to see all three men glowing the same blue, and every single one of them with a raging boner.

Delighted laughter bubbled up out of her. "Aedan, if you don't get that very hard cock over here and follow me back to the bedroom, I'm going to jump your bones right here in front of everyone," Mags called out.

They all stared at her in shock. "What's

happening?" Smitty asked, trying to cover himself. "Fighting doesn't make me horny."

"I'm guessing by the very blue Airiella glow we all have going on, that she just made her connection to Jax," Mags sported a huge smile. "Judging by the feeling inside me right now, it was delicious."

Ronnie swore, then grinned. "I guess that means we all can glow now," he laughed. "Though now I've got to go and take care of something without the help of my angel."

"You and me both, brother," Smitty chuckled. "Not together, you take care of your own."

Mags couldn't stop giggling. "Aedan, damn it! Hurry up!"

"Um, someone should tell Taklishim about this," Aedan mumbled as he tried to walk steadily towards Mags, they all saw his legs shaking though. Mags yanked on his arm as soon as he was close enough and pulled him back to the house.

"This didn't happen with any of the others," Mags thought aloud. "Maybe it's because now her circle is complete and it gave her a whole lot more power? I guess I don't care at the moment because all I want to do is get laid."

Aedan chuckled. "Thank you, Airiella."

"Indeed," Mags pushed Aedan on the bed when they walked in their room. "Thank you." She pounced on him, primed and ready to go.

R onnie bolted awake as the sound of something falling on the floor shattered the stillness. The sun was barely coming up from what he could see of the mostly still dark room. His heart was thundering, and he was no longer glowing.

Then he smelled fresh rain. "Oh. Winnie." He pulled off the necklace and there she was. Grinning like an idiot. "Was that you?"

"Yes. Sorry. I've been trying to wake you for an hour now. I finally threw your phone on the ground in frustration. I couldn't get the music to play. Anyway, I'm free!"

Ronnie's head was still fuzzy from being woken from a dead sleep. "Free?"

"Yes! Jax connected with Airy and it broke the bond he created when I died. I'm no longer tied to this plane anymore."

"Is that good?" Ronnie wasn't sure what to do with that information.

"It's fantastic! I can move on if I want."

"Does that mean you are leaving us?" Ronnie had mixed emotions about that.

She looked sad. "I want to. I want to move past this place I've been stuck in for so many years. I don't know if I can come back, or if that means I won't ever see you again. I need to talk to Onida still."

In so many ways, she was still that fresh and exuberant twenty-two-year-old girl he had loved so much, and in other ways, she was older and wiser than them all, except maybe Airiella. "Whatever you do, Winnie, you have my support."

"If I go, I'll tell you. I want more info before I choose. I was just so excited that I wanted to tell you." Ronnie watched her ghostly figure do a little dance. "It is incredible not to be weighed down by the heaviness anymore!"

"I can't believe all he had to do to set you loose was have sex with her. If I had known that, I would have pushed him harder," Ronnie mused.

"No, it wasn't just the sex. Jax connected with her deeply. You can see the connection from this side as brightly as you can see her. He gave himself to her," Winnie declared more seriously.

"I'm not sure I'm following you," Ronnie was confused.

"He's in love with her, you dope." The grin that split her face was huge.

"We all knew that already, Winnie," Ronnie wanted to go back to sleep.

"Ronnie."

"What?" He didn't get it.

"He *told* her he loved her. He *committed* himself to her. The connection they have is both of their souls intertwined with each other."

"Aren't all our connections like that?" He was still confused.

"To a degree, yes. Not like this. Not even yours is like this, and yours is pretty powerful too."

"He told her he loved her?" Ronnie was catching on.

"Yep. Jax even asked permission from her dad to date her." Winnie beamed like a proud parent.

"You're kidding," Ronnie gaped.

"Nope." Winnie danced around the room again.

Ronnie ran his hands through his hair. He didn't know where this left him, and he was still strongly feeling the effects of being absent from her. "Now what?"

"I don't know. I can see the look on your face, and you should know Airy still loves you. Nothing about what happened with Jax changed how she feels for you."

Her reassurance made him feel mildly better. "Thanks. I think I needed to hear that." He dropped back in the bed. "I need more sleep, Winnie."

"Okay, love. Talk to you later," she said and blinked out.

Ronnie put the necklace back on and fell back asleep almost immediately.

Jax woke up before the sleeping angel in his arms. They had hardly moved all night. Their bodies in the same position as they were when he fell asleep. He felt her the same way he could feel himself. It was like she was an extension of him.

There was a stiff wind this morning, and he thought that was what had woken him up. The curtains were billowing, and the blinds rattled. A trickle of cold air sneaked between the curtains and was drifting over them.

He heard the direction her sleeping thoughts were

going, and he watched her face, knowing she was waking up. Before she could say anything, he captured her lips in a soulful kiss until she melted against him.

She rolled over, straddling him with her legs. If she moved an inch up, he would be in the perfect position to slide right into her. He knew when she latched on to that thought, and before she could make a move, he rolled her under him.

"There was something I forgot to do last night that I've wanted to do for a while now," he smiled down at her. In a smooth motion, he moved so that his mouth was over her left hip. He bit down on it, then sucked it in his mouth, and finally soothed it with a kiss. Then he moved and did the same to her right hip.

"You wanted to bite me?" she asked softly, a smile teasing her lips.

"Your hips are so damn sexy. Soft and curvy, swaying gently, side to side when you walk, calling out to me," Jax crawled up her body. "Good morning."

"At least I'm not alone in this rabbit hole anymore," her smile warmed him as she slipped her arms around his back.

"You never were, siren." He rubbed his thumb over her lip where she had bitten it last night. "Does that hurt?"

"No. Should it?" Airiella looked confused.

"You damn near bit a hole through it last night," he reminded her, then kissed her, wiping out both their thoughts.

Her phone started ringing, and she groaned, reaching for it. Jax saw Dad written on the screen and pulled away as she answered, her face concerned.

"Hi, Dad. No, I'm awake," she answered him. He heard the word grandpa fly through his head, and he got up and went to the bathroom to start getting ready. He knew. He finished as she ran in behind him to start getting prepared herself.

They moved like a well-oiled machine, each knowing instinctively what the other was doing. At any other time, Jax would pause to marvel at it. This wasn't the time for that, though.

"He asked for last rites," she told him as she got dressed, "then he asked for me. I should have known. I heard it on the wind."

Jax slowed his movements as he looked at the windows. As soon as she was fully dressed, he opened the curtains and closed the windows. "The wind talks to you?"

"Yeah. Kind of. It carries messages for me or to me," she answered distractedly.

He led her down the stairs, where she grabbed her purse and keys and a couple of protein bars that she handed him. She didn't want one, and he could feel that her stomach was upset, so he didn't push the issue.

The drive took them less time, as it was still early morning and a weekend. Jax sent a text to Ronnie, letting him know. "Jax, do you feel different?" she caught him off guard with her question.

"What do you mean?" he turned to look at her.

"Inside, do you feel different than you normally do?" she asked again.

He still wasn't sure what she was asking. "I feel more like me. I feel love. A sort of freedom, I guess. Why? Do you feel different?"

"No. But you feel different to me," Airiella puzzled.

He felt a little fear creep into him and try to take hold, but he quickly swatted it away. "Talk it out, siren. I'm not sure I understand what you are getting at."

"Your energy feels different. I don't know if it's the connection, or something else. I don't think it's a bad thing, and it's nothing to do with how I feel for you. There's a difference, though," Airiella chewed on her lip.

He knew it wasn't anything between them. After last night he was positive he would have felt it if something had shifted about her feelings. "One thing at a time, baby. Let's get through this before we dive into the mess that I am."

She took his hand. "You aren't a mess. We are *in* a mess, but you aren't one."

She pulled into the parking garage and took a deep breath, bracing herself for whatever was about to happen.

"I'm with you. No matter what," Jax got out and walked around the car, pulling her door open. "I've got you."

S mitty stared at his computer screen with his brain spaced out. He couldn't focus this morning. No, that was wrong, he could focus, but it was on everything else but the screen in front of him. He felt different, and he wondered if Mags was right, now that she had made all her connections did it do something to them?

He felt, enhanced for the lack of a better word. Giving up, he got out of bed and shut the laptop down. Maybe going for a run would help. He dressed for it and headed down to the kitchen, where he ran into Ronnie.

"You going for a run?" Ronnie asked.

"Yeah, having a hard time focusing today. Figured it might help," Smitty shook his limbs out as he talked.

"Give me a minute, and I'll join you." Ronnie took off upstairs and was back down in two minutes.

"Any news from Airiella?" Smitty asked as they stretched.

"Jax texted, said they were doing last rites today and that her grandpa was asking for her again," Ronnie said evenly.

"Shit. Is that why I feel so out of whack?" Smitty tried to see if it was her emotions that he was feeling and not his own.

"Could be. I feel the same way. I fully plan on going up for the funeral. Just FYI."

"We all should go, she could use the support," Smitty said thoughtfully. He started running a slow pace. "Taklishim answered me about the glowing thing last night. He said there is so much they don't know about the connection that anything is possible. He told me to document everything."

Smitty saw Ronnie staring at something and tried to see what it was. "Did that guy look weird to you?" Ronnie asked.

"I didn't see anyone," Smitty looked back over his

shoulder.

Ronnie shook his head and picked up the pace. Smitty matched him easily, and they ran a mile, then picked up the pace again, sprinting now. They turned around and slowed down a bit, gradually decreasing the speed.

"There, look," Ronnie pointed. Smitty didn't see anything or anyone, just empty road.

"Dude, there's no one there," Smitty retorted. Then he felt a weird feeling and came to a stop. "I have a weird feeling, though."

"Get back to the house, now," Ronnie looked alarmed and started running.

Smitty took off after him, both of them full-on sprinting. "What the hell?" he panted.

"Demon," Ronnie huffed. "That's what I saw, and you felt."

Smitty looked back, still seeing nothing. What the hell was happening? He ran faster.

I held Jax's hand so tight I'm surprised I didn't break any of his bones. The hospital room door was open, and I didn't want to go in through it. Jax didn't push me. The only ones here were my dad and nanie, and I was thankful for that.

My dad must have seen Jax because he came walking out. "He's not making sense. He's rambling about things and you. Nanie said you should be here, sorry if I woke you up."

"I was awake, Dad. It's not a big deal. How's Mom?"

"A mess. Mom's been awake all night listening to Grandpa mutter. Thanks for getting her moved here, at least. She was able to talk to him coherently for a little bit." My poor dad looked wiped out.

"Tell me you went home and slept," I said.

"No. Your mom asked me to stay, so I did. The doctors just gave her a shot a few minutes ago, hopefully she will sleep. If you want to talk to her, you better do it now," he pushed me to the door.

I didn't want to let go of Jax's hand, but my dad forced the issue and pushed me into the room. My grandpa's eyes were closed, so I went over to my mom. "Hi, Mom," I said quietly.

"Ells. I'm glad you are here. He's beside himself about you," she fretted.

"What about?" I smoothed her hair back from her face.

"I don't know. Nanie doesn't know either. His heart is down to eleven percent functioning. It's not good." She started to fade out.

"Rest, Mom." I touched the bruises on her face gently.

"I said goodbye to him already, I feel like a bad daughter," she murmured.

"Why?"

"I feel like I don't believe he's going to make it." She started to cry.

"He *says* he's not going to make it, Mom. Saying goodbye is natural," I tried to console her. "He'd know best if he will or not. You saying goodbye doesn't force the issue."

"I love you, Ells."

"I love you too, Mom. Get some rest so Dad can take you home soon." I kissed her forehead.

"You're a good girl Ella," Nanie said behind me, sounding exhausted.

"Ella?" my grandpa's weak voice called out. "Is that you, my Ella? Are you here?"

"I'm here, Grandpa," I walked up to the bed, Nanie holding on to my hand.

"Ella, some things you can't undo, you need to remember that. It's too late. You can't undo it. Finish it. He'll come back for you. He always will come back," he rambled on.

Nanie gave me a look, and I shrugged. "What can't I undo, Grandpa?"

"It's too late, Ella. Somethings you can't undo. He's

your forever," Grandpa gave me a small smile.

Was he talking about Jax? What couldn't I undo? "Okay, Grandpa. I'll remember that. How are you feeling?"

"It's time, Ella. Where's my love?" he tried to sit up.

"I'm right here, Giuseppe. Standing next to Ella," Nanie said, her voice steady, but her face was sad.

"Ella, promise me you'll finish it," Grandpa said weakly.

"I promise, Grandpa," I said automatically. I had no idea what I was promising, but right then, I would have promised him almost anything.

"I'll be there, and I'll help. You have my word, angel Ella." My eyes filled with tears. He'd never called me an angel before. He knew.

Nanie squeezed my fingers. "I love you, Grandpa. I'll carry you in my heart forever."

"I love you, Ella. Is my love still here?" his eyes had closed now.

"Right here, Giuseppe," Nanie took his hand.

"I love you. Thank you for my wonderful life." The heart monitor flatlined, and I did my best to remain stoic for Nanie, but she crumbled.

I managed to catch her, my legs shaking. I felt Jax support us both, leading us out to the couch where I wrapped my arms around Nanie, both of us shaking and trying to hold back because we were in public.

My dad came and sat next to me, Jax moving off to the side to make room for him. "Ells, I'm sorry."

"It's okay, Dad. Go home and rest. I'll sit here with Nanie and get everything sorted out." He kissed my cheek and hugged Nanie.

"Tell me what you need, Nanie," I kept my arms around her.

"We need to let the rest of the family know. The funeral arrangements are already done. Four days from now is what he wanted. He knew when he was going to go."

"Four days? That's fast," I said, amazed that he knew that much about his passing.

"He wanted you to speak at the service, do you

think you can do that?" she looked at me. Her eyes were vacant. My heart broke. It hurt to see the fire gone from her.

"I'll do whatever you need me to," I promised.

"He never told you, but he loves your writing. You were his favorite," Nanie put her hand on my cheek and rested her head on my shoulder. "Life will be different now. I don't know what I will do."

"We are all here for you, Nanie," I was losing control fast.

"I'll probably sell the house. I hope whatever he was mumbling about made sense to you. He was going on about it all night," she said faintly.

"Nanie, do you want me to take you home?" I bit my lip, trying to keep the tears back, making it bleed again.

"After they take him. I want to stay until they take him," Nanie said quietly and got up to go sit by his bed.

As soon as she was in the room, I broke down. Jax picked me up and sat in one of the armchairs, with me curled in his lap. He kissed me, bloody lip and all and told me he loved me. I let myself cry for five minutes, and then I stopped. I needed to be there for Nanie and my mom.

I stood up silently and went back into the room, sitting next to my mom's bed. Nanie seated between the two, holding my grandpa's still hand. That heartbreaking scene would forever be seared into my memory.

Jax swiped the tears that fell away. The sight of them sitting there, Airiella and her Nanie, was tragic. He called Ronnie. "He died," he told him when he answered.

"How is she?" Ronnie asked immediately.

"Broken. Hang on." Jax switched to his camera on his phone to snap a picture of them sitting there and sent it to Ronnie. "Did you get it?"

"Shit, that's awful. I can feel Airiella's pain, we all can," Ronnie said, his voice gruff.

"Funeral is in four days. Arrangements were already

made. Airiella has to talk at the service." Jax watched her.

"We'll be there. Our angel's not going through this alone," Ronnie stated. "I don't see her as liking public speaking too much. Did she say anything about that?"

"Her family is a lot. She tried to prepare me; explain how they depend on her. It's too much. I don't know how she does it." Jax watched as she moved the chair she was on closer to her nanie. "I don't know what she thought about the speaking part; her emotions were like wild colors all around her."

"She's her. She's love. She will do exactly what she needs to do." There was no hesitation in Ronnie's absolute belief in her.

Jax felt a ghost of a smile on his lips. "She is love. Airiella asked me to make her forget everything last night. She was so hollow sounding. I would have done anything she asked me to."

"Yeah, um, we felt it," Ronnie said sheepishly.

"You felt it?" Jax was confused.

"We all started glowing, and every single one of us got horny as hell. Must have been good," Ronnie chuckled.

"Understatement. There are no words to describe it. We glowed too."

"Find out the time the funeral is, and we will plan flights around it. You guys don't have to come back the same day, but we probably will. The training with Father Roarke is intense and after you connected, we all feel different now. Something changed; we don't know what, though," Ronnie hedged.

"Weird. Airiella told me I felt different this morning," Jax remembered.

"Just be with her, Jax. This death is hard for her," Ronnie changed the subject.

"She hasn't been out of my sight once. I told her I loved her," Jax admitted quietly.

"How did it feel to say it finally?"

"Pretty damn amazing." Jax heard Ronnie's phone ding.

"She just texted me. Asked me if she can call. I'll

talk to you later, bro. Take care of our girl."

Jax hung up with the promise he would. He saw someone lurking out of the corner of his eye, and saw one of the male nurses that had hovered around yesterday. He was standing there staring at Airiella, and Jax felt the hairs on the back of his neck raise.

"She's something else, isn't she?" the nurse guy looked at Jax. "Maybe it's in the way she carries herself. I don't know. She's stoic, though right now, it looks like I could crush her with a toe."

Jax stood. "I wouldn't suggest trying."

"Oh, I wouldn't. I don't want to crush her. I wanted to own her," the creepy nurse said.

"You do realize she's here with me, right?" Jax heard the possessive tone enter his voice, and that darkness in him rolled but didn't do anything else.

"Sure do. Don't really care. See you around, buddy." He saluted Jax and walked off.

I sat in there quietly at first, letting Nanie have her moment of peace. When she started to cry, I moved closer to her. I knew I had to get the calls began, I just didn't want to do it. I waited a bit, then saw that Nanie had fallen asleep with her head on Grandpa's hand.

I texted Ronnie to see if he was busy. I needed to hear his voice.

"Hi, my angel love. I'm so sorry, sweetheart," he answered. That was all it took. The tone of pure love in his voice and I broke again. "It's okay, cry it out."

"He called me angel, he knew," I sobbed quietly.

"Where's Jax?" Ronnie asked.

"Talking to a nurse. I can see him," I told him.

"I love you so much, baby. I wish I could take this from you," his voice broke a little.

"I just needed to hear your voice. I miss you. I might have to superglue you and Jax to me from now on."

Ronnie laughed softly. "You won't get an argument from either of us."

I sighed. "I need to start the phone calls to the family. I had to hear your voice, though. I couldn't start that until I heard you."

"Anything you need, I'm happy to do."

"Can you write a eulogy for me? I have to speak at the funeral, and I'm freaking out about that a little. I don't like being the center of attention. Or speaking in front of people," I said in a whispered rush.

"Whatever you say will be perfect." Ronnie had no idea what to tell me for that part of things. I felt his hesitation.

"Thank you, Heracles. I love you."

"Love you too, babe."

I hung up and started making the calls, oblivious to pretty much everything around me. I knew Jax had come in and sat me on his lap and held me while I called everyone. My aunt Amy and Elena were the first to arrive and said that they would stay with my mom and Nanie, freeing me up to finish the calls and leave.

"Ella," Nanie called out to me. "This is the name and number of the priest, can you make sure that everything's set and ready to go?" I took the piece of paper from her, agreeing. "Also, tell him that you will be doing to eulogy after he says the mass."

I swallowed the lump in my throat, "Are you sure that's what you want me to do?"

"It's what he wanted, Ella. His words to me last night were, 'Have Ella speak. If anyone can make me sound good, it's our very own angel.' I know it's hard for you, and I'm sorry about that."

"It's okay, Nanie. I'll do as he asked." I clung to Jax like he was my lifeline as we headed out of the hospital.

"Do you know that nurse there to your left?" Jax spoke in my ear. I casually looked and only recognized him as someone that worked at the hospital that I had seen around yesterday.

"No. Not really. I saw the nurse yesterday but never spoke to him. Why?"

"He told me you looked like he could crush you with

his toe. He also said he wanted to own you," Jax said. "Something was off about the whole thing."

"Demon?" I wondered.

"Maybe. Remember the nurse's face, in case we come across him again." Jax took my keys. "I'll get us home."

"I don't want to go home. Not yet. I need to speak to Stephanie. Do you mind if we meet her for breakfast?"

He pulled me to him and kissed me sweetly. "We'll do whatever we need to do."

"Hold me exactly like this. I need this." I nestled into his chest, and we stood in the parking garage in that same position for who knows how long.

Chapter Ten

Ronnie started issuing orders, "Smitty, get ahold of Taklishim, let's put him on speakerphone so we can ask questions. Aedan, get us all on a flight for four days from now, that's the funeral. Bring us back here the same day. We are going to surprise her and be there for her. Get Father Roarke a ticket too. Please."

"Do you know the time of the funeral?" Aedan asked.

"3:00, Jax said. If you can get us there by 1:30 or so, it gives us travel time to get to the church. He didn't tell her we are coming, so none of you tell her. Let's give her a nice surprise. As much as I would love to stay with her there for a few days, we need to stick to this plan; things are escalating," Ronnie said firmly.

"How long do you think the funeral will last?" Aedan started searching for flights.

"It's Catholic, so a couple of hours maybe, with the reception and burial afterward. Get a late flight out, like at 10:00 or red-eye," Ronnie answered.

"I'm on it. That also means we will need to shop for funeral clothes. Should I ask Jax if he has something? Wait, never mind. He'll find something on his own." Aedan got busy with flights while Smitty was dialing Taklishim.

"Hey Tak," Smitty said when he got him on the phone. "I'm going to put you on speakerphone."

"Thanks, Taklishim," Ronnie said once he was on speakerphone. "We've got some new little developments happening and were hoping that you would be able to guide us on this. First, you know that Jax made the connection with Airiella already and that we all glowed. This morning we all felt different. Not in a way we can explain. Then when Smitty and I went for a run, I could see a demon, but Smitty couldn't. Smitty could feel one, but I couldn't."

"How did it appear to you?" Taklishim barked the question out.

"At first, just like a guy, I had glanced him out of the corner of my eye. Then when I turned my head to look, he looked less like a guy than I thought. His skin was like smoke," Ronnie tried to describe what he had seen.

"Have you learned about the higher-level demons yet?" Taklishim asked.

"Not other than they are powerful," Smitty added.

"High-level demons can take on human form. They don't need a host to possess," Taklishim informed them.

"Does that mean that we can just kill them and not worry about murdering the host?" Ronnie took some notes.

"I'm not sure that you would be able to kill a high-level demon. I think you'd need Airiella for that. Essentially, that is correct. If Smitty wasn't able to see it, chances are, that was a high-level demon that chose to show itself to you. Smitty, you felt it?" Taklishim asked, trying to clarify the information.

"Yes. I didn't know what it was at first. I felt off. Like something wasn't right. Airiella tells us she has warnings go off in her head, it was kind of like that," Smitty spilled.

"Are you all thinking that that she has made all the connections that her abilities are extending?" Taklishim asked thoughtfully.

"I *am* thinking that," Smitty agreed. "Which

abilities? We all seem to have different pieces of it."

"I don't know. When you connected to Airiella, did you gain something from it?" Taklishim asked. "Hold on." They heard his muffled talking to someone. "Something has happened. Onida said she's showing a blood bond."

"What the fuck is a blood bond?" Ronnie asked, getting frustrated.

"Did Jax ingest her blood?" Taklishim pushed, his voice urgent.

"Well, that's not something that comes up in everyday conversation now, is it?" Ronnie snapped. "What's a blood bond?"

"Find out if he did," Taklishim snapped back.

Ronnie snatched his phone off the table and furiously texted Jax. There was silence until Ronnie's phone dinged. "He said he did not drink her blood. He isn't a vampire." His phone dinged again. "He said her lip was bleeding, and he licked it off her lips, while they were, um, busy."

Taklishim swore. "What does that mean?" Smitty leaned forward. "What are you not telling us?"

"One, we don't know what her blood is capable of, nor do we know how it will react with the energy inside Jax. Two, a blood bond can only be broken through death. Three, the process was started but not finished, which leaves them both vulnerable. Four, Jax will have abilities through that blood that we don't know about," Taklishim listed out coldly.

"Lips don't bleed a lot, how much blood could he have gotten?" Ronnie asked. He wasn't sure this was as big of a deal as Taklishim was making it sound.

"The guy in the park that kidnapped the little kid?" Taklishim reminded them. "She dropped two drops of blood on him from her arm. It healed his mental illness and cancer that was in him. Two drops."

"What do you mean by the process wasn't finished?" Smitty was writing notes down as fast as he could.

"She didn't ingest any of his. It needs to go two ways," Taklishim sighed. "This is dangerous."

Ronnie stood, kicking his chair back. "Dangerous for them both?"

"Yes, Ronnie, both of them," Taklishim gentled his voice.

"Then find them and help them. We will be there Thursday for the funeral. Damnit Tak, don't let anything happen to either of them," Ronnie yelled frantically.

"A blood bond with a connection is extremely powerful. In this case, he's her strongest connection. We know nothing of this. All we are learning is through you all. I'll reach out to Jax. It's also why we told you that they would be after her blood. If she bleeds, leave none of it laying around. Burn anything that has her blood on it," Taklishim ordered.

"How is this dangerous other than not knowing what is going to happen?" Ronnie asked quietly.

"With an unfinished bond, if something were to happen to Jax, it would be three times worse for her. If he dies, she will too. If something happens to her, Jax stands to lose his sanity. With that energy inside him, you will all lose him, even if he's still breathing."

"Perfect," Smitty's sarcastic tone filled the room. "I've had her blood too. Does that mean it applies to me as well?"

"When?" Ronnie shouted.

"When she released that energy. I kissed her, there was blood all over her face," Smitty shivered as he remembered.

"Fuck! Same here," Ronnie said. "What's this mean, Tak?"

"Well, that explains why the two of you are hurting so much being away from her. Also, why the two of you can spot demons now, you'll need to finish it as well then. All three of you stand in danger." The plain words landed with the force of a bomb.

"Why didn't we know this before?" Ronnie demanded.

"Your bonds don't show the way theirs does. There are similarities, but from the other plane, both of yours looks like other connections we've seen. Jax doesn't." Taklishim sighed, and Ronnie heard more talking in the background.

"Fuck. Is she ever going to have a normal life, Tak? She's constantly hammered with shit." Ronnie bent over the table, trying to calm down.

"I can't answer that. There's no one else alive like Airiella," Taklishim himself sounded worried.

"I hope she's more than a science experiment to you all," Smitty threw in, his face pale.

"She is my hope for the future, Smitty. I'll get in touch with her," Taklishim promised.

Smitty hung up. "Now what?"

"We make a hard phone call to Jax and hope he doesn't flip his shit. We can't let him stay like that and have them both at risk." Ronnie fixed his chair and sat back down. "I don't want to find out what it is that breaks an angel. Nor do I want to experience losing Jax."

Aedan cleared his throat. "Mags and I are the only ones that haven't had her blood. Do we keep it that way?"

"Yes," Smitty and Ronnie said at the same time.

Aedan let out a sigh of relief.

J ax was sitting in a quiet diner with Airiella and her cousin Stephanie while they talked. He was currently holding the baby, Emma, and found himself in love. She was a sweet baby, and her dimples when she smiled and giggled made his heart melt. Airiella had just finished telling Stephanie everything. The whole crazy story.

Stephanie was having a hard time believing it, though Jax could tell that she knew Airiella was different. Jax pulled his phone back out of his pocket and opened up his files of pictures from that day on the beach. "Scroll through those. They were all taken with that cell phone, which you can see is just a regular phone. You can even check the picture details and see they're unedited," he slid it over to her.

Stephanie picked it up, and the first one she saw

was the one Jax had framed. He saw her eyes fill with tears as she looked from the phone back to Airiella. "This is the most beautiful picture of you I have ever seen."

"Jax gets the credit for that. That picture healed up a broken part inside me that's festered for years. He showed me I was beautiful; he showed me what it was to look through his eyes," Airiella said, her voice still showing awe over it.

Stephanie reached across the table to touch his hand. "Thank you for that. I've not been successful at it ever. Though I also never knew she had wings." She scrolled through a few more. "It's easy to see how much you love my cousin. I can look at her and see how much she loves you."

"It's not just me, she loves all of us," Jax admitted.

"That was a little hard to swallow, I'll admit," Stephanie said with a smile. "Hearing she had been with all of you was a stretch because that is not her at all. I can see it through in these pictures. Thank you for showing me."

Stephanie looked back at Airiella. "I've got to tell you about Emma. They finally diagnosed her with Rett's. It's a chromosome mutation. It will affect her for the rest of her life. She might not ever talk or walk on her own." Stephanie fought back the tears. "She might not make it to her 20's."

Jax looked at the baby in front of him and wanted to scream at the injustice of it all. This innocent life was marked to be a hard and tragic one, even though all loved her. It broke his heart. His phone rang, startling Stephanie. She slid it back to him, and he stood carrying Emma with him.

"Ronnie, what's up?" Jax answered.

"We've got a lot to go over, bro," Ronnie sounded glum.

"First, I think a demon was stalking Airiella at the hospital," Jax told him. He filled Ronnie in on the conversation the creepy nurse had with him. Emma was making cooing noises at him as she rubbed on his beard. He couldn't help the grin that lit his face.

Ronnie told him about the blood thing that he and Smitty had to finish it as well now. "She needs to drink my blood?" Jax repeated stupidly.

"Um, yeah. Sorry." Emma giggled at something, and Jax grinned again. "What's making that noise?"

"Airiella's cousins' baby, her name is Emma. She has a syndrome that won't give her a long life, which pisses me off because this baby is adorable. Well, not really a baby, she's two, but seems a lot younger," Jax told him, bouncing her up and down.

"You're holding a baby?" Ronnie sounded gobsmacked.

"Why does that surprise you?" Jax moved his phone and took a selfie of him and Emma and sent it to Ronnie.

"In all the years I've known you, I've never seen you once holding a baby. Okay, fine, she's adorable. I'm not sure what to do with that expression on your face." Ronnie bit back a laugh.

"Ronnie, would Airiella's blood help her?" Jax asked suddenly.

"I don't know. It healed the kidnapper in the park, so maybe? Do you think it would be a good idea to mess with the kid's life?" Ronnie sounded hesitant.

"How is healing her and giving her a normal chance at life a bad thing?" Jax asked seriously.

"Messing with fate or some shit like that. I don't know! Why aren't you more worried about all this blood stuff and a blood bond? One where we now all have to feed Airiella blood?" Ronnie yelled.

"My life is already hers, Ronnie. If I had to slice open my vein for her to drink from, I would do it. If I lost her, insanity would be the least of my worries. I know how she feels about all of you. I know how she feels about me. If I suddenly have abilities I've never had before, then great. Maybe I can be more of a help to her now. In the grand scheme of things, this doesn't seem like much," Jax answered quietly.

"No one knows how that energy in you will, or has reacted to the blood. Didn't you just tell me that Airiella said you felt different?" Ronnie asked worriedly.

"She did. A lot going on, though. Something is constantly getting thrown at us. If I want a moment to contemplate helping this little girl's life, which in turn helps out her cousin, why shouldn't I?" Jax asked pointedly.

Ronnie sighed. It was the Jax he remembered from so long ago. Maybe the blood bond was a good thing for him. There wasn't a selfish thought in his desire to help that baby. "Then discuss it with both of them before making Airiella bleed and forcing blood in a baby's mouth."

"I heard everything you've said, Ronnie. I'm not ignoring it. Right now isn't the time to bring it all up to her. She just lost her grandpa, her cousin just learned about her story, she just learned about Emma here, so let's cut her a break."

"You were the right choice to be there with her," Ronnie told him on a sigh. "Mags's kids are going to have a fantastic uncle in you."

"We'll call you later after some downtime. Making all those calls earlier was hard, and Airiella's soul feels heavy." Jax watched the two women talking.

"Take her to nature somewhere, hopefully soon," Ronnie advised. "We'll be there Thursday. Talk to you later."

Jax hung up and called Taklishim before going back to the table. "Hey Tak, it's Jax. I just talked with Ronnie and know about the blood thing. I've got a question. In my arms is a 2-year-old baby. She's related to Airiella. We just found out she has Rett's Syndrome, would Airiella's blood give this baby a chance at life?"

Jax could hear Taklishim typing. "That's a chromosome mutation. It might. I don't think it would hurt at any rate. How are they related?"

"It's her cousins' baby. An innocent life," Jax smiled down at Emma, bouncing her in his arms.

"You continue to astound me, Jax. I *can* tell you that I don't think it's anything we can fix. If she stands a chance, it would be through Airiella. You also know you need to finish that bond with her, right?" He could hear the concern in Taklishim's voice.

"I do know it. I'll talk with Airiella about it in a bit. Oh, the funeral is Thursday at 3:00. I'll text you the address," Jax remembered. "I need to get her away a bit, out to nature somewhere she can recharge. Also, I think a demon was stalking her, or both of us, at the hospital."

Jax told him the conversation. "If that was a demon, it's a high-level one, and you both need to be on guard. Finish that bond. I'll be in touch."

Jax put the phone back in his pocket and went back to the table and sat down. Both women looked up at him, and both looked exhausted. "I have some news that may or may not make you happy-both of you. The first call was Ronnie talking about stuff I'll need to discuss with you later. The second was Taklishim to confirm the possibility that came to me when I was talking to Ronnie."

Stephanie looked confused, "I'm not sure how any of that relates to me."

"Her blood heals." He looked at Airiella and saw the same thoughts going through her head that went through his. "Taklishim confirmed that he didn't think it would hurt to try."

Stephanie was still lost. Jax tried to explain, "When Airiella was interviewing with the council, she stopped a kidnapping from happening. The guy had mental illness and cancer. Two drops of her blood fell in his mouth, and he healed from both."

He watched Stephanie's face undergo a transformation as she put the pieces together. "Angel blood. It heals?"

"It does. If it doesn't work, then it wasn't a wasted effort, if it does work, your baby has a chance for a long and healthy life," Jax added.

"Steph, it's worth a shot," Airiella said quietly.

"What if this is her destiny? Are you supposed to be changing that?" Stephanie wanted to believe.

"We make our own destiny. Emma's too young to decide hers yet. If this works, she will get to choose hers, and you'll get to see it happen. If it doesn't work, we'll know, and we love her anyway," Airiella argued.

"I can't ever tell Bob this," Stephanie looked at her hands.

"You shouldn't tell him anything of what I told you, for your safety," Airiella reminded her.

"Will your blood make her a target?" Stephanie worried.

"I don't think so. Emma's pure of heart, there's nothing to corrupt," Jax said. "All she knows is love."

"Do it before I change my mind," Stephanie looked away.

"I need something sharp," Airiella whispered.

"Papercut," Jax said, holding out a piece of paper.

"I guess." Jax watched as she sliced the paper across her finger, and it welled up with blood. "Don't bite me, Emma," Airiella crooned at her.

She slid her finger into Emma's mouth and wiped the blood on her tongue. More than two drops worth. She cooed at Emma, tickling her and making her giggle. "Rub her throat, it's a signal to her that she needs to swallow," Stephanie said quietly.

Jax rubbed his fingers down her throat and felt her swallow while Airiella put her finger in a napkin. Jax handed the baby back to Stephanie and took the napkin from her. "Ronnie said we need to burn anything that has your blood on it." He stuck the bloody tissue in his pocket.

"When's your next appointment for her?" Airiella asked.

"Next week," Stephanie said, her face pale. "How will I know if it works?"

"I guess whatever motor skills that have been affected by this watch and see if they improve. I guess it happened pretty fast for the kidnapper." Airiella shrugged.

"You know how weird all this is, right?" Stephanie hugged Emma to her.

"Yeah, I do. At least you know now. If I disappear for a while, or you see more weird stuff on the internet, you won't freak out too badly," Airiella took hold of Jax's hand.

"I'll still worry about you," Stephanie smiled.

"Love you, Steph. Hoping this works."

"Thanks for letting me hold her," Jax smiled. "Pretty sure I'm what Airiella calls a smitten kitten."

"You've found him, Ells," Stephanie nodded at Jax.

"More than just me," Jax corrected.

Stephanie held out her hand, "Can I see your phone again, those pictures?"

Jax handed it over without a word. Stephanie scrolled through the pictures until she found the one she wanted. "This is the other strong connection, right?" She pointed to a picture of Airiella and Ronnie.

Airiella smiled a soft smile, "Yes, that's Ronnie."

Stephanie looked back at Jax. "I can see the love they have for each other." She handed the phone back to Jax. "You are right; it's strong. But what you can't see because you are too close, is that what she feels with you, is brighter and stronger than that. It may be with all of you, this connection thing," she pointed at Jax and Airiella, "but this one is different."

Jax could see why Stephanie was her favorite cousin. She pulled no punches. "Thank you, Stephanie."

"That doesn't mean you get a free pass. You better take care of Ells the way she deserves to be taken care of and loved. I have no issues with coming after you if she gets hurt," Stephanie used a tone that Jax associated with protective mothers.

"Hurting her is the last thing I want to do," Jax stood and held out his arms for Emma so Stephanie could get up. "Your mama is fierce, little one." Emma giggled as Jax swung her up and down.

"Yes, I am." She held out her arms for Emma. "Now, Mama wants to go take a nap," she sang to Emma.

"Mama," Emma said and touched Stephanie's cheek.

They all froze and looked at Emma in amazement. Stephanie's eyes flooded with tears. "Yes, I'm Mama, you beautiful little girl. Mama," she said, pointing at herself. "Emma," she pointed to Emma.

"Mama," Emma giggled.

"Ells, you just gave me the greatest gift of my life. That's her first word." Stephanie shoved Emma back at Jax and threw herself at Airiella.

Jax played with the baby as the two clung to each other and cried. "Women! They're crazy," Jax told the baby.

Chapter Eleven

I had four days to come up with a eulogy for someone I hadn't even accepted I'd lost yet. Grief was heavy on me, pulling at every move I made as we walked back to the car. The bright spot of the day was Emma saying mama to Stephanie.

Well, if I was honest, seeing Jax play with Emma was pretty damn cute too. I tugged on his arm and pulled it around my shoulders, needing to feel him close. "I'm sorry I'm acting so needy. It isn't like me at all."

My words halted Jax mid-step. "You think you are needy?" He had a dumbfounded look on his gorgeous face.

"Well, yeah. I'm hanging on you all the time, crying more than I ever have in my life. You're constantly taking care of me, that all adds up to needy."

"You just changed two lives. That's not needy," Jax pointed out.

"You were the one who pointed out the option," I countered.

"Siren, needy isn't a word anyone who knows you would use to describe you. Is there a nature spot somewhere between here and home that is a good place to escape to?" Jax changed the subject.

"Yeah. You want to go out in nature?" I followed as he pulled me along behind him.

"I want to take *you* there to help you recharge a little. I can feel the weight on your shoulders."

My heart fluttered wildly in my chest. "You want to do this for me?"

"It does carry the extra benefit of seeing another place that you love, which allows me to learn even more about you," he grinned. "See? Not entirely selfless reasons."

"The only thing better right now would be Ronnie, so I could work it all out by hitting something," I thought out loud.

"Ronnie is better than me?" I couldn't tell by his tone if he was joking or not.

"At fighting? Absolutely. Sorry, not trying to bruise your ego. The way he trains gets all my aggression and frustration out," I said with surety.

"Don't apologize for that. Ronnie is brilliant at accomplishing that. He does the same for me. There's no way I could duplicate it. So instead, we are going to go out in nature," Jax kissed the top of my head.

He took the keys, and I let him drive, directing him to one of my old haunts that was near my parent's house. I pulled out the parking tag I kept in my car for state parks, and I led him around. I made my way back to a corner in the park where the river makes a bend. The water is crystal clear, and there is a tiny little waterfall across from the rocky beach.

It was lush and green all around us, the snowpack starting to melt as we approach summer. It was one of my favorite spots that I hadn't been to in quite a while. I told him stories of my friends and me here in this park and the wild stunts we pulled. I also told him about white water rafting this river in the rain.

"It's beautiful here," he said, looking at me. "I can picture you here easily."

Feeling wild, and since no one else was around, I stood and started to strip off all my clothes. Not something

I would ordinarily do in the daylight. I don't think the scars all over me were attractive, but in the grief that swamped me, I just needed to let go for a minute.

"Whatcha doing, siren?" Jax had a curious look on his face. "It's not exactly warm out."

I didn't say anything. I just finished stripping and then jumped into the frigid water of the river. "Holy shit, this is cold!" I yelled.

"Are you insane?" Jax was stunned.

"Probably." I dove under the water and swam across to the swimming hole on the other side. "When we were younger, my brother and I would play here." I stepped out on to the rock ledge and pointed up. "There's a rope swing right there."

I started making my way up the little ridge, my bare feet ice cold and my teeth chattering. I reached out for the rope, gripped it as tight as I could, and swung out over the river, letting go right over the deepest part and plunged back in the icy water.

I surfaced, spluttering, and made my way back to him. I climbed out, shivering. "You are going to freeze!" Jax said, running his hands fast over my skin to get the blood circulating.

"I needed that," I said simply. I yanked socks back on and wiped as much of the water off of me as I could before putting my clothes back on. "You should try it. It's invigorating."

"I'd never see my balls again if I got in that water," Jax said, wrapping himself around me, his heat seeping into my skin.

"That would indeed be a shame as they are pretty nice balls," I snuggled into him. "You can take me home now."

"A sleeping bag and campfire would be perfect right now," Jax whispered in my ear.

"Not here, we'd get a ticket. We could go to my beach and do that," I answered. My body was relaxing after the release of all that grief that was weighing on me.

"Your beach?" he kissed my neck. I was definitely

warming up the more he did that.

"Um, yeah," I was distracted by his lips on me. "When I was a kid, my other grandpa and grandma used to take me to a beach where there was family property. It's my favorite place in the world. Don't you remember me telling you about it that day we all went to the beach? Do that some more," my train of thought went sideways as he kissed up my neck to my jaw.

"The sight of you wet like that was one hell of an aphrodisiac, siren. Tell me more about this beach since all I can remember right now is how much I want you."

"Um, yeah, the beach. It's beautiful." He turned my head and gave me one of those kisses of his that were guaranteed to short circuit every single thought in my head.

"Let's go there then," he said against my lips.

"What?" I couldn't even remember what we were talking about, not when he was like this.

He laughed, and I was mesmerized by him. "You need to get warm, let's go home first."

"I'm so crazy in love with you," I murmured as he pulled me up, "I can't even think."

"Ditto, baby. Come on, warm car ahead." He led me back the way we came, handed me his phone, and told me to put my address on the map.

"I know the way home, I don't need GPS," I argued, but did it anyway.

He got me settled in the car with the heat cranked, turned the GPS on, and started driving home. I could have told him the way I was thinking to myself right before I fell asleep.

Smitty laughed as he listened to Ronnie relay the story of Airiella jumping buck naked into the river. "Our girl is one of a kind."

"Jax said his balls would have fallen off if he'd gotten in," Ronnie chuckled. "I can totally picture her flying through the air, naked on a rope swing."

"Are you at all concerned that she's still asleep a day

later?" Smitty wanted to know.

"Not really. Jax said she'd been dealing with her family since she arrived and that they leaned heavily on her. Knowing her, she pulled the heavy stuff from them and took it on herself, on top of her own grief," Ronnie had been looking things up on his tablet for the past fifteen minutes.

"What are you doing?" Smitty was curious.

"Looking for a gym that would allow me to use their equipment after the funeral. Jax said she made a comment about wishing I was there so she could hit something. You know, like how I'd take Jax and work him out to get the aggression out of him. He said she needs that. If I can find somewhere relatively close to the place the funeral is, we can stop by after, and I can do that for her before we leave. I'm just not having a lot of luck finding somewhere."

"I feel like a third wheel," Smitty glumly replied.

"What? Why?" Ronnie looked up, surprised.

"I don't think she needs me," Smitty hated the petulant tone that came out of his mouth.

"Didn't you say she's been texting you?"

Smitty shrugged. "Yeah, but just telling me she misses me and loves me."

Ronnie burst out laughing. "Arthur Smith, are you having a pity party?"

"Why, yes, I think I am." Smitty chuckled. "It's just hard feeling useless. She's going to you and Jax for everything."

"Just Jax. She hasn't asked me for anything. Jax has. Her world has a narrow focus on her family right now, and Jax is her support while she supports all the rest of them. He said even random patients at the hospital were leaning on her. Look, before she left, she told me that you and me right here, learning the stuff we have been learning, is her biggest advantage. It's what we are good at doing. She's relying on us to teach her and Jax when they get back." Ronnie went back to typing. "If you are that upset about it, help me look for a place to do this."

"Give me a list, and I'll start calling," Smitty

resigned himself to the grunt work. He knew Ronnie was right, and he was just missing her badly. "Did Aedan arrange a 7-seater SUV for us?"

"I think so. Why?"

"I can go pack a bit of gear that she will need for the workout to bring with us and the clothes," Smitty suggested.

"Shit. I totally forgot about that. Great idea. We've got to find a place first."

Smitty felt distracted, "Father Roarke will be here today with the equipment he had made and blessed for us, too. So, for the higher-level demons, we will all need you to train us with the weapons. Aedan and Mags, especially."

"That's today?"

"Yeah. The priest will be here in a couple of hours," Smitty called the number of the gym Ronnie just handed him. "Hi, is there someone I can talk to about using the gym on Thursday?"

"Smitty, I'm not sure I know how to fight with weapons," Ronnie looked tired.

"Ronnie, you are the best fighter I know. Incorporate the weapons into the moves you already know. We'll probably need to make some dummies to practice on, though."

"Yeah, I was thinking of that too," Ronnie's face was starting to look drawn.

"Yes, hello? I'm looking for a gym that will let us use the equipment, namely the bags and pads. We don't really need the ring. It would be after hours, for no more than two hours. Is that something that you would be able to accommodate?" Smitty asked the person that came on the line.

Smitty watched Ronnie rest his head on the desk. "Of course, a rental fee is fine. Art Smith. There will be six of us total, probably only two or three that will actually be working out. Yes, I'm that Art Smith." Smitty held a thumbs up out to Ronnie, who sighed in relief. "Yes, Thursday. I'm not exactly sure on the time frame. It would be around seven or eight, I'd think. I'll give you my number. Yes, I'll be your point of contact. Thank you."

Smitty hung up. "We need to go to the studio and get some of the promotional stuff we use for the publicity crap. The guy knew who I was and is a fan. Since it's us, he's not going to charge us a fee. He will be the one to meet us and open the gym. If we bring him stuff that we sign for him, I think he'd let us do whatever we wanted."

"Works for me," Ronnie agreed.

"You and I can go make dummies. I'll send Aedan to the studio to gather stuff." Smitty got up and went to find Aedan and fill him in. He'd been far more subdued with Airiella gone and was eager to be put to use.

"Hey Smitty, how are you doing?" he heard Mags tired voice coming from their room.

He popped his head in, "Hey, little mama. I'm okay, for the most part. How are you? You sound tired."

"It's hard not having Airiella here. It's different when you guys are on a location because you are all together, and I feel the combined energy of the group through the connection. Separated like this, without her, it's draining." She rubbed her belly. "These two keep moving around in there. Wanna know a secret?" She grinned, but it didn't have her usual spark behind it.

"Sure, hit me with it," Smitty smiled and rested a hand on her belly when he sat down next to her.

"Aedan and I picked out names for them. You can't share them with the others, though. We are going to surprise them with it," Mags told him.

"Secret is safe with me," Smitty promised.

"The girl we are going to name Angel Gwendolyn, the boy we are thinking on Jackson Giuseppe. What do you think?"

"Like Jax?"

"Pronounced the same as Jaxon, but we would spell it J-a-c-k-s-o-n. Giuseppe is after Airiella's grandpa. Angel because well, Airiella's an angel, and that's what Ronnie calls her. We aren't set on the boy's name yet, Aedan proposed a new idea, but I think it will be similar to that."

"I think that they all will love those names; did you

tell Winnie?" Smitty rubbed his chest, where he felt the pressure build.

"Not yet. Are you okay?" Mags asked, concerned.

"I'm fine. It was a surge of emotion, that's all." Smitty grimaced. It wasn't all it was, he figured Airiella was awake now and things were becoming more real for her. "Guess what Airiella did?"

"Something crazy?"

"Oh well, kind of, I wasn't referring to that. I can tell you that one first. Airiella stripped naked and jumped in a freezing river and went flying from a rope swing." Mags laughed. "What I was talking about though is her cousins' baby. Emma got diagnosed with a rare syndrome called Rett's. When Ronnie was talking to Jax about the blood, Jax thought maybe her blood could help the baby, Emma. It did. She cut her finger open and saved that little girl."

Mags was crying. "Oh my." She put her hands on her belly. "You hear that babies, your auntie is going to always be looking out for you."

Smitty smiled a real smile this time. He leaned over and talked to Mags's baby bump. "So will your uncles."

"Thanks for that, Smitty." He dropped a kiss on her forehead.

"Do me a favor, pack up a bag of workout clothes for Airiella to bring with us. Ronnie's going to surprise her with a workout so she can punch her grief out," Smitty told her.

"You got it," Mags looked happy to be given something to do.

Smitty went back downstairs to collect the exhausted Ronnie still slumped on the desk, and start making some practice dummies.

Jax had been sitting downstairs while Mel chattered at him, asking questions about the show and digging for information about Airiella's relationship with them all. He didn't mind the questions; Mel was just looking out for her friend. He kept looking at the various pieces of artwork placed around the house.

"You looking at all the glass?" Mel was watching him closely.

"Yeah. It's beautiful," Jax commented inanely.

"She collects blown glass. She started after she got back from a family trip to Italy. She's picky about it. If an artist doesn't sign it or if it's mass-produced, she typically won't buy it."

"I noticed an interesting piece in her room. I've seen one before, though," Jax tried to remember where he'd seen it.

"The phoenix," Mel replied. "It's one of my favorites. She got it at the Grand Canyon."

Jax rubbed his chest, there was pressure there suddenly, and he smelled smoke. He stood up and looked around. "Do you smell anything?"

"No, are you okay?" Mel frowned at him.

An ear-piercing scream rang through his head, and the house in stereo and he bolted for the stairs. He heard thunder booming and panic set in. Something was wrong with Airiella. He ran into the bedroom to find her eyes wild and unfocused, tears streaming down her face as she clutched at her throat like someone was choking her.

Mel was close behind him, fear written across her face as she pushed back. "Ells!"

Airiella turned and saw Mel, but her eyes focused on Jax, and she launched straight off the bed and jumped on him, knocking him into the wall behind him as she wrapped her arms and legs around him. Her sobs were hysterical.

Jax's phone started to ring from his pocket, and he knew it would be Ronnie. "Mel, can you grab my phone out of my pocket, please? That's Ronnie. Can you tell him she had a nightmare, and I'm with her right now?"

Mel nodded, "Later, I'm going to reflect on the fact I got to dig around in your pocket."

He heard her talking to Ronnie as he held a still sobbing Airiella in his arms. He got her sitting on the bed, though she wouldn't unwind from him. "I've got you, siren.

It's okay, baby. Shhh," he murmured in her ear, stroking her hair in a calming manner.

The way she clutched at him was scary. Something had shaken her badly. She was inconsolable. Mel popped her head in a few times, worried, the last time she put his phone next to him and closed the door behind her. Jax just held her and let her cry it out.

When her cries slowed down, she turned her face into his neck; his own heart stopped its mad rhythm. "Nightmare?" he asked her quietly.

"I hope so," came her muffled answer.

"Talk to me, Ells," he prodded her gently. "Lightning struck somewhere outside."

He heard her gulp air into her lungs. "I saw you die," she choked on the words.

"I'm okay. I'm right here, feel me, Ells. Check me over if you need to. I'm okay," he consoled her.

Her grip on him eased a little, and he lay back, rolling them on to their sides. "I couldn't save you," her tears started again.

"It's just a nightmare, baby. I'm okay," he reached behind him to pull on one of her hands, and he placed it between them on his chest. "Feel my heart; it beats for you. I trust you with my life. I'm perfectly fine."

She touched the connection between them, and she let down the walls she'd been maintaining, and then he felt the pain that was ripping through her from the nightmare. He was glad he was already laying down because it would have been enough to drop him. "That's what losing you would feel like to me. That wasn't all of it either, that's only after I saw you were alive."

He understood. That was something he could identify with because it's how he felt at the thought of losing Airiella. He pulled her shirt up to wipe the tears from her face, then kissed her softly. "Do you want to talk about it?"

"No. They can't have you, whoever they are. They won't get to you. I refuse to allow it to happen," the fierce warrior in her came out, and he smiled.

"You summoned lightning for me," Jax said in awe.

"I would burn the world to a crisp for you," she corrected him.

"Do you remember the other day with Emma when I was talking about the blood?" She nodded at him. "There's a piece we didn't talk about that I said we would later. It looks like now is that time. When we were together that first night, remember biting your lip?"

He saw her flush as the memory replayed, and he took a moment to kiss her again, pouring his heart into it. She moaned into him, returning the emotion. He had to stop, or the conversation would never finish. He pulled back, loving the sight of her swollen lips and flushed face.

"Well, I licked that blood off your lip. Apparently, it created a blood bond, but it's not complete yet. There are consequences to both of us if we don't complete it, and maybe whatever or whoever gave you that nightmare knows it," Jax relayed the information.

"What's a blood bond?" she asked quietly.

"More bonding than our connection, I was told. It's not just me. Smitty and Ronnie have also tasted your blood. Both when they kissed you after you released that energy you took from me."

"Oh, no. I've ruined your lives," Airiella whispered.

"What?! No. That's not even close to being true. I say it because if we want to help you, we need to finish it. Tak said that if something happens to you and not us, it will drive us insane from the loss. If something happens to us, it could kill you," Jax repeated Ronnie's message.

"Then let's finish it. I drive you crazy enough. We don't need to make it worse," Airiella told him.

He leaned his head against hers. "You aren't worried about being stuck with me?"

"Not in the slightest. I'm hoping forever isn't too long for you," Airiella calmly told him.

"Forever isn't long enough," he kissed her again. "How do you feel about getting rough with me a little?"

"What do you mean?" her ragged breathing was a huge turn on for him.

"How about you bite my lip, or wherever you want to bite," he said.

"You mean I have to be a vampire now? Suck your blood?" a smile teased at her lips.

"Pretty much. I don't think you have to tear into my neck, though."

Her abundant laughter uncoiled a ball of need in him, and he rolled her back on top of him. "Let's wing it on the location of the bite. See where the moment takes us," she ground her hips down on him, biting down on her lip, so it drew blood again.

Jax bit down on his own lip, drawing blood and crushed his mouth to hers, their blood mingling with their tongues as she tried to pull his clothes off him. He felt the moment that bond took hold of them, whatever mystical forces beyond his understanding took their future and melded it together.

The connection and blood bond began morphing into one impenetrable link between them, a thing of beauty that glowed with its own life force. Jax needed to be buried inside her now. With the frantic way she tore off her own clothing, she was feeling the same. There was nothing gentle in it.

She slammed herself down on him the moment his cock was free, and she rode them both hard and fast, tipping them over the edge in a wild freefall that left them both breathless and shaking. "I'm sorry, Jax," she trembled.

"What the fuck are you sorry for?" He pulled her down on him.

"That got away from me," was her answer, she licked the blood still on his lips.

"Airiella, don't ever apologize for having sex with me," he kissed her.

"It was over so fast, but damn, you feel amazing."

"We've got the rest of our lives to go slow, and you are not going to hear me complain once," Jax nipped at her lips. He felt her heart flutter at his words, and he smiled slowly. "Does that scare you?"

"Should it? Do you have some hidden kink I haven't stumbled on with my dirty mind yet?"

He burst out laughing. "Not yet, but I might try harder to find one now. Is Ronnie still the only sex god?"

"Jealous?" she pulled away to look at his face.

"No. If that's how it will be for the others when you finish the bond with them, I'm going to be laughing my ass off because they aren't going to know what hit them," Jax smirked.

"I think you and Ronnie are tied in the sex god title," she elaborated. "You make it sound like I'm going to run them over like a train."

"Sweetheart, I didn't even get to finish getting my clothes off," Jax pointed out. She blushed, and Jax saw the undiluted dirty thoughts race through her mind. "Easy there, siren. Let's clean up and eat something, so we have enough energy to act on at least one of those thoughts."

"Hey, guys?" Mel's voice sounded through the door, and Jax threw a blanket over them. "I think we just had an earthquake. Did you feel the house shake?"

Jax bit back a laugh at the look horror and fascination on Airiella's face.

Chapter Twelve

wo days of a naked Jax was not nearly enough to quench the lust he set on fire in me. The only break we took was to go to a store where he could get clothes acceptable for a funeral. I thought Ronnie was the master at making me come. I was wrong.

Now here it was hours before my grandpa's funeral, and I had written nothing for the eulogy I was supposed to deliver. I was a horrible granddaughter. Somewhere he was looking down on me, shaking his head, wondering what he had been thinking.

"Stop it, Ells. Maybe you weren't supposed to write anything. He knew you and how you are. Maybe he wanted you to speak from the heart. You aren't a horrible granddaughter." Jax sat down beside me, looking like an underwear model. Holy shit, this man was mine. I needed to focus.

"Right. Because every good granddaughter on the day of her grandpa's funeral can't stop thinking about the way you fill out that underwear and trying to devise every possible plan for getting you out of them," I bit my lip.

"You don't need a plan, just ask." He kissed my

temple. "Come on, before I give in and we are late. I know you don't want to do this. I also know you will be amazing at it. Get dressed; there's only so much temptation I can resist."

"I'm scared, Jax," I whispered, my head hung in shame.

"I know, baby. You are going to be in a room filled with people that love you. There is nothing to be afraid of," Jax tipped my chin up. "Stop hiding those beautiful eyes. Tears are okay, even expected, but not shame."

The awful illusion of the nightmare drifted across my mind, and I jolted. "I love you," my voice came out fiercer than I intended, and Jax raised his eyebrows at me. "Sorry. My thoughts are everywhere."

"Ells, I'm right here."

I nodded. I needed to get my shit together. I felt like I was unraveling as the minutes ticked closer. Where was that mask I had relied on for so long? Snap out of it! I yelled at myself. I grabbed a pair of black slacks that had little white flowers on them and a black V-necked shirt. Not quite traditional for a funeral, I know. I wasn't a conventional person, though, something my grandpa had valued in me.

I couldn't figure out which shoes to wear, so I asked Jax to pick some for me while I went to put makeup on. It's not something I usually wore, and I hoped that if I wore it, I'd be able to control my emotions in fear of ending up a blubbering mess with makeup smeared all over my face. Not that when I wore makeup, it was heavy, I leaned toward the natural look.

Finished with that, I decided to leave my hair down and stepped back into the bedroom. I stared at the sight Jax presented me. Jax, in a suit, was stunning. I think I drooled. "Ells, you are the one who is stunning," he chuckled at the thoughts running through my head. "This is the first time I've seen you with makeup on."

"Too much?" Suddenly I felt self-conscious.

Two steps and he was in front of me, all that sexy man in my reach. The intricate ink that I loved hidden by these sleek clothes. Damn it, Airy! Focus! I told myself.

"Fuck me. You are gorgeous. My personal taste is I like no makeup on you. This look feels like a mask to me that you are hiding behind, and I get the reasons why. With it, or without it, you are still gorgeous. It's not too much, you can hardly tell you are wearing it," Jax assured me.

How did he know how to pull me back from the ledge the way he did? Was this the bond? He handed me a pair of red sandals I hadn't worn in years. "Really?"

"Yep. The sandals will be perfect. And yes, the bond helps me know how to navigate that mess you call a mind. My words are mine and how I feel. I love every bit of you just as you are."

"Damnit Jax, if you make me cry before we leave, I'm going to zap you with electricity," I threatened.

"I have a feeling I'm going to get zapped then. There's just one more thing for your outfit." He pulled a box out of his pocket and handed it to me.

"Is this what was delivered to you yesterday?" I asked, my hands trembling.

"Yes, open it, Ells."

I pulled open the box and saw a jeweled pendant. The center an opal with five stones around it in the shape of a flower on a delicate chain made of links. My breath caught in my throat as I ran my thumb over it. The opal was my birthstone. "Jax, this is exquisite."

He took it gently from me and fastened it around my neck. "I drew it a while ago and had a friend of mine make it in white gold once I found the stones. That part was quick, the making it. Finding the right stones was a bit harder. Each one of these stones is one of our birthstones. You are what holds us together in the worst of times, and you make us shine brighter in the best of times. Your shine is like the opal, all these brilliant colors in one precious stone. Soft and rare."

I threw my arms around his neck and tried to keep the tears from falling. At least I'd had the foresight to get waterproof makeup. "I love you so damn much, Jax. I swear if one of my family members makes a move on you,

I'm going to strike them with lightning. Scratch that, any female, anywhere. Thank you for this."

"There is only one other female that might give you competition," he joked, and I pulled back to glare at him. "Emma. She kinda stole a little bit of my heart."

I grinned. "I can live with that." I held my hand over that pendant and felt the love he had for me seeping through it. "This is so perfect."

"So are you." He kissed me softly. "Come on, let's go."

I didn't want to. Not even a little. I followed Jax like the good girl I was, and he took my keys and handed me my iPod. He did know me. He put an earbud in so he could hear his GPS and let me blast the music to drown out my thoughts.

Way too soon, we were at the church, and I saw the cars of several of my family members. I couldn't make myself open my car door. "This is real. He's gone. I have to talk about him to everyone. I can't do this, Jax." Panic spun through me in wild spurts.

"God, siren. I hate myself for making you go in there, but you know you have to. The guilt you would feel would for not doing this would kill you. I know it hurts, and I know it's scary. I had to do this for my dad, and I felt the same way you do. I was also glad I did it. It gave me a chance to say goodbye in my way. I know the situations are different, and my family is nothing like yours, they don't depend on me as yours depends on you. If for no other reason, do it because he asked you to be the one to stand up there for him. Find the people in the crowd you can look at without freaking out. Focus on me; I'm with you. Focus on Emma, your nieces, whoever works for you."

I nodded, trying to fight back the need to run away. I closed my eyes to take some steadying breaths and found Jax at my car door, holding it open for me. I didn't even hear him get out; I was so far gone. He took my hand and pulled me up; wrapping his arms around me. Whoever put this man on my path, I was incredibly grateful for it.

"I wouldn't be alive if it wasn't for you, siren. Are

you ready now?" Jax kissed me.

"I'll never be ready, but let's go."

"That's my girl." He held my hand securely in his, and we headed in.

I saw my mom first. She was using a wheelchair because it hurt too much for her to use a knee scooter. My dad stood behind her looking lost. Jax led us in that direction, I just followed, numb to my surroundings.

"Ells, did you write something beautiful?" my mom asked, the dagger she hadn't intended landing straight in my heart.

"I couldn't write, Mom. Don't worry; it will come to me. How do you feel?" I leaned over and gave her a one-armed hug, refusing to let go of Jax.

"Awful. Nanie is counting on you," my mom reminded me, that dagger going a little deeper.

"Hi, Dad. How are you doing?" I hugged him tighter than my mom. She was in one of the bi-polar moods.

"Hanging in there. Don't let Mom get to you," my dad whispered in my ear. "Jax, thanks for coming."

"Of course, sir." I almost laughed at his formality.

"Incoming," my dad warned. I turned right as some distant cousins appeared behind us.

"Oh, my God. Aren't you that ghost hunter guy on TV?" the female exclaimed, for the life of me I couldn't remember her name.

"Right now, I'm Airiella's boyfriend, who is supporting her during this painful time," was Jax's thoughtful yet polite response.

"Gina, leave them alone," my mom's acidic tone cut through, and I winced. Well, at least I knew her name now.

Gina ignored my mother. "How did you end up with him? That was a long shot."

"Actually, *I* was lucky enough to land her. She also works with me on the show. She's the best thing that ever happened to me," Jax responded, not even looking at her. He was looking only at me, and my heart thundered in my ears. He wrapped a possessive arm around me and held me close.

Gina apparently had nothing to say to that. "Jax, if I was ambivalent about you before, I'm not now," my dad told him. "Go find Nanie, Ells. Let her know you're here."

I made my escape to where I had spotted Nanie talking with the priest. Jax, making sure he had skin contact with me the entire time. I waited until she finished talking before making my presence known. "Nanie, I'm here. You remember, Jax, right?"

"I'm old, not stupid, Ella. Of course, I remember him. I can see he's taking good care of you. That's a beautiful necklace," she tapped my chest.

"It was a gift from Jax," I blushed.

"Excellent taste, young man." She looked back at me. "I know this is hard for you, Ella. I'm sorry for asking you to do this."

"Oh, Nanie. Don't be sorry. I'll be fine," I reassured her with a confidence that I didn't feel.

"You're an awful liar, sweetheart. I have faith that you will be exactly what is needed today. The first row of pews is for us." She turned to greet whoever came up behind us.

I sat down in the pew and tried to catch my breath. "Ells, this little monster is your responsibility for the next ten minutes," I heard Stephanie come up, and she plopped Emma in my lap. Quietly, she looked at me with tears in her eyes. "She took a step, Ells. With no braces on her legs."

I swooped the baby up in the air, tossing her to get her to giggle. "Emma, you little miracle baby."

Jax grabbed her as I heard a cry of "Auntie!" coming at me. My nieces barreled into me. "You look sad, Auntie," Grace said.

"I am sad, Monkey. It's a sad day. That means you have to be quiet and listen to your parents. No arguing, fighting or being loud. Promise?"

Grace, the little schemer, "If I do, do I get a prize?"

I pulled two little packages of candy from my purse. "You both have to promise me first."

Two little voices made a solemn promise to behave, and I handed them candy. "Sucker," my brother sat down next to me. "Did you hear the good news about Emma?" My brother watched Jax play with her. "Who am I kidding, you were probably the first to know," he answered his own question. "I'll grudgingly admit he isn't the tool I thought he was."

"High praise coming from you," I shot him a warning look.

"Worried about you is all, Ells." Nick patted my leg. "Can't believe you have to deliver the eulogy. I couldn't do it."

"Is that supposed to help? 'Cuz it's not," I growled at him.

"Don't worry, sis. You got this. Grandpa picked the right person."

"Who are you, and what did you do with my brother?" I looked at him stupefied.

"Shut up." He elbowed me and grinned.

"Oh, there you are. Scared me for a minute." I pushed him back.

"Keep it up and I'll feed them nothing but sugar, and promise them they can go home with you. Jax can have their room," he threatened me.

Jax chuckled at my expression. "That was an effective threat," he told Nick.

"Sam wants you two to come to dinner tomorrow night. You aren't headed out yet, are you?"

"No, but it would have to be an early dinner. I need to be in Seattle tomorrow night for a radio interview I'm being forced to do," I grimaced.

"I'll tell her Saturday is better, then?" Nick checked his phone calendar.

I checked with Jax, who nodded. "Saturday works."

"That's my sister," Louis walked up to Jax.

"Hi Louis," I reached out to tickle him. "Where's Amanda and Grace? I thought you'd be playing with them."

He crawled up on to the pew to sit between Jax and I. "What's your name?"

"I'm Jax. It's nice to meet you, Louis," Jax smiled at him. Like Ronnie, he turned out to be a kid whisperer.

I have many talents, siren, his voice popped in my head.

"Brace yourself, Ells; cousins headed this way." Nick stood. "Louis, let's go find the girls, I could use your help," he held his hand out to Louis.

"Okay, bye, Jax," he crawled down and walked off with my brother.

A stream of cousins came through, mostly out of curiosity about Jax than offering condolences. He handled it like a champ, never losing that smile of his that melted my panties. My thoughts scattered again. "Easy, siren." He kissed my cheek. "Take a quick look around and find the people you can safely focus on."

Nanie would be where I was at, Jax was there. My dad would be in the same row, and Stephanie would be behind him. I had my people picked out; they were few. My brain kept blanking out at the thought of standing up there.

Breathe deep, baby. Stay calm, Jax's voice sounded in my head. *Focus on me, feel my love;* he soothed me. *I'm here with you, every step of the way.*

This is harder than all other stuff I've faced, I thought back to him.

I know, love. It is just one moment, though, he told me. *One moment that will mean the world to your family, a moment that only you can deliver. There is no right or wrong to anything you say when you speak from your heart. Your heart is so beautiful and pure that everything around you becomes brighter.*

Jax, thank you. Thank you for loving me.

The priest had started the mass portion of the funeral, and I wasn't paying attention, I was trying to meditate and find balance. I shut everyone out around me and concentrated on slow, even breathing, the feel of Jax holding my hand and the love I felt from him.

Too soon, the mass part was over. Nanie stood and walked up to the pulpit. "I've asked my granddaughter to deliver the eulogy today; it was something Giuseppe had wanted. Thank you all for being here."

The wave I'd been holding back inside me broke,

and I could barely stand. Jax kissed the back of my hand and stood, helping me to my feet and walking me up to the stage. I let my walls down and heard him repeating that he loved me. I felt exposed and terrified as he walked away, my eyes not leaving him.

I took a deep breath in, and my voice immediately broke. "Sorry, folks. I'm not very good at this." I looked at my nanie, sitting serenely with her hands in her lap, her eyes intent on me, and I felt her love. Grandpa, I thought, if you are watching, I could use a boost of your confidence in me.

"For those of you that don't know me, I'm Airiella, the oldest grandchild. For those of you who do know me, bear with me here through this awkwardness. I don't really know why he wanted me to do this, and as hard as I tried to prepare something to say, the words wouldn't come. It's a first for me as I often have an easier time writing than I do speaking. The loss of him hurts deeply," I bit back tears.

"To me, he was Grandpa. He was a hero, a legend, a stoic man, stout in his beliefs, as well as his opinions, which were often colorful when he thought Nanie wasn't paying attention." Some people laughed. I looked at Nanie, who was smiling now. "In honor of him, I wore my hair down. It has the double benefit of driving my mom and Nanie crazy too. When I was little, well, even now, she hated my hair being in my face. She always threatened to cut it off, to the point where she would take me outside and stand me on a bucket and start to do it, and from around the corner of their house, Grandpa would come charging out, telling her that she better not be touching my hair. I always thought he was magic; he always appeared when she had scissors in her hand." There was more laughter.

I looked heavenward, "Grandpa, this mop today is for you." I gathered myself a moment before going on. "Everyone who knew him loved him, learned from him, and valued him. His death is a tragic loss to this world, and it's a bit darker now without him in it." My tears fell, but my voice remained steady. "I've learned though, through these years, he will never be away from me. He's in my soul.

Every hair he kept safe from the crazy woman with scissors, to every lesson he taught me by making me pick berries when I was obnoxious. To every family dinner where he told countless stories of his amazing life, it lives inside me. It lives on in every one of us. Love doesn't die. Memories can get hazy, but love remains. In every single thing we do, he lives on. When we teach others of something that we learned from him, he lives on."

I wiped my tears with a tissue that I saw Nanie had left for me on the pulpit. "Love wins. He's so much a part of our lives, he always was, and he always will be. Each dastardly thing we did as a kid, he never turned away from us. Each failure we've made, he helped us find the lesson in it and keep going. Each success, he celebrated. Each pain, he'd hug it away. He loved what made us different from others; he applauded us marching to our own beat- finding our own way. He was proud of us. All of us."

My chest filled with such strong emotions that if I didn't let some of them go, I was going to drown. "When we moved right after my brother was born, he came to help my dad put sod in the front yard. I was three, and *maybe* a little bit of a pain. He gave me his keys to hold on to, most likely to shut me up or keep me occupied." I heard my mom start to laugh, soon Nanie joined her. "This is a great example of the man he was," I said with a smile. "I, of course, a new toy in my hand proceeded to bury his keys under the sod because why not?" There was a lot of laughter now. "He was furious, not really at me, but because he trusted his keys to a three-year-old. They had to rip up all the sod they had laid to find his keys. Needless to say, he didn't give them back to me after that."

"Now imagine that times eight. Eight grandkids that tortured him with various hair-brained things like that. My brother and I might have been the worst, I can't really say. Grandpa had the patience of a saint. Poor Nanie, though. You all know how she is the world's best cook, sorry, Mom. Every Saturday morning, she would bake. She has that famous drawer in the kitchen that's filled with flour. You can all see where this is heading, right?" Nanie was smiling.

"Grandpa left my brother and me in the kitchen while he went to pick some berries for a pie she was going to make. *Big* mistake. He heard Nanie yelling from where he was out in his garden and came running to find us covered in flour, as well as the kitchen, and all her baking pans. We'd managed to pull the flour drawer out and upend it, *after* we'd pulled out all the baking pans. Grandpa laughed so hard I'm shocked he didn't pee himself. You might ask how I remember something from that long ago, well you don't forget that kind of fury that Nanie displayed. I think Grandpa probably made it worse with the laughter, but it's a story that gets told often."

My aunts and uncles were laughing. "My cousin Mike, he's the youngest boy. He once asked my Grandpa why they had ten years of tuna fish in their cupboards downstairs," more laughter. "Grandpa was the original hoarder. If you were in need of a part for a washing machine that stopped being made in 1938, just ask Grandpa, he probably had a box full of them and could tell you exactly where it was in the mess he called a basement, down to the inch of where it lived and how he procured them."

I choked up again. "There's no replacing someone like that. I know that every one of you probably has countless stories much the same as I do. There is no shortage of memories, from crazy things that you would never expect to come out of Grandpa's mouth to the sage advice of someone that lived through decades of history that we only learn about in school. The loss of him is something that we will feel for a long time. We will feel deeply, and it will hurt."

I wiped my eyes again. "Grandpa wouldn't want us to hurt, though. Maybe this is why he wanted me to be the one up here saying these things because I understand this part of him. Granpda wants us to remember him for what he brought to our lives. He wants us to pass down the lessons, the knowledge, the stories, the history. He wants his legacy of love to continue through us and down the line. That is how he will live forever." A sob broke free as I felt his presence around me. "Tears will happen, and while he wasn't overly emotional, he'll forgive me for spilling a few right now even though it wouldn't be what he wanted."

"Grandpa, I know you are watching us," I frantically wiped the tears, "sorry for making the pulpit wet." Sad laughter broke out. "Family, friends, remember him with a smile. Pass on what he taught you, and he will always live on in our everyday lives. Love doesn't die. Love wins."

I stepped back from the pulpit, blinded by the tears that fell, and I only moved when I felt Jax take my arm and guide me back to the pew. He took the tissue from my hand and wiped my face, kissing my cheek.

Nanie took hold of my hand, "That was perfect, Ella. Absolutely beautiful, and that is precisely what he wanted. No one else could have done that."

The priest dismissed everyone, and they filed out to the parking lot to head for the celebration while the family headed out to the cemetery to lay him to rest. I told Nanie I would wait until it cleared out, I didn't want to get bombarded yet.

"Ells, that was incredible," Jax whispered to me.

I leaned my head on his shoulder. "That hurt. I can't pretend it isn't real anymore."

"You never were pretending, siren. You held it in until you were up there. The strength of the emotions you hold inside is tremendous. Let us help you, baby." He leaned his head on top of mine. "Come on, get up, it's not over yet."

He pulled me to my feet, and he had an odd smile on his face. He turned me around, and I saw them all standing there, all my new family. I didn't care who saw me or what they thought. I broke out into a sprint and jumped at Ronnie, wrapping my arms and legs around him as I sobbed. His arms tight around me. "You're here."

Chapter Thirteen

onnie clutched at her as if she were his lifeline. "Angel, where else would I be when you needed me? There is no way I wouldn't have been here."

She clutched at him, and Smitty came up behind her, "Baby girl, please put me out of my misery and hug me."

Too soon, she was out of Ronnie's arms, and in Smitty's, Jax coming up alongside Ronnie and putting his arm over his shoulders. "Jax, you look fantastic," Ronnie told him. "You feeling okay?"

"Better than I've felt in years," Jax said quietly. "We need to get out to the cemetery, though. They are probably waiting for her."

Smitty let her down, and Jax and Ronnie boxed her between them, each taking a hand. "We're all going with you, angel."

Her eyes were red. Otherwise, Ronnie thought she looked as beautiful as ever. "That was a damn good eulogy, angel. You had them all in the palm of your hands."

"You guys are here," she repeated.

"Baby girl, there should never have been a doubt

about that," Smitty said from the other side of Jax. "Ronnie would have sprouted wings and flown here himself if he couldn't have gotten a flight. I probably would have held on to his legs and made him carry me too."

"We do have to go back tonight, angel. Jax has you both on a flight coming back on Tuesday," Ronnie hated that they were leaving without her. Especially after feeling her in his arms again. That crushing weight that had been tearing at him, instantly went away when he'd seen her.

"I'm going to make dinner for *you* this time, Airy," Mags said with a smile.

"Ronnie will have a whole new training regimen plotted out by then and torturing us all," Aedan added.

Airiella stopped in her tracks, her face shocked. "Father Roarke? Taklishim? Tama? Onida?"

"Hi, Raven. You did a great job up there. We wanted to come to offer our support." Taklishim held out his hand, but Airiella hugged him. Then she hugged the rest of them.

Ronnie saw her bite her lip and the blood well up. That must have been what Jax had been talking about when the blood bond started between them. He elbowed Jax, "Don't let that fall. I don't want her family to see her kissing all of us. I don't think they would be ready for that."

Jax kissed her, "Stop biting your lip, siren." He handed her a chapstick that she quickly put on.

"We'll be there for the radio interview tomorrow," Tama told her. Ronnie again felt a pang that they were leaving tonight.

They approached the burial site and stood back while Jax walked her up to the front. They waited while the casket lowered, and they all had thrown a handful of dirt on it and said their prayers.

Ronnie felt the wind pick up. He knew instinctively that it was from Airiella. It felt like her. He saw Jax touch her and whisper in her ear, and it died back down. He was happy to see how close they had gotten. It had done them both a world of good.

"Angel, can I ride with you to the reception?" He shot a look at Jax, who nodded and handed her keys to her.

"I've got the address already," Jax told the others and headed off with them.

Ronnie pulled her into his arms, which was as far as he felt he could go with her family around. "God, angel, you feel so good."

She leaned into him. "I've missed you so much. Do you really have to leave?"

"I've got to get this training done. We are running out of time. Demons were outside the house; you have them following you here, it's just escalating too fast." He hated it, being away from her.

Someone came running up to them. "Oh my God, it's true! You are dating all of them!"

Airiella sighed. "Gabby, go. I'm not in the mood for this."

"I'm Gabby. I know who you are. You are even hotter in person. I'm her cousin," she held out her hand.

"Nice to meet you," Ronnie limply shook her hand.

"I can ride with you guys," Gabby said hopefully.

"No, Gab. Sorry. No." Airiella stepped away from Ronnie and pulled him towards what he guessed was her car.

She climbed in and rested her head on the steering wheel. "You hanging in there, okay?" Ronnie asked her.

"No. I'm barely holding on. I don't know how I haven't driven Jax insane yet."

"He's a man in love. We put up with crazy well when it comes to those we love. Nothing like this separation to prove to myself how much I fucking love you. It's been killing me every day. When you walked up to the front of that church, it took everything I had not to run up there and fall at your feet."

He heard her giggle. "That would have made for one hell of a eulogy."

"Smitty practically had to sit on me," Ronnie smiled.

"I don't care who can see us, Heracles. Kiss me like you are happy to see me."

He needed no other invitation, he pulled her head

to him and covered her lips with his, letting out all the emotions he'd tried keeping in check as soon as he saw her. She moaned. "I love you, angel."

"Can I keep you?" she whispered.

"I'm yours."

"I wish we didn't have to go to this. I'm dreading it. Those people are going to suck whatever life is left in me right out, and I'll be a useless husk. I'm so damn tired, Ronnie."

"We are all there with you now. One of us will be touching you the whole time. Fuck, we'll probably all be touching you. I see Jax gave you his gift," he touched the necklace.

"You knew?"

"Yep. I knew Jax wouldn't be able to wait until your birthday. It was just as well. I think you needed it today. Come on, angel, let's get this over and done. I have another surprise for you," Ronnie urged her to shut the car off and get out.

"I'm not sure my heart can take any more surprises."

"It'll be a good one, I promise." He helped her out of the car and over to where the rest of the group waited for them. He held her hand the whole way to the reception hall they'd rented because the family was so large.

"Well, I guess you all get an up-close and personal introduction to crazy now. I hope you all prepared for this insanity that I call a family," Airiella took a fortifying breath. "I'll just apologize now, in advance, for whatever shit they throw at you."

"They aren't that bad, Airy," Mags said lightly.

"Mags, the few you met weren't. It's the whole lot now. At once."

"We can handle it," Aedan took her hand.

"In you go," Smitty put his hand on her lower back and pushed a little. Jax came up and took her other hand, Ronnie pushing Aedan out of the way to take the other. He wasn't ready to be without her yet.

As a group, they walked in, and while Ronnie knew

it wasn't silence, it felt like it. Almost all the eyes focused on them, then the hands they were holding. Airiella squeezed him in reassurance and led them to an empty table and sat down.

Luckily, they took up the whole table with the council members. He hoped that sheltered Airiella from the mob she was clearly not wanting to be a part of yet. Ronnie saw right away that wasn't the case as a woman in a wheelchair was headed straight for them.

My bi-polar mom, he heard in his head, *behind her, my dad.* She didn't let go of his hand, so he held it tight. He put the most winning smile he had on his face. He was meeting her parents for the first time.

"Ells, the eulogy was perfect. Thank you for doing it. Introduce me to your friends," she looked a little wild, Ronnie thought.

She was having an episode before the funeral. Expect some drastic highs and lows, Ronnie heard. "Mom and Dad, this is the crew from the show." She went around the table. "You know Mags and Aedan. Mags is pregnant now. This here is Art; he goes by Smitty. Next, we have Taklishim and Tama; they are married. Onida is her twin sister, and this is Father Roarke. They are on the board for the show. And this is Ronnie."

Ronnie held out the hand Airiella wasn't holding. "Pleasure to meet you," he shook their hands.

"A priest?" Airiella's mom asked, confused.

"Aye. A Vatican trained priest specialized in exorcism," Father Roarke said in a thicker than usual Irish accent.

"Exorcism," Airiella's mom gave her a look.

"Mom, it's a paranormal investigative show." Ronnie felt her irritation and kept smiling.

"Why is Ronnie holding your hand?" her voice took on a shrill tone, which caught the ears of Airiella's nanie, who beelined toward them.

"Mariana, what is the matter?" Her nanie went and stood behind Airiella, resting her hands on her shoulders.

"I feel like Airiella is hiding things from me,"

Mariana accused, looking pointedly at Airiella. "Like why it feels like she is in a relationship with Ronnie, while she's in one that looks pretty serious with Jax."

Ronnie was a little startled by that and tried to keep his face neutral. "We all love Airiella," Mags spoke up.

Taklishim stood and motioned Airiella over away from the table. He saw them whispering, and he tried to pick up her thoughts, but she was locked up tight at the moment. Her body language was stiff, and Ronnie felt a trickle of unease.

"Mariana, if she were in a relationship with everyone at this table, it would be her business, not yours. Not anyone's but whoever was involved," her nanie told her firmly.

"Mother, this is my daughter we are talking about," Mariana argued.

"From what I can tell, Jax here is utterly devoted to her. And that warms my old heart. I can also see how much Ronnie, is it?" She looked at Ronnie and he nodded. "I can see plain as day he feels the same way. If they both love her that much you should be happy that she is looked after and taken care of. He's also as easy on the eyes as Jax is."

Ronnie choked on his water and tried not to laugh as Airiella sat back down. "Let her be, dear," her dad Spencer said.

Airiella sighed, "Look, we do need to talk, and soon. Grandpa's funeral is not the time or place for it. Mom, go mingle with your family."

Ronnie heard her nanie whisper not so quietly in Airiella's ear, "I already know what you are Ella, she will have a harder time believing it than I will. Grandpa told me before he died."

Airiella kissed her nanie's cheek. "Is there anyone here that wouldn't be able to keep that secret?"

"A few, why?"

"Because I think I might have to out myself. I promise, I will keep you safe. Can you write down who those few are?" Airiella's skin was practically bristling with anger.

I need you to protect my family. Please? Ronnie heard in his head. He shot a look over at her. *There's a lot of people here, and I know you guys have been training. Just don't let anything through those doors.*

You've got my word, angel.

He saw Jax shift and figured she was talking to Jax. He stood and found a family, the one with the baby he had sent a picture of to him. He was talking to the woman; he figured that was Airiella's cousin at the frightened look that she sent Airiella's way.

"Taklishim, Father Roarke, can you come with me?"

Tama nodded at Tak as he stood, and the three of them walked out of the room. "Guys, we are on protective duty now. I promised we would keep her family safe."

Ronnie never noticed Airiella's dad slipping out the door after them. "Three demons are outside," Onida stated calmly, and Ronnie freaked out a little. "They will be fine, Ronnie. The people in here are in greater danger than Tak and Airiella are."

I froze at the sight that greeted me. "The demons view you as weakened right now, Raven," Taklishim warned me as we peered out the front doors.

"Is that what that prickly feeling I've been feeling is, demons?" I asked cautiously. "It didn't set off my warnings."

"They can't come in unless they break through the blessings we put down when we got here. Three high levels can do that no problem, I'd rather meet them out here than in there, though. That's probably why you only felt a prickly feeling, as you called it," Taklishim explained.

"Father Roarke, if you'd rather be inside with the others, that's fine with me," I put a hand on his arm.

"I'll go where I feel like I'm needed most, lass. It isn't my first encounter with demons," he smiled at me tightly.

"Looks like you'll get to see me in action first hand, Taklishim." I looked around. "Where are they now?"

Taklishim pointed off to the left.

I dropped all my walls and ignored all the emotions that slammed into me. "Easy, Raven. Filter out your emotions," Tak advised me.

I slid a wall up to block my emotions while I left the feelings of others open for me to read. I felt down for the earth's energy and silently asked it for help to protect the innocent. With the tremors I felt underneath my feet, I knew it was ready to help. I reached for the energy of the air and repeated my request and saw the tree branches start to sway. Last, I called for lightning, asking for help against demons. I asked it to enter my body as it did last time, and heard a boom of thunder.

"Raven, whatever you are doing, you have their full attention. And you are glowing. Glowing isn't subtle," Taklishim warned me.

"I can't do subtle, Tak. That's my family in there. I need to end this," I let my anger color my words.

"Father Almighty, bless this angel you've sent us to aid in your work," Father Roarke prayed. "Lass, you have wings."

I looked at my back, sure enough, they were alive and present. I heard a gasp and spun around, seeing my dad standing there. "Shit. Dad, get back in there! Do not come out here. It's not safe. I'll explain later. I promise."

Taklishim gave me a raised eyebrow. "You have a way to explain ink-black wings and a glowing appearance?"

"Stuff it, Tak. I'm not in the mood. I'll have to tell the truth like you just told me to do. And since when do you have a sense of humor?" I opened the front door and stepped out, Taklishim on my heels. "Raven, help me," I whispered, and she appeared on the light pole above the demons.

"You came right to us, Angel, how thoughtful," one of the dark figures stepped forward.

Father Roarke slipped a vial of what I assumed was holy water into my pants pocket. I was glad he hadn't risked touching my skin as I didn't know if it would zap him or not. I didn't have the first clue as to what I was doing.

"You aren't welcome here," I told them calmly. "Leave." That's what Jax and Ronnie said on investigations when they suspected negative energy; it should work, right?

"Lass, the only way you can kill these is to crush and burn their hearts," the priest whispered to me, dashing my hopes that my words were going to banish them.

"How the hell am I supposed to get to their hearts?" I spun to look at him.

"Never take your eyes off them, Raven," Tak said as he started to strip. Before I could ask what the hell he was doing, a gigantic eagle sat there. *I'll get their hearts for you if you can take them down enough for me to get close,* he said in my head.

"Right. Every funeral is like this. Nothing odd or terrifying about it. Or about an eagle talking in my head. Just take down the demons," I muttered. "Like my family hasn't been through enough with the death of my Grandpa. Now I get to traumatize them further by glowing blue and showing up with big black wings." I heard Ronnie chuckle in my head.

I stepped toward the demons. "Come get me if you want me," I taunted them. I called the wind, asking it to make a barrier around them, and it responded. A beautiful funnel cloud formed that I could see through I and caught the flash of red eyes. Creepy.

"Childish tricks won't stop us," one of them said. They had no features to distinguish them. Was that normal?

I called for the lighting again, asking for a strike from the sky, and the loud boom of thunder filled my ears as Taklishim took flight. The blinding flash of the lightning strike pushed Father Roarke back at the energy field it had created.

Smoke rose, an awful stench like rotting road kill filled the air, making me gag a little. I asked the earth to shake them and called the lighting again for a one, two punch. The ground rose and fell; the demons knocked off their feet as lightning cracked through the sky, more potent than it was before.

"Get inside," I told Father Roarke. He'd gotten knocked over that time. He didn't argue. *Sending Father Roarke in,* I sent to Jax and Ronnie.

I walked up to the smoking demons, the funnel cloud separating us. "Your powers have grown. What happens if I kill your pretty bird?" A stream of something shot overhead directly at the raven. At warp speed, and the ground shook again, knocking it off balance.

"Oops, sorry. Didn't your kind learn not to threaten those I love?" Anger tore through me, and I let it loose, whispering to the elements to do as they saw fit. I took the vial of holy water out of my pocket and emptied it in the funnel cloud, telling the energy to use it to hurt them. Letting go of the feelings felt good, my intentions to kill them understood in the power that was flowing through me.

The air tightened around them, the holy water shredding skin like thousands of tiny knives, and a shrieking scream filled the air. A sound that made my stomach roll. And what the fuck was that smell? I reached through the air and grasped what I assumed was an arm and sent lightning straight through it.

In slow motion, I saw Tak drop from the sky, and razor-sharp talons tear through the chest of the smoking demon. In its claws was an oily black, dripping blob of rotting muscle that in no way resembled a heart. It fell at my feet, and in my mind, the raven showed me touching it.

I revolted. Bile rising in my throat, I reached my glowing hand out, and with one finger, touched it. The texture of the rotting thing burning me like hot acid and the lightning in me reacted automatically, a wicked battle of light and dark forces playing out under my finger. "Love wins," I whispered, and the disgusting thing turned to ash.

Hurry, Raven, I heard Taklishim in my head. I quickly reached both hands in to grab the remaining two, and the process repeated. Summoning the last of my courage, I killed the last two hearts, and promptly puked, telling the wind it could stop. That had been awful.

It's not over, Raven, there's one inside, Taklishim's voice filled my head.

"What the fuck!" I screamed, wiping my mouth, fear, and fury battling for dominance.

A naked Taklishim appeared in front of me. "We need to go now. Jax is cornered. He has the baby." Taklishim dressed faster than anyone I'd ever seen.

I burst through the doors, momentarily forgetting that I was glowing and had giant wings until the entire room gasped. Shit! No time for that. Ronnie pointed to a corner in the back where a furious Jax held Emma protectively, faced off against another dark figure.

Is that holy water in your hand, Zeus? I sent Jax.

Yeah, can you do something? I'm in control right now, but not for long, he cautioned.

Put that holy water all over that baby, I told him. Jax did just that.

Father Roarke handed me another vial as I walked past him, casually, right over to Jax, slamming the glass against the head of the unsuspecting demon that had been growling at Jax. I took the baby from Jax while the demon shrieked that unholy sound, sending terror through the hearts of everyone in that room. A lot more terror than had been there before I walked in glowing and with wings. I had a hard time staying on my feet, so much fear hit me.

I handed her off to Stephanie and then shoved Jax over at Stephanie. "Go, watch over them. I love you. Thank you for keeping that little one safe."

I took hold of the arm of the demon and sent lightning through it until it fell on the floor in front of me. Ronnie stepped up with a knife and jammed it into the heart of the demon, and I used the blade like a lightning rod and shot electricity straight through it until it too turned to ash. Chalk this funeral up to a disaster.

"I'm never going to get used to the sight of you walking straight into danger, angel," Ronnie kissed me, right there in front of everyone.

"I guess another kiss isn't really going to ruin how they think of me. I'm glowing and have wings, right?" I said sarcastically.

"Definitely not something you see every day," Ronnie agreed as we stood up. "Were the earthquakes you?"

I nodded. The earthquakes seemed lame in comparison to the giant black wings sprouting out of my back. Ronnie stroked his hand down the feathers, making me shudder. "That feels kinda naughty," I flushed, wishing there wasn't an audience of my family standing there in horror witnessing it all.

"Good to know, filing that away for later," Ronnie said into my ear.

"I think the eulogy was easier than having to explain this," I muttered. I hated the look on the faces of those I loved. *Nothing* was ever going to be the same. My family shouldn't fear me. Not ever. It wasn't right, and I was cursing myself like crazy.

"Auntie, is that a costume?" Grace walked up to me, not scared in the slightest.

I picked her up, and my eyes sought out Taklishim. "Truth, Raven."

I sighed. "No, Monkey. They are real."

Chapter Fourteen

I was still glowing. My body felt like danger was still present, while logically, I knew that it was just the fear of my family setting off my alarms. I walked over to Stephanie, "Is she okay?"

"She's perfect," Stephanie said, her voice trembling a little. "You, on the other hand, are a little more than slightly scary."

"She's beautiful," Jax stepped around her and ran a hand over my feathers. "Did you know the tops of the feathers underneath are white?"

"Nope, this is the first time I've seen them in the flesh. Jax, can you touch me please, make the glow stop. Steph, I'm not going to mention Emma at all. No one needs to know what my blood can do," I told her, in a voice only she could hear.

Jax took my hand, and we walked back over to the group. They all put their hands on me, soothing me until the wings and the glow both disappeared, and I looked like me again. "Your eyes are still angel eyes," Jax kissed me softly. I wasn't sure what that meant.

Taklishim stood on one of the tables to get everyone's attention. A giant gray-haired man wasn't enough to do that apparently without him having to stand on a table. "I'm sure you all have questions, and I'm also sure that all of you just had an awakening to a world you didn't know existed. I assure you, there is no danger right now, you are all safe. Fear is normal, but Airiella is still Airiella."

I wanted to sink into the ground. I felt the rumble under my feet and realized the connection was still open. I quickly thanked the elements and closed down the connection. "Sorry," I muttered.

Taklishim got down off the table, "This is your tribe, Raven. They need to be in your circle."

"That may be. I don't think this was the best way for them to find out, though," I snarled.

"It will be fine. I've got to say, I'm impressed. Your powers are unlike anything I've ever heard of or had the pleasure of seeing before." Taklishim awkwardly patted me on the arm.

"Do I need to memory zap anyone?" I asked wearily. The thought of messing with a family member's mind didn't sit well with me.

"We'll see. For now, we'll help you tell your story without revealing ourselves if you don't mind." Taklishim took a small step back from me.

I laughed a little manically. "Pretty sure that the existence of angels and demons," I laughed at the reference again, "might be enough for them to process in one day. Medicine men, spirit warriors, and shifters might be pushing the limits."

Nanie came up to me, "Did you ask about trustworthy people because you knew that was going to happen?"

"I had *no* idea any of that was going to happen. I'm so sorry, Nanie. I ruined Grandpa's memorial reception. Do you think someone here is going to blab about this? I don't want press coverage, or to be known," I blurted out shamefully.

She pointed out the few that she thought would say something. I looked over at Taklishim, and he nodded at me. I called for the raven again, and she showed me which energy to play with to wipe their memory. I then walked over to them, "I think I heard your car alarms going off," I said casually, and they ran out of the room. Smitty following and locking the doors behind them.

I sighed, and my shoulders slumped forward. "Okay, so you are all still here because Nanie thinks you are trustworthy. If you think that something you just saw, you can't keep to yourself, or you don't want to know because it scares you, please come forward, and I'll make it so you don't remember, and you can leave."

Ronnie and Jax came up alongside me and grabbed ahold of my hands, their energy flowing through me. No one stepped forward, but like a hypnotized audience, they all sat down. Ronnie led me to the stage area, and we sat on the edge of it. It would make it easier to speak from there rather than standing on a table. Smitty had already hooked up a microphone, so I didn't have to yell and handed it to me. Jax and Ronnie sat on the edge with me, the front line. Smitty on a chair behind me, and Aedan and Mags came up to flank Smitty. Father Roarke sat off to the side.

"How do you want to do this?" I asked into the microphone.

Amanda came running up to me, "Auntie, are you a superhero?"

Jax pulled her up on his lap. "She's like one, don't you think?"

My dad came up, "Why don't you just tell us what we saw to start?"

I nodded. "Okay. I'm an angel. Or in native American culture, what they call a raven. It's is all pretty new to me, so there's a lot I don't know." I pointed to the council. "They've been educating me about what being a raven is about." I gestured to Father Roarke, "And of course, Father Roarke has been helping me figure out what it means to be an angel."

My brother stood up, "Does this group have something to do with it?"

Taklishim stood to answer this one. "No. It was

because of this group she was able to discover what she is. In our culture, we have bonds, our bonds help us. This group is what those bonds look like for her. They are her bonds, they make her stronger, and she, in turn, makes them stronger."

Thank God he didn't mention any of the rest of it. "So, Ells, what was that?" he pointed to the pile of ash, his eyebrows almost up to his hairline.

I winced. "A demon. Apparently, demons are after me, and these two," I held up Ronnie's hand and Jax's hand.

Father Roarke stepped forward to speak. "Demons prey on weakness and fear, and with the death of your patriarch, they viewed this as an opportune time to attack. The fear you all had, unfortunately, fed them. Airiella is extremely rare. The last angel on earth was over two hundred years ago is what I was able to dig up in the Vatican records. From what we have been able to find, they appear here when the balance of the world is off. By that, I mean the balance of life. Between light and dark, good and evil if that's better for you."

"Can't ever be normal, can you, sis?" Nick wasn't acting mean. I could see he was struggling with what he had seen but was giving me the leap of faith needed. "Does that mean your new boyfriends will be with you all the time?" And then he grinned evilly, knowing I didn't want him to go there.

"Probably," I mumbled, not in the microphone.

"Sorry, I couldn't hear you, can you speak in the microphone?" Nick pushed, trying to ease the tension in his way.

"Daddy, she said probly'," Amanda yelled. The ice in the room broke at that, and questions were flying through the air. Ronnie took the microphone from my hand and cleared his throat, that beautiful smile on his face. All the females in the room focused on him and Jax, and it was irritating me.

You didn't tell them about the darkness in me. Why not? Jax asked me silently.

Not their business. My family doesn't need to know everything, only enough to explain that shitshow that they saw. I didn't want them looking at Jax like they looked at that demon. Or like they were looking at me.

"Hey folks, too many talking at once. Let's pretend we are all in school and either raise your hands or stand and wait for someone to call on you," Ronnie suggested.

Nick was still standing, his arms crossed now, and his eyes narrowed on Ronnie, then Jax, then finally, me. "One more thing, are you going to be in danger all the time?"

Ronnie still had the microphone, "She certainly seems to run headfirst into it at every opportunity it presents itself."

I snatched the microphone from him and glared at him, only to have it taken from me by Jax. "She is, but as you saw, she's badass, and she's what has kept us all alive."

"She's always been scary like that," my brother joked half-heartedly.

I threw my hands in the air and rolled my eyes, taking back the microphone. "Next," I called out. "Nick doesn't get any more questions."

He smirked at me and sat down. My uncle Joe stood. "Are we in danger?"

"I don't believe that you would be in any more danger than you were before tonight. Demons are after me, not you," I looked at Taklishim for confirmation of that, and he nodded slightly.

"Why are they after you?" he continued, his face screwed up with worry.

"Because I can defeat them is the simple answer." He sat back down, seemingly satisfied with my answer.

My dad stood. My mom was utterly silent beside him. "Will you keep her safe?" he asked, making eye contact with each of the people behind me and with over with Taklishim.

A resounding yes sounded from all around me, including the council and Father Roarke. Jax took the microphone from me. "It's easy for us to say that. As you saw, and Ronnie pointed out, she heads right for the danger to keep us all safe. When I say all, that includes all of you. We are doing everything we can to learn how to help." Jax gestured at the council and Father Roarke.

Ronnie held out his hand for the microphone. "Jax is right. We all say that we will keep her safe, but the truth is, she is stronger than anyone here. She's stronger than all of us combined."

My dad asked, "Then who keeps her safe?" The very same question Jax posed to me that I couldn't answer very well.

"She does. We come in after the fact. When she does what she needs to do to keep the rest of us safe, we step in and take care of her until she's recovered. Whatever that may look like. In that, she has every single one of us that would do anything for her. They," Ronnie pointed to the council, "are documenting, researching, and helping aid us in ways we can't even fathom."

"Ells, what are you capable of?" my dad hesitatingly asked. I knew this was hard for him. Hell, it was hard for me.

"I don't know a whole lot yet, Dad," my voice soft and hesitant. "It's new to me. I don't know what I can do or not do. Things seem to happen when the danger appears like a knowledge that just lies dormant in me until it's needed. So far, I can manipulate the elements. That glow you saw was me containing lightning. The earthquakes you felt were me. I can ask the air to help me too."

I called on the air, asking it to join us inside for a moment, and the doors blew open, making everyone jump as I sent it around the room gently before thanking it and sending it away. "How did we never know?" my dad asked, shaken.

"How could you? It's not like ever I knew." A tiny white lie, I knew of the emotional thing, and I wasn't about to bring that up.

Taklishim walked over to us, "Was there something that happened while you were pregnant with her?" Taklishim asked the question of my mom.

She shook her head, but my dad paled. "What, Dad?"

"You know you were a C-section birth." I nodded. "Your mom was out after they took you out, and there were about a good two or three minutes you stopped breathing. It was perhaps the longest minutes of my life. Nothing they did could get your lungs to work. Out of nowhere, they weren't even touching you, your eyes popped open, and they were golden. You didn't make a sound; you just looked through these eyes that shouldn't have been able to see the way a newborn does. Then the color faded, and I thought I had imagined it."

The entire room was silent, and watching my dad struggle with the memory. Taklishim was looking right at me. *You were born with it, Raven,* he said in my head. *They have no abilities whatsoever. It did not come from them.* "Thank you, Mr. Raven."

Gabby piped up, "Can you make your wings come back out? You'd rock a cosplay convention."

"I have no idea. That's the first time I've ever seen my wings while not in a dream," I admitted shyly.

Focus on them, Taklishim told me. *When we shift, we think of our animal form; we give in to the feeling and essence of the animal inside us. Think of the raven, of being her.*

I did as he asked and heard the feathers rustling behind me. Mags gasped, and I felt them all touching my wings, little shivers rippling through my back. "Okay, I guess I can make them appear."

"Can you fly?" someone asked. I wasn't sure who.

"Not going to try. Sorry. I have a feeling that the landing would hurt a little if I messed it up." My brother laughed at my response.

"Good call," Nick said sarcastically. I wanted to flip him off so badly.

"I think we can finish now." I drew in the calm from Jax and Ronnie and focused on no wings. "If I'd had a choice, I wouldn't have told anyone anything. Please, please, I beg you to keep this to yourselves. I don't want attention, I don't want media hounds after me, nor do I want people who will just try to take advantage of me or want to experiment on me. Please give me that respect. I already feel like a freak show in a bad circus act."

Surprisingly, my cousin Aaron stood up. "Speaking for myself only, I will disavow rumors that I am sure will leak somehow. Your secret is safe with me."

"I appreciate that, thank you. Guys, finish celebrating Grandpa, that's what you are here to do. I'm going to leave now. I'm tired." I slid off the stage and went to my mom. "I'll make sure you stay safe."

She put her hand on my cheek, "I always knew you were special." There were tears in her eyes as she looked at me.

I hugged my dad. "Try not to worry, Dad." He huffed out some sound that wasn't as reassuring as I'd like it to be.

I found Nanie, hugged her, and then made my way out of the room as quickly as possible. I knew the rest would follow me. I needed to not be in the spotlight for a bit. I headed over to where the demons had been and saw that I had cracked the asphalt and left scorch marks.

"Jesus, angel, that's from you?" Ronnie appeared beside me, looking at the burnt and cracked ground.

"Yeah. I had to use lightning from the sky as well as within." Inside I was cringing. I had mercilessly killed.

"Ready for your last surprise?" Ronnie sensed I needed to not talk about this. I shrugged. "Smitty and I arranged some gym time so you can beat the hell out of me and the bags to lose some of the tension I can feel in you."

I gaped at him, my eyes sliding to Jax. "You told him?"

Jax smiled. "Of course."

"I can't fight in this," I reminded them.

"I've got you covered, Airy. Smitty had me pack your workout clothes," Mags spoke up.

"You guys are the best. Let's go!" I raced back to my car, a feeling creeping up on me that I wasn't used to feeling. I was being taken care of by others.

Chapter Fifteen

Smitty felt like he was back in hell. "Tell me again why we had to leave?" Smitty grumbled at Ronnie.

"For the exact reason we are right here trying to kill each other," Ronnie swung a fake knife that Smitty dodged.

"We were pretty useless in there, weren't we?" Smitty acknowledged, trying a tricky combo Ronnie showed him earlier.

"Shit," Ronnie stood up straight suddenly, "I couldn't even keep Jax safe."

Father Roarke walked in. "That was a higher-level demon, Ronnie. You wouldn't have been effective against it no matter what. Cut yourself a break. Remember how I told you they could assume a human shape without possession? You just saw one. I'm not sure what he was masquerading as, but it wasn't human."

Smitty unleashed his frustration on the training dummy. "We're doing all this training, and there isn't anything we can do."

"That's not true, Art. Ronnie is the one who killed the one inside after Airiella weakened it," Father Roarke appeased them.

"She turned it to ash," Smitty argued hotly.

"Yes, she did, after Ronnie stabbed a blessed knife into its heart. Where is your faith, son?" the priest stood his ground.

"It's disillusioned at the moment, Father. She's still away from us, and that display was a blatant show for just how ill-equipped we are." Smitty delivered a fast kick to the dummy knocking it flat.

"Nice kick, Smitty," Ronnie told him, beaming. "He's not wrong, Father. That was awful. You saw firsthand."

"I did. I also saw a team of people band together and give it their all when she asked. It was quite something to be witness to; I'll give you that." Father Roarke didn't budge on his position.

"Is that your first time seeing a team work together?" Smitty fired off and immediately felt terrible. "Sorry, Father. I'm obviously not in the best mood today."

"I understand, son. Everybody has bad days. I was referring to seeing Airiella in action. I do bring news from Taklishim today, though. Are you both at a stopping point?"

Ronnie put his gear down. "I was making Smitty work out some aggression. We've got time."

Smitty glared at Ronnie and checked the time on his phone. "Let's hear it."

Father Roarke leaned against the wall. "Taklishim said that if Airiella can control her abilities as she did with the wings, and calling on the elements, she is much stronger than he suspected, and farther along with her own personal healing. Along with that, he took a closer look at Jax. He saw that the roots that the energy in him had placed in his soul are disappearing. He thinks that is due to the blood bond. Her blood is healing him."

"Does that mean she won't have to pull it from him?" Ronnie asked eagerly.

Smitty thought about it. "No. It means it won't hurt him as much when she does, right?"

The priest nodded at Smitty. "Right you are, Art. There's less chance of him dying if she pulls it from him."

"If it's not all way detached from his soul, are you insinuating that he needs to keep up with the blood?" Smitty tried to predict where this was going.

"We aren't sure. Tak is going to talk to them about it," the priest stated.

Ronnie scowled, "She still has to die then, just not him. And we don't know if she will come back, right?"

"I don't know, Ronnie. Taklishim is basing his knowledge on what he has found, seen her do, and what he can see on the other side. As well, Tama, Onida, and he keep looking inside the both of Airiella and Jax and tracking changes. She's still quite the mystery. He does feel that the control and power she is exhibiting makes her harder to kill permanently. At least in that way."

"I don't know that I can watch her do that again, Father," Smitty added.

"Me neither," Ronnie paled at the thought.

"Aye, Ron. That was very bad. The last bit of news is that Tama and Onida talked with the money men, and the council both, and told them of the need to have an exorcist on location given the demon activity. With their eyewitness account of demons at the funeral, they were on board with it."

Smitty sat straight up from where he slumped. "Wait. They told everyone what she could do?"

"No, we all agree that would be bad. The three told the council that I dispatched the demons, even though, as you saw, all I did was provide holy water and a blessed knife."

"Are they going to ask you to do it, or are they going to hire some two-bit hack?" Ronnie growled.

"They asked me if I could make the time. I agreed that I would, and I also agreed that the investors could promote that you added a priest to your team. I will let them exploit me to keep her safe, so don't fear," Father Roarke replied with bravery.

"Can I ask why, Father? Is this a ploy for you to

gather information about her?" Smitty fought to keep his tone even.

"No, son. I've grown rather attached to the hard-headed, soft-hearted lass. She feels like family to me," he admitted, and Smitty softened his look.

Smitty's phone rang, and he glanced over at it and snatched it up the next second. "Baby girl, you okay?" He saw Ronnie shoot him a look and check his own phone. Smitty himself was surprised that she called him.

"Yeah, I'm okay, I think. I needed to talk to you, that's all," Airiella's soft, sexy voice penetrated the dark shadows in him.

"What about?" He nodded at Ronnie's questioning look about her being okay.

"Nothing in particular. I didn't get to spend a whole lot of time with you yesterday, and I miss you. I need my voice of reason."

"You still need me?" Smitty heard the pain in his voice that sounded desperate to his own ears.

"Very much so, Smitty. Why would you think that I didn't?" her soft tone melted his lousy mood away.

"Jax and Ronnie have kind of taken center stage. I'm okay with it, don't get me wrong. I was pretty ineffective yesterday and just assumed you didn't need me as much as you needed them," he answered truthfully and without blame.

"I'm always going to need you, Smitty. I wish I was curled up next to you right now," she sounded sad.

"God, baby girl, I wish you were too." His eyes filled with tears. "Where is Jax? You don't sound as okay as you said you were."

"He's here. He's on the phone with Taklishim."

"Talk to me, what's going on in that pretty head of yours?" He felt Ronnie sit down next to him but didn't look over at him.

"I feel like I'm stuck between two worlds, sometimes more. I'm in a literal demon-infested hell and this world with you guys that you filled with love. It's like I'm losing my mind. This weight's always on me, and it feels like I'm letting everyone down all the time. I don't know that I am worthy of being what I am. I never asked for it," she said. Her words were breaking his heart.

Smitty swallowed the lump in his throat that formed. "If you feel like that, it's us that's failing you."

"No. You all are my safe place." He could hear the tears in her voice.

"What aren't you telling me?" Smitty pushed her gently.

"I took four lives yesterday, Smitty. What kind of person does that make me? How can I be hope for people when I killed? That doesn't make me any better than them."

She needed a voice of reason, and that was him. "Baby girl, those weren't people. Those were demons."

"You saw the fear my family had on their faces! They were scared of me. They watched me kill," she sobbed quietly.

There it was. Smitty knew she'd eventually get to the heart of the matter. "You think they are disappointed in you."

"How could they not be?" her shocked whisper was an arrow to his heart.

He could hear the tears falling. "That's not what I saw, love. I saw awe, inspiration, love, and pride. You kept everyone you loved safe. Besides, Father Roarke said Ronnie dealt the killing blow, so it's not you that's a killer, it's your boyfriend," he said with a smile. "The fear you saw was fear of the unknown, not of you."

"Are you afraid of me?" her voice sounded so fragile and small.

"No. I trust you with my life. With all of our lives. How many times have I seen you stand between us and death? Baby girl, you walked straight up to a demon; a demon! You shattered holy water against its nasty forehead, so you could get that adorable little girl to safety, as well as Jax. That had to have been the most badass move I've ever seen."

"It scares me, Smitty. I let my rage take over. I also

told Jax I would burn the world to a crisp for him. And I meant it." She was so sure she was awful.

"I think that's true of anyone you love," he told her quietly. "Degataga said you were an unconventional angel, and that is not a bad thing. Your belief in love and protecting it and the precious lives of others is your motivation. It's the disregard for life that sets you off. Allowing rage to take over to save innocent lives is not a bad thing, baby girl. It's admirable. Your anger is at the injustice of what's happening. It's not hatred for the sake of hate."

"How could you possibly ever think I don't need you? I would not have come to those conclusions on my own. You have a way of finding me in this in-between place and pulling me safely back to your world. To the path I'm supposed to be on and shining a light on it. I love you, Smitty," Airiella said reverently.

"In your defense, you've got a lot going on. I'm not going to lie and say it didn't do me any good to hear you say it, though. I thought I was losing you. I've been an ass all day because of it."

"I'll do better at making sure you know you are not in danger of losing me. I can't wait to be back with you guys." He heard Jax in the background and shuffling sounds.

"Jax with you now?" he asked, a smile in his voice.

"Yeah."

"Things okay between you two? You looked pretty close yesterday," Smitty commented.

"I had a nightmare where I watched him die at the hands of a demon. It was so real that I summoned lightning while I was asleep. I really would burn the world to a crisp to keep him safe. Any of you, you were right about that." He heard Jax rumbling. "In answer to your question, things between us are good. He told me he loves me."

"Baby girl, he told the world he loves you," Smitty said with another smile. "Whatever you two have going is working for him. He's so much closer to how he used to be, but an enhanced version that's way better. Less of a prick.

You make us all better people; it's one of your gifts."

"You are a gift," she protested.

"I love you, baby girl. Nervous about the interview tonight?" he changed the subject.

"A little," Airiella admitted faintly.

"You'll do great. We'll be listening. When you get back, be prepared to be smothered."

She laughed, making Smitty smile. "I can't wait to be smothered. Thank you for being my voice of reason."

"Anytime. I'm happy to be whatever you need, whenever you need it."

He hung up and stared at his phone. Airiella needed him still, relief flooded through him. "Why didn't you say something to me?" Ronnie butted into his thoughts.

"About what?" Smitty asked, getting defensive.

"Feeling like only Jax and I are what matters to her."

"It's my issue, not yours." Smitty felt a stab of irritation and pushed it back.

"If we are monopolizing her, then it's our issue too. She's made it clear she loves all of us and wants to spend time with all of us. At least to both Jax and I, she has made it clear," Ronnie said, adamant.

"She's said the same to me. I know the connection between you all and her is stronger than the one with me."

"It doesn't mean she can't spend time with you, that she doesn't need you," Ronnie glared at him.

"It's not that. I felt like I wasn't needed anymore. I know Airiella loves me. She's barely spent time with Mags and Aedan too." Smitty shook his head, feeling foolish. "Honestly, I think the separation from her is screwing with my head."

"It is for me, too. Aside from the physical pain, I was starting to think along the same lines as you. About Jax, though. She wouldn't need me now that they have the blood bond and the connection. It's not true; she needs us all." Ronnie bumped into his shoulder. "Don't keep that shit from me. We are all in this together."

"Thanks, Ronnie. Did she tell you about the

nightmare she had?” That concerned Smitty.

“No. Was it prophetic?”

“Fuck, I hope not. Airiella said she watched a demon kill Jax. She summoned lighting in her sleep,” Smitty relayed.

“Holy shit. Remember the pain both of us had in our chest? I bet you anything that is what that was!” Ronnie shuddered.

“Good thing he’s with her then. For damn sure, we couldn’t keep him safe. She said she’d burn the world to a crisp for him.” Smitty smiled.

“She’d do it for any of us,” Ronnie corrected him. “Have you noticed how much she has changed all of us?”

“Yes. And that’s what I told the angel.” Smitty looked up and saw Father Roarke still standing there. “Sorry, Father, we kind of ignored you there.”

“Not at all. I’ll admit, the changes in you all are incredible.”

Chapter Sixteen

Jax stared at the woman he loved. "Did you know that you have a different tone for each of us?" Jax shifted her, so she sat sideways across his lap, her back against the arm of the chair. "Was that Smitty?"

"Yeah, sorry. I needed to talk to him."

"Why are you sorry?" Jax brushed the hair out of her face.

"I didn't want you to think I was ignoring you. What did Tak have to say?" she tried to switch the focus.

He studied her face. He had seen her crying, so it was evident that something was on her mind. He'd caught the end of her conversation about the dream as he'd picked her up and sat down with her. She'd gotten good at shutting him out of her thoughts when she focused on it.

She slipped under his arm and nestled into him. "Remember how you said I felt different?" He felt her nod. "Taklishim said that the darkness inside me was losing its roots in me. He thinks your blood is slowly healing it. That means that if you have to pull it from me, then there is less risk of my soul being so shredded that I die."

She pushed her face into his shoulder, and he heard

her muffled response of, "It's not a risk I am going to take."

"I heard the last part of your conversation about that dream. Is that what has you down today?" The week had been beyond emotional for her, and he wondered if this was the fall out now.

"One of many things," she admitted so softly he barely heard her.

"Is this something you don't want to talk to me about?" He laced his arms around her loosely and held his breath.

"It's not that. I think we are so close that I can't be objective about you."

He felt a bolt of fear at her words. "Why do you need to be objective about me?"

"I hear you say that there is now less risk of death, my brain processes it as there is still a risk, don't even attempt it or you'll find out what it's like to live without him. And you'll be the reason for his death, not a demon," she breathed out, shaking.

"Siren, I have to say, when you said you couldn't be objective, I immediately thought of you changing your mind about me. Now that I understand what you meant, maybe it's not a bad thing. If I am going to die, at least I have hope that now I will be dying for something. I'll die knowing I've truly loved."

"Jax, I can't. I can't even think about it," she clung to him, her nails digging into his skin through his shirt.

"Taklishim also told me that he thinks because of your blood that I will be harder to kill, and that's why the demon just had me cornered and hadn't attempted anything yet. Tama told him it was scared."

"This is what I mean. You've told me good things, things that should encourage me, and still, all I can think of is the danger is still there. I can't seem to see the silver lining. I just see threats everywhere when it comes to you." Her voice was gravelly and rough, and when he tipped her head back to look in her eyes, he saw raw pain.

"No one has ever loved me enough to feel that way before. My beautiful siren, that's how both Ronnie and I, probably Smitty too, feel every time we see you jump headfirst into a shitty situation. If you've taught me anything over these months, it's that love isn't objective. It defies logic and reasoning, and that's what makes it so special."

"What if that dream was a warning or a vision of what's to come?" She bit right through her lip again, and Jax kissed it, sucking the blood from the wound and reaching for the chapstick he now kept in his pocket to try and help stop the bleeding.

"Stop biting your lip, baby. It won't heal if you keep doing that. If it's a warning, then we accept the warning and work on changing the outcome. It could also be that you've had an incredibly shitty week, and your emotions are on overload. What else is bothering you other than the dream?" Jax asked, sensing there was more.

"Me killing. In front of my family, no less. Thrusting them into a world, I'm not sure they are better off knowing exists. Also, I feel stuck between worlds and a little like a science project gone bad."

"Sounds like you have *plenty* of room left up in that beautiful chaos you call a brain for more issues. Is this why you called Smitty? You needed his reasoning?" Jax guessed.

She shifted against him, tucking her toes in the crease of the arm. "Yeah. Only now, his reasoning is battling the original thoughts for control."

"Are you cold?" He reached for her fingers and found them icy. He stood, setting her down in the chair and started moving the coffee table off to the side and turned on the fireplace. He grabbed pillows off the couch and pulled her down to lay with him in front of the fire.

She tucked into his side, sliding her cold hands up his shirt, causing his skin to pebble up and threw her leg up over his. "Okay, let's break this down. Why do you feel like a science project gone bad?"

"The way my family looked at me, the way that everyone keeps studying me. I'm starting to feel like one of those volcanoes' kids make. Let's push this button and see if she explodes," her tone caustic.

"Your family wasn't looking at you like a science project. That was more shock than anything. It's not every day you see someone that's glowing with blue lightning, and giant black wings walk into a room. They weren't scared of you either. As for the studying part, I know that the rest of the council wants to do that to you. Taklishim, Tama, and Onida are doing their best to keep that from happening. We can talk to them and let them know you bothered by it."

"No. That's okay. I know why those three are doing it," Airiella sighed unhappily.

He kissed her forehead. "Then, the killing part. You did what you had to do to protect a room full of your family."

"That's what I tell myself, but there's this part of me that is condemning myself for it. From everything that I've read about demons, or fallen angels, whatever you want to call them, they aren't all bad. What if those weren't bad, and I just slaughtered them for no reason? Even Lucifer, or whatever name people use, is an angel. Take the religion out of it, and you have someone who made a bad decision and becomes scorned for all time. Yet countless stories tell of him wanting back into heaven. What separates what I did from what he did? Or any of them for that matter."

"Intent. It's not my first go-around with demons, and I can tell you that it intended to cause harm. Yours is never to cause harm. Big distinction and what separates you from them."

"How can you tell?" she asked.

"The way it was aggressive was a big tell. For you, I think your alarms only go off if there is danger. If they had been there only to observe or to try and talk to you, I don't think you would have gone full angel mode."

"Okay."

"Wow. Okay? No arguments?" Jax was stunned.

"That's an answer I can accept. No arguments."

"We fly back Tuesday. How about Sunday we head down to that beach you were talking about the other day? Give you a chance to unwind and let go?" Jax wanted to do something that mattered to her.

He heard her breath catch. "Really?"

"Yes, really. This week has taken a heavy emotional toll on you. Life-altering for both of us, and we find ourselves in a war, others know nothing about outside our circle. We can take a day and spend some time in your favorite place before we dive back into everything," Jax was determined to make it happen.

She pushed herself up and kissed him. "Yes, please."

The months of sexual tension between them hadn't eased a bit, and he found himself rock hard in a matter of seconds. "Is Mel home?"

"Yeah, she's asleep still. Why?"

"Trying to decide if I wanted to put on a sex show or not." He shifted his pants, trying to get more comfortable.

"She'd probably try to join in," Airiella warned him. "By the way, Smitty said you told the world you loved me. What does that mean?"

Jax groaned. "I should have known one of them would have told on me." He fished around in his pocket, trying to get his phone free and brought up his Instagram account. He held out his phone to her and watched her face.

He'd used one of the pictures from the beach he'd taken. Airiella still had the skirt on and was standing there, hair and skirt blowing in the breeze, staring out at the waves. It was a great shot, and it kept her anonymous enough unless you knew her. He'd captioned it with, "Never would I have thought that I would find something so beautiful in which to place my heart."

She was statue-still, and Jax was afraid it had upset her that he posted a picture of her. "Let me in, siren," he pleaded with her.

She dropped her walls, and his mind became flooded with love. Bright swirling colors of pure love washing over him, through him, showing him all the ways how he had a hold of her. Love so potent that everything else fell away from them.

Chapter Seventeen

ou ready, Raven?" Startled out of my thoughts, I looked up from my phone.

"No. I hate this." I looked back down, waiting for Mags to reply. I asked her which of the photos Jax had taken would make an excellent gift for my parents and my nieces. I wanted them to have something beautiful to look at when they thought of what I was instead of what they had seen at the funeral.

Jax sat slouched next to me, his arm across the back of the chair I occupied. He thought both of the pictures, in a side by side frame. He reasoned that one showed the outline of my wings, the other just showed me, so that they had both images of who I was.

"Beautiful girl, I know you don't like this. I don't either. Keep it simple and use your natural charm. They are broadcasting locally too, playing it as the hometown girl, hero angle." Tama tapped me on the head. "Stay locked up." Done deal with that. My walls were up before I had even left my house.

Mags replied with the same answer as Jax. Figures. He smirked at me and sent both to a local drug store to get printed. We'd pick them up after the interview. I had ordered the book Alice in Wonderland for the girls, and it would be delivered to my house tomorrow. I planned to write a little letter and put it in the book for them, telling them to always believe in magic and impossible things.

"Raven, I know it doesn't seem like it at times, I do have your best interests in mind though," Taklishim sighed.

"I know, Gandalf. Jax told me earlier he thought I was on overload. I think he's right. I just also really hate being in the spotlight. I promise I'll lose the attitude before it begins."

"I didn't think you had an attitude," Taklishim corrected me. "Your facial expression is one of someone undergoing extreme torture."

I pasted a fake smile on my face, "Is this better?"

Tama laughed. "Definitely not. Use what Jax calls your siren voice, and this guy will be eating out of your hand. For that matter, Tak probably would be too."

That got a real smile out of me. "Really Tak? That's all it takes?" I used the tone Jax liked so much, and he immediately shifted next to me, growling.

"It is rather persuasive," Taklishim admitted, glaring at Tama. "I prefer the attitude. I rather like that sarcastic wit of yours."

"His reaction is a bit different than Jax's; otherwise, we'd have some issues. When you use that tone, he wants to bend reality to give you whatever you want, or change into his animal and tear apart whoever is hurting you. He thinks of you like a daughter, or a little sister, though he will never admit it." Tama just spilled all of Taklishim's secrets with a sweet smile. "Degataga, too."

"I don't need to admit to anything with you around, now do I?" He crossed his arms and raised his eyebrow.

"Your secret is safe with me, Gandalf. You're not such a bad, old man yourself," I grinned at him.

"There she is," he squatted down in front of me. "We will be in the next room watching. Jax will be in there with you. The stations are going nuts for it because he's here with you. Follow his lead if you get confused."

"Got it," I confirmed.

"One more thing that I have a feeling they are going to try and spring on you. The investors added a day to the live show. It's now a two-night event, two locations. They were supposed to notify Aedan today, but I don't know if they did. Something smells off to me about it, and I'm working on trying to confirm it. Dega is too."

"Seriously?" Jax got a hard edge to his voice as he remembered the last live show.

"Yeah, sorry, Jax." Tama pulled Taklishim up to his feet. "Both locations here in state at least. The first night will still be Northern State Hospital as planned. The second will be a little place called Franklin."

"Franklin? The ghost town?" I sat up, more interested now.

"You know it?" Taklishim looked curiously at me, surprised.

"Yep. I've hiked all over there. Both locations. They want us to cart all that equipment uphill for over a mile to even get to the town?" I looked over at Jax. "There's not an easy way to get there. It's out in the sticks. Not too far from me."

"What's there?" Jax asked warily.

"Nothing, really. Foundations of where buildings used to be. It was an old mining town in the late 1800s, I think. If I remember right," I amended. "There was a big mine fire that caused a scandal back then. They suspected the fire had been set deliberately by someone that opposed the union or was pro-union; I can't remember. A lot of people died. There is a tiny little cemetery there, too. Sadly, it's overgrown and not taken care of, but it is creepy. So many of the headstones have matching dates from all those that died in the fire."

"Can you get into the mine?" Taklishim asked, worry creeping into his tone.

"No. At least, not from there that I know about or remember. The shaft at the top of the hike up is grated over. Some people died there in the 90's I think that was repelling down it. It's not safe."

"So, there is a lot of confirmed death there, sabotage, resulting in death that could be considered murder? In other words, a lot of negative energy." Jax ran his hands through his hair. "With demons at play, that does sound like a setup. But why? I thought the one guy was bound now."

"I didn't want you to be blindsided by it in the interview, that's the only reason I told you right now. Don't let it bother you, and don't act surprised. The investors want the reaction from you," Taklishim advised.

"I know the game." Jax stood and paced a little. "Siren, you know this place well?"

"I wouldn't say well. I can show you pictures from my hikes there. I've been to Franklin many times. I researched its history a couple of times and looked at photos of what it used to look like when it was a functioning town. There's really nothing left of it. It's disappeared and reclaimed by nature."

"Thanks, Tak." Jax saw someone coming and put his show smile on. "Game face on, siren."

"Airiella Raven? Hi, my name is Forrest, and I flew up from California to do this. I wanted to meet you in person," he stuck his hand out to shake mine.

"Hi, Forrest." I shook his hand, my senses tingling. *Something's off;* I sent Jax.

Danger? He sent back.

I don't think so, but my senses are tingling. I switched to talk to Taklishim. *Tak, my feelings are tingling with this guy, something is up.*

I'm watching on the other side, Tama is with you here. Pay attention and walls sealed tight, Raven.

Forrest led us to a studio. "The infamous Jax. I feel honored to meet you, as well. When I heard you were going to be here, it became a must for me to do in person instead of through the broadcast."

"Why is he infamous?" I couldn't stop myself from asking, my defenses on high.

"You've watched the show, right?" Forrest looked at me like I was crazy. "He's volatile."

"I disagree," my tone hardened.

"How could you disagree with that?" he asked as he handed us headsets and sat us in front of a microphone setup.

"Because I've been on location with them." Damn it; this guy already had me on edge with his passive-aggressive statements to Jax.

Relax, siren. It's not my first interview with people like this.

Fuck that. I won't let this guy get away with it, I sent back, angry, and trying to hide it.

The look Jax gave me was comical, and my smile started to hurt my face. I was trying so hard not to laugh. Forrest mistook the smile for nervousness. "Don't worry. It will be easy and fun."

"Sure. Right. Got it." I grinned at Taklishim as I used the siren voice.

"Good evening listeners, Forrest here with Night Shadows, coming live to you from Seattle tonight. Our special guest is Airiella Raven, and the guy everyone loves to hate from Shadow Seekers, Jax Walker. Welcome, you two."

Jax grimaced. "Hello."

With the best voice I had, I said, "Good evening, Forrest. Thank you for having us."

"Airiella, I understand you are back here on your home turf for a family situation?" Forrest started in immediately, his eyes glued to me.

Jax stiffened beside me. "Yes, my family has suffered a loss. Jax was kind enough to make sure I got here safely and has been an immense help to me during this difficult time. The support of the show and crew mean so much to me."

Forrest appeared surprised. "He came to support you for a death in the family? Jax, were you hoping for a ghost sighting?"

Fire lit my veins. "That's kind of crass of you to say. Jax has been helping quite a bit. My family was very impressed by his kindness. It was a tough loss for us."

"I apologize," my voice appeared to be working on Forrest. "So, tell me how you came to be on the show."

"They were looking for an empath to help them on locations, and I applied. I interviewed with the crew, and here we are today."

"Can you tell us what an empath is, for those of us who don't know? I'm aware Jax claims to be one, though I hardly see empathy from him on the show," Forrest kept the barbs on Jax going.

"Well, an empath is someone that can feel the emotions of the others around them and often take them on to ease burdens of others. We feel things differently, more passionately. Situations, where emotions run high, would be very intense for an empath. Likewise, being in crowded areas is difficult. As for Jax, he *is* an empath. The reason you don't see it on the show, or you are mistaking what you see, is a more accurate statement; is because the situations with the paranormal run to the extreme emotions. It's a battle inside, to try and keep the emotions of a spirit separate from your own. A lot of what we encounter on the show are emotions from someone who died violently, and they want their story heard. What you see as aggression or anger, is really Jax trying to keep things separate to get the message of the deceased across without it taking over him, or damaging him. Emotions are powerful."

Nicely played, Raven, came Taklishim's calm voice.

Forrest was flustered now. "I see. Uh, can you tell me why then they needed another empath if Jax was already there?"

"To help back him up. I'm not in the investigation. I'm on the outskirts getting readings to make sure they are safe and to notify personnel if Jax is in danger, or any of the crew, actually. I'd be able to tell if their emotions got to a dangerous level and have them removed before possession or harm could come to them."

You have him wrapped around your finger, siren. Your voice is making me want to jack off or take you here and now in front of him, but it's working. I smothered a laugh.

"Fascinating. In your opinion, are ghosts real?" Forrest asked.

"Very much so, just as their emotions are. Tell me, Forrest, have you walked into a building and thought what a great place? Or on the flip side, that you didn't like somewhere?"

"Of course. I think everyone has done that," Forrest readily agreed.

"Why do you think that happens?" I asked.

"Wait, are you telling me there are ghosts everywhere?" I got the crazy look again.

"I couldn't answer that if I wanted to, I'm not a medium. I can tell you that you are picking up on emotions that have been left there or currently reside there. If you are in a historical place and you feel like the place is awful, something bad must have happened there. Yet, if you think the place is wonderful, chances are it was at one time, filled with love. Or for a currently occupied place, it is still filled with love. That's the power of emotions. They leave a lasting mark. You can forget a place or a memory, but you rarely forget how something made you feel, especially if it was a strong emotion."

"You make a compelling case," Forrest said with admiration. "There have been rumors floating around that you are dating one or more of the crew, is this true?"

"Are you one of the people that believe rumors, Forrest? What *are* rumors? Emotions of jealousy, or spite usually. My personal life is personal."

"Jax posted a picture recently of someone on Instagram. Was that you?" Forrest pushed harder.

"I haven't seen it, I couldn't say. I don't play with social media a whole lot. Does it look like me?" I asked innocently.

"Uh, I'm not sure. It's a view from the back." Thank God that Jax had told me to wear my hair up for that exact reason. It, for sure, would have given it away. I even wore makeup and nondescript clothes that didn't look like anything close to the picture.

"Ah, I see." I winked at him. "Wise people don't

believe everything they hear on the internet. Wasn't it Abraham Lincoln that said that? I think I read that someone online." I grinned at Forrest.

In case you didn't know this yet, I love you, witch.

"You're a funny one. I bet the filming locations are fun with you around," Forrest smiled.

"I *definitely* keep things interesting. They'd probably all tell you that," it was hard to keep a straight face. I had to applaud Jax for not busting out laughing at that one. Pretty sure I caught a faint cackle of laughter from Ronnie as well.

"Take me back to that live show that almost ended in tragedy for you guys," Forrest asked, glancing down at his notes.

Careful, Taklishim warned.

"That was a scary night," I shuddered.

"I bet. It looked intense. What happened?"

Tak? How far do I take this? I frantically asked.

He's putty in your hands. Use your judgment to make you all shine in the best light without giving anything away, other than the empath stuff, Taklishim suggested.

"Well, I started to pick up a dangerous feeling emotion. We tried to use the communication devices we had, but something cut out the electronic signals. You ever had that sense that you need to move or get away from something?" I took a wild stab.

"That tingly sensation on the back of your neck? I've felt that," Forrest nodded, staring at me in fascination.

"Okay, then you can understand this. What I felt was a thousand times stronger than that. It was an emotion so full of rage that I just reacted when we couldn't get through. I ran inside and followed the sound of voices until I found Ronnie and Aedan and sent them outside. I think that showed on the video that appeared on YouTube."

"It did, but there wasn't audio," Forrest confirmed with a nod of his head.

"Something was definitely in that house. We had uncovered occult ties during the research phase, and others have concluded there must have been some sort of ritual that had taken place with the owner. After Ronnie and Aedan got out, I ran down the stairs and found Art and Jax getting threatened by the owner. My appearance had thrown the owner off of whatever he was doing, and he attacked me," the tremble that went through me wasn't at all fake.

"Did whatever happen to the communication devices get figured out? How did it knock out the audio on the camera but not the image?" Forrest asked in fascination.

"I don't have the know that equipment to answer that. I deal with emotions, not electronics." Forrest was giving me an odd look. "It could have been something as simple as atmospheric pressure. I don't know."

"Some of it you can clearly read the guy's lips. You took some pretty hard hits," Forrest stayed on the same path he was on.

"As I said, it was a scary night."

"What happened after Art left? How did he leave? It looked like you were pushing him out," Forrest checked something off his notes.

"I was. I was trying to diffuse the situation and get both guys out safely. Sometimes empaths are like magnets to some people, they want to unburden themselves, and you find a bad situation eased relatively easily with a little empathy," I tried to deflect.

"It doesn't look like that is what happened here. Art left, then what happened? Were you aware that lightning had struck the house?"

"No. I didn't know. I wasn't surprised that it burned as quickly as it did. It was poorly maintained, and the wood was brittle. After Art left, I kept talking to him to keep his focus on me and circled to get us closer to the stairs. Smoke poured in fast. Like crazy fast, and he took off. As you've seen from other episodes, Jax has asthma, and the smoke affected him pretty quickly. I was trying to get him up the stairs when Ronnie came to the rescue and got us both out," I lied.

"You could have died. Both of you could have died. I understand you were a part of an attack that happened before that too?" Forrest prodded.

Shit. How the hell had he known about that? I tried to play it off. "My first experience with a fan. People are passionate about the show."

"How do you feel about being called a hero?" The look in Forrest's eyes shifted a bit.

"Heroes are different things to different people. If someone thinks what I did was heroic, I would ask them what they would have done in my situation if that had been their friends in danger? We all have a hero inside us."

"You are an enigma." Forrest turned to Jax. "Jax, tell me about the girl in the picture? In all these years of you doing the show, I've never heard of you being in a relationship."

"It's the first relationship I've been in since my girlfriend died twelve years ago," Jax said easily.

"That's a long time to go without a relationship," Forrest smirked. I wanted to smack him.

"No one's been right for me, until now." Jax shrugged as if the questions didn't bother him.

"What's she like? Will you tell us her name?" Forrest leaned forward eagerly.

"No. The beautiful woman wants to remain unnamed. She's the reason my heartbeats, the oxygen that keeps my flame burning."

Jax, I'll always be in the rabbit hole when it comes to you, I told him through the connection.

"Romantic words for someone like you," Forrest said sarcastically.

"Forrest, that's kind of offensive, and you aren't even talking to me. How do you know what kind of person he is? All you know of him is what you see on TV in situations where emotions run high. That's not a fair statement."

"I find it oddly coincidental that he is now in a relationship after you join the show. Plus, you keep defending him," Forrest pointed out as if he knew everything.

"I defend all of them. It just seems to me that you are dead set on attacking Jax's character needlessly when you don't know him." I was sitting stiffly now, and doing my best not to zap him with lightning.

"Okay, we'll switch back to you then. Can you demonstrate the empath abilities?" Forrest asked as if I had played into his hands.

"Well, I can tell you what I am picking up from you. It will be your word against mine, though, since there is no way to verify." I wasn't going to give an inch.

"How about if I write down what I am feeling right now and hand it to a person, not in the room with us?"

"That's not a true test. You can write down anything you want. An empath is not a mind reader. I can't tell you what you are thinking. I can only feel the emotions you are feeling. I can't tell you why you feel them. I can look at your body language and make assumptions. I try not to do that though because I am not in your shoes. It's not my place to judge or assume," I kept my voice even.

"I guess I hadn't looked at it that way," Forrest sounded unsure for the first time.

"Most people don't. You aren't alone in that. It's what makes empaths so different from others."

"Does the rest of the team take your advice when it comes to things you are picking up on?" Forrest wondered.

"Yes. The crew trusts my assessments. I've been able to pinpoint locations where strong emotions are at, resulting in them getting some great paranormal evidence that you'll see on the upcoming episodes we've just filmed," I said with pride.

"You said you believe in ghosts. Do you believe in demons?" Forrest's pointed question got the attention of the raven in me.

Danger! Tak's voice shouted in my head. I didn't have any alarms going off, so I opened a small part of my senses to filter through the energy around us. The electronics threw off some of the signals I was getting, though I thought I had a handle on it.

"I think, and this is my own opinion, that people call negative emotions demons pretty readily. I am not going to say they do or don't exist. I will say that if ghosts are real, and I've seen that they are, then other things would have to be real too. You can't believe in one narrow scope and not have your mind open to the rest because it makes you uncomfortable. If bigfoot exists, that means aliens probably do too."

"Diplomatic answer," Forrest nodded.

"Not diplomatic, honest. I believe in keeping an open mind."

"Does that mean you believe in bigfoot and aliens too?" Forrest tried to use my words against me.

"Can you prove to me they don't exist?" I countered his attitude with my own but in a sweet voice.

"Point to you, Airiella. Lastly, I heard through the grapevine that they added a night on to the live show that will be happening here in Washington. What are your thoughts on that?" Forrest tried again to get one over on us.

"I think it will be fun to be part of an investigation on my home turf no matter how many nights it is," I replied with fake enthusiasm.

"Can you tell us about the locations?"

"I don't know if that is something I am allowed to talk about or not, so I will play it safe on that and say no," I told him with a smile.

"Not even a hint?" he said flirtatiously.

"Okay, here's your hint. The locations are both somewhere on the western side of the Cascade mountain range," sweet sarcasm laced my tone.

"You are feisty. I love it. Okay, folks, you heard it straight from the mysterious Airiella's mouth. Until next time we meet in the shadows of the night. This is Forrest, signing off with Airiella and Jax."

He did something with the recording equipment, and I refused to speak until I saw the lights go off that said we were on air and recording. "Thank you, Forrest."

"Would you be interested in grabbing something to eat with me before you leave?" I was so stunned I just looked at him blankly.

"Are you asking her out?" Jax's voice was not friendly.

"What does it matter to you?" Forrest had an odd glint in his eyes that came off as aggressive, and my alarms did go off then.

"I think he asked that because I am still recovering from the death of a very close family member, and I need to get back to my family. Thank you for the offer, but I am going to have to decline." My hands itched to grab Jax and hold on to him, but I kept them at my sides.

"Sorry for your loss," he forced a smile on his face.

"Thank you. It was nice to meet you." I stepped to the door and headed out, Jax, on my heels.

Taklishim, my alarms are going off. What's happening? I shouted through my head.

I don't know, Raven. Do not drop your walls. You will glow like a beacon on this side if you do, Taklishim warned me.

I put a little speed in my step as Taklishim and Tama came out of the viewing room. "You never told me who these guys are, Airiella." Forrest pushed again as he followed us out.

"Family," I said sweetly. Tama's facial expression wasn't a friendly one as she looked at him. I took both of their arms between mine like it was a natural thing for me. "Thank you again."

Jax damn near shoved me in the elevator. Once the doors closed, he expelled a rush of air. "What was that energy?"

"I don't know, but it wasn't good." Taklishim was edgy, and Tama still looked pissed.

"Jax, did you feel any pressure in your head?" Tama settled a penetrating gaze on him.

"Yeah. I thought it was because Forrest was pissing me off, though," Jax growled.

"No, either he or something else was trying to get in your head." Her response startled Taklishim.

"How? I didn't sense anything on the other side,"

Taklishim asked his wife with disbelief.

"I don't think it was a demon. I think it was Forrest. He has some sort of mental ability; I couldn't get a good read on it. He had protective walls up like Airiella's. Almost impenetrable. You sensed something, didn't you Airiella?" she turned to me.

"I did when he shook my hand. My senses tingled. I warned Jax and Taklishim both."

"Jax, did you use walls?" She looked back at him.

"I did, I'm not very good at them though," Jax said sheepishly.

Tama had an intrigued look come across her face. "Are you protecting him?"

Hmmm. Was I? "Can I do that?"

"I can usually read Jax like a book. He is as closed up as you are. If I had to guess, I would say you somehow shielded him."

"Well, that's kind of cool. I can still read him," I said, thinking.

"Love is the strongest motivator." She finally smiled. "Keep your guard up until you are away from here."

"You did good, Raven. I especially liked how you turned the insults around that he was firing at Jax," Taklishim praised me.

"What I wanted to do was strike him with lightning." I touched Jax's hand lightly as we exited the elevator.

"That would have made for an interesting interview," Jax said dryly.

"We'll be in touch. Take care you two. Raven, you weren't wrong. We are family," Taklishim's voice was soft.

The unexpected compliment stopped me in my tracks. "Holy shit, Gandalf!"

Tama smiled widely. "Right? Every once in a while, the human side comes through."

Taklishim rolled his eyes, "Women."

Chapter Eighteen

edan shot to his feet. "She did it!" he crowed. He looked around the room at the grinning faces. "He never stood a chance against her."

"Did you seriously doubt her?" Mags pushed him as she walked past where he stood.

"She was nervous and didn't think she could do it." Aedan started after his wife.

"Don't push, she's pregnant," Ronnie joked.

"I wasn't an ass. Airiella's had a rough week." He plopped back down. "Damn."

"We got what you meant," Smitty threw him a bone.

"She shut that asshole right up about Jax and explained how easy it is to misconstrue a situation." Aedan pointed out.

"I wonder if she used that voice on purpose?" Smitty thought out loud.

Ronnie laughed. "It *was* pretty distracting. I wanted to tune out and just rub myself. Bet Jax was struggling too!"

Aedan laughed too. "I agree! I bet it was driving Jax crazy to sit there quietly and listen to it. He calls her siren for a reason."

"Speaking of, we should call them about that second location since we couldn't warn him." Smitty went to pull out his phone, but Aedan beat him to it.

"I'll put it on speaker." He dialed. "Hey, good job, you guys. Put me on speaker. I've got you on speaker here."

"Hi, Aedan." Airiella's voice floated across the airwaves.

"Fantastic job, baby girl," Smitty praised her.

"Yep. Guy didn't know what hit him, angel. Jax, how was it to sit there and listen to that voice?" Ronnie chuckled.

"Fucker asked her out in front of me after the interview! After trying to get us to admit to a relationship," Jax spat out.

"Seriously? He asked you out, Airiella?" Aedan was outraged, and he wasn't sure why.

"He did. I had some alarms going off in my head, so we made tracks pretty quick."

"I saw red." Jax snarled.

"Well, I just wanted to touch base about this second location. You didn't sound surprised. I'm guessing Taklishim gave you a heads up?" Aedan asked.

"He did. Said he thinks something is up with it too. Airiella said that she's been there quite a bit. She's hiked there," Jax's tone was too guarded.

"Smitty said it's the site of the largest mining disaster of the state. What's the site look like?" Aedan wondered.

"Forest, pretty much. There're some old stone foundations along either side of the trail, no original buildings, so to speak, everything is gone. About a mile hike up to where the mineshaft is. Gravel path. After the mineshaft, it becomes a dirt trail, that in the dark, would be treacherous. That leads back to the cemetery where I think they buried a lot of the people that died in the mine fire. It's super overgrown with sticker bushes and other vegetation. It's right by the Green river," Airiella described.

"The river the killer dumped all those bodies in?" Aedan grimaced.

"Yes, but I don't think in that particular area. The gorge to that river is right there. Beautiful area. I will say on my first hike there, I did hear women singing, and there was no one out there with us," she remembered.

"She also said that there were two deaths in the mineshaft from people repelling down it," Jax added. "She the hole's covered with a grate. Before dinner at your brother's, do you think we could go out there?"

"Sure," she answered Jax.

"Have you ever picked up on bad energy there?" Aedan wanted to know as much as possible about this new location.

"No. I can't say I've ever really looked. There are a few creepy spots, some really cool history, and a sense of sadness in the cemetery. For me though, it's nature and near a river. I'm usually lost in the energy of the life surrounding me," Airiella clarified.

"Will you check tomorrow?" Aedan pushed her. "I'm with Taklishim on this. I think something's up with it."

"Airy! You were brilliant in the interview!" Mags called out.

"Thank you, Mags!" she replied.

"When you have a moment, send some pictures of what the place looks like, or do it tomorrow after you are there. Send them to Smitty or me," Aedan instructed her.

"It won't have changed much building wise. The only difference will be the amount of vegetation. It's easier in the winter to see things. It will be close to autumn then, so it might not be awful, but the ground will be slick with the start of falling leaves," she told them.

"How far apart are the two locations?" Aedan had tried to find Franklin on the map but couldn't.

"Not close at all," she said quickly. "Northern State is probably about two and a half hours from my house. Franklin is about thirty minutes from my house."

"I can't find it on a map." Aedan tried to look again.

"It doesn't exist anymore, that's why. Look up Black Diamond, that's where it is now. Black Diamond used to be a coal-mining town. My grandpa's baby sister has a plot in the historical cemetery there. He had family that worked the mines when they immigrated over from Italy," she informed them readily.

"Shit. Is this a set up for Airiella?" Ronnie broke in, his voice expression concern.

"Could be." Aedan thought about it. "You've been to the other location, too, right?"

"Yes, I've hiked that area as well. I haven't been to the hospital itself, just the grounds around it. There are about five miles of hiking trails that weave in and around the remaining structures on the grounds. The hospital is behind a fenced-off area with posted no trespassing signs," she recalled.

"Maintained trails?" Aedan wondered why they were both in such an outdoor area.

"For the most part. The terrain isn't even on all the parts, so footing will be tricky in the dark," Airiella warned.

"How's this going to work with trying to get the research done on the surrounding towns with them so far apart?" Smitty asked.

"No idea. We may have to split up or go a couple of days early." Aedan made a mental note to go over the schedule again.

"It's a lot of driving and traffic for the hospital. I'd suggest after flying in, you do the Black Diamond interviews first before heading north," Airiella suggested.

"Alright. Smitty and Ronnie will be all over the research on this. Don't worry too much about it. Just finish up what you need to with your family before coming back." Aedan leaned back in the chair. Could this really be about her?

"It's a fascinating history, at least, for both locations. Full of political strife at a weird time in our country's history. As for the rest, we are having dinner with my brother tomorrow. I suspect my parents will magically be there, after the whole demon display. After that, don't worry if you don't hear from us. Jax is going to take me to my beach for some downtime. Sometimes cell reception is spotty," she told them, sounding tired again.

"Fuck, thank God, Jax. I was hoping you would do that." Ronnie sounded happy about that.

"She needs it." Jax sounded a little strained.

"Love you guys. Can't wait to be back there with you all," she sounded sad, and Aedan felt the pang of her absence.

"We love you too, angel. Take care of you," Ronnie called out.

Aedan hung up. "Would they really go so far as to research Airiella's family to find a spot that has ties to her grandfather that just died?"

"Hearing that, I'm inclined to believe there's some other motive here." Smitty crossed his leg over his knee, making a table for his elbows.

"Is this the council? Or the money men?" Ronnie asked Aedan.

"I'm not sure where the decision came from, the council knows what she is. We also know some of them don't like her. I'd lean towards them over the money men. To them, she's a cash cow. Ratings have skyrocketed because of her." Aedan steepled his fingers. "Let's try to cover all angles with this."

"The good news is, if she makes lightning happen, it's likely to be wet by a river in the fall, so there won't be a forest fire." Smitty pointed out.

Ronnie barked out a laugh. "No, we'd just have to dodge falling trees."

"Not funny, you two," Aedan scolded them.

Chapter Nineteen

J ax looked around as they pulled into a muddy parking lot that said you had to pay to park there, but he saw no attendant to pay. "Who do you pay?"

"In offseason like this, there is a little lockbox over there." She pointed to a wooden box.

"Don't people just break it?" It didn't look very secure to him.

"I'm sure they have. This place is private property, and maintenance isn't cheap." She got out and stretched. "Follow me back out to the street. I want you to see the view from the bridge."

"Heights aren't my thing, siren." Jax looked hesitantly back to the street.

"Mine either. It's solid. You can hold my hand even," Airiella teased him.

He grumbled but followed her. "Jokes on you, babe. I was going to hold your hand anyway."

She pulled his arm over her shoulder and stretched to kiss him. "Good."

They walked out on to the bridge, and Jax fought back a wave of vertigo. "Siren," he pleaded.

"Trust me, Jax. Don't look down, look out until your equilibrium re-balances. Look at the cliffs surrounding us, the aqua color of the river on a clear day like this. Here is the Green River Gorge."

Jax looked out like she said, and it was beautiful. His brain was just processing the height, not the beauty. "Okay, nope. Gotta go back." He pulled her back.

"Do you want to walk down there? Or just go to Franklin?" she asked.

"Is it a bridge to get down there?" Jax looked warily back over his shoulder at the bridge.

"No, it's a little trail, a steep one. There are cliffs," Airiella pointed out.

"Franklin, it is. Sorry. I get vertigo. We can try after Franklin, how about that? I would like to see the river, just don't want to go down a cliff to get to it," Jax compromised.

She gave him a soft smile that made his heart skip a beat. "With spring here, we might not get to see much of it because everything is in bloom. It will give you a good idea of what it will be like. The muddy factor will probably be the same, depending on how long summer decides to stick around. Also, you've already seen the river; this is the same one I jumped in, just farther down that way," she pointed.

She stopped back at the car and grabbed her backpack. "Do you always take a pack?" he asked out of curiosity.

"If we are going to be in a remote area like this and the woods, yes."

"We aren't that far from civilization, isn't the town just a few miles away?" Jax wondered.

"Yep. Though this is all uphill, a steep drop-off on one side, and muddy conditions, so it's very slippery. While it's large enough to get lost for a really inexperienced person, that isn't my concern. There're animals out here, as well as questionable terrain. Injuries happen. I'd rather be prepared."

"What kind of animals?" Jax halted his momentum.

"Cougars, bears, coyotes, I'm sure," she ticked off and looked back at him.

"Cougars and bears? Here?" Jax looked around nervously.

She laughed. "This is Washington. Cougars and bears are pretty common."

"And your pack will keep us safe from those?" He put a hefty dose of skepticism in that question.

"A gunshot will scare off a bear. So will stomping your feet and making loud noises. A cougar on the other hand and I'm talking about the animal, and not old single ladies, you'll never see that coming or hear it," she told him truthfully.

"Oh, I feel totally safe now," Jax couldn't help the sarcasm. He wasn't a great outdoors person. "You have a gun in there?"

"I do. Not a large caliber one." She patted the pack where Jax assumed the gun was.

"You are a total badass. Back to the cougar, are we in danger?"

"Not likely. I'm always prepared. You're more likely to step in poison ivy than be attacked by a cougar," she grinned at him, her eyes twinkling.

"Great. Touch nothing, Jax," he mumbled.

She grinned at him again. "These here are all blackberry bushes. They go most of the way up and are all over up there. They tend to take over. When we are here next, they'll be at the end of their bloom. I pick them and eat them as I walk up."

"You eat them right off the vine?"

"It's not like we are in a pesticide area. The berries are juicy and sweet." She danced up in front of him, walking backwards. "The other thing I used to like to do when I was involved with someone, and we went hiking, was find a quiet spot and have trail sex."

As a distraction from the scary stuff about cougars, bears, and poison ivy, that was pretty effective. "Really? That's a thing?"

"You bet your sweet, sexy ass it's a thing."

"You think my ass is sexy?" Jax smiled wickedly, his brain filled with dirty thoughts.

"Jax, you are all sexy. Every last bit of you. Especially when you take your shirt off, and I can see all that beautiful ink."

Something in the woods next to him cracked, and he jumped sideways. "You're going to kill me. Now all I'm thinking of is being buried inside you and having a cougar take a bite out of my sexy ass."

Her delighted peals of laughter warmed his heart. "Come on, tough guy. Keep up." She turned and walked facing forward now, swaying her hips exaggeratedly.

"Damn, woman. Hiking with a hard-on to a ghost town, this is what my life has become," he growled good-naturedly.

"You love it," she said over her shoulder.

"I do," he admitted. "Because I'm here with you." He snapped a couple pictures of the trail on the way up and saw he still had signal. "Hey, we have signal out here." He labeled the photos trail to town and sent them to Ronnie.

"You aren't far from Black Diamond. They have a great little bakery there too. We'll stop and grab a loaf of bread to bring to my brother's tonight. Maybe get a few things to take tomorrow too."

They finally came to an intersection in the trail. There was an old black coal mining car sitting there, he snapped a picture and sent it to both Ronnie and Aedan. The path forked to the left and the right. "Which way?"

"Both. Let's go right first. That's where you'll see most of the old foundations that are still here. From what I had been able to gather, this was the road through the main part of the town. I am almost positive that under all this brush is more of the town. No one's ever cleared it though," Airiella said a touch sadly.

"I'm starting to think there is no flat ground in this state," Jax huffed. "Why aren't you breathing hard?"

"This isn't all that steep. I'm sweating," Airiella took his hand and wiped it across her forehead. "See?"

He threw back his head and laughed, wiping his hand on his pants. "That was a shit move, siren."

She giggled, and he lunged for her, wiping his

sweaty face all over hers. She pulled her shirt up and wiped her face off. "So was that."

They walked up the road, and she pointed out the foundations that were left, though she couldn't remember what they were. Jax took photos of everything and kept sending them as they went along. He knew Smitty would try to match them up to whatever he found.

She stopped and looked around. "I feel some sort of energy right now. It's not bad energy. I can just feel something."

He stopped next to her and closed his eyes, trying to get a feel for whatever she picked up on. He felt it, but for him, it was faint. "Yeah, I feel it."

They kept going back and headed up. It was steeper here, and while Jax considered himself to be in good shape, he wasn't used to inclines like this, and his legs ached. When they got to the top, he looked around. He could see the mountain in the distance, and it was a serenely beautiful spot with all the lush green trees around.

"This is the mineshaft," she told him.

"This is where the two people died?" Jax looked around curiously. There was a giant hole in the ground. "Someone actually thought it would be a good idea to repel down that? Fucking insane."

"Yeah, wouldn't be on the top of my list of things to do either. That's why they grated it up." She ducked between the rails and stepped out onto it, standing over the hole. "You should try it. Big adrenaline rush if you look down."

"No. Siren, get off there. You are going to give me a heart attack," Jax's palms got clammy.

"Calm down, it's fine." She looked around for a small rock and dropped it. It was a few seconds before Jax heard it hit something. "Long way down."

"Please, get off there," Jax hated the tremor in his voice. "I thought you were afraid of heights?"

"Okay, fine. I am." She reached for the railing and took a step, her muddy shoes slipping on the metal grate as her knee slammed into the concrete. "Ouch. That hurt."

Jax's heart had stopped when he saw her fall. He reached under the railing and bodily dragged her out of there, sitting her on the little stone plaque. "Are you okay?"

"I'm fine. It'll leave a mark. It's not the first time I've fallen. It's why I carry the pack," she dug through and pulled out a first aid kit and rolled up her leggings.

"Damnit, Airiella. I'm not supposed to leave any of your blood lying around." Blood was dripping down her leg. He swiped his finger up to capture it. "Shit." He wiped it on a gauze pad she pulled out. "Are you sure you are okay?"

"It's fine. It's just a scrape." She used an alcohol pad and cleaned it up and bandaged it. He took the items that had her blood on it and put them in a plastic baggie she had with her and stuffed it in his pocket.

"Scared the shit out of me, siren." He yanked her to him in a hug after she rolled her pants back down.

"Better get used to it. I tend to do that a lot. Get some pictures of the shaft to send the guys, and then take a picture of right here," she pointed to a narrow trail. "That's the way to the cemetery. The footing is tricky, so watch where you walk."

They wound their way through dense forestation at times, passing more old foundations, thick rusted out cables embedded into the ground. She pointed out a track above their heads where little coal cars would roll to be loaded.

Jax thought the whole place was cool. She was right; some areas you got a little creepy vibe, but in broad daylight, you just saw where nature reclaimed its home, and an echo of the past remained. They finally arrived at the cemetery, and Jax felt a wash of sadness roll over him.

"There're emotions here I'm picking up on," Jax looked around. "If I can feel it, I know you have to be feeling it."

"Every time I come here. I feel like the spirits are sad that their final home is so neglected. This town was once a large hub of activity, and now, it's gone. I try and find as many headstones as possible when I come here and read their names out loud to let them know someone remembers," she pointed to different spots.

Her soft reverent tone and facial expression had Jax riveted. "Siren," he stepped closer to her and touched her face. "Your grace and love are so breathtaking when you set them free like that. I'm sure whatever spirits are here are grateful to you for remembering them."

"It makes me a little sad that the show wants to come here and disrupt them. Despite nature reclaiming so much of this, it's still a beautiful and peaceful spot for them to rest. Maybe something good will come of it. Maybe it will bring some funding to the area to get it cleaned up and maintained for them. That's what I'm going to hope for anyway. It's living history."

She leaned down and righted a fallen headstone and traced her fingers over the name. Jax snapped a picture of it, the silhouette of her wings showing in the filtered light from the trees. He sent the image to the entire team and an idea to raise money to get the cemetery cleaned up. He took some more pictures and sent them along as they weaved in and out of sticker bushes.

"You're right, look at how many of these dates match each other," Jax mused quietly, as he read the names. He felt the sadness wash over him again. "There is a lot of residual emotion here."

"It was here I also heard the women singing. Back by the large cable in the ground is where I could hear children laughing in the distance like they were playing in the river below," she still had that soft tone. "I'm sure there are ghosts here. I don't think they are angry ones, though."

"I don't think so either. The mineshaft gave off a weird vibe." Jax pondered on it. "There has to be another entrance somewhere."

"Probably. I assume it's blocked off or buried. If there are angry spirits, I'd think they would be down in the mines where the murders happened, and the fire was where miners were trapped. I doubt that anyone could get down there."

"Even if they could, it's probably not stable. Smitty is going to love this place for the history alone." Jax touched another headstone he found sticking out of the bushes. "Now that I'm here, it begs the question of how they came to know about this place and why they are sending us here. Ronnie may be right; it's tied to you somehow."

"It won't be an easy location to shoot in the dark, that's for sure. With how spread out it is, it's also not a location where it will be easy to keep track of anything that might pop up. You can't exactly come running out of here in the dark and not risk breaking a bone or falling down the cliffs that are back that way."

"Let's head back so I can get some shots of those spots too. This *is* an odd choice. It calls to me in a way to bring it back to life and share the stories of those that died here, but it doesn't call to me in a rid the place of bad energy way." Jax followed as she led them back the way they came.

"So many people don't even know of this place, or have never heard of it. The hiking communities know. There's another one by my house that's kind of like this place, but I don't know what it used to be. There are just shells of old buildings and foundations along the trail. Franklin though, feels special to me. It always has," she said softly.

Jax reached out and tugged on her pack, getting her to stop so he could take a few photos. "I feel it too, siren." He put his phone back away and pulled her close to kiss her. "I won't let them exploit it."

"Black Diamond has tours of mines still going, and I think they even do one through here. There is also a historical society and museum I think in Black Diamond. Another avenue to think about incorporating. Since this shut down in the early 1900s, I doubt there is anyone still alive that remembers what it used to be," she mused.

"Did you have family that used to work here?" There had to be a connection here, Jax just needed to find it.

"Maybe? I don't know. There were a lot of immigrants here, and there was a large community of

Italians that worked the mines. I'd found pictures of them when I attended an Italian fair years ago that was at the Seattle Center. I asked my grandpa about it once, but that was before he was born. He did tell me that he had family that worked the mines though, he just didn't know which ones. His family didn't speak a whole lot of English and stuck to the Italian communities that had sprung up."

"You don't have any family left in this area?" Jax asked as he took a few more photos and stopped to admire the lush green landscape. If she heard children laughing out here, it had to have been ghosts. He couldn't even hear the river that he knew wasn't far beneath them.

"No. When the mining shut down, my family moved north into Seattle. During his heyday, Beacon Hill in Seattle was where most of his family and my nanie's family settled. It's crazy to think that he watched Queen Anne hill get constructed. He saw the counter-balance being installed there. He lived through so much." Since she was in front of him, Jax couldn't see her face, but he felt that jolt of sadness like he'd walked into a brick wall at full speed.

The loss was still so fresh for her. Jax gently stopped her and hugged her to him as she cried quietly. "Your family has an amazing history, it's no wonder you are so damn incredible," he said into her hair. "I love you."

Chapter Twenty

Smitty swiveled his chair around. "Okay. Here's what we are working with, seven Italian men died in that mine fire. Four of them still had family in Italy. I think it's those four we need to focus on to look for a connection. If there is one, that is. It could be any of them, but with Airiella's story of her family, I think it's probably one of the four who still had family in Italy. Her great-grandparents came over here after they had family here already." Smitty handed the list of names to Ronnie.

"Want me to research the names while you dig through the history of the place, or do you want the names?" Ronnie asked, looking it over.

"I think we should tag-team it. I'll start with the town, you the names, then we'll switch. Two sets of eyes on both is better than just one." Smitty printed a bunch of pictures he'd found, and then the ones Jax had sent.

"Any more ideas on why they would go after her?" Ronnie stressed about it.

"No. It feels personal to me, which makes me think it's a council member, not the money men." The backers had never met her.

"Dr. Stone is who I suspect." Ronnie threw his pen down. "He had an attitude about her from the start."

"That was my thought, too. Dr. Fields and Asher are suspect too, in *my* mind, at least." Smitty had a feeling he couldn't outright dismiss about Asher.

"Should we be researching them too?" Ronnie was out for blood.

"Maybe Aedan can dig on them. He's more political-minded than either of us." Smitty sent him a text. He didn't feel like yelling to get his attention. "Father Roarke may be able to help him there too."

W innie popped in on Ronnie. "Hey there, good looking," she smiled at him.

"Hey, sunshine. Any news?" Ronnie glanced up at her.

"I think you guys are right; there's a council member or two involved. One of them has been talking with spirits over here, feeding information to them. Make sure you all stay buttoned up about what she can do. They are trying to find her weaknesses, other than you guys, that is," Winnie said helpfully.

"They think we are her weakness?" Ronnie looked unhappy at that.

"You *are* her weakness. She'd run in front of a speeding train to save all of you. They know it, too. They've even started trying to target Onida. She's a force I would *not* want to have pissed off at me." Winnie shuddered at the thought.

"Still no idea on who is behind all this from the demon perspective? No names?" Ronnie asked, hopefully.

"Not that I have been able to find out. I did see both of Airy's grandpas, though. They shine bright like she does, but without the angel glow. I introduced myself. Both are great men. She was lucky to have them in her life." Winnie smiled wistfully. She'd never gotten to meet her grandpa's.

"Did you tell her that you've met them? She'd probably like to know they are there."

"I haven't been able to get to her. She hasn't taken that necklace off once. I'm okay with that. I think she needs the extra protection. Now that I'm free, I seem to have less power here to do things. I think when I was bound, I was able to draw power from Jax, possibly even Airy," she said thoughtfully.

It was okay with Winnie. She liked the feeling of being free, having none of the heavyweights that she'd had when bound to Jax. She still felt their emotions, especially Airy's, when they were sharp like they had been lately. The magnitude was enough to zap her energy entirely out.

"You are still okay?" concern laced Ronnie's voice.

"Yes, I'm okay. Free reign to come back and forth and if I wanted to reside only on the spiritual realm I could. I'm not ready for that yet. I've made some nice friends now that the binding broke, and I can see them."

"Good. You deserve happiness, Winnie." Ronnie looked wiped out. "I can't wait until she's back."

"Do me a favor. Tell her I've talked to her grandpa's, both of them and that they are watching over her. I think it will do her some good to know that. Also tell her to leave that necklace on. She's the talk of the town over here," she reminded Ronnie.

"You got it, Winnie. Thanks for all your help. It's nice to have you as part of the team."

Winnie's heart soared. He thought of her as part of the team! She was over the moon happy about that and did a little dance. He smiled at her antics. She loved these talks with Ronnie; they were precious to her.

"Love you. Get back to work, no more slacking off talking to ghosts."

He gave her a heart-stopping smile. "Yes, boss. Love you, too."

Ells, I have the picture frames, don't forget the book," Jax called up the stairs to me.

I came down the stairs, and my heart slammed against my ribs as I caught sight of Jax. He'd shaved when we got back from Franklin, and he had a nice, neat little goatee now. His chiseled face slightly sun-kissed, hair perfectly messy in a sexy way.

And he looked damn good in red. Nice form-fitted t-shirt that fell just below his belt and those blue jeans he filled out so nicely. I had to remind myself not to bite my lip. This sexy creature loved me. I still had a hard time believing it.

"You better fucking believe it, siren," his deep voice rumbled, sparking little fires in my veins. "We are going to be very late if you keep thinking about how sexy I look."

"Nosy much?" I quipped as I jumped down the rest of the stairs.

"Those thoughts were pretty loud. Why don't you hear mine all the time?" Jax looked at me, quizzically.

"I tune them out. I have enough shit in my head already. Otherwise, I'd hear you all the time," I patted his ass.

"How do you tune them out? I'm not sure if I feel insulted by that, or not. You are already tuning me out like we an old married couple."

I laughed. "I listen when I need to. I'm not sure how I do it. Mentally it's like my walls. I picture filters in there and just put them in place. When it's just us, I tend to keep my walls down around you because you like it that way."

"Will you be putting them up when we leave here?" Jax quizzed me.

"Yep. Our link will be open though. I won't shut you out." I kissed his cheek. "You smell fantastic."

"Not like you. Your smell is things dreams are made of. And you look unbelievably cute right now."

"Cute? I'm not sure what to do with that." I walked past him to grab my phone and purse.

"You just say thank you, Jax. That's all you do with that," he frowned and quirked an eyebrow up at me.

"Thank you, Jax," I managed with a straight face.

"Smartass," he mumbled.

"Ready?"

"Let's go. I'm hungry." He pulled me to the garage

and stuffed me into the car. "Keys." He held out his hand.

"Wow. Bossy." I handed him the keys.

"Well, I'm hungry and horny now, thanks to your dirty mind. Since we have to be somewhere, I can only fulfill one of those," Jax said with a small growl as he started the car.

"I thought you liked my dirty mind."

"I fucking love it. It's just not very helpful when I have to be around your family, and my dick is trying to pop out of my pants," he said in a matter of fact tone.

I snorted, which made him break out laughing. "I'm going to tell my brother you are a vegetarian and to only give you salad."

"Witch."

"Did you put your coat in here? He usually has a bonfire at family dinners, and it gets cold at night still."

"It's behind you. Tell me where I'm going." I gave him directions, and we arrived five minutes later.

"Prepare for wild girls," I warned.

"I'm ready. Bring on the monsters." He stepped out the car. "I smell barbecue."

"That's how my brother cooks, kind of like you. Samantha will have made all the side dishes," I informed him.

"Auntie!" The girls came tearing from around the back of the house.

"Monkeys!" I yelled back, handing the book to Jax right before they launched at me. I caught Amanda mid-air before she crashed into me, but Grace landed, and we fell back on the grass to their delighted squeals.

"Hi, Ells!" Samantha called from inside the house. "Hi, Jax. Your parents should be here any minute."

"Do you need help with anything?" I asked from under my nieces.

"Nope. Got it all covered. Keep those two occupied that will help."

"Okay, girls. Let's play tag. Jax, you're it!" I yelled and tagged Jax and ran, the girls chasing after me as they tried to keep away from Jax, who launched right into the game.

I saw my brother peek around the corner and shake his head. I was breathless and ready to drop when my parents pulled up. I exited the game and walked out to meet them and help my mom get out of the car.

"Ells," my dad pulled me in to hug him. "I'm not sure how to act now."

"Act like my dad. Nothing has changed. I'm still me, you're still my dad," I frowned, the feeling of not fitting in coming back to the surface.

"Looks like the girls have taken to Jax," my mom remarked. I got her in the wheelchair and pushed her around to the back of the house.

"I'm surprised myself since they are usually so prickly around others." I loved watching him play with my nieces. It made me warm and gooey inside.

If they are important to you, they are essential to me; I heard him answer my thought. He started walked towards us, a girl hanging on each of his legs.

"Hello, Mrs. Raven, Mr. Raven," Jax said as he walked up.

"Oh, jeez. Call me Mariana after the totally inappropriate things I said in the hospital. Call him Spencer." I smothered a laugh. "Ells, are you really dating him and the other big one that was at the funeral?"

Shit. Should have seen that one coming. "Kind of," I mumbled. "It's complicated, Mom." Now my brother snorted and I shot him a nasty look. "It's part of the whole angel thing. The truth of that is, Jax is my future. It's unclear right now what part Ronnie will have in it. I just know he will be a part of my life forever."

"How do you know Jax is your future and not Ronnie?" I was surprised my dad asked that.

I tapped my heart. "I just know."

"Does that mean Jax will be my uncle?" Grace asked. Damn kids. I blushed and tried to change the subject.

"I brought a present for you girls," I said and damn near ran out to the front where Jax had put them when we started playing tag. Amanda was right on my heels. "Give that to Grandma."

"Grandma! Auntie brought you a present too!" Amanda squealed.

"Actually, Mom, it's from Jax." I smiled at him.

"What she means is, it's from both of us." Jax took my hand, and I handed the girls the book and wrapped picture frame.

"Spence!" My mom called my dad over. "Look at this!" She showed him the picture and damn it; he got tears in his eyes.

"We got one too, Grandma!" Amanda jumped up and down. "Look, Daddy! Auntie is a superhero!"

"Ells, this is stunning," my Dad whispered.

"The girls get one, but I don't?" my brother said quietly, looking at the picture.

I cleared my throat. "Nick, you can share. Here, go read them this letter in the book." I pushed him away. "Mom, Dad, Jax took those pictures at a beach in California they took me to."

"Jax, you are very talented. These are beautiful," my mom said softly.

"Airiella was worried that you would look at her differently because of this. This picture here, where you can see the outline of her wings, might be the best picture I've ever taken. She's had a hard time seeing what we all see when we look at her, which is how beautiful she really is. How rare and special. When I turned and saw this, I figured this was the best way to show her what I see, when I see her. I told her to add this second one, where you don't see the wings as a way to show you that she is still her. The same person she always has been. No less beautiful than this picture."

My dad wiped his eyes. "Jax, I can't thank you enough for this. It's exactly what *I* needed to see. I hope it was what she needed to see as well."

"It was, Dad. Jax has been monumental in my recovery from the past." I squeezed his hand.

"I absolutely love this." My mom tugged Jax down

and kissed his cheek. "I'll be forever grateful for this."

I heard the door open, and Samantha barreled at me. "Thank you." She sobbed into my shoulder.

"What? Sam, are you okay?" I was a little alarmed.

"The letter, the book, the photo. It's perfect. I was so worried about what the girls would think. It's also exactly what your brother needed to see. That's the most beautiful picture I've ever seen." She wiped her eyes.

"That's Jax's handiwork. I didn't even know he was taking them. I was worried too. I figured since they were so young that telling them to believe in magic was the best route to go. They don't need to know the photo is real. Not right now."

"It's perfect. Thank you," Sam hugged Jax and went back inside.

Nick came around the corner. His own eyes wet. "Thanks, sis."

J ax looked back over at Airiella, sitting on the porch swing with her nieces tucked up into her on either side as she read them Alice in Wonderland. He pulled his phone back out and got another great picture to add to his growing Airiella collection.

"You really love her, don't you?" Nick asked quietly.

"More than I ever thought possible," Jax told him. They were sitting around a fire pit, just as Airiella had told him. He wasn't cold, though.

"Tell us about yourself, Jax," Mariana asked him.

"There's not a whole lot to tell. The major parts are Ronnie and I grew up together along with another person, her name was Winnie. She became my childhood sweetheart. Twelve years ago, she died in a car accident. It broke me down; we decided to prove that ghosts are real in hopes we would get to speak to her again."

"Oh my God," Samantha breathed out. "That's tragic."

"It wasn't until I met Airiella that I finally believed love was possible again. She's brought new meaning to all of our lives. Changed us in ways, we didn't even know we needed to change. She breathed life right into us," Jax let the honesty ring from his voice.

"If I know my sister, it was probably by force, a kind force, but still force. She's got a way of smacking you upside the head with something," Nick chuckled.

"That's no lie." Jax smiled.

"She had us so worried after her divorce, then Michael. I've never seen her so devastated before," Mariana looked at him. "She was just a shell of a person."

"Now, she's this bright beacon of hope again," Spencer looked over at Airiella. "She's always been so strong and fierce. It was hard to see her so broken."

"What's your family like?" Samantha asked.

"Nothing like this. My parents divorced when I was in high school. My mom found out my dad had a whole secret life going on. Aedan is my half-brother. We never knew until we met in high school. It took us a while to get used to each other, and now I'm so happy to know I have a brother. Smitty, Art, we met then, too. My dad died our senior year. Neither of us has large families like this, and the family we do have isn't close like you all are."

"Airiella and Nick used to fight like crazy," Mariana said with a laugh. "They drove me nuts. He was the biggest instigator, he used to purposely push her buttons to get a reaction, and she never could turn the other cheek. She always gave him the reactions he wanted."

"Oh, yes. I can still do it. Ells never let me get beat up, though. I was a scrawny kid, small and weak, someone the bullies loved. She would beat down boys three grades above her to protect me," Nick told him. "It's kind of nice to know that hasn't changed. She's got a streak of fire in her that is not to be messed with."

"Oh, I've seen it," Jax commented wryly and immediately wished he hadn't. She hadn't mentioned anything to them about the situations she'd been in that were less than favorable.

"Yeah, I figured based on the radio interview we heard last night. I'm surprised she didn't lay into that guy more for attacking you," Nick laughed.

Phew! Jax felt saved on that one. He felt a breeze stir around him and smelled her scent. She'd heard him. *Sorry,* he sent her.

"You won't keep her away from us, will you?" Spencer looked directly at Jax.

"No! Why would I do that?" The question had taken Jax off guard.

"You don't live here. Ells is the type that would follow you wherever you wanted to go," Spencer put it bluntly.

"I love the way you guys are together. I think it's fantastic, and I wish I had been lucky enough to grow up with a family like this."

"You know I was a Navy SEAL, right? I can kill you forty-six different ways with my thumbs," Spencer said so sincerely that Jax didn't know what to think.

Nick burst out laughing. "Dad, I don't think that will work on him. Maybe show him your secret Navy SEAL sign instead."

Spencer grinned and flipped Jax off, who now realized that they were joking. *He really was a SEAL,* he heard in his head. *He used to tell my guy friends the thumb thing; it freaked them out.*

Jax laughed. "If you get the opportunity, use that on Ronnie."

"What can you tell us about him?" Mariana asked.

"He's one of the best men I know. He's known in the fighting circuit for his skills and strength."

"He's a fighter?" Spencer was suddenly serious. Jax studied him for a moment and then understood that he was worried about Airiella being around violence.

"Ronnie grew up with an abusive dad. He witnessed his mom getting beaten often, and when he got older the beatings turned to him. As a way to try and learn how to stop it from happening he started to take martial arts at school. Once the school finally found out and intervened, a shelter stepped in and offered him boxing lessons as an outlet for his anger. He entered tournaments and was undefeated for quite a large stretch."

"That's not concerning to you?" Mariana clutched Spencer's hand.

"No. Ronnie is the gentlest person I've ever met. The only time I've seen him aggressive with anyone outside of high school testosterone is in the ring. He despises violence, as do I. He's been the one training Airiella in defense skills, so she feels more confident. I think the only thing that would make him react aggressively is if she was in danger. He's even more protective of her than I am," Jax tried to reassure them.

"You don't fight?" Spencer pointedly asked.

"No. Ronnie has trained all of us, and he works us out regularly to keep us up on our skills and in shape. He's very disciplined."

"He sounds like a good guy," Nick said to his parents. "Stop worrying. After what we saw, I'm confident Airiella can handle herself." Jax kept his mouth shut and nodded.

Tell Nick that the girls are asleep. Just look at me first like you were checking on me or something, Airiella spoke through the connection.

Jax looked over at her and smiled. "Hey, Nick, I think your kids are asleep."

"Thank God. The magic of auntie at work. Made my night easier. I'll go put them to bed," he stood and walked over to them, lifting Amanda and going inside. A few minutes later, doing the same to Grace.

Airiella joined them. "Are you done grilling him?"

Samantha laughed. "I think so. How'd you know?"

"Come on. Like I didn't know that's why you wanted us over for dinner," Airiella joked.

"No! The girls have missed you and wanted to see you." Samantha defended herself. "That was just a bonus."

"Well, we fly out Tuesday. Tomorrow we are going to the beach for some downtime, so don't get worried if you don't hear from me. I'll be back to visit soon. The two live shows will be here. At least that way, if I don't see you before then, you'll see me then."

"Are you leaving to go home now?" Mariana looked sad.

"We can stay longer," Jax broke in. *She misses you, siren.*

I know. Airiella stood up and went to grab a chaise lounge chair and brought it out to the fire pit. *I want to sit with you.* Jax stood and moved to the chaise lounge, and she settled between his legs, resting against him. *Much better.*

They spent hours out there sitting under the stars talking until the fire burned out, and they said their goodbyes. Jax felt her pang of sadness at leaving them, and the worry underneath it all that they wouldn't be safe. He texted Taklishim her concerns asking if he could do a blessing on their house. At his confirmation, he relayed the information to her and her brother.

Nick came to shake his hand as they were leaving. "She's in danger, isn't she? Play it straight with me." Jax simply nodded. "She's my only sister, angel, or not. Do your best."

"You have my word."

Ronnie bolted out of his chair, "I think I may have something! Spellings are different though, but this is close. A lot of immigrants had their names shortened or changed when they came over due to language barriers; if that happened with Airiella's family, we might have our link. Think of whatever English person was at Ellis Island back then and hearing thousands of foreign names in a day. Her grandpa's last name is Rosetti. One of the people who died in Franklin was Rosati. Possibility, right?" Ronnie was excited.

"If the link is through her grandfather, then that is an outstanding possibility. Make sure to rule out her grandma, though," Smitty played it carefully.

"Here's what's interesting about that. I found a family tree her dad had done on Ancestry, and through her grandma's side, there is also the last name of Rosalla. I felt that was more of a stretch to Rosati, but there are similarities. Based on this family tree, I think her dad's name got shortened to Raven from Ravenna. They all stem from the central region in Italy."

Smitty came over to look at the family tree Ronnie had found. "Holy shit, that's a huge family."

"No joke. Airiella's dad put in a lot of work on this tree. It's full of information, photos, and immigration dates in some cases. I haven't come across the Franklin guy's name yet, but he doesn't have a whole lot about the extended family here in some cases. Most likely, due to some of these smaller villages not keeping great records." Ronnie tapped on a map, "I think these would have been small villages or towns, and possibly quite poor."

"Okay. Maybe in that case we research back on this Franklin guy then and see if we can find a link back through him. Or a similar enough name in his own history that ties to one of these. We'll get there." Smitty clapped him on the back. "Good work, man."

"Thanks. Sadly, that means we are most likely right that Airiella is the intended target of this little subtle attempt. I don't like that. She hasn't done anything to deserve this." Ronnie smacked the desk in frustration.

"If it's Stone, we already know he is petty and childish. She showed him up during the interview and won the respect of the most powerful council members. It's no big jump to see how he'd create some sort of vendetta against her. He's a tool." Smitty had a point.

"Two more days until she's back here with us. We can try to gather as much as we can to present it to her." Ronnie sat back down. "I wish we could do more."

"Need a training break? Father Roarke is supposed to be here today with more blessed weapons, and he said Kalisha added a potion of some sort that we can dip said weapons in to make them more potent," Smitty told him.

"No, let's wait until he gets here. If I leave this computer now, I won't come back to it. My brain is taxed to the max. I didn't even mean to rhyme there." Ronnie thumped his head.

"Well, let me show you an old map I was able to find. There *was* another mine entrance other than that shaft that is covered. From old articles talking about it, they did try to bury it, and some explorers of the area stumbled on it. From their descriptions in the article, it sounds to be somewhere past this old foundation up the hill," Smitty showed one of the pictures Jax sent.

"We aren't going to try to find it in that mess, are we? That's all overgrown bushes and vines." Ronnie didn't even want to think about the hazards they could be walking into going into that.

"It's something we'd have to discuss with the whole team. I was more thinking we could use some of the equipment and investigate the general area. I'm not too excited about walking into a patch of poison ivy in the dark," Smitty twisted his face up.

"I don't want to walk into it in the daylight either," Ronnie commented. "This is a huge nightmare of an investigation for a live show. We'll be lucky if we don't fall down a cliff."

"Good thing she knows this area. I don't think they were expecting that or that she would take Jax there. We have a few tools under our belt walking into it at least. Even Taklishim was surprised she knew about it. I need to believe that works in our favor," Smitty punctuated his words with a fist in his hand.

"Any advantage we can get is a good thing. If we can find the link to this location, we can trace it back to what these guys are hoping will happen, what their motive is in this. That will be our biggest advantage walking into it." Ronnie's gut told him it had to do with Airiella. He needed to figure it out to help protect his angel.

Chapter Twenty-One

I'd stopped at the store and gotten some food to pack for our little beach trip and made us up salami sandwiches and grabbed snap peas and carrots as well. We had the cookies and pastries we'd gotten from the bakery, and I threw in some trail mix as well.

I dug out the wind tube chair I had; I called it the vagina chair. Filled up, it looked like a brightly colored vagina. I also found the beach sleeping bag and blankets that I didn't care if they got sandy. I grabbed some towels and extra clothes. If it rained on us, we could always put the seats down in the car and sleep there.

Garbage bags, toilet paper, lighters, and flashlights in waterproof bags were all set and ready to go. It was all way more than I usually took with me to the beach, but I was thinking of Jax and how he wasn't used to this the way I was. It wasn't as warm here as it was in California, or even close to what it's like in Wyoming where he lived.

When it was just me, I grabbed water, nuts, and a flashlight and my pack. Sometimes I brought the sleeping bag. Jax came back in from doing manly things like checking the oil in my car and tire pressure because I told him it took two hours to get there. I laughed, but if it made him feel better, he could do whatever he wanted.

We loaded up the car and headed out. My excitement grew the closer we got. "Tell me about this place again? The last time we were talking about it, you got distracted," he grinned at me.

"Right, distracted. I spent a lot of time on this beach when I grew up. It stretches for miles. My other grandpa used to like to tell people that as soon as I hit the beach, my clothes came flying off, there's a nice tidbit for you to think about."

Jax burst out laughing. "Oh, I'll definitely be thinking about that. What else?"

"When the tide goes out, there are usually tons of tide pools left. I used to play in them all the time. We'd walk for hours up and down the beach. It became a place of peace and only happy memories for me. The skies can be moody as small weather systems roll through, or they can be clear and blue. There's always a breeze, or flat out wind sometimes, tons of shells. Generally, pretty secluded. We may see a few people, not a lot, and all of them local," I filled him in.

"Your tone of voice when you talk about it is soothing."

"That's what this beach does to me. It's also where we spread my grandpa's ashes when he died. Now when I go there, I talk to him. I had a surreal experience once, after Michael," I tried to keep my tone even when I said his name.

"Which one is Michael?" Jax had an edge to his voice.

"The most recent ex. Anyway," I moved past Michael; I didn't want to talk about him. "I was upset and needed to rebalance my life, and I went there. I'd walked a couple of miles and turned to go back. I was just looking out to the waves, it had been breezy, but warm out. I started talking to my grandpa, and out of nowhere, I kept feeling like someone was watching me. Every time I turned around, there was no one around me. I kept going for a little bit, then felt like I needed to stop, so I did. The breeze died. Like, zero air movement. The sound disappeared, and the tide went out. Tide pools everywhere. I just knew he was with me. I broke down crying and started wading through the tide pools. It was perfect."

"You are extraordinary, siren. I can't wait to see it," Jax laced his fingers with mine.

"It's rare for me to bring people there, you are one of a very select few."

"I won't ruin it for you." He kissed the back of my hand. "I'm honored you are taking me there."

Quietly, I said, "I'd share anything with you, Jax." The intensity of the emotions he brought out in me rendered me silent for the rest of the ride. Once we got there and parked, I stood there and just breathed it in.

"Siren, this smell, it's you," he stood next to me. "Wow. This place is nothing like the beach in Cali we visited. This place is raw beauty. Like Mother Nature, herself is letting you into her backyard."

"I'm glad you like it. Tell no one, or I'll zap you," I kissed Jax's cheek and tore off my shoes and socks, throwing them in the car and handing Jax my keys. I beelined for the beach. I was home.

Jax didn't think he'd ever get enough of seeing her like this. With the way their bond worked he could feel exactly what this place felt like and meant to her. The wild beauty a draw she couldn't resist. The roar of the waves was deafening the closer he got to them, trailing after her.

He caught up to her as she was wading through a tide pool. She was murmuring, her words lost in the sound of the surf and breeze. Her face a picture of serenity as she connected to the earth, water, and air.

She pointed out jellyfish to him as they walked, picked up a few shells here and there. They saw seal pups playing, and she gave them a wide berth, so they didn't feel threatened. She fit here in a way Jax was starting to understand that was very important to her well-being.

In the hours they had been walking, they had only encountered one other person walking their dog. Jax was amazed at how secluded it was. There were signs of life everywhere, from the litter that she was picking up, to pieces of houses that had gotten washed out to sea.

Being here, Jax felt like he was seeing her for the first time. Her guard entirely down, at one with her surroundings. Her gentle nature was rivaling the beauty of the location. She called her house her safety zone, but it wasn't, not compared to this.

She took his hand and turned them back around. He almost felt bad that Ronnie wasn't here to see her like this. Skin pink and glowing, soft, serene smile, grounded in nature in a way Jax had never seen before. She felt whole here.

Maybe someday I'll bring Ronnie here. Like I told you earlier, it's very few I bring here. Very few, I will let see me here, he heard her say to him through the connection.

Why me?

You're different. You are just as much a part of me as this place is. This place is my grandpa's love for me, a place I have never felt bad about myself. I can be wholly me and this place accepts me. Her honest words shook something loose in him. Some fear he hadn't known he had been holding on to where it concerned her and how he felt about her. *I think you needed to be here just as much as I did.*

Jax felt a pull inside, and he gave into it. He pulled his shoes and socks off and let her lead him to the surf, the cold water washing over his feet as his toes sank into the sand. It was like he was wading in her, the energy so pure and fresh, dislodging more of that darkness inside him.

They came to a spot, and she stopped, the words of her story about her experience here coming back to him. Just like then, the air stopped moving, and the sun warmed his skin, the sound of the waves becoming distant. He heard the sound of her wings before he felt one of them behind him.

"Hi, Grandpa. I'd like you to meet Jax," the untarnished love in her voice washing over him. Water lapping at his toes, the receding tide depositing a perfect sand dollar in front of him. "He likes you," she told him, a beatific smile on her angelic face that tipped up to his.

"Angel eyes," Jax whispered and lost himself to that gaze as he kissed her. She wrapped her arms around him, and then her wings enfolded them both in their downy feathers. Jax felt the sand dollar bump across the top of his foot.

He broke the kiss and bent over to pick it up, washing the sand off in the water. "There's a religious story about sand dollars," Airiella told him as her wings disappeared. "It represents God and his love; some say, Jesus. This part here," she traced the star pattern, "the star of Bethlehem." She flipped his hand over, "the Christmas poinsettia. When you break it open, inside, you'll find five white doves to spread peace and love."

"Do I need to break it open?" Jax didn't want to. It was beautiful, pure white and perfect.

"No. Grandpa Jack was giving you a gift," she smiled.

"His name was Jack?" She nodded at him. He looked out to the waves. "Thank you, sir." Just like that the sound came back. "He's really here," Jax was in awe. It had been perhaps the most profound moment with a spirit he'd ever had. It meant even more to him that it was someone she loved.

"I think he wanted you to know he approves of you," she started walking again. "And he's happy we are here."

"Me too, siren." Jax held the sand dollar carefully and turned his head to the waves, whispering, "I'll take care of her."

Aedan hung up his phone, swearing loudly. "Mother fucker!"

Mags was at his side in an instant. "Uh, honey, you okay?"

Aedan threw his phone against the wall, smashing it, fury overtaking his mind. This second location was an attack on Airiella. Degataga confirmed it and was still working on the why. Someone wanted to hurt her and had uncovered the same information Ronnie had been working on tirelessly.

Mags had run out of the room and came running back in with Ronnie and Smitty. Smitty walked over to the phone and picked it up. "Care to explain?"

Ronnie stood back and assessed Aedan as he spoke, "That was Degataga."

"He pissed you off to the point of breaking your phone and cussing?" Smitty challenged him.

"No. What Degataga told me did. That Franklin location *is* an attack on Airiella. He hasn't figured out why yet, but that link you found Ronnie, is the thread to pull. One of the council members is behind this. Also, they are sending Asher to be a part of the shoot as someone who can talk to the dead. He could still be the one behind this, or part of it anyway," Aedan snarled, his voice dripping in disdain.

Aedan saw Ronnie cross his arms over his chest, and his eyes narrow. "Why not go after one of us?"

"Degataga said this would hurt her more. Fuck! I'm sick of feeling like a goddamn puppet!" Aedan needed something else to throw.

"Dude, relax, this isn't you," Smitty tried to calm him.

"Let's go." Ronnie didn't give him a chance to argue, just grabbed him in a vice grip, and pulled him out of the room. "You're scaring Mags. Knock this shit off."

Aedan fumed. "No. Fuck that, Ronnie. Know what else he told me?" Aedan yanked his arm out of Ronnie's grip. "Her ex-husband was at the reception where her wings and the demons made their presence known. He's trying to expose her through the station. To what end, I don't know."

"Gym. Now." Ronnie's cold tone penetrated Aedan's anger.

Somewhere behind him, he heard Smitty swear quietly and calm Mags. "I'm allowed to be pissed. You guys don't hold the rights to that."

"No, we don't, and yes, you can. But explosive violence in front of your pregnant wife, who has never seen you do that before, might not have been the best way to go about it," Ronnie growled.

Aedan sagged. "Why are they out to get her? Hasn't she been through enough?"

"More than enough, and we'll figure it out. Hit the damn bag until this shit is out of you." Ronnie laced the gloves on him.

"Why aren't you, out of all of us, more pissed off than you are?" Aedan snipped, getting in Ronnie's face.

"You think I'm not mad?" Ronnie's aggressive tone was a warning that Aedan heeded and backed off. "I'll find a way to destroy whoever is behind this and threatening her. Violence isn't the answer."

Somewhat mollified, Aedan took his anger out on the bag, logic creeping back in, and he was ashamed of how he acted in front of Mags. He started to plot out his thoughts, an action plan taking the place of the rage that took over.

Dripping sweat, he stopped and held the gloves up for Ronnie to unlace. "Sorry, bro."

"Never let me see you do that again. Even not directed at Mags, unrestrained violence like that is not the answer. I know you wouldn't hurt her, that isn't my beef. It's a gateway to behavior that *will* hurt her. Seeing you lose control hurts. I understand the emotions behind it, but there are better ways to go about it. Got it? If Jax had been here, he would have kicked your ass." Ronnie's eyes were hard.

"Got it. I'm aware it was wrong. I'll fix it with Mags. Thanks for the intervention," Aedan said remorsefully.

"Is your head in the right place now?" Ronnie hung the gloves up.

"Yeah," Aedan promised.

"Good. Figure out a way through this shit hole then.

I'm fucking sick of people trying to hurt her when all she does is love." Bare fisted Ronnie slammed a punch into the bag that sent it reeling.

"That's why I got mad," Aedan said quietly.

"I know. Now let's redirect the anger into something productive so we can help our angel."

"The more we uncover about this person, the less the shock will be to her, right? Also, Asher. If he is going to be there, he will be trying to channel this person. That's all I can think of as to why he would be there. Can we use Winnie? Also, since her dad has done a lot of work on that family tree, we might be able to tap him to looking through old family stuff that we wouldn't have access to online. Pictures and whatnot, or names of people we could talk to," Aedan spewed out the ideas that came to him.

"Take your necklace off and talk to her. You know she'll help however she can." Ronnie's quick stride gave away the emotions he was trying to suppress. "As for her dad, we need to run that through her. I don't think she told them of the danger aspect of all this."

"What do we do about the ex-husband?" Aedan hurried after him.

"We tell her. She knows the ass better than we do. If there's something we can do on this end, we help. We can't keep this from her; it involves her. If we go behind her back to pull some satisfying move that makes us feel better, it will hurt her," Ronnie bit out.

"Shit. I know. I really want to punch the ass, though." Aedan kicked at the ground.

"Oh, me too, bro. Me too."

Chapter Twenty-Two

Mags was pissed. "What the hell was that?" Mags paced around Smitty, rubbing her back to ease the sharp pain that stabbed at her.

"That, I believe, was Aedan finally snapping," Smitty said calmly.

"Smitty, he threw his phone! Against the wall!" Mags spun around. "Look at this! I'm supposed to be the crazy one, not him." She held out the mangled phone. "It's bad, isn't it? If he did this, it can't be good."

"Mags, slow down. This reaction could just be a culmination of everything catching up to him. He's in good hands with Ronnie. Why don't you and I go get him a new phone?"

"I can go, shouldn't you stay here, and I don't know, supervise? Ronnie looked pissed." Mags rubbed her back harder.

"No one goes out alone. We can go together. Ronnie is fine. Have you ever seen him beat the shit out of Jax for being an asshole?" Smitty asked her.

"No, though he probably should have." She slumped her shoulders. "I'm worried about him."

"Jax? Or Aedan?"

"Aedan. Jax, I'm always worried about him. But he's with Airy, and if he got out of hand, she'd be able to handle it. Aedan, on the other hand, represses all this inside him and tries to rationalize it out, and there is no rational explanation for any of this shit that's happened. He's always been the calm through the storm, and now he's the storm!" Mags blew up.

"Ronnie was right to haul him out of here. Come on, let's go get a phone. The change of scenery will do you a bit of good." She let Smitty lead her out. "I'll text Ronnie, so he knows we aren't here."

"What if he can't come to terms with this? What happens then?" Mags asked quietly.

"He will. Look at it from a different perspective. Maybe he needed to snap to get his head right. Think positive, Mags."

Mags was a little astonished that Smitty came to that conclusion before she did. "Wow. Airy has been good for you."

"She's good for all of us. Aedan will be fine," Smitty promised her.

"Ronnie really won't hit him, will he?" Mags knew Aedan could hold his own against Jax, Ronnie was a different story though.

"I can *guarantee* you that Ronnie didn't even glove up. He would have set Aedan loose on the bags. Ronnie will probably have some harsh words for him, but Ronnie didn't even hit back when Jax punched him. He hit the wall instead. There's nothing to worry about there. You *know* this."

"I know. Ronnie looked so furious at Aedan, though." Mags had felt fear when she saw the look on Ronnie's face.

"He *was* furious. Think about it. Think about what he went through with his mother. About the things that Airiella has told him about her past. Aedan will be fine," Smitty reasoned.

"What happens if Airy's ex-husband outs her to the world?" Mags couldn't get past that part.

"Who is going to believe an alcoholic ex-husband with a history of violence, trying to discredit his ex-wife at her family's funeral?" Smitty painted an elaborate picture.

"Well, when you put it like that, probably no one. You're pissed too, aren't you?" Mags noticed his tight jawline and heard the undertone of his voice.

"Sure as hell am. All we can do is cover our tracks and get to the bottom of this. Letting the anger take over won't help. Let's redirect it to fuel our need to figure it all out before it's too late." Smitty's grip on the steering wheel was making his fingers white.

"I understand. Thank God, you two are here. Jax would have lost his mind if he'd seen Aedan flip out like that." Mags felt another sharp pain in her back, making her wince and gasp.

"Mags? What's wrong?" Smitty looked at her; concern etched across his face.

"Sharp pain in my back. Feels like a hot knife jabbing through me." She adjusted the car seat to lean back a little. "I'll be fine."

"We aren't far from the hospital, I can swing by there, and we can get you checked," Smitty suggested.

"I'm fine. Let's just get the phone and get back. I have a doctor's appointment tomorrow." The back pain had been more frequent than she'd let on. She wasn't going to tell him that. It had prompted her to schedule the appointment before they'd left for the funeral.

"Are you sure?"

"Positive." She saw Smitty giving her a look from out the corner of her eye. "We had insurance on the phone, right?"

Smitty laughed. "Yeah, though I thought for sure it would be Jax or Ronnie that would have to use it before Aedan. They are hard on phones."

"Not as hard as this," she remarked sarcastically, holding the phone up.

We were sitting on the air tube chair that Jax had filled up, our bodies relaxed and intertwined. Jax had laid down first and draped his legs on either side of the chair, and I sat between his legs, then Jax wrapped them around me. We looked like a human pretzel.

We sat on the side of a sand dune to protect us from the wind, the waves not as loud since we were farther from them. The sun shone down on us, warming our skin, yet I was still a bit cold. I wasn't about to move.

"Damn stubborn woman," Jax growled good-naturedly. "You seem to forget; I can hear your thoughts."

He unwound himself from me and went back to the car, grabbing the bag of food, and the one with blankets. He was right, I did keep forgetting. We'd made up a fire pit earlier, found some fantastic dry wood to burn, and a bunch of dry grass to use as a fire starter.

He got a small little fire started, enough to throw off low heat, and we sat down next to it to eat. A ranger had driven upon us, and I wondered if there was a fire ban. "Just wanted to make sure it wasn't an unattended fire," he'd said when he spotted us. "Also, to remind people to stay away from the pups on the beach."

"Thank you," I said kindly.

He did a double-take at Jax. "You're the guy from Shadow Seekers!" Oh, he was a fan. "It's one of my favorite shows. You must be Airiella, I heard you on the radio, great interview by the way."

He shook Jax's hand and stared at me curiously. Jax offered an autograph, and the ranger went back to his truck to grab something for Jax to sign. He came back with a ticket book, and I choked back a laugh. "Don't fill this out after I sign it," Jax joked. "What's your name?"

"Ben," the ranger told us. He tilted his head, looking at me again. "It *is* you in that picture he posted."

Jax stiffened. *It's okay;* I sent him. *It's a different pace of life out here.*

I looked over at what Jax had written. 'Ben, thanks for being a fan. It's people like you who help make the world a better place. Jax.'

Ben took the autograph and read it, blushing faintly. "How am I helping the world?"

Jax gestured around him. "You keep this safe and alive. Also, you are going to keep our secret, right?"

"Oh. Yeah. No worries, man. Your personal life is your business. I hope it's okay if I say that the picture you posted was amazing. How did you come to be here? This beach is kind of an out of the way place."

"I grew up spending summers here," I told Ben. "My family used to own that little corner store."

"That's why I recognize you!" Ben said excitedly. "When you and your family were here spreading ashes on the ground, I was patrolling the beach. I gave someone in your group a ticket for doing donuts on the beach."

I flashed back in my mind to the day. "Oh yeah, I remember that happening. I'm sorry that I didn't recognize you."

"Why would you? We'd only met that one time." Ben smiled. "I remember you, though. Your hair was shorter than it is now. You were standing off away from everyone else in the water, trailing some ashes. The sight always stuck in my memory; you looked so sad I wanted to hug you. Yet there was this fiery glow about you that set you apart from the rest of them."

"It was an interesting day. I was pretty irritated with my cousins and happy you had ticketed them. I was the only willing to walk into the water to spread ashes; that upset me too. My uncle had told me that what we were doing was illegal. He also told me that you wouldn't stop me," I remembered.

"No. I was captivated by the picture you presented to me. I think when I saw the picture of you Jax posted, it reminded me of that. I wouldn't have matched the face since you can't see it in the photo, but your hair gives it away. The sunlight through it makes it this red color. I've not seen a color like it since that day on the beach, and his picture, until now. That's what made it click for me," Ben snapped his fingers.

"Small world," Jax muttered.

Ben sat down and openly stared at me, causing Jax to shift closer to me. "Can I ask why you don't want people to know about you two?"

Jax cleared his throat. "I don't care if the world knows. She's private, though."

Ben shifted his glance to Jax. "You're protecting her, then?"

"As much as I can," Jax looked at me, his voice so full of love.

"So, what brings you out here today?" Ben looked back at me.

"Much like the last time you saw me, a death in the family. The time you mentioned, it was my grandpa's ashes we were spreading, the one who brought me here all the time. Today I'm here healing from the death of my other grandpa," I choked up a little.

"I'm so sorry. Are you guys staying the night here?" He asked both of us but was looking at me, and I could tell Jax was getting uncomfortable.

"Most likely," I admitted.

"The orange car back there yours?" He gestured back to the road.

"Yes. Do I need to move it?"

"No, it's fine. I'm on patrol tonight. That way, if I come back this way, I'll know who's it is and not to try and look for you both. You might get a few locals down here for the sunset, otherwise, it should be quiet for you. Here's my card," he handed it to Jax. "If someone bothers you, just give me a call. It was nice meeting you both. I promise your secret is safe with me."

"Here," Jax held out his hand, "give me your phone, she'll take a picture of us. I don't care if you post it or tag me, just leave her out of it."

Ben handed me his phone, and I took a picture of them both, handing it back. "Is it the press that's after you?"

I nodded. "And jealous female fans of the team."

"Ah," he looked back at Jax. "I get it. For what it's

worth, I think it's great you are protecting her from that." He looked at me again, then back at Jax. "She's special, I think. There's something about her."

Jax sat behind me and wrapped his arms around me possessively. "Damn right, there is."

Ben smiled genuinely. "Thanks again. Watch the tides, they come pretty far up here, and have a great night." Ben walked off, and we heard the truck drive away.

"That was nice of you to take a picture with him," I leaned against him.

"I'd rather have him on our side than stalking us," Jax said into my ear. "You bewitch people everywhere you go."

I laughed. "I think Ben was smitten with you, not me."

"Oh siren, he remembered you spreading ashes. I may have given him the opening to talk to us since he recognized me, make no mistake though, you are what kept him here."

"He wasn't a bad guy. He won't stalk us," I replied.

"That's why I suggested a picture. People will still draw the conclusion that I am here with you, but they already knew that from that interview. Besides, I don't think he will tag me. He doesn't strike me as that type."

I fed some more wood into the fire, letting the heat seep into my hands before I pulled them back. "Is my hair that recognizable?"

"For people trying to figure out who you are? Absolutely. He was spot on with that. When the sun hits your hair, it's a totally different color. With me, it's just brown. With Winnie, it was red. It was always red. With you, when you appeared on camera for that live show, it was dark. So people watching that will see someone with dark hair. In that picture I posted, the sun was shining right on you, your hair was glowing a coppery red, the wind had caught it and was blowing these curls all around. It's distinctive. If that's how it was the day he saw you here, I can see why it would stick out in his memory," Jax ran his hands through the ends of my hair.

"That why you were so insistent on me wearing it up for that interview," I commented.

"Yes. You can see the color tones in artificial light, too. I wanted it up, so it only showed as dark, and so Forrest couldn't see the curls or how long it was. Your eyes are like that too. From a distance they look like this milk chocolate color, then when you get closer you can see the lighter tones. And when the sunlight hits your eyes, they make me think of sunsets. Even your wings are a contrast of light and dark." He brushed the hair from my face. "You know I'm not afraid to tell the world I'm with you, right?" He grabbed my hips and turned me.

"Yes, I know. I never thought you were."

"I do hate all the speculation about my private life, and if I can keep that from touching you, I will. There's a large part of me that wants to shout it to the world, that you're mine. It's not fair to Ronnie for me to do that, though," Jax gave a soft and sad smile.

I pushed myself to my feet and spread out one of the blankets on the sand and deflated the air chair enough to make it a pillow and stretched out on it, patting next to me. "Join me."

He crawled up next to me as a large flock of seagulls flew overhead. "I hope we don't get shit on," he mumbled.

I giggled as I slid my cold hands up under his shirt, and he grimaced. "What's better, cold hands, or bird shit?"

"As long as they are your cold hands, I'm fine with it. Bird shit, that might be a mood killer," he smiled down at me. "Siren, we are still very much in broad daylight and a public place," he kissed me. "You might want to be careful where you put those hands."

"Raven," I called out softly. "Can you stand watch, let us know if we aren't alone?" I saw her settle on the top of the sand dune. "Problem solved. Do I need to be careful where I put my mouth?" I asked Jax, letting my dirty thoughts speak for me. He was rock hard under my hand.

I watched his eyes darken. "Do I get to return the favor?" he growled, crushing his lips on mine in a bruising kiss.

"What if I say no?" I teased him, stroking slowly.

"You would deny me?" he slipped a finger down the front of my pants, dragging it along the most sensitive places, pulling it out and licking it clean.

"Fuck, that was hot, Jax," I moaned.

"Will you come for me?" He tugged my pants down and settled his mouth over me, licking into me, my hips arching up into him.

"God," I moaned. "Wait, how did this go so far off track?" I panted.

"I'm selfish. I wanted to go fist," Jax flicked his tongue fast and curled a finger inside me.

He didn't stop after the first orgasm crashed through me, until he wrung another one even more intense out of me, my voice calling out his name. He gave me a satisfied smile as he came back up. "We'll see if that smirk is still there when I get done with you," I whispered as he nuzzled my neck.

I took my time, bringing him close and taking him back down. I pulled out all the tricks I had until he was begging me, and then it gave it my all. His hoarse cries lost in the breeze as he bucked under my mouth and hands, losing control and coming in wild spurts as I coaxed every last drop out of him.

"God, I love you," he panted and hauled me up his chest and buried his face in my hair. "I don't know how you do that."

"I got skills," I said as I grabbed another blanket and settled it over us. "Keep us safe, Raven, and don't let me miss the sunset." I nestled into Jax's arms as we took a nap to the sound of the waves.

Chapter Twenty-Three

Ronnie looked up at the sound of Smitty's voice, "Did you text him?" Smitty asked as he came back from getting Aedan a new phone.

"Yeah. I don't think Jax will respond. Not sure if they even have a signal. I hope he doesn't. She needs one quiet day. One day where the world isn't out to try and take her down because of what she is." The anger still simmered in Ronnie, just under the surface.

"Aedan, okay now?" Smitty's tone was careful with that question.

"I don't know about okay; he's focused on finding answers."

"Mags was worried," Smitty hedged. "I told her you wouldn't hit him."

"She should know better. So should you. I wouldn't hit any of you." He needed to move, though. He had the itch for a fight. The sun would be setting soon; maybe he could find a circuit fight to jump in. The last gym visit flashed through his mind. Nix that, bad idea.

"Need a run?" Smitty guessed.

"Fuck. Yes. Badly." Ronnie dropped and started stretching.

"Give me a minute to change," Smitty jogged off, and Ronnie kept stretching, so his arms kept busy.

Smitty came back down and did a few light stretches with him, and they took off. Ronnie set a brutal pace trying to run the anger out of him. Thoughts of Airiella's ex-husband running through his mind, along with opinions of the traitorous members of the council that wanted to hurt her. Harder and harder, he pushed himself.

He heard Smitty's harsh breathing, his own heart thundering in his ears. Every sacrifice she'd made haunted him; every time she'd saved them, dying for them; each person that tried to hurt her while they couldn't do anything to stop it from happening. The love she had for them pushed him over the edge, and he hit his breaking point.

He collapsed on the grass that ran alongside the road they were on, body heaving, retching. Pain tearing through his muscles as they cramped up. He was vaguely aware at some point that Smitty was coming up to him, but the tears in his eyes and ringing in his ears prevented him from seeing or hearing anything.

Smitty must have called Aedan to come to get them because he was lifted between them and put in the car. *You better be okay, Heracles,* she said in his head.

Stop worrying about me, he told her. *Take care of yourself.*

I'll never stop worrying about you. I'll leave you be for right now, but you aren't off the hook. We'll be talking. I love you. Ronnie felt it, the love pouring across the connection, and he broke down in tears.

I love you too, angel.

"Jesus. It has got to be this separation that's doing this to us," Aedan said from the driver's seat.

"I'm fine," Ronnie choked out. "Just drive."

"Dude, that's not fine. You just sprinted six and a half miles. Balls to the wall sprint. I was a full thirty minutes behind you," Smitty looked back at him. "No water to hydrate either. What the fuck were you thinking?"

"I couldn't escape my thoughts. All this shit, all

Airiella's done for us while we have done nothing."

"I don't think she sees it the same way," Smitty said gently. "You need an Epsom salt bath and a whole lot of liquids. Come on."

Ronnie let Smitty help him out, his leg muscles painfully cramping with each step. Aedan ran ahead to have Mags start a bath for him while Smitty carefully got him up the stairs. "Sorry, dude, but I'm not bathing you," he tried to joke lightly.

He did help him get undressed and into the tub, though, and brought him three sports drinks. "Thanks, man."

Smitty sat outside the bathroom. "Aedan may be on to something with the separation thing. It's pushing all of us to the edge. That wasn't your smartest move, the run. You got on my case for not talking to you about it, why didn't you talk to me?"

"I don't know. I'm just trying to hold it together. Be strong like Airiella is," Ronnie groaned and sucked down a drink.

"We aren't her. She needs us to be us." Smitty's reminder hit him.

"Fuck. I know. It's the longest I've been away from Jax too. It's fucking me up. I know he's fine, she would have told me if he wasn't. I can't explain it. Seeing Aedan lose it like that brought it all home to me. I'm sorry." He truly meant it too.

"You'll be really sorry if your ass ends up not being able to move because of this. How do you think Airiella would react to that?"

"Damn. Enough. I get it. I know I fucked up." Ronnie cringed as another cramp tore through his legs. "It was either run or find a fight. If I would have fought, I don't know that I would have been able to stop. I'd rather hurt me than someone else, scratch that. I want to hurt her ex-husband," he grumbled.

"I think that is a unanimous feeling there," Smitty chimed in.

"Did Mags use Airiella's bath salts?" Ronnie asked,

the scent finally breaking through his pain and filling his nose.

Ronnie heard Smitty's muffled laughter. "She sure did. She thought it would calm you down."

"I smell like a girl," Ronnie smiled. "Don't you dare tell her it worked!"

"Too late! You giant pain in the ass!" Mags called from Airiella's bedroom. "That's what you get for being a bonehead."

"Thank you, Mags," Ronnie said weakly.

"It will serve you right if Smitty sneaks in in the middle of the night to cuddle you because he smells Airy." She retorted hotly. "Am I the only sane one in this house?"

"Sane?" Ronnie snorted.

"Wrong answer, dude," Smitty laughed.

"Sorry, Mags." Ronnie tried to hide the smile that crept into his voice.

Smitty tossed him a washcloth, "Better cover-up, here she comes."

Ronnie barely got the washcloth over his junk as she stormed into the bathroom. "What do you think it does to me to see them practically carrying you in here? You are supposed to be calm," she shrieked. "That way, when the rest of us freak out, we don't kill each other!"

"Hey!" Smitty called out. "I'm right here! I haven't freaked out."

"Really?" She spun around to face him. "You let that happen!" she pointed to Ronnie.

"Fine. My freak out wasn't as bad as theirs was. And *you* try to stop Ronnie. He's a damn brick wall," Smitty whined.

"I get it, Mags. I'm sorry," Ronnie said contritely.

"It's just a couple more days," her anger deflated. "Can we hold on for a couple more days? It's not even a full two days."

"Yes," Smitty and Ronnie answered at the same time.

"By the way, Ronnie, you look good naked." She grinned wickedly at him and left the bathroom.

Smitty howled with laughter. "Oh, to have a photo of the expression on your face right now."

"Fucker. Go get me some ibuprofen." Ronnie threw the wet washcloth at him, chuckling as it smacked him in the face.

"Notice Aedan was the only smart one and stayed away from the hormonal pregnant angry lady?" Smitty stood, throwing the washcloth back at him. "You smell pretty."

"Ass." Ronnie smiled as Smitty went to get him another drink and ibuprofen. He couldn't help but think that Airiella would have been just as pissed as Mags was, but she would have laughed at the bath salts. Perfectly evil of Mags.

Jax woke to the sound of the raven cawing at them. It was still daylight; they couldn't have been asleep long. He checked his watch, just over an hour. He couldn't talk to the raven like Airiella could, so he wasn't sure why it was cawing. He looked at the bird, "What is it?"

She cocked her head sideways and flew down and landed on Airiella. It unnerved him the way the bird was looking at him. He shifted sideways to look at Airiella and found her ice cold. "Airiella," he shook her a little, trying to wake her. "Siren? Talk to me, baby."

He shot a look at the bird, "Do something. What's wrong with Airiella?" The bird flew back up to the top of the dune and returned to its watch over them. Jax could see Airiella was breathing. That didn't tell him why she was ice cold and non-responsive, though.

Damn it! What the hell was happening. He pressed his lips to her forehead. "Come back to me, siren." The raven bobbed its head and cawed at him again. Was the bird telling him yes? "Kiss her?" he asked the bird, feeling like a total whack job. She bobbed her head at him again.

He kissed Airiella, their connection sparking to life and buzzing between them, he pulled back and looked at the connection between them, seeing it faded. Panic set in.

"No. Siren, listen to me, wherever you are, come back." He kissed her again, pouring his love into it, and saw that flare of light that let him know she was still with him.

"Wake up, baby. Please wake up." He touched the connection with his fingers, stroking it, and he felt her move. "That's it, siren. Come back to me," he kissed her again, wrapping his arms around her, hating the feel of her unresponsive skin against him. "Please, Airiella."

"Jax?" he heard her whisper.

"Oh, fuck. Thank God!" he crushed his lips to hers and fought back the tears as she responded to his touch.

"What's the matter?" she asked sleepily.

"Where were you? What happened? Why are you so cold?" Jax fired off questions between kisses.

"What do you mean?" she looked confused. "Not that I mind waking up to you kissing me, you're just throwing off frantic energy right now."

Jax rested his forehead on her. "You were totally unresponsive and ice-cold like a deathly cold. The connection we had was dim, not bright like it usually is. The raven woke me up."

"Dream," she said warily. "I was dreaming and talking to someone. I can't remember. I felt a shock, and then you were kissing me."

"What new fresh level of hell is this now?" Jax was worried.

"Let's not think about it," she begged him.

"I don't think it's a good idea to ignore it. The raven woke me up. I don't think she would have done that if it wasn't important," Jax insisted.

"I know, you're right." She sat up and wrapped her arms around her legs. "I'm going to go back to the water for a bit. Can I try something?"

"Try what? I'll come with you." Jax sat up.

"No, I want you to stay here with our stuff. Can I pull a small bit of that energy from you and see if I can use the saltwater to get rid of it?"

Jax froze, fear taking over. "Isn't that how you died?" he asked her quietly.

"Hear me out." She held up her hand, and he took it, holding it tighter than he meant to. "That was when I pulled a large amount. The only way to test if saltwater works is to try it. I'd only pull a little."

"I won't agree to it unless I come with you. I'll put all the stuff back in the car." Jax's heart was hammering at his chest, and fear was trying to make him irrational. "Non-negotiable, Ells. The tide is still far enough out that if something happened, it would take too long for me to get to you."

"Did the saltwater hurt you?" she scooted closer to him.

"No. It didn't hurt."

"Jax, I don't know that I want you to see it," she was honest with him. "I don't know what it will do to me or if it will even work."

"I'm not moving on this. If you are going to do this, then we do it together. I know I usually let you do what you think is best, I can't agree on this, though. Every instinct in me is telling me to be there," Jax pushed.

"Were you dreaming when the raven woke you?"

"What? No. I don't think so. Why?" her switch in topic threw him off.

"I think it was the energy in you that was talking to me. That's why I want to try this. If I can get a little more out of you safely, it weakens it more," Airiella rationalized.

"Even more reason you aren't doing it alone. I'm serious, Ells. I might not like what happens, but I'd rather deal with that than something else happening and me not getting to you in time. You could pass out and drown. Be reasonable," Jax argued.

"Okay," she agreed quietly. "Let's clean this up, and you need to work on finding calm in yourself."

"There isn't anything calming about this. What made you come to this conclusion?" Jax stood, his hands shaking as he picked up the blankets and shook them out. He was trying to tamp down the anger that was growing.

"It's one of the possibilities I've discussed with Father Roarke and Taklishim. Other than holy water as a solution to get it out of me. Also, that feeling of cold I've been having is the same sensation inside you when I have to feel for that energy. It's this icy cold, oily feeling. And when I was asking the raven where I was when you woke me, she showed me darkness. It's a jump, I admit, but we are here. I might as well test it."

"I don't like this," Jax folded the blankets up and looked at her. "I'm terrified of losing you."

"I know. But out of every beach in the world, here is the safest place for me to test the theory. My grandpa is here. The sooner we can get this out of you, the less of a target you will be. I don't want to lose you either, Jax." Those big angel eyes gazed into his.

"This sucks." Jax closed the distance between them and dipped his head down to kiss the fear out of him. He felt the calm she brought him flooding through him as he deepened the kiss, their tongues dancing erotically.

"I love you," she whispered into him.

J ax clutched my hand so tight I thought the bones were going to crack. I didn't ask him to ease up. The closer we got to the water, the tighter the grip. "Hey, wait." I stopped and pulled my hand away, trying not to shake circulation back into it.

I reached into my pocket and pulled out a vial of holy water I'd grabbed from my purse. "This is as a last resort. If the saltwater doesn't work, I'll need to drink this." I handed it to him. He slid it into the pocket of his hoodie, where it wasn't in danger of being crushed. His face a controlled mask that looked about to crack.

I sat down in the cold surf, letting it wash over my feet and legs. Jax didn't sit but stood next to me, the water washing around his shins. I reached out for the much smaller strand of that energy that was in him and found it so much easier to pull than previous times.

So much more comfortable that I almost pulled too much and had to force myself to let go. The intensity of the energy was no less potent inside me, and I fought hard against nausea that cramped my stomach violently. Jax moaned painfully next to me and was breathing hard, his eyes glued to me.

The energy fought me hard. I couldn't hold in the cries of pain as it tried to break me apart from the inside. I refused to give in and reached for the earth's energy around me, and my senses told me it wasn't enough. "Raven, help me," I whispered. "Grandpa," my whisper broke as I felt my shoulder separate again.

"Get it out, baby!" Jax cried.

I closed my eyes, and the raven was showing me the ocean. "More," I told her. "I'm in the water." I didn't understand what she wanted me to do, and I was about to blackout. I searched out all the energy around me, and then I realized. I needed to pull energy from the ocean.

I didn't have much time because I really didn't want to die in front of Jax at my favorite place in the world. That would most assuredly ruin his memory of here. I reached for the water's energy as a wave of excruciating pain slammed into me, and I didn't even try to rein in the scream that ripped from my lungs. I grabbed the energy and pulled it hard, telling the earth and water to take it from me and cleanse it.

I imagined it leaving my body, the ocean purifying it, and returning the energy to the earth to feed life and continue the cycle. That dark energy contained a violent rage that unleashed the wings from my back in a rush, and thunder rolled through the sky.

"Fuck, get out of the water, Jax," I tried to scream at him, but my voice was a harsh whisper.

"Not without you, siren," he gripped my arms and hauled me to my feet, wrenching another scream of agony out of me as my shoulder moved. My stomach heaved, and I pushed the energy out of me, pulling in the clean energy to offset it. "Love wins, baby. I love you," Jax kissed me gently.

I refused to lose this battle. I called the lightning into me, allowing it to run through my veins and burn it out of me while the good energy ran through me in a loop. "Kill it," I told the lightning as a searing hot pain tore through my body with the force of an exploding bomb.

Jax stumbled back as the energy blast lit me up, and the moment the dark energy was out of me, I dropped hard, landing on my knees. The air around me stilled, and I felt my grandpa's arms around me, then Jax's as he lifted me by my waist to avoid hurting my shoulder more.

I let him support me as I lifted my arm to pop my shoulder back in place with a sickening crack. "No more. You are not doing that again," he tipped my head, tears streaming from his eyes.

"I'll do what it takes to save you," I whispered, my voice still cracking. "Besides, I didn't die."

He led me out of the water, the air around us warm and still, and I knew my grandpa was still with us. "Airiella, that isn't worth it," Jax's tender touch was warm on my cheek.

I wrapped my wings around us, not caring at all if anyone saw me or not. "Jax, you don't get to decide what's worth it or not. I'm here for exactly this reason, bound to you, with or without this connection or a blood bond. I'm in love with you because of you. In my eyes, that makes everything I've been through worth it. This experience taught me that I could beat this without holy water. It might just take longer. I didn't die; this was a success."

He sobbed into my hair, "It hurts you."

"Yes, it does. What about my life hasn't hurt me, though? Saving you from this gives me a chance at a future with you. I'll die as many times as it takes for that. Don't you dare think for one second you aren't worth that to me. Nothing worthwhile is ever easy."

"I don't deserve you," his raspy words hurt.

"Please don't say that. It's not true. It's also one of those things you don't get to decide. I choose that. I choose you. Hearing you say that hurts me," I cried.

"There is no one on this earth that deserves you, siren. I wasn't insulting myself, at least that wasn't my intention. How much worse does it get than what I just saw?" he still hadn't lifted his head from my shoulder.

"That's a better question for Ronnie. From my standpoint, the pain of last time was about a thousand times worse than what you saw. Plus, well, I die," I pointed out the most significant difference.

"You going through that is not ever going to be okay with me. I know it's not for me to choose, but you argue with me all the time. This is just me arguing back for the sake of argument, I guess." He trembled around me. "Your wings smell like jasmine." He pulled back to look at me. "Also, you lost a feather, and I'm going to keep it."

"Okay, just that one. Any more and my wings will go bald. No one wants an angel with bald wings," I said with a smile. "I know you aren't okay with that," I ran my fingers over his cheek, and another tremor ran through him. "Neither is Smitty and Ronnie. We all want to save you, and look at the bright side; you got an angel feather out of it. I hear angels are pretty rare."

A weak laugh bubbled through his lips. "There are no words for you and your twisted sense of humor. Holy fuck, I love you."

The air around us started to move again. "I think you had my grandpa worried." Sounds were filtering back in, and I unwound my wings from around us to the sight of an astonished ranger Ben. "Shit," I mumbled.

Jax hadn't let go of me yet. "What?"

"We have company," I looked behind him.

He rested his forehead on mine. "Will we ever get a break?"

"Once this shit is out of you, yes, we will. I will use all my angel powers to make it happen," I promised with a whisper.

Jax turned. "Hello, Ben."

Ben's mouth moved, but no words came out. I gave my brain a second to catch up and make my wings disappear, which apparently, didn't help his speechless moment. Jax snorted. I elbowed him and stepped toward Ben, and he reeled backward.

That halted me. I didn't want Ben to be afraid of me. Jax wasn't happy about it either. "Look, Ben, can we go sit down? You can follow us and try to find your words, but I need to get my girl warm and dry. We are no threat to you."

An errant thought popped in my head. "Shit. The guys can usually feel when that energy is in me. I bet you they are freaking out right about now. I don't have a cell signal either. We may need to head to town until we can get a signal and call them."

"Oh, I can guarantee you they felt that. That sucked sweaty, hairy, gorilla balls." Jax glanced behind him to see Ben trailing a few feet behind us.

"That was a great visual," I rolled my eyes.

"I have a hotspot in my truck. You can use my phone," Ben finally found his words.

"Thank you, Ben. Jax, you want to call? I'll, uh, talk to Ben here." Jax settled me down on a log and fed some more wood on the fire to restoke the flame.

"Let me go get the blankets, hang on." He jogged back to the car and came back with the blankets, the food, and the sleeping bag.

"I'm fine. Go call Ronnie before he sends out a search and rescue helicopter," I gave him a little push. Ben silently held out his phone, and Jax went to sit in the truck and make the call.

"I'm sure there's a logical explanation," Ben shook his head.

"You'd be wrong. There's nothing logical about my life, Ben. I can tell you the truth and hope like hell you will respect my privacy and keep my secret, or I can offer to erase your memory of everything you saw."

"Truth. Where did the wings go? Were they real?" Ben's tongue seemed to be working quite well now.

"I don't know where they go, but yes, they are real. In basic words, I'm an angel. I'm here to restore the balance of good and evil. Sounds like the plot of every book, right?" I gave him a crooked smile.

"I have no idea if you are joking or not," he said gravely.

"Dead serious." I focused until my wings

reappeared, and his eyes bugged out. "Go ahead, touch them," I offered, bracing myself for the touch.

He reached a finger out and brushed a fingertip over the closest feather. "Oh, jeez. That's a real feather." He looked a little pale.

"You okay, Ben? Sure you don't want to take door number two?" I suggested and made the wings disappear. "I won't be offended."

"An angel?" He stuttered.

"In Native American culture, they call me a raven. Different cultures call me different things. I just found out myself not too long ago. It was quite the mind fuck."

"What was that out there?" Ben pointed behind him like it was still playing out.

"How much did you see? Wait, scratch that. Never mind, that doesn't matter. What you saw was me releasing dark energy back out after pulling it. That's where the empath part of me comes in. I can give and take emotions. When I take the bad ones, if I don't release them back out, they will take over me. Imagine bad energy with the angel stuff. Not good, right?"

"You'd be the devil?" I laughed. Oh, oops. He was serious.

"No, I don't think that would happen. But the wrong side would have a whole lot more power than they do now."

"Doesn't letting that bad energy go just put it back out there to stay?" Definitely a fan of the paranormal then, Ben was.

"Also, part of the empath thing, or maybe it's an angel thing, I don't know. When it cycles through me back into the earth, the pure energy of the earth cleanses it of the bad. In this case, the ocean, the saltwater purified the bad energy before it dissipates. I don't know the science behind it. Hell, I don't even know if there is science behind it."

"This sounds farfetched," Ben showed some skepticism.

"I know. I felt the same way. Allow me to demonstrate. Pay close attention to the emotions you have right now," I told him. I felt around and pulled his fear; he didn't need that. I then took it and fed back my own energy into his curiosity and excitement.

"Wow!" His enthusiasm now was a little much, but I'd rather have that than the fear.

"Keep watching. That fear I took from you? I'm going to release it. Fear isn't bad, so you won't see me glowing or anything." I grabbed the earth's energy and asked it to wash the fear from me, a small little tornado appearing in front of me, and then whoosh, it was gone. I sent out a thank you, adding in thanks for the other part I forgot to do.

Jax walked back up in time to hear Ben exclaim, "Holy moly!"

I tried to hide my smile because I didn't want to laugh at Ben. Jax stood me up, "Ben turn around, please. These wet clothes need to come off her, so she doesn't freeze." He pulled out my dry clothes and waited while I stripped off the wet ones, then dressed me, wrapped me burrito-style in a blanket, and sat me down in front of him.

"Okay, Ben, you can turn around," I said with a smile.

"Man, I totally get your need to keep her protected and private. Now I know why you fascinated me so much the last time I saw you," Ben was almost vibrating with excitement.

I pulled his fear and replaced it with curiosity and excitement; they were the easiest ones, I explained to Jax through the connection.

Jax coughed a little to hide his laugh. "You gonna keep our secret, Ben?"

"Totally! I always knew paranormal stuff existed. I never dreamed I'd meet a real angel. Today is the best day ever!"

"Not something I ever thought I would come across either, man," Jax smiled.

"Thank you for understanding, Ben. It means a lot to me," I shook his hand.

He looked abashed. "I appreciate the trust, ma'am," he said.

"No, don't call me ma'am. That makes me feel old. Call me, Airy. That's what friends call me."

"Airy. I have a friend that's an angel, and I met the star of my favorite show! Today just can't get any better," Ben crowed with delight.

I ducked my head to keep from laughing. He was over the top excited. Jax cleared his throat. "In all honesty, man, thank you. I'd do anything to keep her safe."

"Me too! Oh! Hey! I'm going to go pick up some teriyaki for dinner, can I bring you guys some?"

"Sure. Food would be good," I agreed. I considered calming Ben down, but he looked so damn happy that I couldn't make myself do it.

"I'll be back in ten minutes." He took off running.

"Well...that just happened," I replied, doing my best not to crack up laughing.

"Wow, siren. How much excitement did you give the poor guy?" Jax rolled his eyes.

"Not *that* much. I think that's just Ben. It's kind of cute, and he got to meet you, and an angel, and we get dinner out of it!"

"Cute, huh?" he growled.

"Jax, there is nothing cute about you," I turned a little to see him. "You are sharp edges, dripping in raw sexuality and sensual lines. Heat and silk. Fire and ice. Cute is a puppy dog."

"Have you ever had sex on the beach?" his hot breath fanned across my ear.

"The drink? Or what we did earlier?" I teased.

"What we did earlier was an appetizer," he promised.

"For the record, no. I've never had sex on the beach, nor have I ever done anything on this beach. You will be the first."

"I'll be the only," he revised.

"What did Ronnie say?" I changed the subject before I jumped him then. Ben didn't need to walk up on that too.

"Yeah, they felt it, and they freaked the fuck out.

Don't be surprised if Ronnie or Smitty chain you up somewhere when we get back," Jax said with a snort.

"I'm not a fan of chains," I told him drily.

He swore. "Sorry, siren. That's not what I meant."

"I know. Don't worry so much. Look, Ben's back with food." Now I rolled my eyes as he ran back up to us.

Chapter Twenty-Four

Mags was ready to punch Ronnie. "Fists up, keep them up, Mags. Jab!" Ronnie called out.

"I'm going to jab you if you keep yelling at me!" she snarled at him.

"You wanted to get some aggression out. Boxing was your idea." Ronnie said smartly.

"I know!" Mags stopped and rubbed her back again. "I'm done. I'm sorry. Today has just sucked."

"She's okay. Jax promised she was fine," Ronnie softened.

Mags threw a glove at Ronnie. "Don't use logic with me right now!"

"Sorry, Mags," he ducked before the glove hit him.

"Ronnie, I'm scared something is wrong with the babies," Mags blurted out.

"What? Why?" he dropped all attitude and focused on her entirely.

"My back keeps getting sharp pains. I have an appointment with the doctor tomorrow, but I'm scared to tell Aedan." She walked over to him.

"You thought telling me was better? *I'm* the emotional one!" Ronnie practically shouted.

"No. But the words came out before I could stop them," Mags replied hotly. "That shit that hit us earlier scared the life out of me. It felt like Airiella was dying. Did you tell Jax about the ex-husband and possible family connection and all that other shit?"

"No, that stuff can wait. Yeah, the shit earlier almost tipped me over the edge, too. Maybe you are worrying about nothing. It could just be stress," Ronnie guessed.

"Could be. I'd rather be safe and get it checked out." She fidgeted with the gloves.

"What else? You never want to train at fighting," Ronnie pressed her for answers.

"If something happens to her, what will happen to Jax?"

"Don't even go there. Power of positive thinking, let's practice that," he said immediately.

"Ronnie, you can't tell me you've not thought about it," Mags got quiet. "I've had bad dreams lately."

"Me too. I think it's the separation, coupled with all the shit that's been raining down on us. It could just be crazy pregnant lady hormones with you. Don't pregnant ladies get wild dreams?"

"Yeah. I did read that somewhere. What the hell was she thinking, pulling that energy from Jax?" Mags threw the other glove against the wall. "Damn reckless if you ask me."

"It was legitimate reasoning on her part, and I hate to admit that because I agree with you."

"What would have happened to Jax if he saw what you saw happen? That shit in him could have taken over." Mags had angry tears rolling down her face. "I just want my family all back together and safe."

"I know. We all want the same thing. Hang tight. They'll be here soon."

"Yeah, and I still won't get to see her because you and Smitty are going to be hogging her!" Mags sighed. "Okay, I may have a little hormonal situation going on. I'm driving myself crazy."

Ronnie laughed. "You're excused. Want me to help

you make dinner Tuesday?"

"Now, you're crazy. You don't cook. Not well, anyway." Mags leaned against him. "You smell pretty."

"That was a brilliantly evil little plan on your part," Ronnie laughed. "I'm not ever going to live that one down. Smitty will be reminding me of this for years."

She stood. "Yep. I'm good like that."

"Just wait. I'll teach your kids plenty of practical jokes to pull on you."

"And I will feed them full of sugar and dump them with you while I go away for a weekend." She gave him a wicked smile.

Ronnie put his hands up in surrender. "I give up."

"Thought so. Thanks for the cool down." She waited until he stood. "Now be a gentleman and carry me back to the house. I'm tired."

Ronnie burst out laughing. "You only hit the bag three times!" He swung her up in his arms and pretended to sag under the weight.

"You'll pay for that. Now march."

Jax was ready to be alone with Airiella. Ben sat there and ate with them until the sun started to set. Airiella's effect on him was humorous. He was like a sugar fiend in a candy store. At least he had the foresight to leave when the sunset started. Airiella warned him not to come back, or Ben would see parts of Jax that he couldn't un-see. The poor guy blushed, wished them goodnight, and left.

A few clouds had rolled in and given the brilliant colors of the sky a dramatic look. It was almost like broad brush strokes across a canvas. It was breathtakingly beautiful to behold the myriad of colors morphing across the expanse of sky stretched out before them.

Airiella sat between his legs again, her knees up to her chest as she leaned forward. Jax leaned forward too, keeping their bodies in contact, his chin resting on the uninjured shoulder. She didn't speak, and he could feel the peace she was radiating out.

Despite the energy thing earlier, this place was right for her in a way he hadn't ever expected. She had deep roots here, and there was a piece inside of him that wanted to plant his own roots here. "Thank you for letting me be a part of this, siren."

"I wouldn't have it any other way," she turned her head to say to him.

He pushed her hair off to the side, gathering it over the injured shoulder, then wrapped his arms around her middle and nuzzled her exposed neck, loving the little sparks that lit inside him when he touched her. "You are magnificent."

"You're just saying that because you are hoping to get lucky," she snickered.

"I'm already lucky, Ells," he lightly sucked on the spot between her neck and shoulder. The sun was almost below the waterline, the sky above a deep dark blue, a few stars already making their appearance.

He let her go and stood up to feed their fire, spread the other blanket on the ground, and put the food bag back in the car. The thought of animals seeking them out, especially larger ones, didn't excite him. He looked at their lumpy makeshift bed, picked the blanket back up, and smoothed out the sand before putting it back down.

"Hey, come lay with me on our deluxe sand-crafted one of a kind bed. Let's star-gaze from our five-star open-air suite," Jax called to her.

She stood up and gave him a sexy smile. "Only the best for you, babe. Raven, keep watch for us," she told the bird who took flight at her request.

He lay there with his hands behind his head, watching her saunter up to him. A primal growl started low in his belly the closer she got to him. She slowly pulled her shirt off, and her wings appeared, along with the visible connection between them. She ran those fingers of hers along it seductively, and his body responded immediately.

She straddled herself over him and slowly lowered herself until she was sitting on him. "What would you do if you had an angel at your mercy?" Jax groaned at the siren tone she used.

"I'd argue that it was I who was at her mercy," his voice had taken on a guttural sound. He arched his hips up into her as she ground down against him. "Light and dark," he whispered. In the rapidly fading light, her skin had an almost translucent glow contrasting sharply with her dark wings, black lacy bra, and black leggings.

She slid her hands up his shirt, dragging it up along his body until he leaned forward so she could pull it off him. The wind direction had shifted a little, and she curved her wings around them, placing the tips under his shoulders as he lay back, creating a barrier from the breeze. "You are a piece of living art," she breathed, her eyes burning into him.

He raked his gaze down her body and jolted as he noticed the fresh bruises on her torso. He reached out and brushed his fingers over them. "Siren," he tried to sit up only to have her push him back down.

"Not now," she silenced him.

His emotions were all over the place. "Do you truly think I am sharp edges?"

His question caught her off guard. "You have them; it's not all you are." She traced his collarbone. "Aedan is my foundation; he grounds me in the here and now. Mags is my adventure; she challenges me to accept the wild side as okay." She traced over the planes of his chest. "Smitty is my reason; he brings me back from the edge and shines a light on what I should have seen."

She brought her other hand up and used both to trace every muscle in his torso, scraping her nails across his abs, his skin and muscles twitching under her soft touch. "Ronnie is my safety. He never lets me fall. I'm never afraid with him. I can be vulnerable with him."

Jax's self-doubts were fighting to take control. "You are afraid with me?"

She ignored his question and dragged her fingers up his sides. "You, Jax, you are my salvation. It's in you that I was reborn. You scare me all the time. You also stand right by my side and let me fight the fears. You let me fall, but you help me back up. Your edges are sharp, but they are ones I would gladly let cut me repeatedly. Your edges are beautiful; they don't scare me. I love them. You are the reason I still breathe; you are my hope, you save me, you see me." She put her hands over his heart, and his skin hummed under her touch.

"You are as much light and dark as I am." She pushed light into him, his heartbeat erratically as he tried to process the words that started putting more pieces of him back together. "You make my light shine brighter, my dark, less scary. You are my salvation, Jax." She moved her hands and kissed the skin his heart lay beneath.

"You scare me in the ways you challenge me," she ran her hands up his neck, and her fingers traced his cheekbones. "You scare me in the way you light my soul on fire and give me purpose, make me believe in myself. You scare me in all the right ways. Your edges aren't dangerous to me. They rub against me and show me how to feel." She swiveled her hips on him.

His eyes stung with the intensity of the feelings she was evoking in him. She slid down and was sitting on his knees, her head bent, and licked up his chest. Crawling up him, she went up to his neck, over his jaw, and licked at his lips before she took them with a passionate kiss that stole all the air from his lungs.

"Look at me, Zeus," her throaty voice commanded. The heat of her gaze had him groaning. "I can feel your hunger, the raw sexuality," her fingers were back to tracing his chest, "in every contour, dip, and edge in your body. I feel the heat," she kissed him again, "in every touch we share."

He watched as she stood and pulled off her pants, bent to remove his. He lifted his hips, helping her slide them off, and she settled back on top of him, her wings tips sliding back under him. "I also feel your fear; it matches my own." She grabbed his hand and placed it over her own heart. "Feel me, Jax. It's all here for you. Everything I am is open to you, fears and all. I won't back away from them."

She slid against him, slick, wet and hot. "Ronnie

may try to protect me from the fire, you Jax, you walk with me right through it." She shifted, and he sunk into her. "You are my reason."

Helpless to stop the tide of emotions that crashed over him, he surged up into her, trying to make his body say the things he was scared to voice. Things he knew she saw anyway. He gripped her hips hard, pushing himself deeper and deeper into her as she rode him, wild and free, their bodies a perfect fit.

He let go of the tethers holding his feelings back and let them fly, gave everything to her as she brought him to the edge, and jumped right over it with him. The night lit up around them as the wind carried their cries to the heavens, the very air they breathed glowing blue.

He sat up, their bodies still connected, and he buried his face in her neck as sobs took him. She wrapped her wings around them both, keeping them warm against the chilled night air. "I love you will never be enough to describe how I feel," Jax let his tears soak into her hair.

She traced the wings tattooed on his back, "You don't need words."

"All I've wanted to do is save you, so you know you are worth the time and effort. All you've done is save us, over and over. Now you just gave me those beautiful words and told me exactly what I needed to hear. I want to promise you everything," Jax felt himself growing hard in her again.

"I don't need everything," she told him. She groaned as she shifted against him, her heels pushing into his back to bring them closer.

He trailed a hand down her back between the wings, his fingers splayed out to touch them both. "What do you feel when I touch them?" he saw her soul shining in her eyes.

She took one of his hands and placed it between their bodies, pushing his finger against her swollen button. "I feel it here," she used his finger to play with herself. Then she drew his hand up to her heart, "And I feel it here. It feels like you. When someone else touches them, it's like a tickle."

Jax moved his hand back to between them and slid his finger back over the bundle of nerves and stroked a wing at the same time. Her head fell back a wild moan escaping her lips, and her body clenched tight around him. "Jesus, siren, those sounds you make undo me," he nipped his teeth at her exposed throat.

The glowing air around them hummed with the electricity they felt in their veins. Each stroke Jax made against her caused her body to tighten around him. He shifted his legs to get a better position to thrust with as he stroked her wings and her bud in an alternating rhythm, slowly drawing out the pleasure.

As they made love, he felt the energy around them being drawn inside them, building into something big. Her body trembling let him know she was close, and he surrendered to the sensation she was wringing out of him with each squeeze. She shattered, tightening so hard around him that he came, his cock jerking wildly inside her.

The energy blast that tore from them sent weeds, wood, and sand flying out in all directions as if a bomb had detonated. Lightning lit up the sky in a wild display of power, and the heavens opened up, big fat raindrops falling on them. The wind ripped through the area, and she cocooned them in her wings, laughing.

"I think mother nature approves," she giggled and kissed him. "Let's grab our stuff before it gets soaked or blown away."

Chapter Twenty-Five

Ronnie groaned and stroked himself as another wave of desire swept through him, the intensity almost enough to make him come. Damn those two. They were going to give him tendinitis in his wrist. He hoped he wasn't going to feel it every time they had sex now.

He finished up and buried his face in her pillow. He pulled off his necklace. "Winnie, you around?" He waited a few minutes and asked again.

It took about another five minutes before she appeared. "Hi, handsome!"

"Hey, sunshine. Have you talked with Aedan?" he wondered.

"Yep. It might take me a few days to find anything out about this guy, and if I do, I need to find a translator because he probably doesn't speak English."

"I hadn't thought about that. Anything else new?" Ronnie tried to draw out the conversation.

"No. Not that I can tell. I thought something was going down, but then everything went quiet suddenly. Kind of weird."

"I got a weird question for you," Ronnie was embarrassed to ask, though he wasn't going to let it stop him. "Am I going to feel it every time they have sex?"

Winnie laughed. "I don't know. That last one lit up this side with that blue light of hers."

"They are going to be the death of me. Death by masturbation, or cold shower," Ronnie groaned.

"In all seriousness, are you okay with them?" she asked.

Ronnie leveled a look at Winnie. "I am. He's almost back to normal, Winnie. She's in love with him, and I am okay with it."

"She's in love with you too," Winnie said honestly.

"I know. I'm not blind to the ways it's different."

"I can't tell you what the future holds. The stronger Airiella gets, the more it changes. She's changing it as she grows and heals. Things I used to think of as set in stone have crumbled and turned to dust."

"I think that's probably a good thing. I don't want to know the future. I just want Airiella back here. I'm happy to play second fiddle to Jax." Ronnie ground his fists into his eyes. "That sounds awful, even to my ears."

"She doesn't see you as a second fiddle. I know how she feels about you. I can't lie and say it's as powerful as what she has with Jax, but I can tell you it's damn close. She isn't going to break your heart, Ronnie."

"I know that too. I think this being apart has fucked with all of us. Today was just awful. Then when Airiella pulled that energy from Jax, and we felt the pain, I swear to God we were all about to kill each other we went so crazy. No fucking cell signal for them. I had no idea if Jax was hurt. Or if she had died again or if they were getting attacked. Jesus, Winnie, I wanted to hit something," Ronnie shook.

"Don't lose your belief. Airiella can hear you, remember? You just have to focus on it. Your connection with her is almost as strong as the one with Jax. Use it."

"Feels stalkerish," Ronnie argued.

"Not in those situations."

"Do you think that ranger is going to out her?" Ronnie flipped over on his side and bunched the pillow under his head.

"No. The ex-husband is a concern. I can't tell he's the danger, his son, or her ex-friend. I can tell there is danger there. Actually, now that you have me thinking about it, I think the demons on this side are using her past to get to her," Winnie tapped her chin.

"I thought about that too. How much stronger is Airiella now?" Ronnie thought about what the powers she held could do in the hands of a demon.

"The glow of her on this side is almost blinding. She exists here too, but I don't think she knows that. She's completely visible, but not touchable. I can put my hands on where her glow is, and she doesn't know I am doing it. I don't know if that's the case with everyone. It is for me."

"Theoretically, if she becomes touchable on that side, she becomes killable from that side, too, right?" Ronnie felt fear slide through him.

"I don't know. Airiella's the first of her kind that has held as much power as she does. No one knows. That's why they want her so bad." Winnie shrugged her shoulders.

"They won't ever turn her. I don't know what they think would sway her."

"Ronnie, losing one of you, would have the power to sway her. That's why she shuts you guys down all the time. No one is kidding when they say you guys are her weaknesses. She knows it too. Imagine how you would feel if Jax died."

"Fuck. Times like these, I wished I still drank," Ronnie groaned.

"No, you don't. You do need some sleep."

Ronnie rolled onto his back. "I know. Now that you've filled my head with too many disturbing thoughts, you can go away."

"It's nothing you didn't already know. Goodnight, Ronnie."

"Goodnight, Winnie."

Chapter Twenty-Six

Mags woke up with her back hurting worse than it had been. She figured the night of rowdy sex probably hadn't helped, but they were helpless against the waves of lust and desire that had hit them. She sure hoped that Airy had been having some fun.

Aedan was still sprawled out dead asleep, and Mags checked the time. Her appointment was for first thing in the morning, so she had to get going. "Aedan, time to get up, we need to get ready for the doctor's appointment."

All she got for a response was a mumble and him rolling over. She flopped out of bed and took a shower, figuring he'd get up while she was getting ready. She was wrong. She came back out of the bathroom, pulling her wet hair into a ponytail and saw him in the same position she'd left him.

She was feeling a little evil due to the mood swings she hoped were hormonal; otherwise, she had more significant issues. She stalked up to Aedan and twisted his nipple sharply, and bit back a laugh as he woke with a yelp.

"What the hell, Mags?" Aedan rubbed his offended nipple.

"I told you to get up unless you don't care if I go to

this appointment alone," she stomped to the dresser and pulled out some cute stretchy leggings and grabbed one of Aedan's shirts because they fit her better than her own did.

"Why are you so bent out of shape over a checkup?" Aedan grumbled, getting out of bed. "You know I want to go. You didn't have to kill my nipple to get me up."

"It's not just a checkup," Mags yelled unintentionally. "Ooops," she lowered her voice. "I've been having bad back pain."

"Why would you not tell me that?" Aedan put his hands on his hips, mimicking one of her moves.

"Because you act like an overgrown ape when you are worried, and I am already stressed enough about it. Go get ready," Mags pulled on her tennis shoes and glared at him until he got in the shower.

She went down to the kitchen and sliced up an apple and a chunk of cheddar to eat. The food helped settle her stomach a bit, and by the time Aedan came down and made himself a cup of coffee, she was feeling better. She was almost sorry for the purple nurple she'd given him.

He dropped a kiss on her forehead and sipped his coffee while she finished her apple. She wiped her hands and stood up, wrapping her arms around him. "I'm lucky to have you."

Aedan chuckled. "Are you sure about that? I've been stumbling around like an idiot with his foot stuck in his mouth lately. How about this, instead? We are lucky to have each other."

"I'll take it." She stretched up to kiss him.

Aedan grinned, "You just kissed me to taste coffee, didn't you?"

"What?! I would never do such a thing! You're my husband, and I love you," she fluttered her lashes at him and kissed him again.

Aedan laughed. "Come on, let's go." Aedan tugged her to the door and got her loaded up in the car. Mags didn't speak the whole way there. The tension in her kept growing the closer she got, and by the time she got there, another mood swing took over, and sarcasm spilled from her lips every time she opened her mouth.

She ended up snapping at the nurse for telling her to change into a gown; then she cried because she felt terrible for doing it. Aedan had no idea how to calm her down, so he just held her hand. The nurse came back in and drew some blood and asked for a urine sample, to which Mags handed the container to Aedan and told him to go pee in a cup instead.

"Mags, you need to relax, honey. You wanted to know what was going on with the pain you are having; they are just checking all avenues."

Mags broke down in tears again. "I'm unhinged."

"I can't argue with that right now. Go pee in the cup." Aedan pushed her to the bathroom and waited outside the door.

Mags saw the stirrups out on the exam table and cringed. She hated those things. They didn't have to wait long before the doctor came in smiling, her face all bright and shiny. "Good morning, Mags! I understand you are here because of some pain you are experiencing. Let's get you laid back and in the stirrups to get this part over and done with first."

Mags obliged while the doctor poked her head and hands around between her legs. She liked it a lot better when Airy or Aedan was down there. Finally, when the doctor finished, she was allowed to sit back up. "Physical exam shows everything is okay. Tell me about what's been happening."

"For a little over a week now, I've been having sharp stabbing pains in my back. Like someone is sticking a knife in me slowly over and over." Mags described the pain and showed her the general area it had been happening.

"Back pain is pretty common in pregnancies. With your frame being so narrow, it might be a little more pronounced as these kiddos try to make room for them to grow. You also haven't gained any weight, and you should have. Are you eating enough?"

"I feel like all I do is eat," Mags widened her eyes.

"Try to up the calorie intake a little. We also might

need to discuss a c-section birth instead of natural, but I'd like to see how things progress first." She pushed on Mags' back, "Does this hurt?"

Mags almost groaned, it felt so good, "Nope."

The doctor laughed, "I think I'm going to suggest massage, and possibly a chiropractic adjustment, both of those should help with the pain. We also need to have you add some exercises that will strengthen your back. You aren't used to carrying the extra weight, and it throws off the spine a little bit. Walking is always good, just make sure you are eating enough. Has sleep been okay for you?"

"I think so. I'm always tired too. Sleeping and eating is my life." Unless the doctor wanted to include coming unglued, wild sex and the three punches Ronnie had gotten out of her.

"Let's add some exercise to that. So, massage, chiropractic, and exercise combined with more calories. Also, try to stay low key, avoid stress. Let's do an ultrasound and take a look, shall we?"

Mags lay back as the doctor adjusted the gown and blanket over her and spread the gooey gel over her belly. Mags loved the sound of the little heartbeats she heard when the wand slid across her bump. She happened to look at the doctor right as she made a concerned face and moved the instrument to her side, pushing it harder than usual.

"What's wrong, doctor?" Mags heard the fear in her voice.

The doctor didn't reply for a minute and instead pushed harder again, adjusting the position of the wand and took a few pictures. Mags barely heard the, "Oh my," that escaped from the doctor's mouth.

Immediately Mags burst into tears. "Is something wrong with the babies?" Aedan was at her side, clutching her hand in his.

She moved the wand again and tapped the screen. "Look here, see this?" she was pointing at something on the screen. Mags saw whatever she was pointing at, but she didn't know what it meant.

"What is it?" Aedan whispered, his voice holding a

slight tremor.

"A baby. It's not twins, it's triplets," the doctor said with a smile.

"I'm sorry, what did you just say?" Aedan's eyes got wide and voice incredulous.

"Triplets, this little guy is hiding right behind his brother. Their heartbeats identical, one was disguising the other. You have two boys and a girl residing in you."

"Three babies?" Aedan repeated, his face dumbstruck.

The doctor printed out the photos where's she'd circled each of the babies. "They are okay?" Mags asked.

"They all appear healthy to me. We'll run the blood tests to make sure there isn't anything we can't see. I'll have you come in a little more frequently than normal because you do not have a lot of space inside you. We'll keep a close eye on these little ones. Go ahead and get dressed, leave the door open when you are ready, and I'll come back in, and we can discuss any questions you might have."

She stepped out of the room while Mags wiped her belly clean, her emotions a wild roller coaster. "Doctors orders, you have to massage me," Mags told Aedan. When she didn't hear a response, she looked up at him. "What's wrong?"

"Join me here in what the fuck just happened land for a second, please, Mags. Three babies!" Aedan hissed wildly.

Mags burst into tears again, fear once more creeping inside her. "You don't want them?"

"What? Why would you think that? Of course, I want them. I'm just scared shitless of three babies and what we are going to do trying to take care of three babies. Three!" Aedan paced.

"You sound mad," Mags whispered, pulling her pants back on.

"No, I'm not mad. I told you, I'm scared," Aedan's eyes looked a little on the wild side.

"Well, that's not how to avoid stress," Mags fired off, her temper flaring.

"Shit, sorry, Mags. I'm happy we get our dream, we've both always wanted a big family. Now bam, in one shot, we get instant family, no time to practice raising one before we add another, we get three at once."

She understood his fear, "I get it, Aedan. It's not like we can undo it. We just do our best."

He dropped to his knees in front of her and kissed her belly. "Kiddos, I love you. Please don't all shit at once."

Mags threw her head back and laughed. "Looks like your third name option just became a reality. There's one less decision to have to worry about."

"This doesn't scare you?" Aedan stood and squished her cheeks as he planted a kiss on her lips.

"Oh, it does. But you aren't the one who has to push three bowling balls out of a garden hose, or get gutted and have them pulled out of you."

Aedan winced. "I'd rather not picture you getting gutted, that's a bit macabre."

Mags pulled Aedan's shirt back on and cupped her breasts. "At least I have big boobs now."

Chapter Twenty-Seven

I woke up slowly, breathing in the scent of the man who had turned my world upside down. I'd gotten so used to waking up with him that it would feel weird not to have that. I didn't even know how things would play out now back in California. How would I feel not to wake up and see how his dark lashes fanned out against his cheek when he was sleeping peacefully, or not to experience the possessive way his hand rested on my hip?

Everything was different now. My heartbeat started a crazy tempo at the thought of leaving here again, of leaving my family after shaking their entire world off its axis. I hadn't realized how much I missed being here and how much I missed them until I was back here. It was a conundrum I was having a hard time with because I missed my new family down in California just as much as I missed the ones here. I couldn't wait to be back with them.

Those thoughts led me to wonder how things would be adding in the new relationship with Jax. How would they handle it? How would Jax handle it if I wanted to spend time with the others? Would things get tense? I needed them all, but if I had to choose, I would pick Jax. If he asked me to, I'd follow him anywhere. That was a thought that scared me and exhilarated me at the same time.

I was trying to figure out how to get out of the car without waking him when I looked up and found those gorgeous chestnut eyes of his penetrating right through me. All thoughts of getting out of the car vanished as he kissed me.

"Good morning, siren," he said quietly. "Are you trying to avoid a morning-after scene?"

"I was trying not to wake you up; you looked so peaceful. We are a little late for a morning-after scene. I've been waking up next to you for a week now. I wanted to see the beach after the storm. See what treasures were left."

"You mean the storm that we created?" Jax clarified.

"Um, yes?" My brain flashed back on last night and the way we molded together so perfectly.

"That was kind of crazy. What was that?" Jax looked different.

"For me, something else healed in me, because of you. I'm guessing that unleashed some sort of new ability in me that created that." I looked at him with narrowed eyes. I couldn't put my finger on it; something was different, though.

"Something healed in me too, the moment you said I was your salvation." Jax kissed me again. "Instead of doing what I want to do right now, I like your idea of getting out of the car. Stretching would be nice."

I giggled and opened the car door, sliding out. Jax followed behind me, and I beelined for the bushes needing to pee. Jax laughed at me, heading for his own shrub to pee on. He didn't hide behind it as I did. I peered from around the bush at him and noticed the colors surrounding him.

Was that it, his colors changed? Had I noticed colors around him before? When I used my empath senses, his energy and emotions had colors; I knew that. I shook my head and went back to the car where Jax had dug into the pastries we'd brought.

"Making love with you works up one hell of an

appetite," he smiled as he popped a whole pastry in his mouth.

I raised my eyebrows and snatched one of them before he ate them all. "You still have to share." I took another bite, "Let's give it at least an hour before we head back. Allow the morning traffic to ease."

He took my hand, and we walked over to the little dune that led us to the beach, and we both froze at the scene of destruction that lay before us. It looked like a war had taken place. "Holy shit." Jax looked up and down the beach.

"That was one hell of a storm," I whispered in the wind. The beach had become littered with logs, uprooted plants, clumps of grass, trees, shells, rocks, kelp, and seaweed.

"We unleashed that," Jax looked down at me. "See how much power that took? That's how I feel for you," he tried to form the thoughts that were in his head.

I knew what he meant, what he was trying to convey that his love for me was as powerful inside him as this storm had been on the land. Before I could respond, I heard Ben from behind us, "Glad to see you guys made it through that."

We turned to look at him, and as I did, it struck me how different he seemed to me, too. I could clearly see the colors around him, the goodness in his heart, the dark spots he held close, and his shame. His intentions and nature were plain to see.

It hit me then when the raven appeared in my head. I could see his aura. That's what I saw around Jax. The raven cawed in my head, telling me there was more to it than that. My brain spun around fast, trying to put it together, and as Ben was giving me a curious look because I was flat out staring at him, I understood.

"Holy fuck! I can see souls!" I shouted in surprise.

"Siren?" Jax glanced at me; his face was concerned.

"Um, I'm not sure what to do with that statement," Ben said, confused.

"What am I supposed to do with this?" I muttered. I

bent over and took my shoes and socks off and handed them to Jax.

"Ells, are you okay?" Jax asked quietly.

"I need a minute alone. Do you mind? I need to go down to the water." I needed to talk to my grandpa, or the raven or whatever had done this to me. I needed to figure out if I could turn this on or off because seeing colors and souls could get a little distracting. I kept my eyes downcast, not wanting to look at either of the men standing there.

"Will you let me know when you're ready for me to join you?" Jax asked softly, not pushing me.

I nodded, and he kissed the top of my head. I shut down the flow of information between us, needing my thoughts to be my own, and I took off, leaving Jax behind to talk to a perplexed Ben. I headed straight for the tide pool, where the raven perched waiting.

Jax watched her walk away and noticed when she shut the connection down. He had no idea what it meant that she could see souls, but he felt her uneasiness about it. He wondered what she'd seen when she looked at him.

"Will she be okay off on her own?" Ben looked wearily after her.

Jax laughed. "More than okay. She's a force."

"Okay, then. I'm not sure what to think about what Airy said. I just wanted to make sure you both were fine. That was quite the display mother nature put on last night. Power got wiped out in the surrounding towns, and the surf was crazy."

"We are good. At the raindrops we loaded up and slept in the car. We still don't know what all her abilities are like she told you, we are still learning. It sounds like she figured out another one." Jax smiled to try and ease his discomfort. "There was something peaceful in the chaos of the storm," Jax told him honestly. When he thought about the destruction on the beach, it felt like the bad emotions he'd been holding on to about someone being able to love him like Airiella did, were set free and tried to destroy everything in their path.

Her words to him had started a violent storm in him that had matched what they had witnessed last night. She'd healed up another part of him, and at the loud thoughts she'd had this morning that she didn't seem to remember seeped into him, he'd started to form a plan. He gave Ben a careful look.

"Can I ask you a huge favor? Please do not feel like you have to accept it, saying no will not hurt my feelings."

Ben shot a puzzled look at Jax, "Sure."

Jax tried to figure out how to word things without giving too much away. "You are familiar with this area pretty well, right?"

"Yes. All up and down the coast, really," Ben explained.

"I'm plotting a surprise for her, so once I clear it with my brother, I'll ask you to communicate with him, not me, that way it stays a surprise. But if you wouldn't mind keeping an eye out for a house along the coast for sale, that would be great. Send listings of things you think would be good."

"You want me to find a house for you?" Ben looked stunned.

"Kind of, maybe? I know how much this area means to her, she's attached to the mountains too, though. I'm undecided and torn between locations." Jax tapped on his chin, thinking of where she lived now.

"There's always the Olympic peninsula, just north that way. The Olympic mountain range starts and goes up the peninsula and is along the coast. Kind of both worlds in one," Ben suggested.

"Would you be willing to help me with that? Since you know the area, you'd know way better than me what is a good place, good price, that kind of thing."

"That you would even trust me with something so monumental honors me," Ben's enthusiasm came bubbling to the surface.

"Do you have a paper I can write down some key points on?" Jax smiled.

"Hang on," Ben ran off to his truck and came back with the same ticket book Jax had signed the previous day.

Jax laughed, "Ticket books will never look the same to me now." He wrote down some features and specifications he was looking for and his phone number. "Don't call me, though. Once I talk Aedan into being the point person on this, I'll call you and give you his contact info. Send listings to him, which he'll filter through and find good ones. I may ask you to tour through one of them. I'm willing to pay you for your time as well."

"Don't even think about it. It'd be a pleasure to help you out. I'm more than happy to do that. It also helps that my wife is a real estate agent," he winked at Jax.

"Perfect! She has my commission then. Remember, though, it's a surprise, and I have to be very tricky about this. She knows way too many things. There's a lot of things I have to put in place back at home too. I'll have to talk with the others first." Jax wasn't sure how that talk would go either.

"I understand." Ben folded the paper Jax had written on and put it in his wallet.

"We'll be back in the area for the live shows soon. I can add you to the list of approved people to be on-site if you'd like. We don't usually allow it, and as long as you stay out of the way, we can make it happen for you," Jax offered, spur of the moment.

"Seriously? That'd be awesome!" Bens grin lit his face.

"Consider it done. And really, thank you for allowing me to abuse your goodwill like this," Jax added.

"It's not an imposition, honestly. I'll make sure my wife knows to keep it discreet and not throw your name around as well," Ben promised, holding out his hand for Jax to shake.

"Fantastic. Consider me your new friend."

I'm ready, he heard in his head.

"I'm going to head out there now, check on her. Thanks again, I'll be in touch."

Ben saluted and walked back to his truck, and Jax

put Airiella's shoes in the car, taking off his own before he set out to find her. *I'm coming;* he sent her.

He found her sitting on the sand in front of a tide pool, the raven next to her, and a pile of what looked like glass on her other side. "Sorry about that," she told him as he sat down. "I wasn't trying to shut you out. I just needed my thoughts to be my own for a minute," she apologized.

"You don't have to explain yourself to me siren. I didn't think you were shutting me out. I was a little confused about why you wouldn't look at either of us."

"Because I kept seeing this mix of colors that didn't make sense to me, and along with the colors were all these things I shouldn't know. Like when I saw Ben, he had about three little dark spots that held things he was ashamed of, and then there were all the colors associated with his emotions, and colors associated with his overall being. It was a lot to process."

"Are you talking about aura?" Jax wondered.

"I think that's part of it, but it's more than that. I could see Ben's soul. I can see yours." She gestured to the raven, "I can see hers, which confuses me because I think hers is mine."

"I can tell this bothers you," Jax picked up her hand and wove his fingers between hers.

"It does because it makes me feel like I am judging them, and I don't like that. I'm not judging, I can just plainly see the truth, and the emotions they try to hide behind to cover the truth. Well, I saw that when I looked at the raven, which told me it was me," she muttered.

"You are hiding behind your emotions?" Jax asked, surprised.

"Yeah, I always have. It's just that same mask I wear. Only now, I can see it. I see my soul, and I can see what you guys have been telling me about the glow I put off. I can also see what is good, and I can see the parts that are still damaged. It's unnerving."

Jax wanted to ask, but he was afraid. What if she saw something not redeeming in him? He kissed the back of her hand, and she leaned against him.

"Jax, your soul is the same color as mine, stop worrying that you aren't worthy. I can see the darkness in there, and it's significantly smaller than you think it is. I can see the trauma of the past, and I can see your doubts. Your emotions are clear as day to me. I don't know how to describe it to you, but our souls are woven together, like our fingers," she held out her hand. "Our colors mesh; they are almost the same."

"Not possible. You are damn near pure of soul," Jax argued.

"So are you when you cut through the bullshit," she smiled to ease the sting of the words. "Jax, there is no hate harbored in you, despite what you think."

"Have you figured out why you now can see this?" he veered away from that.

"No. Though the raven did guide me in learning how to mute it, it's not quite as distracting. It will take a bit of practice."

"What is one man's blessing, is another man's curse," Jax quoted, unable to remember who said it. "You are my blessing, and the curse for the demons who wish to destroy us."

"Thanks for the reminder. I need to focus more on the positive side of this instead of how it confounds me."

"Siren, you are always focused on the positive. Just because blinking blinds your vision as your eyes close, it doesn't mean you still can't see when they reopen. All this is, is a blink. It will take a few of them to figure things out."

"Surprisingly, insightful. I almost thought I was talking to Smitty," she elbowed him. "I had another disturbing thought as I was sitting here," she finally looked at him. "All this, I know we caused it, but it feels like it was the result of a blowback."

"I think I understand, but explain," Jax requested.

"That pressure of energy that built between us last night was for me at least, fueled with emotions I didn't want to let go, the fears I had inside of finally admitting to myself and you, how important you were. Accepting that I truly did hand over my heart to you to do with as you wanted. I'm not saying that I regret it, or that it made anything I admitted before then less viable. Just that admitting it all allowed some damn potent emotions to be set free," she tried to put it to words.

Jax let out a rough sigh. "I came to the same conclusion myself. For my own emotions, though, not yours. I didn't think it was blowback, but I felt that it was from emotions. When you were telling me, I was your salvation, and what the others meant to you, things inside me were moving around. Some parts of me healed, pieces clicking into place."

"I think all those bad emotions were pulled out of us and took out their wrath on the earth," she looked around. "There's a strange beauty to it."

"Funny enough, I told Ben almost the same thing. That I found a peace in that chaos," Jax rested his cheek on the top of her head.

"Something that powerful and destructive was inside us, and it did it's best to destroy us. Once unleashed, it tried the same with the earth, yet life still goes on as if nothing happened here. The local wildlife will sift through the wreckage using what they can, and the tide will reclaim the rest. There's a lesson in that."

"One, I think we both are learning," Jax added.

Chapter Twenty-Eight

Smitty sat back with a satisfying thump as the printer spit out the pages he'd just uncovered after going through archives of online publications about the mine fire. He'd managed to dig up a little about the couple of names they'd narrowed their focus down on.

It felt good to have something more concrete to help them finally. The rest of the team were out back with Father Roarke, looking like a medieval group of warriors. Of all the things Mags could have requested, a bow and arrow were the least likely that Smitty would have guessed.

He'd been mildly shocked to learn she had been really into archery as a kid, competed in competitions, and won. Ronnie's request for throwing stars hadn't surprised him at all. He had a deadly aim. and those were easier for him to conceal.

Aedan had requested a sword of all things. His reasoned he wanted something with a longer reach. How Aedan and Mags planned on concealing their weapons of choice baffled Smitty, but they certainly looked mean. Maybe a little bit funny too, like something out of time.

Ronnie had suggested a dagger for Jax, the same as Smitty had wanted. Jax and Smitty both preferred to get in close range of their opponents. When they sparred, the closer they were, the harder it was for their opponent to get a substantial hit. Airiella *was* a weapon and didn't need one.

Smitty headed out to join their training session with the weapons now that he had accomplished one of his goals. Mags and Aedan had come back in an odd mood from their doctor's appointment; they hadn't looked devastated, so Smitty didn't ask.

Smitty now watched as Aedan wielded his sword with a skill that shocked him. It was like it was an extension of his arm; the movements were so natural. He used the moves Ronnie had taught them all, adding the sword as the finishing touch to his kill moves.

Smitty was impressed. He took his dagger out and started practicing on the dummy Ronnie had set up for him and was getting into the swing of it when terror struck him hard and fast. Next to him, Mags fainted, and if Smitty hadn't thrown himself at her, she would have hit the ground instead of landing on Smitty.

Ronnie and Aedan were braced against each other, looking for the threat that they all felt, though no one could see anything. Smitty eased Mags off him and stood over her as he joined them in looking around.

He wasn't sure when it came to him that the threat wasn't with them, but with Airiella. "It's not here, it's Airiella," Smitty said quietly. The certainty in his heart, leaving no room for his brain to doubt him. "Something is happening."

Smitty's phone rang at that moment, scaring them all with the sudden sound. "It's Taklishim."

"It's Onida," Taklishim said as soon as Smitty answered. "She's trapped on the other side in her animal form by a demon, while one is after Raven. Onida is hurt."

Smitty repeated the message as they all stood there, helpless against the threats they couldn't see on their friends. "What do we do?"

"Nothing we can do. I can't get through to Jax or Raven. If they call, I need Raven here. Tell her."

I felt the danger and couldn't see anything. I heard the raven cawing frantically. Faster than I thought possible, I grabbed hold of the air and earth energy readying it for use. We were on the highway, a deserted stretch where there weren't many other cars at this time of day.

"What the fuck?!" Jax yelled and slammed on the brakes.

I barely had time to register that a human shape had appeared in the middle of the lane ahead of us when something hit the front end of the car and lifted the back end, the airbags deploying with an explosion of air.

The car was flipping through the air, and I didn't have much time before crashing back onto the highway. I asked the air to catch us and the earth to soften the landing, having no idea if that would work. I was terrified we were about to die.

The air caught us as we were upside down, and the airbags deflated enough for me to see a dark soul staring directly at me. In a flash, I understood the ability now. I was able to spot a demon even if it looked human.

"*I won't hurt you, Airiella Raven,*" I heard echoing in the car's space. "*I just want to talk to you.*"

"Siren, I don't know who that is, but can you put us down? If another car sees us hanging upside down in mid-air, it might cause questions we can't answer," Jax said with panic in his voice.

I asked the air to put us down right side up and got rewarded with the car flipping back over and landing with a thud on the tires. My heart pounding, I looked around for the demon. "Where are you?"

"*Watching you closely. We will meet soon,*" the demon promised, the eerie voice giving me chills.

"What do you want?" I felt unhinged, talking to empty air.

"*You. After I take apart what holds you here.*"

On the hood of my car, a raven that wasn't mine appeared, at first, it felt menacing; then it switched positions like it was standing guard. "That doesn't look like yours," Jax said uneasily.

"It's not, and I don't know what it's doing, but its soul is an odd color. Muddy almost," I answered quietly.

"Your friend's life hangs in the balance, go now," the raven said.

Panic settled in my blood that was racing through my heart. "What, friend?" I shouted as Jax stomped on the gas pedal, shooting us forward and sending the bird flying off.

"The hawk," came the distant voice.

"Onida," I whispered. "Jax, take that exit for north 101 up ahead," I told him, unbuckling my seat belt and turning to try and find my phone in the mess that had been my purse from the car flipping.

"Was that one demon or two?" Jax asked, shaken.

"Two. The raven was a different one, and I think it was trying to help? I don't know. Its soul was a different color than the one on the road. The one on the road was dark. Black," I told him frantically.

"Onida is a hawk?" Jax's hands were trembling now, and I wondered if he was in shock.

"Yes. I don't know if you are supposed to know that or not. Are you okay? Are you hurt?" I looked him over carefully. "Do you want me to drive?"

"Not okay, but not hurt. I'll keep driving. It will keep me from freaking the fuck out," Jax's words came out harsh. I knew it was a reaction to what had just happened.

"Yes!" I shouted, making Jax jump. "Sorry. I found my phone. We should be in signal range shortly. I know they live up the peninsula, so if we head that direction, we will be good. Keep going this way. Do you want me to pull some of the fear from you?"

Jax nodded tightly, and I separated the strands and pulled the fear from him. I left the anxiety alone because I knew it would just return, given the situation. I pushed some love into him and felt him calm. "Thank you."

"I got a signal, calling Tak," I told him.

"Raven, where are you?" Taklishim barked.

"North on 101. Text me the address where I need to go," I told him.

"What did Smitty tell you?" Taklishim asked.

"Nothing. I haven't talked to Smitty, but two different demons just visited me. One of which looked like he was trying to help, the other flipped my car right off the road," I relayed.

"Are you hurt?" his voice tightened up.

"No, I caught us with the air," I told him in detail what happened and what they had said.

"Onida's caught on the other side. She went to her animal form because she felt things moving and wanted a better perspective. Something hit her. Her wing looks broken, and she's not responsive. A demon is holding her there. You can get her free."

"How?" I asked, stunned.

"You are in both worlds. We can see you there." Taklishim wasn't making sense.

"I don't understand," I was firmly right here, not on the spirit plane.

"You need to go to the other side and cut the tie that's got a hold of her. I can't do it. I can't get through," Taklishim insisted.

"Taklishim, I've never been there unless I've died. I don't know how to do it. Why do you think I can?"

"You are the only one who can exist in both places at once," Taklishim revealed.

Ronnie paced. "What did she say?" he demanded an answer from Smitty.

"She's on her way to Onida right now. She's not sure how to help, but Taklishim seems to think she's the only one who can."

"Of course, she is. Why would it be anyone else? Are they okay?" Ronnie felt frantic and paced around again, trying to calm himself.

"She said they were both shaken up, but physically fine."

"Fuck. Are they still coming back tomorrow?" Ronnie thought he'd lose him mind if she didn't.

"She'll call us. Chill, bro," Smitty put a hand on his shoulder.

Ronnie remembered Winnie's words about the connection and him being able to reach her. He walked away from the rest of them and went back outside, sitting on the bench in the garden. *"Angel?"*

"I'm here. Are you okay?" Ronnie heard her say almost immediately.

"No. I feel like my soul is getting ripped in half," he told her honestly.

"Why?" her tone was worried.

"Because I'm not with you and Jax. I never thought I'd miss that grouchy old bastard this much, but it fucking hurts, angel."

"I know, love. I'm coming back tomorrow. If I don't figure this out today, I'll just bring a broken bird back with me."

"Onida is a bird?" Ronnie hadn't known that.

"Um, yeah. Pretend you don't know that. And Jax isn't as irritable as he was before," he could hear the smile in her voice.

"Just come back to me. Both of you." Ronnie hung his head low.

"Does this have anything to do with the crazy emotions that came from you yesterday?"

"Yes. I think the separation is literally driving us insane. We've all snapped; it hasn't been pretty." Ronnie felt like he was laying down a guilt trip though that wasn't his intent.

"I'm sorry," the remorse in her voice came through loud and clear.

"You don't have any reason to be sorry. You made the right decision. I didn't say it to make you feel guilty; I said it because I'm honest. Every single one of us has broken down in tears the past couple of days. It's like Mags's pregnancy hormones have taken over us all."

"When I get there, promise me you'll kiss me like

you've missed me," her request had him shaking.

"That's a promise that's easy to make. Please be careful," Ronnie begged her.

"I will. I love you, Heracles." He felt love pouring into him from across the miles.

"I love you, angel. Go save the bird." He pulled away from the connection so she couldn't tell he was crying again.

Chapter Twenty-Nine

It felt like it took way longer than it had to get there, and when we pulled up, a beautiful giant cougar met us.

Jax freaked out when I got out, and I remembered that he didn't know what their animals were. "Jax, it's okay. It's Tama."

"Fuck, this is going to take some getting used to," he muttered.

Tama butted her head against my hand. "Where is she? We'll follow you."

She led us into the woods where I saw Taklishim standing watch over the hawk. "Raven, she's fading. I can feel her life force draining."

"The hell she is. Tell me what to do," I demanded, kneeling next to the enormous bird.

"I don't know. I can see you on the other side," Taklishim's voice was distant, and when I looked at his face, I could tell he wasn't fully here. "I can see you here too. She was right. She told me that you were in both places."

"How do you switch to over there?" I asked him, trying to figure this new development out.

"In my head, I see a clear line between the two

worlds. For me, it's as simple as stepping over the line. I can see both worlds without being in the other. I can only be in one, though. If I step over the line, you would see me here, but all you are seeing is a body."

"Isn't that astral projection?" Jax asked.

"I guess, in a sense, it is. I can't go to all worlds or planes of existence; I can only go to the spirit world."

Jax looked at me. "Meditation. Your mind needs to be relaxed, and you need to visualize," he explained. "That's what I learned about that from someone who does is. He said there is a silver line from your astral form that connects to your physical form. If that line severs, you are stuck there, and your body would wither away and die here."

I looked at Taklishim, "Does she have a tether line like that?"

"If so, it's not something I can see. My skills allow me to feel life force, so if that line is what you are looking for, chances are, it will be dim because she's fading. Try what he suggested; it's a starting point," Taklishim urged me.

"Tak, tell her what the place looks like, or what to visualize," Jax suggested.

"It looks exactly like right here. Some people say that the spirit world is all in shades of gray to them. So maybe picture a gray version of exactly where she is?" Taklishim was agitated, and Tama's cougar eyes were pain-filled.

"Tama, is that the best way to get there?" I looked at her.

"She said touch her," Taklishim said quietly. "Be very careful when you do that. Animal forms are the animal, and most predator birds don't like to be touched when they are in pain."

"Will my blood help her?" I thought out loud.

"I don't know that either. It will heal Onida, most likely. I don't know if it would bring her back. A demon has a hold on her."

I put my hand on the very tip of her uninjured wing

and forced myself to relax and open my senses. I felt Jax sit down beside me and put a hand on my lower back, which had an instant calming effect. Instead of picturing where she was, I asked the earth to bring me to her.

I felt the energy surge through me, and it was confused because I was already with Onida. I tried a different tactic. I asked the earth and the air to guide my soul to hers. The flow of energy changed, and I felt the air around me, responding, and I opened my eyes.

It had worked. At least I figured it had because the hawk's eyes were on me, and I couldn't see Jax or Tama, though I felt them both. "Can you communicate with me?" I asked her.

"You shouldn't be here!" her voice was insistent in my head.

"I'm here to get you back," I told her, looking for the thread Jax had been mentioning.

"Hello Airiella," my head shot up, and I looked around. "I knew you'd come."

"Who are you? Show yourself," I demanded.

The light figure that I knew was Taklishim shifted, and I saw him step into this world. "Hurry, Raven."

"The demon wants you here. You played right into the demon's hands," Onida's tone had fear in it now.

"What's your name, demon?" I recklessly asked.

"Do you think it's that simple, Airiella? That I will just give you my name?" a dark figure stepped into view.

"Are you the same one who tried to crash my car?" I asked the lightning that had never let me down to come into me. To aid me, and fight for me.

"You didn't like that trick? I wouldn't have let you get hurt. I can't say the same for your friend. I don't need him. Nor do I need this one here, she has served her purpose now." It stepped closer to us, and I felt the lightning surge in my veins.

"I wouldn't come closer if I were you," I warned heedlessly.

"Raven, time is low," Taklishim whispered fiercely to me.

"Can you hear me, Onida?" I asked her.

"Yes, Taklishim is right. My life is almost over. He's been draining me slowly."

"If I cut my finger on your talon and put it in your mouth, will my blood keep you alive?" I kept my face blank.

"Yes, but I will still be trapped, and he will still be draining me," her tone had a sense of finality.

"Well I don't have a habit of giving up that easily. Where's the tether Jax told me to look for?" I asked.

"If you share your blood with me, it creates a link between us, Airiella. If I get hurt, it will cause you pain," Onida warned.

"I don't care, Onida. You aren't dying here today." Jeez, she was stubborn.

"Do not let your blood spill anywhere other than on me. Don't use my talon. I'll cut your finger with my beak," Onida relented.

I held my hand out to her beak and let her bite me, my blood welling and spilling into her mouth. The tether that bound her to the demon flared with life. "Ah, there it is."

"You think you are clever, don't you?" he stepped closer again, and I could feel the anger radiating from him.

I pulled energy to me and fed it into the lightning that was snapping through my veins, ready to be unleashed. I directed it to the tether and asked it to fry the connection. *"Sorry, if this hurts,"* I apologized to Onida.

The demon launched at us right as I fired the lightning bolt out. It fed up the tether and right into the demon's chest, leaving Onida alone. I saw smoke rising from whatever his form was and heard the inhuman howl reverberating in my head.

It had worked because Onida got to her feet, shifted, and held my bleeding finger in her mouth until she stepped back into the living world. Unfortunately, I was too transfixed by what was happening with the demon and didn't go with her.

I curled my finger into my palm and stuffed my

hand in the pocket of my coat. "That must have hurt," I said sweetly.

"You will be mine. All it takes is one decision, one mistake, and you'll be mine. It's so easy to fall, one little misstep. All that light will get extinguished, all that power mine," it hissed at me.

I stood up and saw Taklishim shift back to the living world. "You seem to think that I am afraid of the dark. I'm not. Even in the dark, there are things to love."

I felt the danger to Jax the minute the demon moved, and my instincts responded before I knew what was happening. I was back in the living world, but so was the demon. In a human body so unbelievably attractive, I had to remind myself that it was a demon headed right for Jax.

Help me; I told the lightning. A glowing blue circle appeared around me, Jax, Taklishim, Onida, and Tama. It looked like a blue ring of fire, and it stopped the demon in its tracks. I pushed Jax behind me towards the others, and I saw Taklishim pushing him back farther to where Onida sat on the ground cradling her arm.

Tama stepped in front of Jax and Onida in her cougar form, but it was Taklishim who demanded attention. His telling me he was a warrior came back to my mind, and he looked every bit of a warrior. I could feel the power radiating off him.

I had no idea how to beat a demon other than the lightning, and that hadn't killed this guy. I was running out of ideas and felt the ground moving beneath me. "You think you are the only one who can play with the elements, my angel?"

"I'm not yours in any way, shape, or form," I snapped back, asking the earth to fight back against the threat.

I felt around for the energy signatures around me and could identify all of them. Instead of pulling from the demon, which sounded like an awful idea to me, I fed into Taklishim's energy, giving him my strength.

The demon laughed. "Wrong choice. You are now weak."

"Think again, asshole." I shot a bolt of lightning down on him and watched as it crackled against his skin, smoke rising but no real damage.

"No, Airiella, it's what he wants you to do. He wants you to harm him. If you hurt him and he hasn't done anything, it could cause you to lose your light," Onida's voice filled my head.

"That makes no sense, Onida. He hurt you. I'm defending, not attacking."

"He's not attacking you. He's not attacking anyone. It's a threat. A trap." Onida's voice was getting stronger.

I was out of my element. *"But, I killed those demons at the funeral."*

"Those were openly attacking. Technically, Taklishim killed them by removing their heart. You just made it permanent by burning them."

"Fuck!" I yelled. Oops, that was out loud. I looked over at Taklishim, who was utterly still yet more menacing than I'd ever seen anyone be. Well, fine then. I found his energy and poured more into it until he glowed with the same glow I had. "Do your worst, Gandalf."

He nodded at me and stepped right through the blue fire and stood in front of the demon. "Leave."

"I came for my bride," the demon replied, not looking intimidated at all.

The tension in the air was thick and suffocating. I hated to admit it, but my energy was weak. "I'm not ever going to be your bride. As long as there is life in my body and soul, I will never belong to you."

The smell of sulfur and sickness washed over me, making me gag. "Never is a dangerous word, Airiella Raven."

"No, it's a promise. I will never belong to you," I repeated.

The ground beneath me shifted, throwing me off balance and I fell right out of the ring of blue fire I had created, landing somewhere behind Taklishim. The deep laugh of the demon chilled my bones, and I felt the energy flow around me change.

I stood up and glanced at the others to make sure they were okay and then stepped closer to Taklishim, who had begun to chant in a language, I could only assume was that of his tribe because I didn't recognize it.

"You can't defeat me, warrior," the demon taunted.

All around us, I saw animals popping up with a natural glow to them, their eyes not of this world. While I had warned Jax of bears when we were out in the woods, I had never seen a black bear before in the wild. Yet, a bear the size of my car appeared behind the demon, and behind the bear, was a reddish-brown wolf that was almost as big.

My instincts were screaming at me to run, but I felt no danger from the animals. I did feel it from the demon. Whether it was the demon's reaction to the animals or not, I didn't know. He was a powerful demon, much stronger than the ones I had faced before, and now I knew what he wanted.

I was about to do something stupid; I was sure of it, because Jax reacted with a loud, "No!" Before I could do anything though the flow of energy once again changed, and became dark and cloudy, toxic like a poison spreading through us.

The next thing I knew, I was flying through the air, watching the huge jaws of the wolf snap down on my wrist, yanking me to the ground as a terrifying howl split the night. Then all I knew was blackness. Everywhere I looked was black. I wasn't on earth.

www.ingramcontent.com/pod-product-compliance
Lightning Source LLC
Chambersburg PA
CBHW060238100726
47907CB00003B/686